LOVE AND WORLD WAR IN THE NEW AMERICAN CENTURY

J R Ortiz

American Amaranth is a fictional novel.

Any resemblance of characters in the novel to real persons, living or dead, is purely coincidental and not intentional.

ISBN: 061557825X
ISBN-13: 9780615578255

Library of Congress Control Number: 2011945731
J. R. Ortiz, Miami, FL

For Alina, Ali, and all the beloved women of our family -
past, present, and future.

Contents

RUSSIA
Astana
KAZAKHSTAN
Ulaanbaatar
MONGOLIA
Beijing
CHINA
New Delhi
NEPAL
Kathmandu
Thimphu
INDIA
Dhaka
BURMA
LAOS
Hanoi
Vientiane
THAILAND
Bangkok
VIETNAM
TAIWAN
Manila
Bay of Bengal
SRI LANKA
Colombo
Male
MALAYSIA
Bandar Seri Begawan

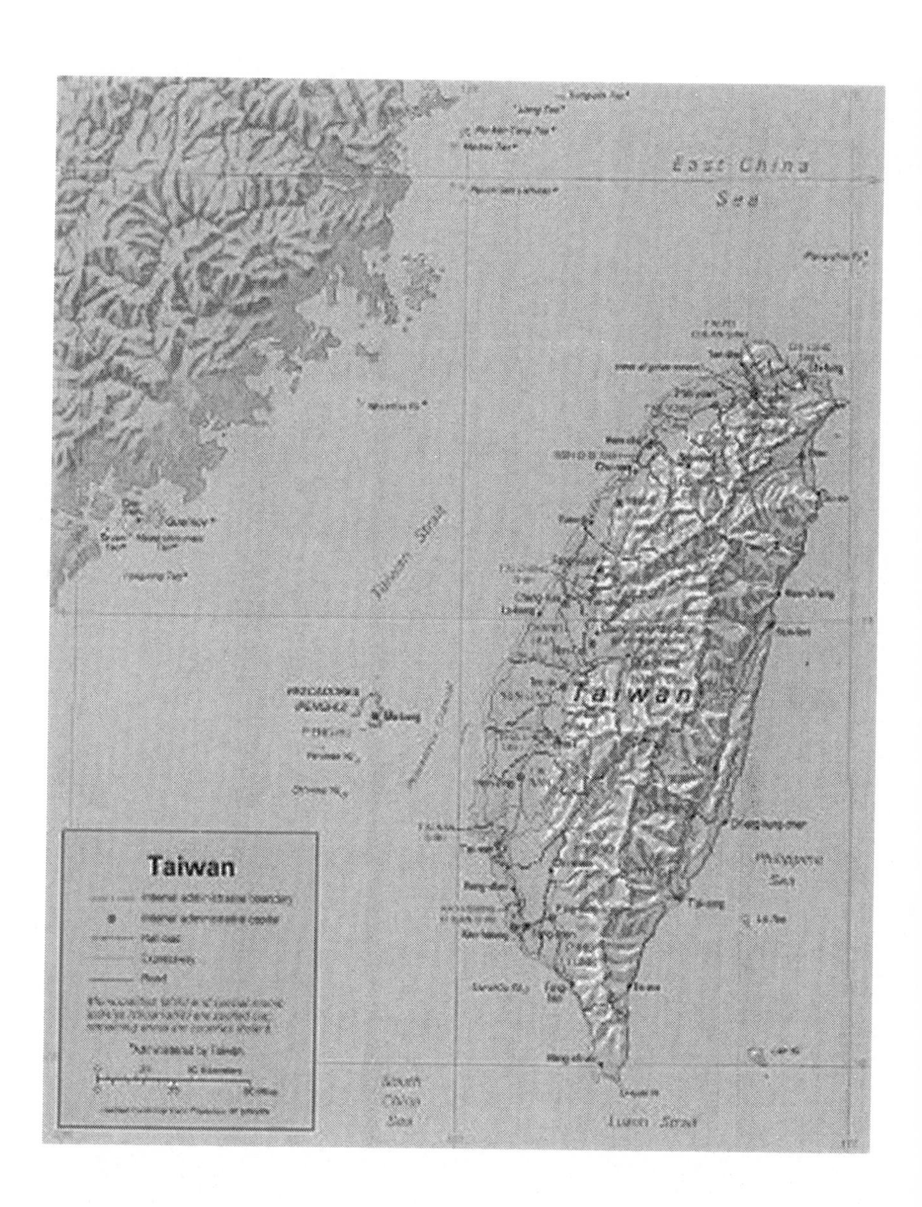
East China Sea
Taiwan
Philippine Sea
South China Sea
Luzon Strait
Taiwan

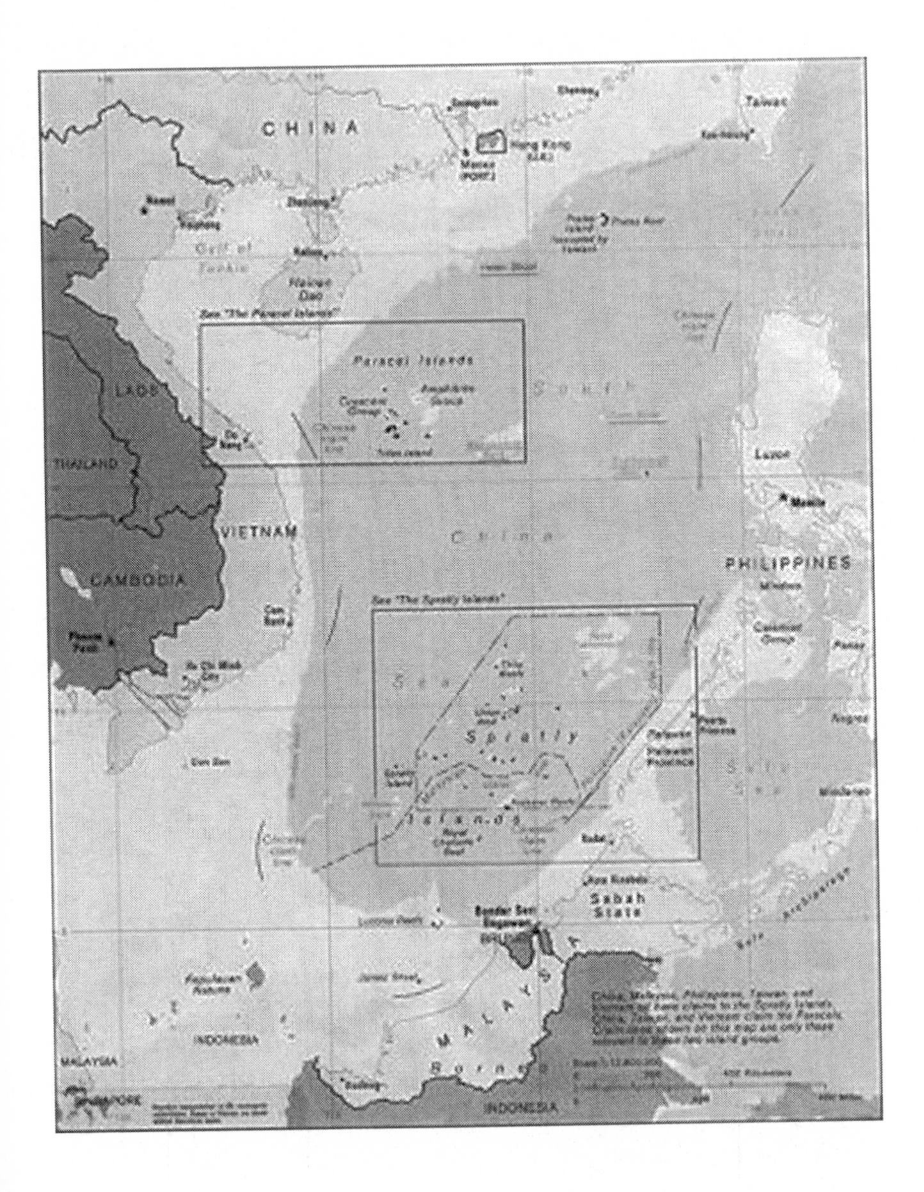
CHINA
Hong Kong
Gulf of Tonkin
Hainan Dao
See "The Paracel Islands"
Paracel Islands
LAOS
THAILAND
VIETNAM
CAMBODIA
South
China
Luzon
Manila
PHILIPPINES
See "The Spratly Islands"
Sea
Spratly
Islands
Sabah
State
MALAYSIA
INDONESIA
Borneo
SINGAPORE

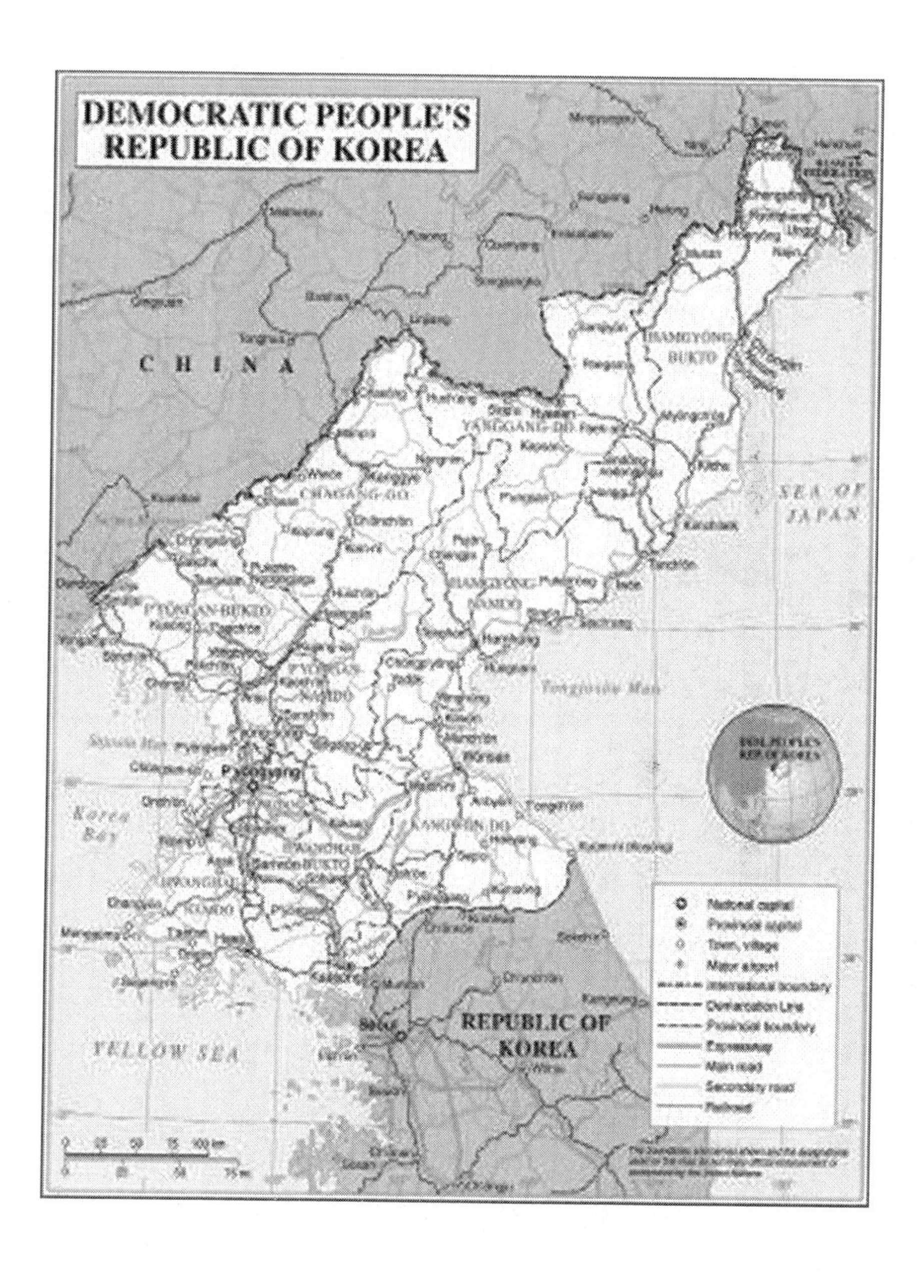
DEMOCRATIC PEOPLE'S
REPUBLIC OF KOREA
CHINA
HAMGYONG-BUKTO
YANGGANG-DO
CHAGANG-DO
SEA OF JAPAN
P'YONGAN-BUKTO
Pyongyang
Korea Bay
YELLOW SEA
REPUBLIC OF KOREA
Seoul
National capital
Provincial capital
Town, village
Major airport
International boundary
Demarcation Line
Provincial boundary
Expressway
Main road
Secondary road
Railroad

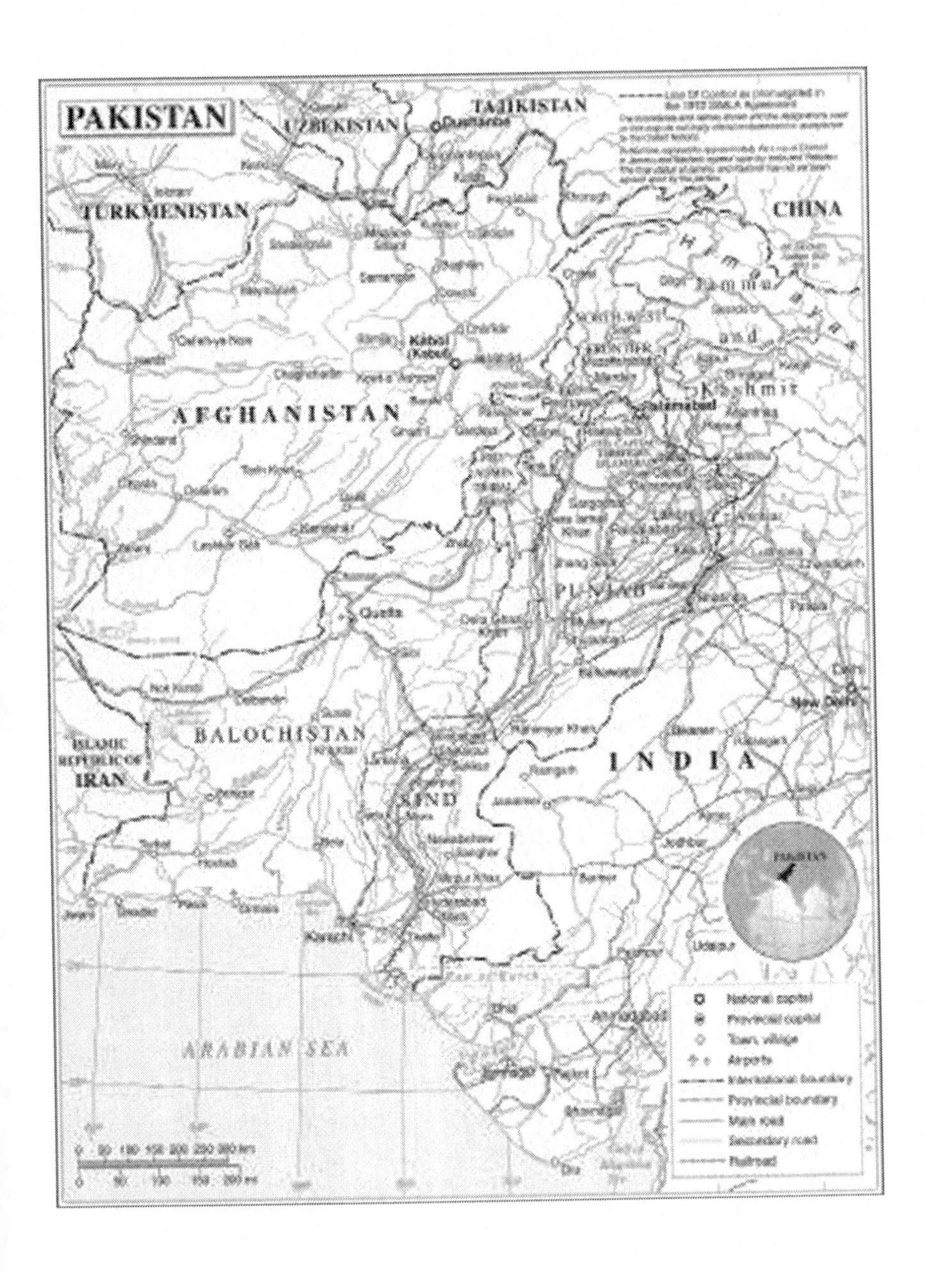
PAKISTAN
UZBEKISTAN
TAJIKISTAN
TURKMENISTAN
CHINA
AFGHANISTAN
Kabul
Islamabad
Quetta
BALOCHISTAN
ISLAMIC
REPUBLIC OF
IRAN
SIND
Karachi
PUNJAB
INDIA
New Delhi
ARABIAN SEA
National capital
Provincial capital
Town, village
Airports
International boundary
Provincial boundary
Main road
Secondary road
Railroad

Kashgar
Upal
Yengisar
China
Yarkand
Ghez
Tajikistan
Tashkurgan
Afghanistan
Khunjerab Pass
Sost
Passu
Gulmit
Karimabad
Chalt
Nagar
Gilgit
Bungi
Skardu
Khaplu
Chilas
Karghil
Chitral
Dasu
Line of control
Besham
Srinagar
Mansehra
Abbottabad
Haripur
Islamabad
India
Peshawar
Pakistan
Rawalpindi
Indus

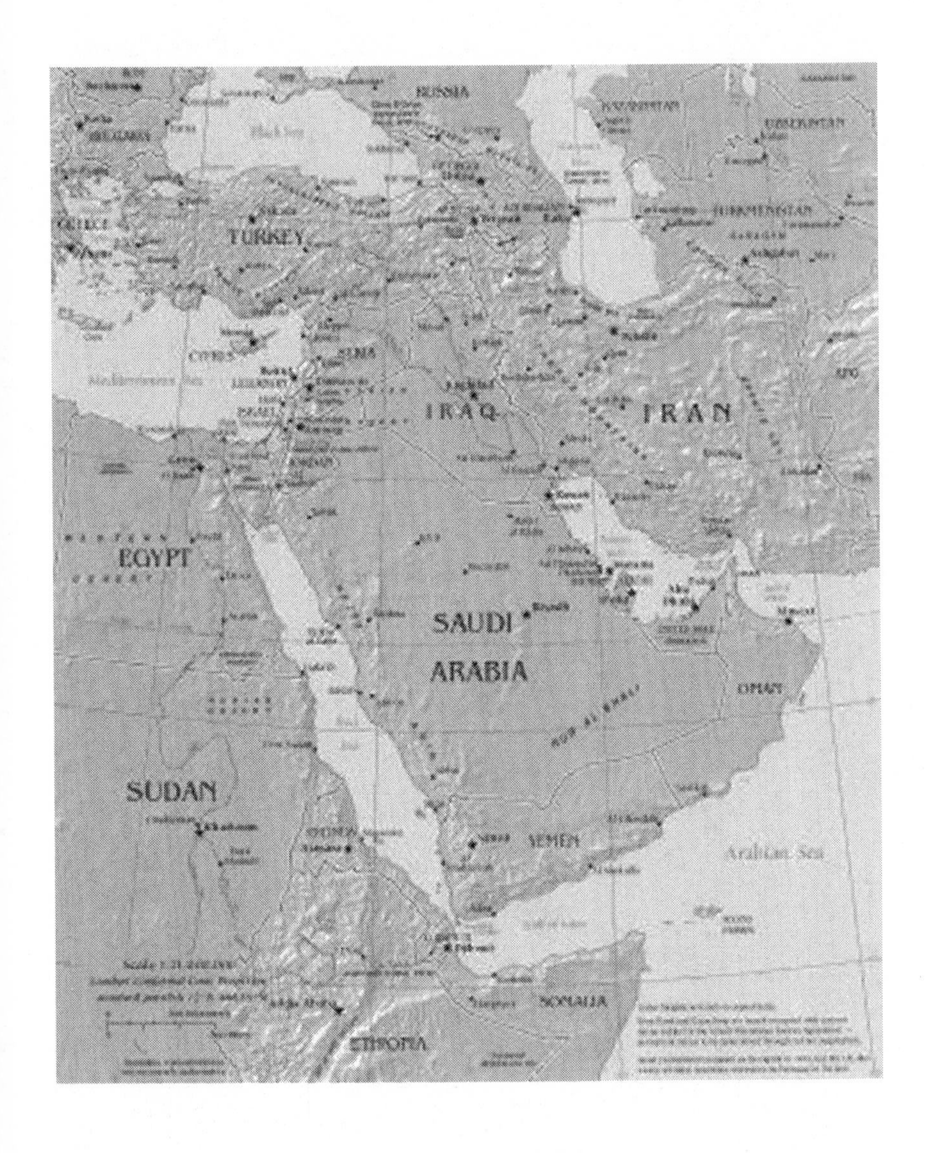
RUSSIA
TURKEY
IRAQ
IRAN
EGYPT
SAUDI
ARABIA
OMAN
SUDAN
YEMEN
Arabian Sea
SOMALIA

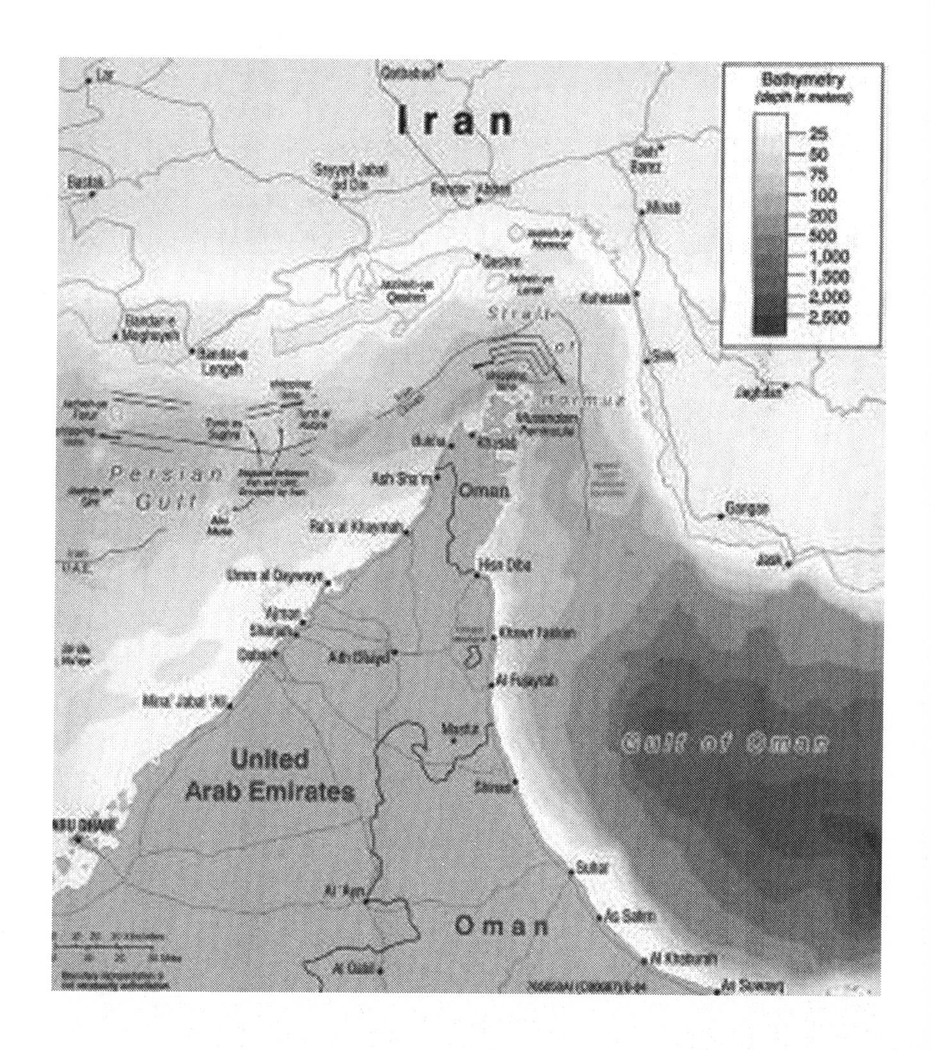
Iran
Bathymetry
25
50
75
100
200
500
1,000
1,500
2,000
2,500
Bandar Abbas
Persian
Gulf
Strait
of
Hormuz
Oman
Ra's al Khaymah
Umm al Qaywayn
Ajman
Sharjah
Dubai
Mina' Jabal 'Ali
Al Fujayrah
Madha
United
Arab Emirates
Gulf of Oman
Suhar
Al 'Ayn
Oman
Jask
Goragan

ISLAMIC REPUBLIC OF
IRAN
TURKMENISTAN
TURKEY
AFGHANISTAN
KHORASAN
IRAQ
KUWAIT
PAKISTAN
KERMAN
SAUDI
ARABIA
QATAR
Doha
UNITED ARAB
EMIRATES
Abu Dhabi
OMAN

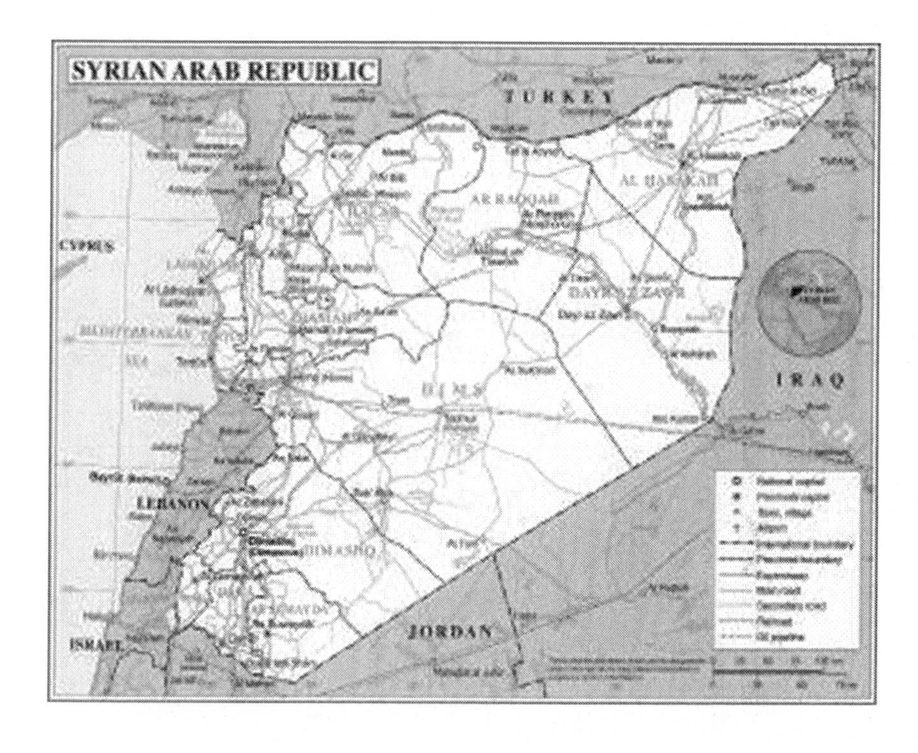
SYRIAN ARAB REPUBLIC
TURKEY
CYPRUS
IRAQ
LEBANON
ISRAEL
JORDAN
AR RAQQAH
AL HASAKAH
HIMS
DIMASHQ

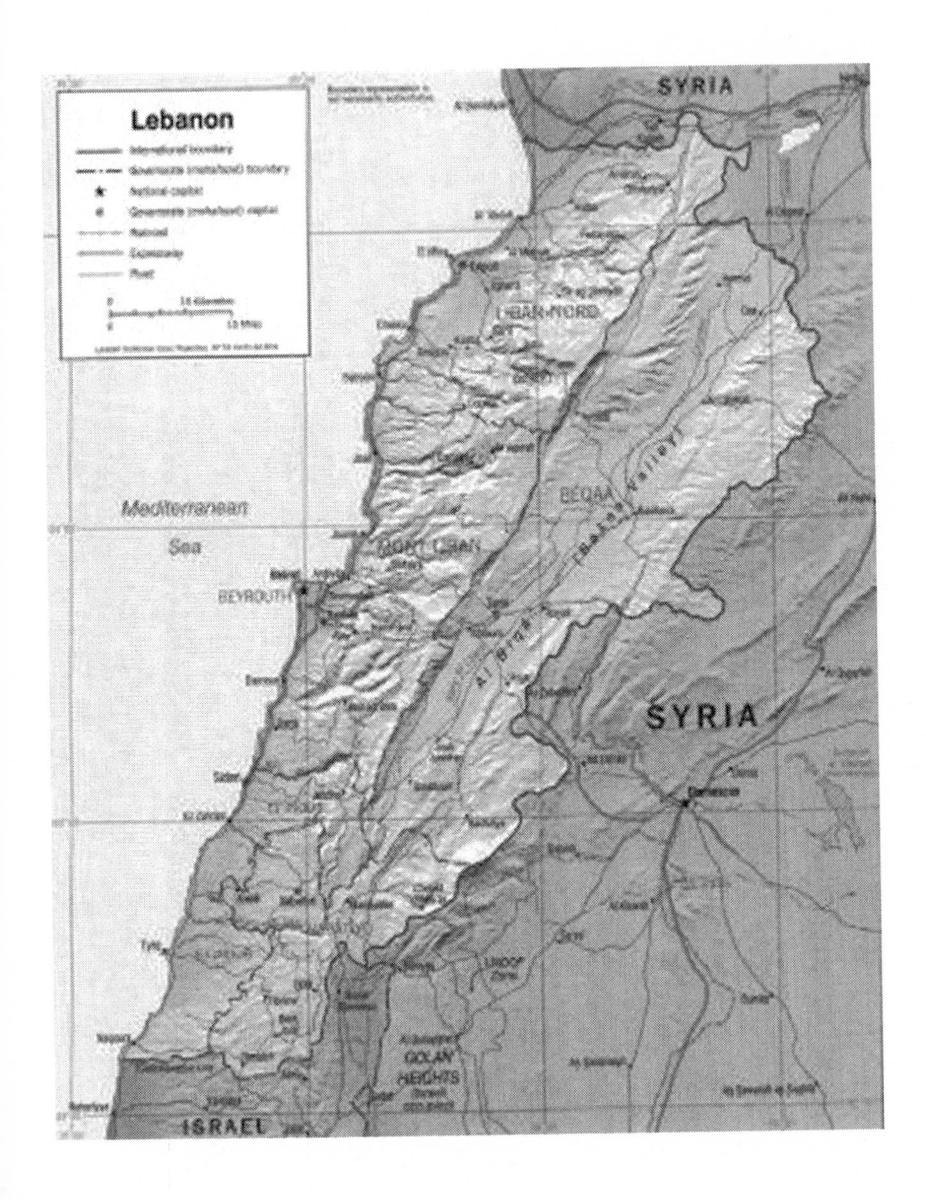
Lebanon
SYRIA
Mediterranean
Sea
BEYROUTH
BEQAA
SYRIA
GOLAN
HEIGHTS
ISRAEL

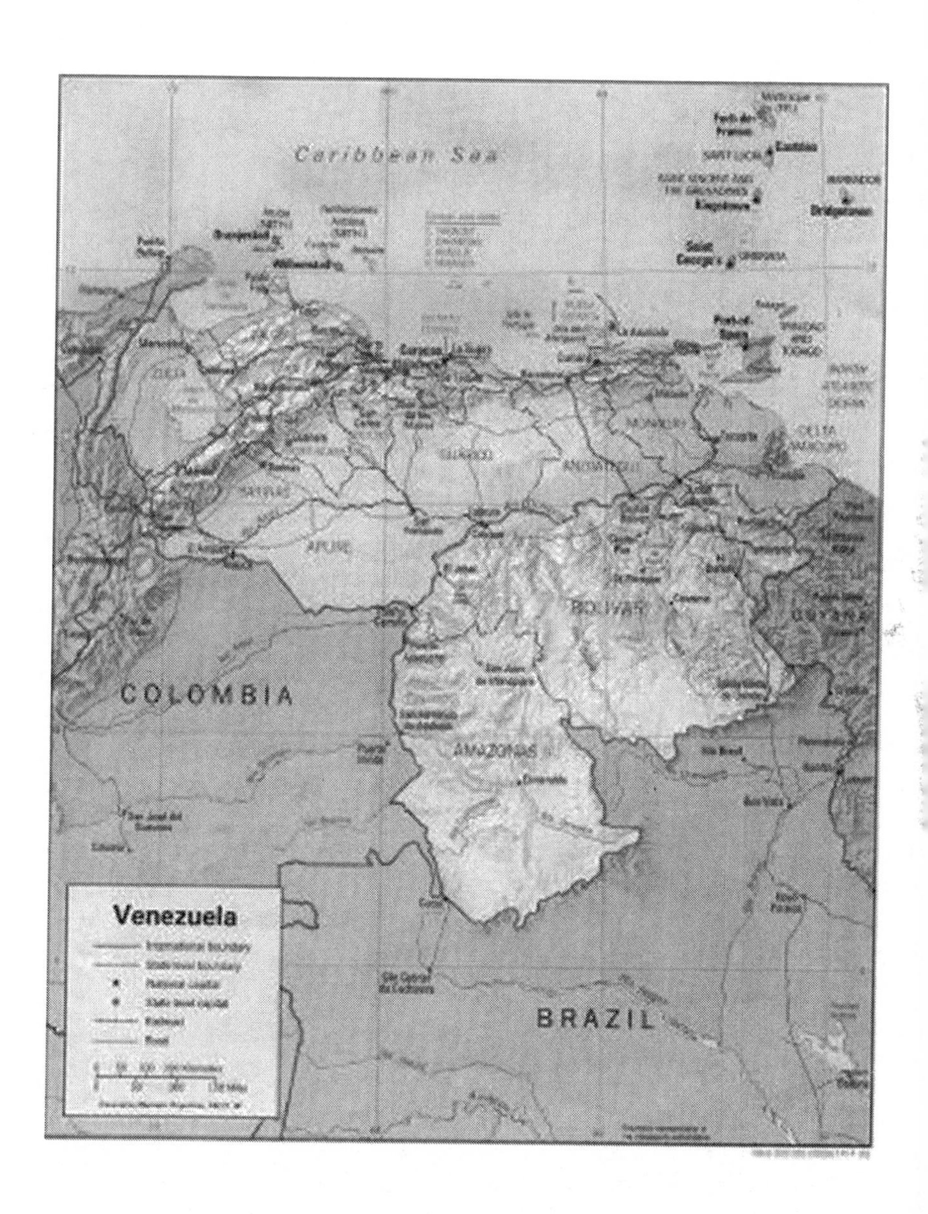
Caribbean Sea
APURE
BOLIVAR
AMAZONAS
COLOMBIA
BRAZIL
Venezuela

Preface

America had overcome many dangerous foes in the twentieth century. Surmounting the challenges of the Great Depression, International Fascism, and Soviet Communism had led the United States to believe in a bright future for her people. However, the twenty-first century began with an ominous tone for all Americans. The terror attacks of September 11, 2001, had exposed the soft underbelly of America's civil liberties and the potential power projection of international radical Islamic Terrorism. 9/11 had also revealed the future risks to America from rogue nuclear regimes in Iran and North Korea, and uncovered their close supportive relationships with the People's Republic of China.

The Great Economic Collapse of 2008 in the developed world, followed successively by the destabilizing Arab revolutions in North Africa and the Middle East, and the Euro Meltdown in 2011 with its consequential implications to the future world economy, have brought the planet to the brink of chaos. National austerity measures in the Western democracies are leading to progressive protectionism and isolationism. Currency wars are expanding into trade wars. Natural resource, economic, and demographic competitions between nations with vastly different cultural and political ideologies are leading to increasingly more belligerent relations and inflammatory rhetoric.

The development of a nuclear weapons program in Iran, and her theocratic government's public statements of annihilating the state of Israel, have generated great paranoia throughout the Middle East and disrupted the region's balance of power. The Persian Gulf's critical oil reserves have potentially become open to coercive blackmail.

In addition, China's illegal claims on the gas and oil riches of the East and South China Seas have created disharmony with Japan in the north, and her Southeast Asian neighbors to the south. Political and potential martial conflict has put in jeopardy the future of the free commercial sea routes through the regions. The world's fragile economic condition is susceptible to further collapse with rising oil prices. To say the world is advancing towards international military conflict would be a great understatement.

The novel you are about to read is of love and war in this new 'American Century'. It is set in the near future, when the disposition of nations will likely be more aggressive and intolerant. It is told in a time of an angry world dominated by general discord. A globe disjointed by economic, ideologic, and religious fracture. A moment which possibly could be America's most challenging and dangerous in her history.

American Amaranth is a tale of a man's love for his country, family, and most of all - his wife. It is a story about the eternal nature and grandness of love between a man and a woman. It reflects the hope and faith one can have in themselves. It speaks of loss, revenge, and redemption. It highlights the perseverance of the 'American Spirit' in the face of danger and sorrow. It reveals how people remain dutiful under extreme stress, moving forward against perilous adversity - when there is no other choice. It shows how love truly conquers all in the end.

The moral essence of *American Amaranth*, its quintessential virtue, will be required in all of us to keep our great nation free and the planet at peace. The children of the world demand our strongest effort. It is for them that we sacrifice, toil, and bleed.....

CHAPTER 1

The Dream

There is nothing more difficult to take in hand, more perilous to conduct, more uncertain in its success, than to take the lead in the introduction of a new order of things.

***Niccolo Machiavelli* (1469 to 1527)**

I was in a dream, lost alone without you. I sensed your absence next to me. You had left me in a dark void. There was deep lonely emptiness. I was hollowed out. Lifeless dust I was. There was no sound or color, just black silence..... In the despair, somehow and from somewhere, my place became injected with the light of life. Color was restored. An overwhelming sensation of goodness, deep peace, serene joy, and contentment began flowing into me. I felt your soul return. Although amorphous, you were there with me again. The lightness of your presence filled the darkness..... I was again young and strong, and able for all things. I was at the helm of our boat as we sailed towards the eastern horizon and an early morning sunrise.

The Cape Florida Lighthouse stood tall and white next to the sun. A full moon and a bright Venus were still visible in the morning sky. Around me were our three young boys. Their smiles lightened my heart. Their love, and your love, glowed in me. Like in days past, we were all together in spirit. We had the warmth of the sun on our faces again..... Cruelly and without warning, a rogue wave swept our sons into the sea. I dove frantically into the water but could not find them..... They were gone. You were gone. Life had vanished from my eyes. Darkness had returned.

I WAS AWAKENED FROM a short and difficult sleep by the ringing of my cell phone. "Admiral Stansfield, this is Lieutenant Commander Stevens. We've lost the *Spokane* in the Indian Ocean with all 134 men on board. It was tracking and gathering intelligence on a Chinese PLA naval convoy traveling east towards the Strait of Malacca, 800 nautical miles away. The convoy, composed of three guided missile destroyers and three frigates, had left the PLA naval base at Hambantota, Sri Lanka, and was en route back to the South China Sea. Helicopters off the destroyers, using dipping sonar and sonobuoys, localized our submarine and destroyed her with torpedoes....."

For the past several months, Chinese naval ships had protected North Korean flagged freighters carrying ballistic missiles and nuclear materials to the Persian Gulf and the Islamic Republic of Iran. PLA convoys were routinely tracked by US attack submarines, leading to constant challenges on both sides.

My young adjutant Stevens added, "Admiral, we're already working on a plan to intercept these ships as they return to the South China Sea through the Strait of Malacca. We're going to concentrate a pack of subs just east of Singapore.

"Needless to say, the *Mount Olympus* plan has been activated. The entire staff has been ordered back to the

Pentagon by 3 AM this morning. Your staff car will pick you up in 40 minutes."

After finishing the call, I lit a cigarette and took two deep drags. The bedside clock showed 1:50 AM. I was still in a profuse sweat. Reality was now reflective of my recurring nightmare.

Just hours before, an American guided-missile destroyer had been hit by anti-ship cruise missiles fired by Iranian Revolutionary Guard troops on the Syrian coast. She sunk into the eastern Mediterranean Sea with the loss of 80 men, including its commander. In less than a quarter-day, we had lost two fighting ships. Many men had died. America was at war again.

A few months earlier, with war feeling imminent, I had traveled on a *Zumwalt*-class destroyer from Pearl Harbor to Guam. I wanted to inspect the new-generation intelligence systems on the ship and at our naval base in the Mariana Islands. While in the western Pacific, I witnessed a total eclipse of the sun.

I stood on deck in bright daylight and watched the sky darken in a matter of minutes. It became like night. The heavens and the blue Pacific became the color of coal. Only a faint solar corona lit the blackness.

The thin ring of yellow light seemed to shimmer around the silhouette of the moon. The central black roundness appeared like a hole ready to swallow me and the Earth.

In a strange way, I saw the eclipse as I saw my life and the world. I sensed a sullen darkness that was complete. Eventually, I hoped, the world would return to an enlightenment. For myself, I was much less hopeful.

On Christmas evening years ago, my late wife Olivia and I had observed the Comet *NOSI* from a dark beach on Cape Florida. We lay in the cool sand at midnight, admiring its sparkling tail across the sky. We were inspired by its presence. It was natural beauty of the first degree, like Olivia.

It's odd how the celestium can offer such different emotions. It can present to you joyous light or somber darkness. One with Olivia, the other without.

It was now nearly 9 AM in the Persian Gulf and 2 PM in the South China Sea. The activation of *Mount Olympus* virtually assured that major US combat operations would begin within six hours. All US and NATO forces in the Middle East, Indian Ocean, and the western Pacific Ocean had gone into higher alert and were under orders to engage enemy forces showing hostile intent. The definition of "hostile intent" had been recently broadened to include virtually any offensive movement by enemy forces.

Upon further review of the present situation, and of the preparation status of US forces by the Pentagon and the President of the United States, the plan would likely be upgraded to *Climb Mount Olympus*. The upgrade would set in motion a full-scale aerial and naval assault on the Islamic Republic of Iran and its interests throughout the Middle East. We would also bring war on all Chinese and North Korean interests in the South China Sea and East Asia.

In the past month, there had been an extreme increase in terror attacks against American and NATO forces in the Middle East. Over 1400 military personnel had been killed, including the 80 seamen lost last night in the sinking of the *USS Patrick Henry* off the coast of Syria.

US intelligence services had concluded that late generation, Chinese-made anti-ship missiles had sunk the *Patrick Henry*. Even without considering the loss of the LA-class *USS Spokane* in the Indian Ocean, Chinese involvement in providing modern weaponry to Iran and it's clandestine operations in Syria and Lebanon was unacceptable to the United States. Additionally, their provision of military advisers and advanced satellite intelligence made the PLA a full-fledged enemy combatant.

War with the People's Republic of China had finally come; and her military interests in Africa, Central Asia, Pakistan, Sri Lanka, Bangladesh, Burma, Cambodia, and the South China Sea Island chains would be in play. China's ally North Korea, a nuclear terror regime, would also become another theater of war.

A tipping point had been reached over access to natural resources and energy supplies. Diplomacy had failed. Dire economic consequences had forced nations to consider aggressive action to prevent the demise of their political systems. The primal instincts for survival had turned human nature towards war.

As Director of US Naval Intelligence (DNI), I would help lead my country into a major global war. My duty was to win this war with the least number of American casualties possible. To achieve this conventionally without nuclear war, US naval power would have to be overwhelming and inflict catastrophic losses on the enemy in a short amount of time. The enemy would be forced to see their inevitable destruction early in the fight. They would be made to see the 'light' through the 'dark'.

I took two more puffs on my cigarette and rolled my legs over the side of the bed. I wiped the sweat off my face with the palms of my hands and reached for the stereo remote control on the night table. My daughter Rebecca's recording of Ravel's "Pavane for a Dead Princess", from her Royal Albert Hall concert in 2013, began to play. French Impressionistic music from the late 19th century, particularly this Ravel piece, had been a favorite of Olivia; and no one could play it as beautifully as our world renown concert pianist daughter, Rebecca. Olivia had always said that it evoked in her the image of a young Spanish Renaissance princess dancing a slow and elegant courtly dance. To me, it simply evoked an image of Olivia. And I needed that more than anything in this world.

Eternity with her..... The thought was ethereal, but it sustained me. I had never imagined being without her. Alas, life doesn't usually evolve as you expect it to. How do you live without your life's most essential element? She was the very reason for my being.

Without Olivia, I was slowly dying. And I welcomed it. I was seeking that eternity. My heart was broken, and no doctor could mend it. In an unusual kindness, my material end was part of the plan. With every beat of my heart, my life drained from me..... But there was one more thing remaining that I needed to do.

I walked into the bathroom and threw the cigarette into the open commode. I faced the mirror. I had become aged. White hair and a disfigured left eye made me appear older than my age. I was thinner than I used to be, with less muscle mass. Early cardiac cachexia, the doctors called it.

As a US military observer with the Chinese PLA during the Sino-Vietnamese War in 1979, I had suffered a devastating traumatic injury to my left eye. Several surgeries at the Johns Hopkins Hospital had not prevented a slow progression to functional blindness in this eye. The cornea opacified, giving the eye a marbled appearance. I usually covered it with a black patch. It had become my trademark at the Pentagon.

Serious cardiac problems had forced me to consider retirement. The Navy, needing expertise and experience, requested I become Director of Naval Intelligence two years ago. With coaxing from my wife, who was already terminally ill with cancer, I accepted the position three months later.

Over the past twenty years, I had become an authority in anti-ship ballistic missile technology. I knew well how best to sink a ship, and also how best to prevent it. With war fast approaching, the United States understood her enemies would use asymmetric warfare against the American surface fleet, particularly the aircraft carriers.

It was cheaper to build missiles than naval ships. Russia, China, Iran, and North Korea had developed advanced missile technology and amassed thousands of ship killers. America, in turn, developed excellent defenses against them. Even so, in closed bodies of water like the Persian Gulf, the Red Sea, and the eastern Mediterranean, high volumes of anti-ship missiles from multiple directions could inflict severe losses on the US Navy. *Operation Mount Olympus* would certainly test America's new naval defense systems, and my ingenuity in implementing them.

There were also deep personal reasons for not retiring and accepting the DNI position. I had three sons serving in the United States military.

Julius, my oldest, was the captain on the *USS Oregon*, a Virginia class nuclear attack submarine in the South China Sea. He had been in the thick of the international intrigue for over a month. He was measured and cool in his decisions and actions. His calculating demeanor made him an excellent undersea commander. He took risks, but never unnecessarily.

Michael had been in the Navy SEALs until being transferred to the CIA Special Activities Division in 2013. Knowing exactly where he was in the world was difficult, even for me. Michael was very smart and witty. He had an excellent sense of comedic timing which could provide appropriate levity to seemingly tense situations. My second-oldest son was never afraid, and he was rarely wrong in his actions. Michael was a 'survivor'.

Mark, the youngest, was a Special Forces Marine Raider. He was presently involved in an operation along the Hunza River in northern Pakistan. He was absolutely fearless in battle. At times, I thought, almost to the point of recklessness. His men on the ground loved him because he would never command them to do anything he wouldn't do first. He was always first in and last out. I worried most about Mark. He was perhaps too brave.

Maybe, I thought, my intelligence analysis could help keep the young American warriors safe. Like as for all the star-spangled boys and girls destined for conflict, I wished to increase my sons' chances of returning to their families unharmed after the war. If I could force the enemy to realize rapidly the futility of making war with the United States, then all our children - friend and foe - could return home faster. I had promised this to Olivia, shortly before losing her fifteen months ago.

I dressed into my dark blue Navy uniform. I placed a strapped black patch over my left eye and holstered a .40 caliber pistol into a shoulder harness. Since last year, all US-based military officers had been personally armed with concealed weapons. Furthermore, our official transport vehicles were armored against small arms fire, RPGs, and roadside bombs.

As I walked downstairs, I gently glanced at an old portrait of a young Olivia on our sailboat in Biscayne Bay, Florida. It was my favorite depiction of her. Although Olivia's physical beauty was the centerpiece, her unique and precious smile dominated the painting. I stopped and stayed in front of it for a while, admiring her. I remembered all the good times. Olivia was a bright and charismatic girl, and she had instantly captured my love in those first moments after meeting. There was a great power between us. I had never felt anything like it. That feeling remained my whole life with her.

Without Olivia, as in a cold and total eclipse of the sun, my life was dark and difficult. It had no rhyme or reason. All its colors had faded. It was like watching a rainbow form over Biscayne Bay after a summer storm, alone, without having anyone to share it with. It was dancing slowly by myself without music, or eating alone in darkness late in the evening. It was shallow breathing inside a tight enclosure with my only eye closed. I was very uncomfortable with all of it. I didn't belong anywhere - anymore. I had been too long without her.

I knew I would see Olivia again in time. It was my hope, my faith. The thought sustained me. Her love fueled me to do what I needed to do now. She would guide me on my mission for the United States.

I exited my Georgetown home to the waiting staff car and drove off towards the Pentagon. A dangerous chapter in world history had begun, perhaps its most threatening. America and the world held their breath. I held my breath. It was 2:30 in the morning on May 12.

CHAPTER 2

The Pentagon

It is only the dead who have seen the end of war.
***Plato* (428 BC to 348 BC)**

IT WAS A SILENT DRIVE to the Pentagon. My mind drifted in thought..... I had given several decades of my life to America..... My journey in the Navy began at Annapolis as a first year cadet in 1969. I graduated at the top of my class in 1973 with the highest examination grade point average at the Academy since 1913. I was a particularly strong student in the biological and physical sciences. But I had loved literature, history, and philosophy. The Navy urged me to go into the submarine service, where scientific innovation was occurring on a daily basis..... While serving on the USS Tunny, a nuclear submarine, I met Olivia on a cruise layover to Miami, Florida, in December of 1975. By all judgement, Olivia was the most beautiful woman in South Florida at the time. She was graceful and impeccably educated. Olivia was the granddaughter of a very wealthy Cuban industrialist, and the daughter of a famous Cuban patriot who had been executed by Fidel Castro's regime after the failed Bay of Pigs invasion in 1961. Love was immediate, and we married in 1976..... I was transferred to a Pacific submarine division in San Diego, California, and later recruited into Naval Intelligence. At the end of 1978, I was sent to China as a military observer during the Sino-Vietnamese War. This assignment led me to believe strongly that China would be a future battlefield antagonist of the United States..... With Navy Intelligence, I was granted special permission to acquire a masters degree in Chinese Studies at Princeton University. I became a scholar in Chinese military history and tactics, and fluent in the Mandarin Chinese language..... I had spent most of the past two decades becoming the Navy's top authority in offensive and defensive missile technology..... My making in the United States Navy had been long and complex.....

My mind continued to wander. I thought of how my young life before the Navy had become very distant to me in time. The central details were clear and distinct, but the edges were fuzzy. Many years had passed.

I remembered the first time my father took me sailing on Lake Michigan, and how he taught me to prepare a ship for open water. How Father had stressed the importance of a safe harbor in a storm. I was very young, but I learned his lessons quickly.

I thought of Bobby. The unexpected death of my older brother had been a very traumatic event for me and my parents. As a child, I couldn't reason his absence. Worse, it contributed mightily to the death of my father and mother, a few years later. I was forced to become a man before my time. I had much anguish in my heart as a boy.

I reminisced of the first time I went sailing with Olivia in Biscayne Bay. Her gentle sensuality struck me like lightning. She was devilish and angelic at the same time. The curves of her hips and thighs were matched by her lips and smile. I couldn't keep my eyes off of her. She generated spontaneous combustion in me. I truly became a man with Olivia. Her fire was amazing. She had been so easy to love.

I remembered the births of our children. Olivia had closely guided their development into great human beings. She was important in all the stages of their lives. We all missed her much.

During Olivia's final days, she asked me for a promise. Knowing a global war was coming, she asked that I help protect her boys in my duties. She pleaded for me to get them home safely, after victory. I made this promise to her.

Olivia also requested her ashes be scattered into the waters of Biscayne Bay. She wanted her physical remains to stay where she had fallen in love with me. I always agreed to her wishes.

Last year, on a cold but brilliantly beautiful early February morning, we sailed a strong wind onto Biscayne Bay and released Olivia's ashes into its blue-green waters. Under a bright cobalt sky, I returned toward the Cape Florida Lighthouse without her. It was the first and only time I sailed the bay without Olivia. I never came back to the place where it all started. The cape had been our sanctuary - the very spot where my life began, and then, where it had also ended. That sunny February morning was the last time I saw Cape Florida.

If there was a constant in my life, it was love. Love for the family I lost as a boy, love for Olivia and our children, and love for the United States of America and its Navy.

These were my thoughts as I rode in the backseat of my staff car to the Pentagon early in the morning of May 12. I reviewed my life in vivid moving picture flashes. I had lived a good life. I was very appreciative of its quality. I had no regrets.

Arriving at a back entrance, I began the long walk down the empty corridor to the Naval Operational Intelligence Center. My footsteps echoed off the walls loudly in regular cadence. The sounds reminded me of the drums on the parade grounds at Annapolis as a young cadet. I had spent many years preparing for this moment, always hoping it would never present itself.

America had not been taken flat-footed. Since the early 1990s, the United States maintained detailed war plans for China, North Korea, and Iran. It was a common belief at the Pentagon that war with these countries was inevitable. The plans entailed securing the Persian Gulf oil fields and the Strait of Hormuz, through which 40 per cent of the world's seaborne oil traveled. The Strait of Malacca and the South China Sea would be denied to the PLA Navy. Chinese vessels would not be allowed into the Pacific through Japan's southern chain of small islands. The Japanese Navy would combat a circumnavigation of the larger northern home islands via the Sea of Japan. A Chinese invasion of Taiwan would be prevented at all costs. All Allied territories would be defended against sea, air, and land attack. The Korean peninsula would be reunified under a democratic government. Finally, Chinese and Iranian political, economic, and military influence would be eliminated in Central Asia, Africa, and Latin America. In essence, the plans required world war.

Armed U.S. Marine guards opened the double doors to the Navy Intelligence Center. I took a deep breath and entered the room. Waiting for me near the conference table was my personal aide, Lieutenant Commander Louis Stevens.

Stevens had been with me for a good while. He was loyal and hard-working. He reminded me of my sons.

The young man had the unusual distinction of being born and raised in Fredericksburg, Texas, the birth town of Chester William Nimitz – famous Fleet Admiral of the United States Navy in the Pacific during World War Two. He was very proud of the rare fact.

Louis had graduated with Mark from the Naval Academy. A mathematical genius, he served briefly on a guided missile cruiser in the Persian Gulf after graduating from Annapolis. Quickly transferred to Navy Intel, Louis had done research and intelligence development prior to America's war in Libya in 2011. He had also managed the intelligence gathering for the clandestine US involvement in the Amazon War between Colombia and Venezuela two years ago.

Lieut. Cmdr. Louis Stevens spoke fluent Spanish. He provided my only opportunity to speak in that language since Olivia passed away. He was kind and personable. I always appreciated his company.

"How are you feeling, Sir?" politely asked Stevens as I took my seat.

"About as well as you can expect under the circumstances, Louis," I answered. "The reality of being at war is unpleasant for everyone, but especially so for an old man who has spent his entire life trying to prevent it. We can only do the best we can to limit its magnitude for the world. I will depend on you greatly over the next few weeks."

"Weeks, Sir?"

"Yes, Louis..... Weeks!" I said forcefully. "The might of the US Navy will limit it so."

"I will do my earnest, Sir, to be of your assistance."

"Oh, I have no doubts, Louis, that you will perform for your country with best efforts. You are a patriot. I saw it in your eyes the first day we met. Eyes don't lie. I am proud to have you working with me. We will be busy, I assure you."

"You have quite a schedule today, Admiral."

"We'll have a tough schedule every day going forward.

"By the way, Louis, what would your Admiral Nimitz do under our present circumstances?"

"He'd kick ass, Sir! Just as you will, Admiral."

I smiled at the boy to acknowledge his faith in me.

"I hope I have a better start than 'Old Chester'. He sweated out the first few months," I said.

"Oh.....You will, Sir. You're older and wiser."

"Older for sure, but wiser? I don't know about that. Perhaps more beaten in," I laughed.

The Naval Operational Intelligence Center at the Pentagon was a large square room. At the center was a round table where intelligence officials were seated. Aides sat behind their superiors in a circumferential manner. There were real-time live video screens on two walls, which provided active data analysis and live video streaming from all the operational theaters. A third wall held a teleconference system that connected anyone, anywhere, anytime, instantly.

Present at the meeting via teleconference were the Navy Intelligence representatives from - the US Seventh Fleet bases at Pearl Harbor, Guam, Subic Bay in the Philippines, Okinawa, Sasebo and Yokosuka in Japan - the US Fifth Fleet base at Bahrain in the Persian Gulf - and the Sixth Fleet base in Naples, Italy.

Present in person were the base commanders from Norfolk, Virginia, and San Diego, California, as well as the deputy directors of Homeland Security and the CIA.

Additionally, directors of the US Missile Defense Agency (MDA) and the Space Tracking and Surveillance Systems (STSS) were seated at the conference table.

The Deputy Director of the CIA began the meeting by describing recent intelligence received from American agents inside Iran, showing Iranian scientists had finally adapted their nuclear warheads to intermediate and long distance ballistic missiles. The weapons were capable of reaching Europe and the continental United States.

Furthermore, Iran had recently purchased ready built nuclear missiles from North Korea and Pakistan, and had placed them in the hulls of freighters which were destined to sail close to US international waters. The cargo ships were prepared to fire the rockets against America if the need arose.

Iranian agents had also smuggled disassembled mini-nukes into the US. They were under orders to deliver them to safe houses where technicians would assemble the bombs before distributing them to predetermined target sites.

America was under a multi-pronged nuclear assault threat. Although prepared to an extent, a nation can rarely count on all her defensive mechanisms for fail-safety. Somewhere along the line, the protective net usually collapses and a catastrophe occurs. It is difficult to avoid a bite from *Cerberus*, the three-headed dog guardian of the mythological ancient Greek God of Death – *Hades*.

Orders would soon be given for US Air Force B2 Stealth and B52 bombers out of Diego Garcia Island in the Indian Ocean to deliver nuclear earth-penetrating bunker buster bombs (B61-15 NEP) to key Iranian atomic facilities holding offensive missiles. US Naval aviation would provide support for these missions, as well as attack other key military and commercial facilities throughout the country.

The US Navy was ordered to seek and destroy the clandestine freighters bound for waters off of the United States. These freighters were believed to still be at Persian Gulf and Red Sea ports. Only one had left port from Tartus, Syria, and was still in the eastern Mediterranean. All the freighters were flying false flags.

CIA, FBI, and Homeland Security agents were on the trail of the Iranian terror cells responsible for the smuggling of the mini-nukes into the US. Two safe houses had already been discovered and were under surveillance.

Intelligence reports showed that Iranian terror cells had been activated in Central and South America. There were over 800 units, of twenty men apiece, prepared to assault American establishments with light arms, RPGs, and suicide bomb vests. The radicals also had small planes and helicopters outfitted for offensive combat operations. The United States could expect attacks on their interests in these regions within a short period of time. Most of the activity was forming in Mexico and Panama. US military intervention would likely be required at the US-Mexico border and in the Panama Canal Zone.

The CIA revealed Iran had amassed depots of biological and chemical weapons. Large stores had been secretly transferred through Iraq into the Levant. The presence of over 150,000 rockets and cruise missiles in Syria and Lebanon would allow Hezbollah and Islamic Jihadi fighters to attack Israel from short range. The use of biochemical WMDs on population centers in Israel was expected to generate tens of thousands of casualties. The Mossad knew where the storage sites were and felt they could be neutralized through covert action.

Urgently, the Israeli prime minister would proceed with plans to invade Lebanon and Syria within hours. The invasion was being coordinated with the Pentagon and NATO forces in the Middle East. It would also involve a seaborne invasion of Lebanon and Syria by British and French military forces.

Israel would not reveal the locations of the WMD depots. Mossad had full control of those operations and did not want to risk the loss of surprise through inadvertent information leak.

For the past several months, the CIA had provided secret shipments of weapons to anti-government rebels in all major Iranian cities. They believed open rebellion would break out soon after US air attacks on military facilities. American Special Forces were dropping by air into key areas to help lead the insurgencies. Heavy loss of Iranian and US military lives were expected behind enemy lines early in the battle.

Homeland Security then presented their readiness report on *Operation Red Tide*, a country-wide federal net to attack and asphyxiate all known terror cell operatives inside the United States. Hundreds of cells were scattered throughout America with orders to blow bridges and dams, attack public buildings and transportation, sports venues, schools, and hospitals. They were trained to shoot down commercial airplanes with shoulder held rockets. It was expected that some attacks would be successful and lead to a significant loss of civilian life.

Biological and chemical weapons were expected, and major metropolitan hospitals had been placed on high alert for mass casualty events. A state of martial law was now in effect.

Operation Galea was activated by the MDA (Missile Defense Agency). Named for the Roman legion's helmet, the plan protected the US homeland from ballistic missile attacks by foreign powers (i.e. China, North Korea, Iran). The system used land, air, and sea based kinetic energy interceptor missiles, arrayed in a coordinated net around the world. Terminal phase defense systems using Arrow and Patriot Advanced Capability 3 missiles (PAC-3) were scattered throughout friendly territories in the Middle East, Asia, and Europe, as well as throughout the American homeland. Boeing YAL-1 Airborne Laser systems on military 747 planes were deployed around the globe for airborne defense against ballistic missile attacks in the boost and ascent phases - before the missiles reached apogee.

Homeland Security and the US Navy were tracking several Chinese nuclear attack submarines off the West Coast and in the Gulf of Mexico. Two carrier battle groups, the *Eisenhower* and *Nimitz*, were in eastern Pacific waters in defense of the US West Coast. Several hundred stealth "Ghost" ships were patrolling America's coastlines. Combat conditions were in effect, and battle was expected at any moment.

The Director of the Space Tracking and Surveillance Systems (STSS) showed satellite images of Chinese troop concentrations in southwest China along the Pakistani border. There were over 250,000 PLA troops preparing to cross into Pakistan down the Karakoram Tri-rail highway to Islamabad, and further south into Balochistan, in development of an offensive front against US forces in Afghanistan and southwestern Pakistan. Top-secret US raids along the highway had destroyed critical bridges only a few nights before, causing a major disruption to the Chinese plans.

More satellite images of Chinese troop concentrations at ports along the Fujian coast opposite Taiwan, and several PLA divisions crossing into North Korea, were presented. The movements of several hundred thousand North Korean troops toward the DMZ (Demilitarized Zone) were shown on satellite maps.

Satellite images of PLA naval forces on Hainan Island, Woody Island in the Paracels chain, and several Spratly Islands in the South China Sea were discussed. China's "String of Pearls" naval bases in Pakistan, Sri Lanka, Bangladesh, Burma, and Cambodia were noted to be on high alert.

America's anti-satellite (ASAT) and cyberwarfare plans were activated. They were shown to be far ahead of similar Chinese programs.

I then presented the Navy's plan to protect the Persian Gulf oil traffic through the Strait of Hormuz, and our directive to gain total air superiority within the first 24 hours of combat operations against Iran. The Navy would land three Marine divisions along the Iranian gulf coast - concentrated mainly at Bushehr in the southwest, and Jask in the southeast. An additional 250,000 US, British, Canadian, and German troops would enter by land and air from Azerbaijan, Iraq, Afghanistan, and southwest Pakistan.

A small US surface fleet would help support the British and French Expeditionary Force (BFEF) landings along the coasts of Lebanon and Syria.

Soon, a US carrier strike group would leave Subic Bay in the Philippines and attack the Chinese garrison on Woody Island in the South China Sea. It would support the landing of the First Marine Regiment. They expected to confront the PLA South Fleet out of Hainan Island in a naval engagement.

Several US submarine-supported Navy SEAL raids on PLA South China Sea island bases would take place prior to the American landings on Woody Island.

The Strait of Malacca would become impassable to Chinese shipping within the first week of combat operations, and little oil would reach the Chinese mainland. All foreign PLA naval bases would be blockaded, and their vessels attacked and sunk.

Nearly 35,000 US Marines were already stationed on Taiwan, supporting 210,000 Republic of China (ROC) troops in their defense against a PLA invasion. US Task Force 93, composed of three carrier strike groups, would engage the Chinese in the Taiwan Strait and help prevent the landings. They would be supported by US air elements on Taiwan and Okinawa, two unsinkable aircraft carriers.

From the Sea of Japan, the *John F. Kennedy* and the *Gerald R. Ford* carrier strike groups would help support Allied military operations on the Korean peninsula. Seven hundred thousand US, South Korean, Indonesian, Japanese, and Australian troops were poised to strike into North Korea.

At the end of the meeting, the CIA Deputy Director spoke briefly on Russia. Since the 'Ukraine Crisis', and the deaths of thousands of innocent Ukrainian civilians, bad blood had simmered between Russia and America.

Nevertheless, it was essential to keep the Russians out of an enemy axis in a global war. Maintaining open communications with them would hopefully decrease the chances of dangerous misunderstandings. Dealing with Russia was not easy, but there were few other options.

Like many times in the past, the US government had again advised Russia to remove all personnel from Syria and Iran.

Russia had been playing a dangerous game of geopolitical hypocrisy for years. They would switch support from America and her allies to the 'Evil Axis', and back again, on almost a weekly basis. It had become a comedy.

The Russians would sell military equipment to China and Iran, and the next week reprimand them for unacceptable behavior. They had built much of the Iranian nuclear infrastructure, while pushing them to sit down with the West in negotiations. The Russians called the North Koreans 'animals', while selling them ballistic technology.

But when looking at the bottom line, America understood Russia's predicament. The Slavs needed the West more than the West needed them. Russia could not avoid two major realities.

The Chinese expansionists needed energy. They wanted to regain old lands in the Russian Far East, heavily laden with precious oil. Lands stolen from them by the Tsars, they believed. China had requested a diplomatic meeting on the issue. As their military power expanded, the PLA could be expected to be more forceful with their intentions.

Secondly, why would Russia ever want a strong radical Islamic empire to their south? The Caucasus would be exposed to Iranian fundamentalist machinations.

Russia's chances for future war with the Chinese and Iranians were much greater than with the West. Besides, It was better business to sell their oil and gas to the West. Also, America was a better drilling partner for Russia in the Arctic.

America's position on Russian Arctic policy had been thoroughly argued and explained. Russia was told America would support Canada and Norway in their Arctic claims against her, but that also, the US was willing to negotiate a settlement which would benefit all parties.

Likewise, the US would support her ally Japan's claims on the Northern Territories. Yet, there was room for settlement in favor of Russia.

The US would vigorously pursue her own interests in the Arctic Circle and would not allow Russian meddling. But also, America was agreeable to the financial potential of 'joint venture' with the Russians.

America informed Russia of her willing desire to negotiate new contracts for the future purchase of Russian mineral and energy resources. There was also American support for Russian sales to Europe.

Most importantly, the US reminded Russia of the ongoing Chinese demographic re-population of Russian territories in their Far East, and its implications for the future security of Russian natural resources. They were being invaded slowly, and would soon lose control of the region.

Additionally, America was willing to cooperate with Russia in Central Asia to mitigate increasing Chinese economic influence and military involvement in this region. The US was amenable to exchanging Chinese 'hard power' with Russian 'soft power'.

Simply stated, the US wanted friendly relations with her old enemy - perhaps even an alliance with Russia. Although the US blamed Russia for much of the world's misfortune at the present time, we were willing to 'forgive and forget'. America could not allow Russia to cooperate with the enemy alliance militarily. It would be a formidable negative for our strategic planners.

The US was annoyed at Russia's positions on the never-ending Syrian Civil War. Russian economic and military aid to the nefarious Syrian government, and her support of Iranian military involvement in the conflict, had prolonged the war unnecessarily. The rebels, supported by the West, had failed to destroy the stronger Axis Alliance. Slowly, the war spread regionally. The long conflict had bled into Lebanon, Turkey, Jordan, and Iraq. Eventually, growing Syrian and Iranian losses led to a closer cooperation between them and China. North Korea also increased its support of the Axis. A world war evolved. The lessons of the Spanish Civil War from long ago had been forgotten. In the twenty-first century, nations had once again been irresponsible. History had repeated itself.

After years of wrangling, eye-opening American diplomacy and economic stiff-arming were finally turning the Russians away from the Axis. Russia was seeing the greater dangers of an aggressive Shia-Persian Empire and a hungry China at her doorsteps. She had much more to lose from a victorious Axis than from a democratic West, led by the US.

Overall, the US intelligence community was now comfortable with the hypothesis that Russia was more willing to work with her old nemesis, the United States, than deal with the rapidly expanding, insatiable, economic and military power of the People's Republic of China. America was hopeful and confident of Russia's non-involvement in the developing conflict.

The intelligence conference ended by 6 AM. I was ordered to the White House for a meeting with the President and his national security inner circle.

While I gave instructions to my driver, the sun was rising over Washington and our national monuments. Louis Stevens had escorted me to the car.

"I hope the sun continues to shine on America, Sir," said Stevens as he squinted at the sun and saluted me.

Sitting in the back seat of the staff car, I turned my look towards the lieutenant commander. I returned his salute and kindly smiled at him.

"I wouldn't worry much about that, Louis. The sun will always shine on truly free governments. It's simply 'Natural Selection'. 'Survival of the Fittest'.....

"I'm much more concerned that my efforts don't entail a blotting out of the sun for the rest of the world. There is no victory in total catastrophe. Darwin wouldn't have approved of that calamity, Louis."

I gazed at the sun through my window and added in a low voice, "No..... I don't wish to blot out the sun..... That certainly wouldn't be achieving 'Peace on Earth'. My duty is as much to save the world as it is to save the United States of America, Louis. I will honor that duty to the best of my ability. We all owe that to mankind. The sun is God's business only....."

I looked again at the lieutenant commander and smiled, "Honor and Duty, Louis. Honor and Duty..... You can't perform the latter without much of the former. Let's pray for the courage to see it through."

Louis Stevens nodded his head. "I have faith in your honor, Sir. Let it guide you and our country to a righteous victory. I have trust in your wisdom, Admiral. I don't believe there is any higher power 'under' the sun."

CHAPTER 3

The President and The New American Century

We, and all others who believe in freedom as deeply as we do, would rather die on our feet than live on our knees.

***Franklin Delano Roosevelt* (1882 to 1945)**

I RODE PAST the Washington Monument. Early sunlight reflected off its capstone top, creating almost a halo effect. I thought of its symbolism and how its 555 feet of granite and marble represented the strength and power of the United States. America's virtues of liberty, freedom to think and express, and personal growth, all supported by military might as an agent for preservation and national security. The 20th century had been challenging. America dominated much of it. Although it entered both the First and Second World Wars late, the United States was the deciding influence in the outcomes of both. America was the first to develop atomic energy and used its power to end World War II. We rebuilt Europe and Japan after 1945, and made them economically competitive in the world marketplace. America's enemies embraced democracy. The United States fought a long ideological battle with Communism throughout the century, eventually leading to the fall of the Soviet Union in 1991. The US finished the 20th century as the world's sole superpower. It truly had been the "American Century".

However, the 21st century began poorly. The stunning attacks of September 11, 2001, paralyzed America economically. 9/11 led to a world wide war on terror. Conflicts in the Middle East, Asia, Africa, and Latin America bled America dry politically, economically, and socially. The Great Economic Collapse of 2008 created a long painful recession which weakened governments throughout the world, directly leading to domestic and international conflict. A great wave of inflation caused insurmountable hardship at all levels of society. Sovereign debt led to bankrupt nations and even the dissolution of the European Union. Currency wars between nations transformed world trade and culminated in several shooting wars. Depletion of natural resources and unstable weather patterns forced nations into a mad chase for energy supplies, minerals, food, and clean water sources.

America was at a critical crossroads. Did the United States have the vision and resolve to shape a new century, favorable to American principles and national interests? Or would international chaos, and the rise of China and radical Islam, lead to a greatly diminished America and a lessened influence to advance democracy throughout the world? Would America become unrecognizable to the citizens of the United States? These concerns passed through my mind as I drove by the Washington Monument on the way to the White House.

The encrypted radio in the car sounded.

"There's an incoming emergency message for Navy Intel at the Pentagon, Sir. It's being shared to you here, Admiral Stansfield," said the driver.

"Turn up the volume," I said.

"Special Report from US Observation Post 4..3..6..7, atop Uotsuri-shima in the Senkaku Islands - approximately a hundred nautical miles northeast of Taiwan Island..... This is Lieutenant Commander Timothy Gardner, US Navy..... It is early evening with twilight of dusk. I'm in an observation cave built into the rock at 1000 feet above sea level..... With night vision, I'm observing a heavy exchange of fire at unusually close distances - between opposing forces of a PLA naval destroyer squadron of nine ships, and a grouping of eight Japanese vessels..... The battle is happening in a channel separating my position from Kuba-shima Island, several miles to the northeast. The rocket, shell, and torpedo shooting is at extremely close range. It is intense, accurate, and destructive. Ships on both sides have taken crippling blows..... Twenty miles west of me, I see two Chinese vessels in the process of sinking. Three others are on fire..... Beginning five miles to the northeast of my position, there are six Japanese ships ablaze; three of them will be 'deep-six' below water in the next few minutes..... There appears to be heavy loss of life..... It is surprising to see neither force has air cover, being that the engagement is occurring so close to bases..... I venture to say both commanders involved showed poor judgement by getting so close..... Or perhaps, it's an example of 'old school' stubbornness and bravado. To me, it looks like a knife fight in a dark alley of a bad neighborhood..... This is Gardner, Post 4..3..6..7, out....."

"What do you think, Sir?" asked the driver.

"I think these two nations hate each other, Lieutenant. Killing at long range doesn't satisfy either of them. They want to see the enemy burn in front of their eyes..... Both commanders had risky nerves. They challenged the enemy to cut their throat at arm's length. They were very brave, and also very stupid..... We have an old-fashioned war on our hands, young man," I answered.

Our car turned onto Pennsylvania Avenue and approached the outer security perimeter of the White

House. Concrete fortifications, heavy machine gun bunkers, and uniformed military personnel made the area appear like a war zone. We stopped at multiple security checkpoints - where our identification papers were checked, our irides were scanned, and our bodies were searched. The car was inspected for explosives, nuclear materials, and weaponized chemicals and biologicals. The entire process was completed in less than fifteen minutes. The tight precautions had been added after last Thanksgiving's suicide attack on the White House.

A group of seven terrorists, armed with automatic weapons and suicide vests, had attacked the perimeter of the White House grounds. All were killed before they could enter the building. Ten US security agents died in the assault.

US intelligence analysis quickly confirmed the identities of the terrorists. Their origins were traced to an Iranian supported terror cell which had entered the United States through Mexico six months prior. Their initial point of entry to the Americas was even further traced back to Venezuela, three years ago.

From South America, the terrorists slowly dispersed into Central America and Mexico. In Mexico - they provided logistical support for the drug trafficking cartels, before entering the United States through drug smuggling tunnels across the Texas border.

Similar combat security measures had been established around other important US government sites, including the Capitol building and its surrounding offices. Up to now, there had been no further attacks on American government centers.

After the White House attack on Thanksgiving evening, the President of the United States ordered the Pentagon to finalize their plans for war with Iran. More recently, military plans were completed for China and North Korea. The US military directive called for a coordinated global effort by America and her allies. The US Navy was at the point of the spear in the Persian Gulf, Indian Ocean, and western Pacific.

It had become a matter of national survival. Radical Islamic fundamentalism, and China's relentless drive to secure its energy needs around the world, could not be allowed to suffocate freedom and Western democracy. It was an existential issue. I had a clear military directive to stop America's bleeding before it was too late. Washington, Jefferson, Lincoln, and Reagan demanded it.

On the front lawn of the White House, I saw my old friend Joseph Mitrano, Director of the CIA.

"How are things at Langley?" I asked.

"Quite hectic and confusing, Julian. But that's the norm for us, as you know."

"It'll get much worse very soon. When the bullets and rockets start flying, the 'fog of war' rolls in. Hold on to your pants, Joe."

"I've already strapped in for the trip....."

"Do you know of your son, James?" I asked.

"He's in Taiwan, waiting with his fellow Marines. I spoke to him last week before all personal communications were stopped. He sounded well and confident.

"Do you think he has reason to be, Julian?"

"Confident?

"I suppose so, Joe. He's got over 30,000 Marine brothers with him, all armed to the teeth and fully supported. I have a lot of hardware going that way. Three carrier strike groups will defend Taiwan from invasion. We have significant air power on the island, and Okinawa will send several squadrons.

"The Republic of China troops are also tough kids. Their air and naval forces are formidable. Jimmy will have 200,000 Taiwanese soldiers on the beaches with him. They'll be defending freedom on their home turf."

"What do you expect on the other side, Julian?"

"The PLA is prepared for the invasion. They have been for years. They've been licking their chops for a long time. I suspect their planning and logistics are tuned, and their troops are fired up. They're well disciplined and fit.

"I think they lack in battlefield leadership, though. In the heat of combat, poor junior officer ground leaders bite you in the ass. Losses are always greater under bad field command.

"I do worry that China does have their strongest naval and air elements assigned to the assault.

"But on the other hand, so do we."

"How many Chinese do you expect in the invasion force?" asked the director with poorly hidden concern.

"Anywhere between two and three hundred thousand PLA marines, Joe. They can double that number, if need be," I uttered softly.

"That's a lot of flesh and bone, Julian. Even with poor battlefield officers, it still takes many bullets to bring down a horde of humanity."

"No doubt.....

"But we'll be fine..... Jimmy and his brothers are ready. The US Navy will destroy most of the enemy before they see sand. You have my word on that, Joe."

The director smiled and patted me on the back.

"I hope your sons are well, Julian. My wife and I are praying for all of you."

"Likewise, Joe.....

"We thank you.....

"Our sons, and you and I also, need all the prayers we can get....."

I let Director Mitrano enter the White House alone. Joe needed to regroup himself and mentally prepare for the President's meeting. I needed to do the same.

Fathers in war are a bad bunch. Particularly so when the fathers are writing the command orders, and the sons are doing the fighting and dying.

Envisioning one's son in a bloody battle trench under heavy fire - facing an onslaught of rabid, angry enemy in a massed frontal assault - is a horrible thought. It sends shivers down your spine. Regardless of personal mental toughness, everyone is entitled to worry a bit. I have been guilty of this many times.

Upon entering the White House, I was escorted to the Situation Room in the basement of the West Wing. General Samuel Powell, Chairman of the Joint Chiefs of Staff, had ordered me to attend this meeting with the President.

Sam was a four star Marine general who had graduated from the Naval Academy several years after me. We had become close friends over the past few years.

General Powell agreed with my analysis of the upcoming conflict. We both felt US naval power would be decisive.

Projection of American naval power depended on its ability to defend against speedy ultrasonic anti-ship missiles. Although not extremely accurate, Russian and Chinese anti-ship missiles were possibly the most destructive in the world. They were difficult to detect and neutralize. They could be shot from multiple platforms - land, air, and sea. The technology was made available to Iran in large quantities, and had subsequently been disseminated throughout their terror network in the Middle East.

In a confrontation in the Persian Gulf, the US Navy could expect thousands of anti-ship missiles to rain down on our fleet. They would be launched from coastal sites in hidden mountainous terrain, Iranian Air Force fighter bombers, and Iranian Navy fast boats. The eastern Mediterranean and Red Sea would also be in harm's way.

Doubtlessly, the Chinese PLA Navy had these missiles in unlimited supply. PLA island bases in the Indian Ocean, South China Sea, and East China Sea were outfitted with thousands to defend against the powerful US Navy and her aircraft carriers. Naval engagements would be high risk affairs indefinitely into the future.

I passed through a final security check and took my place at the conference table. Seated to my immediate left was General Powell. Around the table in clockwise direction were the Vice President of the United States, the Secretaries of State, Defense, and Homeland Security, the National Security Advisor, the US Ambassador to the United Nations, the US Attorney General, the FBI Director, and finally, Joe Mitrano.

The President of the United States entered the Situation Room and took the final seat at the conference table. He made slow and deliberate eye contact with each of us, and began to speak.

"Early this morning, I activated *Operation Mount Olympus*. You are all familiar with the details of this plan and have been updated on the situation prior to attending this meeting.

"We are under siege at home and abroad. The loose radical Islamic terror network alliance - between the Iranian Revolutionary Guard Corps (IRGC), al-Qaeda, Hezbollah, the Islamic Jihadi, and Hamas - has increased its activity in the Middle East and the Persian Gulf region. Over the past six weeks, 1400 US and NATO personnel have been killed by their direct action. This culminated in last night's attack on the *USS Patrick Henry*, a guided missile destroyer in the eastern Mediterranean. We lost nearly 100 men in the sinking off the coast of Syria. The ship was attacked by elements of the IRGC and Hezbollah. The *Patrick Henry* was hit by two anti-ship ballistic missiles, and sunk quickly with the loss of her captain and entire executive staff.

"Twenty-four hours ago, US Naval Intelligence discovered that the Iranian Navy had deposited over 300 mines into the Strait of Hormuz. Most are believed to be late generation Chinese mines with remote control capability. PLA naval advisors assisted in this massive deployment from Iranian submarines and fast boats. Information from one hour ago indicates the mines have not yet been activated. But we can expect that shortly.

"Besides the obvious danger to Allied naval and oil tanker traffic, this will lead to decreased flow of commerce and a panic in the oil trade. We've already seen a marked spike in oil prices over the past month. The evolving situation will certainly cause economic collapse in the equity and commodity markets.

"Most alarming, Iran has successfully adapted nuclear warheads to intermediate and long range ballistic missiles – easily capable of reaching Western Europe and the continental United States. In addition, they have purchased ready built nuclear missiles from North Korea and Pakistan, and placed them in the hulls of specialized freighters with orders to sail toward American waters.

"The Department of Homeland Security has also revealed that Iranian terror cell operatives transported nuclear bomb materials into the United States. The CIA and FBI believe multiple component parts have been smuggled separately, in redundancy. In other words, six, seven, or more copies of the same components were smuggled individually by different enemy operatives. These operatives are under orders to deliver their parts to different safe house locations, where experts in building functional bombs may share the pieces. Completed bombs are then transported to the target sites. Therefore, even if our intelligence services track down some of the terrorist operatives, others may escape capture and deliver their cargo to target. Shared redundancy assures the construction of several bombs.

"These terrorist smugglers are unknown to each other; thus, interrogation does not help in uncovering other plotters. Each smuggler has to be tracked individually, and each safe house has to be discovered separately.

"Iran's actions - and the complicit behaviors of China, North Korea, and Pakistan - have forced America into her decision. They wish for war, and war they will get. But it will be conducted on our terms.

"Their unified front of belligerence will not scare America into a negotiated settlement. Their evil and brutal positions are unacceptable to the democracies of the 'Free World'.

"More than two hundred years of gallant American history require us to defiantly confront this threat to freedom loving people everywhere. Future generations of Americans will look back at this time as one of the most critical in our history. We can not betray our children and grandchildren, and allow them to live in a world less safe, less free, and less American.

"The objectives of *Operation Mount Olympus* are the following:

1) regime change in Iran, North Korea, and Syria
2) reunification of the Korean peninsula under a democratic government
3) contain and restrict Chinese economic and military influence in the Persian Gulf, Central Asia, and the Caspian Sea Region
4) neutralize Chinese sea lines of communication (SLOC) by eliminating their military presence in Pakistan, Sri Lanka, Bangladesh, Burma, Cambodia, and the South China Sea
5) contain and restrict Chinese naval operations out of Hainan Island and the Sayana Naval Base
6) prevent the Chinese invasion of Taiwan
7) the US Navy must safeguard the Malacca Strait and inhibit the PLA Navy in the South China Sea
8) prevent oil shipments to the Chinese mainland
9) maintain a strong military alliance between the US, Britain, France, Germany, Canada, Israel, Australia, India, Japan, and South Korea

10) disrupt the Shanghai Cooperative Organization (SCO) between China, Russia, and the Central Asian states of Kazakhstan, Kyrgystan, Tajikistan, and Uzbekistan
11) contain Pakistan with help from Indian military pressure
12) eliminate the nuclear weapon programs in Iran, North Korea, and Pakistan
13) maintain a strong US missile defense system to prevent nuclear ballistic missile attack from China, North Korea, Iran, and Pakistan on the US and friendly nations
14) eliminate forever the Islamic terror network and its support from China, North Korea, and Pakistan
15) pry Russia away from the enemy alliance by: a) negotiate fairly on Arctic policy, b) allow her to become the major energy supplier to Europe, and c) allow Russia to increase her influence in Central Asia at the expense of China

"These are our objectives in *Operation Mount Olympus*. They are difficult and may take several years to achieve. But in the end, we must persevere and eliminate state sponsored terrorism from the face of the Earth....."

The President clasped his hands together on the table and turned toward General Powell. With tired but determined eyes, he asked, "What can America expect in the early stages of the operation?"

"Thank you, Mr. President, for your leadership. Let me begin by saying that the armed forces of the United States stand ready to serve with all our might in defense of our great country..... We are here to serve the people of America.....

"US Special Forces and CIA operatives are presently engaged inside of Iran, supporting armed rebellion in the democracy-seeking civilian population. These brave men and women are leading multiple sectarian freedom movements, particularly in the Kurdish northwest and the Balochi southeast. British commandos are involved in similar activities in Kuzehstan to the southwest.

"A mine clearing operation is under way in the Strait of Hormuz. To this point, none of the mines have been detonated by our enemy. The reasons are unclear. Perhaps they're waiting for us to position a second carrier strike group near the strait. They may be planning suicide attacks with subs and fast boats at night. The mines could be used to confuse us in the mayhem. We won't have all the mines cleared for another 48 hours. Admiral Stansfield will have more to say about this shortly.

"On your orders, Mr. President, we will begin a sustained naval and air campaign to neutralize all Iranian nuclear program sites, offensive and defensive missile sites, military installations, land based radar centers, seaports, oil facilities, and supply depots. A 'no fly' zone over Iran and the Gulf will be created.

"The Israeli Defense Force will invade southern Lebanon and strike into Syria across the Golan Heights. They will re-take territory given back after last year's punitive incursion. This time, however, the IDF is rolling into Damascus and beyond.

"We don't expect Egypt to involve themselves in this conflict against Israel. We've picked up communications from Cairo to the Syrian government, indicating their inability to assist them in any way. Egypt is heavily engaged in their war with Ethiopia and South Sudan over the control of the Blue Nile waters. Russian military aid to Cairo has dried up at the worst time. A big Ethiopian offensive began last night.

"In coordination with the Israelis, the British and French Expeditionary Force from Cyprus lands on the coasts of Lebanon and southern Syria. The Russian Black Sea Fleet will not impede these landings. It withdrew from the eastern Mediterranean and returned to Sevastopol.

"Two Turkish Army corps will enter Syria from the north along the coast and move east into the interior. They won't stop until they reach the Iraqi border. The Iraqi Shiite forces supporting the Iranians have been advised to cross over to their territory or risk annihilation by the Turkish Air Force. We have granted the Iraqis safe exit out of Syria for the next 24 hours. They will oblige. The Turks don't expect strong opposition. Most of the stronger Iranian, Hezbollah, and Syrian units have been pulled south to face the Israelis.

"There are over 10,000 uniformed IRGC troops supporting the Syrian regulars, as well as several thousand Hezbollah and Islamic Jihadi fighters in southern Lebanon. Much of the Sunni Syrian Rebel Army has gone over to the government side. They would rather kill Israelis and Western Europeans than their Shiite enemies.

"To our knowledge, Russia has removed her 5000 special forces troops from Syria. They have vacated their defensive positions at the naval port in Tartus. However, contrary to what was indicated to me at the Pentagon four days ago, the Russians 'abandoned' their S-300 anti-air batteries and Yakhont anti-ship mobile carriers to Syrian and Iranian operatives. A lot of dangerous hardware was 'left behind'. We are uncomfortable with this fact. It will increase IDF, British, and French losses. I personally tongue-lashed the Russian top brass over this misadventure. In retaliation, we secured the disappearance of two of their spy planes over Romania last night. It's a dangerous world, and we have reminded the Russians of that reality.

"We expect that all US naval and air campaign goals over the Iranian landmass and Persian Gulf will be achieved by the third day. This will allow a three-pronged invasion of Iran to begin.

"US and NATO forces will enter Iran from bases in Azerbaijan, Iraq, Afghanistan, and southwest Balochistan. The US Navy will land three divisions of US Marines along the Persian Gulf coast. A total of 300,000 Allied troops will be inside Iran by the end of the first week of combat.

"On the other side of the world, US attack submarines will support landings of Navy SEALs on several South China Sea islands. Their missions are to disrupt PLA naval communications and signals, as US Task Force 94 leaves Subic Bay on Luzon in the Philippines and heads northwest to Woody Island in the Paracels. Supported by the *Carl Vinson* Carrier Strike Group, Task Force 94 will land the First Marine Regiment on Woody Island. We can expect a naval engagement with the PLA Southern Fleet off of Woody Island.

"A US wolfpack of attack subs will drive towards Singapore and intercept the Chinese convoy responsible for the sinking of the *USS Spokane*. We'll hit the bastards as they exit the Malacca Strait.

"US Task Force 93 out of Guam, composed of three carrier strike groups, will repel the impending Chinese invasion of Taiwan. We have over 30,000 US Marines on Taiwan in defensive positions, supporting over 210,000 Taiwanese troops. US air elements based on Taiwan and Okinawa will also assist in the defense.

"There are 700,000 Allied troops south of the Demilitarized Zone ready to defend against a North Korean invasion. They have detailed order plans to counter-attack deep toward Pyongyang. Two carrier strike groups are in the Sea of Japan to help support the Allied forces.

"All foreign Chinese naval bases will be blockaded. Their remaining ships will not leave port.

"It's not a pretty picture for our enemies, Mr. President."

"Thank you, General Powell, for your concise summary," said the commander in chief.

The President looked at Julian Stansfield. "What are your thoughts on the Strait of Hormuz, Admiral? And what are the greatest risks to the early operations?"

"Mr. President, we can expect suicide attacks on our ships in the Strait of Hormuz within the next few hours. They will detonate any mines which have not been neutralized. They will use jets, subs, and fast boats in their attacks. We are ready for all of these approaches. Rest assured, we will not lose control of the strait. But there will be losses. Perhaps, many of them.

"In general terms, the Chinese and Iranian navies have developed very effective asymmetric warfare tactics. Strong technology programs have developed reasonably accurate supersonic anti-ship cruise and ballistic missiles which can be delivered from coastal and island bases, fighter bombers from great distances, and by capable surface vessels and submarines. Our countermeasures are very advanced, but unlikely to stop all attacks. We will have surface ship losses in all theaters of operation.

"In addition, the Chinese have also developed a large attack submarine force with accurate torpedo and missile technology. They have sold, and freely given, several stealthy diesel-electric submarines to the Iranian Navy. We believe Iran may have 30-35 quiet submarines with fully trained crews.

"Finally, new mine technology has greatly increased the profile of the sea mines. They have become high-tech smart bombs with multiple applications.

"In summary, we are facing formidable enemies. We can expect significant losses of ships and men in the early operations. It is not inconceivable that even our aircraft carriers are at risk. In the end, however, our technology and training will be overwhelming. We have too much firepower and too many advanced systems to concentrate that firepower on the enemy.

"I don't believe the final result of the conflict is in question. Yet, I strongly suspect the road to conclusion will be ugly and bloody. It is difficult to avoid significant loss of precious life when modern armies and navies do battle. It is not easy to accept the consequences of our decisions. Even in victory, we have great sorrows."

"Yes, we do, Julian..... We certainly do," sadly said the President.

"How about nukes, Julian? Do you think the Chinese are capable of using atomic weapons in the conflict?"

"No, Mr. President, I don't feel it's a reasonable possibility. China's military will not consider the use of nuclear missiles. They appreciate the accuracy of our missile defense systems and fear the consequences of our retaliation.

"This will be a conventional naval war with very high-tech destructive weapons on both sides. Our technology wins out."

"Thank you, Admiral," said the President with a somber face.

He turned his gaze to the FBI Director and asked, "How confident are we on stopping the nuclear threat inside the United States?"

"The FBI is confident, Sir. We have many leads and secret contacts that appear to be credible. They should direct us to all the terrorist smugglers. Evidence shows there are likely four bomb-building safe houses. We have already identified two of these houses. The clock is ticking, and practically all our assets are on this case. I am optimistic that we will prevail."

The President stood and thanked us all for our loyalty to America. "*Climb Mount Olympus*," he said intrepidly, before slowly turning and walking from the room.

General Powell requested I ride back with him to the Pentagon. We walked out of the White House together, talking of family and our country.

"Julian, you look strong. You still have that agile mind I remember," smiled Powell.

Sam laughed. "I heard so many stories about you at the Academy, it got me sick. You were a god-damned legend!

"What did they call you? 'Mind Fencer'?

"Yeah, that's it.

"You'd cut people up with your brain!

"You kicked ass in everything difficult. It didn't matter who the professor was. You knew more than they did.

"You were a savant, Stansfield, pure and simple.

"So, tell me – can you still think at light speed?"

"Well, if you're asking me if I can think of two things at once? The answer is yes. I can still take a crap and read at the same time," I laughed.

"How's your health holding up?"

"I'm still alive, Sam. The heart is still beating, although sometimes - a little irregularly," I answered....

"The doctors at Bethesda say I have mild congestive heart failure. They believe it can be controlled with medications. I just need to remember to take them," I said as I lit a cigarette.

"They also stressed that I stop smoking," I added, in between drags.

"You're still smoking those god-damned cheap cigarettes, Julian?" smiled Powell. "They've been with you longer than that patch over your eye."

"You've known me too long, Sam. Way too long!

"I don't think this is a good time to stop smoking.

"Hell! I'm too old to save my own life.

"Besides, the last few years have been the most stressful and painful of my life.....

"It's not easy getting old, Sam. I don't think I'd recommend it to anybody," I laughed.

"I understand, Julian.....

"Just don't smoke yourself to death before we win this god-damned war!

"Our country needs you more than ever, Julian. You're a good friend and I need you also," said the general.

Sam looked over at me and hesitated....

"How are you doing personally, Julian?"

"What can I say?

"I miss Olivia.....

"I try to keep occupied with my duties, but there's much loneliness.

"Freud was correct about feminine love and affection.

"I've always been a passionate idealist and romantic; but lately, I've turned into a mystic. My mind never sleeps. It constantly searches for what I can't have.

"Over the years, Olivia taught me to recognize beauty in all aspects of life. I'm having a hard time seeing that beauty without her," I said quietly.

"How are your sons, Julian?"

"As far as I know, they're all alive and well. I hope for the best. They are strong men. I have faith in their good fortune."

"So do I," said General Powell. "So do I."

"No, Sam.....

"I don't think I can stop smoking my cheap-ass cigarettes, right now. Now is not the time.

"I have three sons scattered around the world, in the most dangerous conditions.

"My country is facing the most critical time in its history, and it's asked me to direct its naval intelligence service.

"Why would they want an old sick war horse like me to decide the fate of the US Navy?

"Stop smoking?

"These cigarettes are my friends for the time being.

"Besides, I've heard smoking helps prevent dementia. I never want to be old and dumb," I joked.

"No..... I don't think you'll ever be dumb, Julian.

"But if you wish, keep sucking those tobacco pencils!" laughed the general.

We both prodded each other like kids as we walked to the general's car. It felt good to laugh a little.

General Powell looked at me more seriously.

"America knows how much you love your country, Julian.

"Your intelligent mind and intuitive senses have decided your course.

"Yes! You are a passionate, romantic idealist, god-damn it!

"But you are also a passionate, romantic realist.

"The thought of taking life has always betrayed your personal core beliefs. But you realize you must for the defense of your country. It's this struggle inside of you that makes you the great patriot warrior you are.

"You were way ahead of your time in the understanding of Chinese culture and history. You saw the light before any of us.

"Your understanding of science, and your expertise in naval missile warfare, makes you a critical component of our national defense.

"Having a sick heart and a blind left eye does not detract from your remarkable abilities, Julian.

"This country loves you as much as you love her."

We drove away from the White House. Instead of returning directly to the Pentagon, General Powell asked the driver to go to the Vietnam Memorial.

Following closely behind was a car with three heavily armed men of General Powell's security detail.

CHAPTER 4

The Walk

Melancholy and sadness are the start of doubt.... doubt is the beginning of despair; despair is the cruel beginning of the differing degrees of wickedness.

***Isidore Ducasse Lautreamont* (1846 to 1870)**

WE ARRIVED AT the Vietnam Memorial. General Powell ordered the driver to wait outside with the security team. Sam and I remained in the car.

"You and Olivia were fond of classical Greek culture, legend, and mythology.

"Why was that, Julian?"

"It's a long story, Sam. Perhaps on another day, when we have more time, we can sit over a beer and discuss it."

"All right, I'll hold you to that."

I could sense concern in Sam's voice. It was more than worry over the coming storm of war. It was more like apprehensive fear.

"What's wrong, Samuel?"

The general stayed silent. He seemed to be measuring his words in his head. This wasn't characteristic of Sam's way. Usually, the general was direct and clear with his mind. He never ruminated over things he needed to say.

"Do you remember the legend of *Damocles*?" asked the general.

"Sure, Sam.

"He was a fawning panderer to Dionysius II, the 4th-century BC tyrant of Syracuse, Sicily.

"*Damocles* commented to Dionysius and his court of how fortunate the king was to have such great power, wealth, and magnificent and exotic female carnal companions.

"Dionysius offered to switch places with *Damocles*, so he could taste the splendor for himself. The panderer eagerly accepted the king's offer.

"*Damocles* took his place on the king's throne, surrounded by beautiful women, gold, and jewels. But Dionysius ordered a large sharp sword to hang above the throne, held by a single hair of a horse's tail.

"*Damocles* stared at the blade of the executioner, hanging over his head. He studied the tenuous grip of the horse hair.

"The scared panderer begged the king that he be allowed to relinquish the opportunity for great fortune and power, realizing that with it came also danger.

"The *Sword of Damocles* is a metaphor, Sam, for the fact that with omnipotence comes great peril."

"Have you heard of the *Ulfberht*, Julian?"

"Yes, I have..... The *Ulfberht* was the famous ancient Viking sword, made of an incredible, high-quality steel. It was much stronger and durable than enemy steel. It was invincible in battle."

I wondered why a Viking sword and an ancient Greek legend were on Sam's mind. What could possibly be bothering him?

"The armed forces of the United States are powerful, Julian. Your submarines alone could destroy the Earth several times over.

"Our military might can be wielded like an *Ulfberht*, or it can hang over us like the *Sword of Damocles*.

"In order to be successful in world geopolitics and war, we must stand strong and united. The American military must not have fractures!" said Sam loudly.

Fractures? I thought.....

"How is the morale at Navy Intelligence, Julian?"

"Excellent.

"Why are you asking me this, Sam?"

"You are well aware of the disagreements at the Pentagon over the past few years, concerning our previous lack of initiative against China, North Korea, and Iran. Many officers have been reprimanded for their public disclosure of disgust with the US civilian government. They were unhappy with the appearance of appeasement we projected at the Geneva Conference with Iran. They have also been uncomfortable with our inability to stop China's expansionism across the globe. They blame diplomatic weakness and lack of leadership at the Defense Department. It's been like a small rebellion within our ranks, Julian.

"I have been told the movement is growing. A larger division between the statesmen and soldiers is forming. If this is truly the case, it bodes poorly for us in the coming struggle. The feeling is the war could have been avoided altogether, if only our politicians had remained strong and united against our enemies in the past years.

"What is your opinion, Julian, regarding this matter? Where do you stand?"

"You and I know the officers who have been castigated. Many of them are personal friends. But to say a movement is growing, which may jeopardize the future of our country, is a far stretch of the imagination.

"As a unit, the US Navy is a strong and unified entity. We are a Viking sword against the throats of our enemies. The Navy was not, is not, and will not be a *Sword of Damocles* over the head of the United States Government."

"I am confident of your words, Julian. I am relieved. More than ever before, the military must stand as a firm structure and continue to support the President, the Congress, and the US Constitution. The continuity of the American way of life depends on it."

I was weary of Sam's words. I was aware of the same issues and situations that concerned him. Yet, he seemed to be more worried than I. Perhaps, I was a stronger believer in the pillars of America, or maybe, I simply knew something he didn't. Either way, I didn't have a lack of faith in the communion of my country or my military. To me, they were one and the same. America since the Civil War had always been 'One Nation Under God'. My allegiance to her was pure and total.

We walked east along 'Memorial Wall'. The security men walked to our sides, protecting us from all directions.

Sam slowed down and finally stopped. Bending down on one knee in front of the Memorial, he passed his right index finger along the name - *Jeffrey S Powell.*

The general looked up at me and said, "My father was a Marine colonel in Vietnam. In February 1968, during the height of the Tet Offensive, he was in a forward combat headquarters outside the city of Hue. They had come under heavy attack by forces of the North Vietnamese Army. In the chaos of the fire-fight, a suicide bomber breached the US base's defensive perimeter, entered the command tent, and detonated his explosive vest. My father and his entire staff, 14 men in all, were killed.

"I was only seven years old at the time. I remember coming home from school on a cold winter afternoon, and having my mother tell me the sad truth.

"She had been crying. Her eyes were red, and her eyelids were swollen. She whispered in my ear that my father had died in Vietnam. Mother said he had been protecting us and our country.

"I'll never forget the despair I felt and how helpless I was without him at my side. I had never felt sadness in my life before that day. It was a horrible milestone for a child.

"For years afterwards, my mother's words haunted me; that he had died protecting me. I perceived I was guilty in some way; that if he hadn't been in Vietnam protecting me, he wouldn't have died.

"Of course, when older, I realized he had been doing his duty as a military officer of the United States. He was protecting the world from the scourge of advancing international Communism. I was not at fault.

"They never found his remains on that battlefield. His name on this wall is like his grave to me. I come frequently to look at it. It reminds me, in the most personal way, of all the Americans who have died protecting our country in the past and of all those who will die in the future. It seems there is no end to this dirty business of war. Human nature is wicked."

Sam passed his finger across his father's name one more time and prayed on one knee. He got up, put his right arm around my shoulders, and asked me to take a walk along the reflecting pool towards the World War Two Memorial.

"You know, Julian, thousands of lives will depend on our decisions over the next several weeks and months. But you also have three sons in forward battle positions. How do you deal with that?" asked Powell.

It was a beautiful and cool spring morning in Washington. There was a cloudless blue sky. Sunshine and blooming flowers were all around.

As we walked along the reflecting pool, Sam and I passed a number of homeless persons who had been sleeping near the Vietnam Memorial. Poorly clothed and protected from the environment, they slept huddled together. Many of them were barefoot. I stopped my walk for a moment and stared at the unfortunates. I gazed over at the Lincoln Memorial and closed my eyes. I thought of how people dealt with loss. And much had been lost in America over the previous years.

All three of my sons had attended the US Naval Academy at Annapolis. They had chosen their own career paths. Two of the three were married and had beautiful children of their own. Unfortunately, America had entered into a dangerous world after the attacks of 9/11. Suddenly, all our lives were at risk. How do you deal with that? I thought.

"Let's face it, Sam. Our country is in disrepair. Somehow, we've become a three-ring circus. The politicians, the banking and business elite, and the people are divided. There's a lack of trust for our institutions. There is little faith in the proper management of government, or in the conduct of corporate business. The people believe everything is shown to them through a prism – deflected, misdirected, and obscured. These are dangerous developments for our future, Sam.

"America is suffering from a general malaise syndrome. We are losing the 'American Dream'. Politically, economically, and socially, we are a lesser nation than we once were. Like scavenging hyenas, our enemies sense the weaknesses and are congregating around us. They wish to destroy us.

"They perceive us as morally bankrupt. Perhaps, we are. They see drug abuse, alcoholism, and the breakdown of the American family. Our enemies believe that we may be more susceptible at this time of our history than ever before.

"I still see the embers of freedom in my country. I still have hope and faith in my people. I truly believe in the greatness of America. We may not be now what we were in the past, but I know we will come back stronger than ever before. I love my country. I am willing to give up my life for her.

"Americanism is not a birthright. It is an ideology. It stands for justice and liberty for the fair-minded. It symbolizes and supports the natural rights of all men. With hope and faith, it is dedicated to a brighter and stronger tomorrow. Its pillars are courage and honor. Its essence is a respect for the right to free self-determination under international law.

"Olivia termed this special spirit, 'American Amaranth'. She lived by it. An ideology such as this can not die. It should be urged to grow. These are my beliefs.

"So how do I deal with the sad possibility of losing my sons? I stand up and love them that much more. I respect their moral courage to protect their country and give it vital time to hopefully find its way again. That's how I deal with it. I have faith that they will be safe.

"I promised their mother that I would do everything in my power to protect them and bring them home in one piece after victory. I perform my job thinking of every American son and daughter coming home safely from this conflict. This is my solemn oath to the United States of America."

The general nodded his head, agreeing with my beliefs. We continued to walk towards the WWII Memorial. We walked in silence for a while, as both of us collected our thoughts.

Sam softly spoke again. "Our depressed economy over the past several years has been responsible for much of our country's present disillusionment. The Collapse of 2008 led to a chain reaction of progressive international political conflict and resource wars throughout the world.

"At present, the United States and China have established two belligerent and opposing poles which are each vying for the world's minerals and energy supplies. Nations have allied themselves around these poles. Many of the free democracies have lined up behind America. Russia, North Korea, Iran, and radical Sunni Islam have formed an axis with China.

"In the last few years, numerous proxy wars have developed around the world. Wherever you look, Americanism is or has been at war with the axis of authoritarian despotism.

"In Latin America, we had the Mexican drug wars, the Honduras-Nicaragua conflict, and the Amazon War between Colombia and Venezuela. We saw the various 'Freedom' rebellions in Cuba, Ecuador, and Bolivia.

These conflicts have all died down a bit over the past few months. But I expect them to re-kindle soon.

"In Africa, we had the Libyan Civil War, and the Egyptian Muslim Brotherhood Revolution and subsequent military coup. We have the ongoing sectarian wars in Nigeria and Mali. The conflict between Egypt and Ethiopia is causing thousands of deaths on both sides. South Sudan and Sudan are at war again. Somalia and the Congo are chronic conflict disaster areas. The natural resources of Africa are being fought over by the two axes of world power.

"Presently, as before, the natural resources of the Persian Gulf and Central Asia are essential to the economic future of both ideological poles. Chinese western expansion has led to their increasing influence in this region. They support terror regimes financially and militarily, in order to keep America preoccupied.

"America's wars in Iraq, Afghanistan, Syria, and Pakistan have allowed China to increase her profile in East Asia and the South China Sea. They've also extended their secret tentacles into central and southern Africa, and returned to Latin America.

"North America has abundant minerals and energy supplies. Our continental natural resources would likely satisfy our needs for more than a hundred years. However, if we abandon the Middle East and Central Asia to the Chinese and their allies, our country would become relatively much weaker and vulnerable throughout the world. Europe would become impoverished, and Israel would eventually cease to exist. Democracy, as a political concept, could slowly die.

"From a strategic perspective, America must contain Iran and its vast terror network. We need to neutralize

China's support of nuclear and ballistic missile technology transfer from North Korea to Pakistan and Iran. China has become an active conspirator in the nuclear terror threat to America and other free democracies around the world. This is unacceptable, and it must be stopped at any cost.

"I believe Russia is critical for our strategy. They must be pried away from the enemy axis. My sense is that we may be able to reason with them. Our many common interests may allow for negotiation. Besides, they stand to lose much more from radical Islam and the Chinese than what they could ever lose by associating with the United States and the rest of the Free World.

"We have a very complicated geopolitical problem on our hands, Julian. A great tug-of-war has evolved between the Judeo-Christian Western democracies and the fanatical authoritarian China/Islam axis. The Chinese wish for hegemony in Asia and the western Pacific. Radical Islam wants a return of the Caliphate and empire control over North Africa, the Middle East, and Central Asia. Russia appears to be standing on the sidelines, waiting to join the winning side.

"We need to create a reform revolution in our enemies. China must be weakened economically to slow their march around the world. The Chinese people must be made to see their government's misadventures. The people must clamor for more freedoms.

"Radical Islam must be pacified. The Sunni/Shia divisions need reform to alleviate social pressures. Governments must be made functional for their people. A return to the empire days of the Egyptian pharaohs, Ancient Persia, the Moors, and the Ottomans is not possible. Islam should incorporate into the 'world culture'.

"Ataturk, the founder of modern Turkey, had the foresight needed to progress his people. He saw the future clearly. He wanted a social integration and a modernization in government rule. Leaders like him are needed today.

"Western foreign policy in the Muslim lands after World War One, particularly ours, committed many misjudgements. We concentrated too much on the access to oil. We dealt with corrupt governments which abused their people. We didn't play according to our own principles of justice and liberty.

"Later, we were too decidedly in favor of Israel's existence. Perhaps, we didn't listen to the cries of other peoples in the region until it was too late. We were too late on the 'Peace Train'. Animosities between religions and cultures built up quicker than what we expected. The damage was done before we had time to blink. There was room for everyone in the Middle East. We should have insisted on it before the hatred became permanently established.

"In the end, Julian, there are great risks for America. The world is a huge mess. Radical religious thinking and despotic authoritarian governments have infected the planet. Our government refuses to give in to their ideologies. There is room in the world for religion, if it is pacifist and tolerant. Cultures must cooperate in building a more cohesive world, where differences of opinion, race, or creed are not the subject of violent discord. One culture for Earth is the ultimate goal at the end of the road. If not, there will be no Earth.

"The next decade will decide the remainder of the twenty-first century. Likely, the future survival of mankind hangs in the balance. The consequences of battle in the early twenty-first century are potentially more grave than those of a hundred years ago. There may be great loss of life, both military and civilian. Still, we have chosen action. Any postponement of war would be catastrophic for us in the long run," said General Powell.

"You know, Sam, war is synonymous with failure. It means that diplomacy has been unsuccessful. We, as human beings, are diminished by it.

"Many years ago, on my mission to China as an observer with the PLA in their invasion of Vietnam, I saw something that has remained with me since. Outside Lang Son, a town near Hanoi, I deployed to an observation ridge with a Chinese assault infantry battalion. My liaison - Captain Shang Wei - introduced me to a young PLA officer in charge of 800 troops preparing to attack the town in a frontal daytime raid.

"The officer handed me his binoculars to view the movements of Vietnamese troops in the buildings of the small city. While he explained his plans for the upcoming raid, he received a sniper round into his neck. I heard the sound of the gunshot as I peered through the binoculars at Lang Son. I turned towards him, and he fell into my lap.

"A large hole had torn into his anterior neck at the base. A torrent of blood shot up into my face. With every heart beat, the fountain would spray me. I quickly placed my hand over the hole, but the blood simply sprayed from the exit wound in the back of his neck onto my leg.

"His eyes became big and glassy as he gasped for air. Blood began pouring from his mouth. He seized once and died. He was the first man I saw die in combat. He was not American. In fact, the PLA officer would now be an enemy. But it was a horrible sight to see a young man die violently in front of you. I felt very sad for him, and I didn't even know the boy.

"War is hell, Sam. Many American boys in this war will likely see their end in similar fashion. I don't want to think about it, but I must. The wickedness doesn't seem to end.

"The conclusions of wars simply set in motion the beginnings of the next one. It's a never ending process. Eternal power, like eternal life, is a myth.

"In ancient Greece, the amaranth flower was considered a central symbol for immortality. It was believed to grow on Mount Olympus, the home of the deities. It was said the amaranth flower never died. They were given as crowns to express the wish of good fortune to those who would receive them. They were also spread on the graves of their fallen warriors. Immortality remained only in the minds of the living and grieving families left behind."

Sam and I remained silent while we walked the last hundred feet to our waiting car by the World War Two Memorial. It was 2:30 in the afternoon in Washington, 9:30 in the evening in the Persian Gulf, and 2:30 the next morning in the South China Sea.

CHAPTER 5

Silent Attack

Mine honor is my life; both grow in one; take honor from me, and my life is done.

William Shakespeare (1564 to 1616)

IT WAS 0300 HOURS on May 13 in the South China Sea. The *USS Oregon*, a fast attack Virginia class nuclear submarine, was southwest of Mischief Reef in the Spratly Islands. She was cruising at a depth of 150 feet. Captain Julius Stansfield studied the display console in the control room of his ship. Four passive sonar blips had shown up on the high definition screens. The enemy was 40 nautical miles northwest of the *Oregon*'s position, bearing down on her at 22 knots. Sound signature profiles identified them as a PLA Navy Luyang II class destroyer, two Jiangkai class II frigates, and a Yuzhao class troop transport ship. Stansfield's order was to support a commando raid on a Chinese naval installation at Mischief Reef Island. Specifically, he was to control and deny the ocean approaches to hostile naval forces while two Los Angeles class nuclear attack submarines landed 20 SEALs by submersible delivery vehicles. The covert team would sabotage the PLA communications center on the island, destroy the airport and seaport under construction, and neutralize any Chinese troops encountered. The satellite relay base was critical to Chinese operations in the South China Sea. Similar operations were being conducted at the same time against the signals camp on nearby Fiery Cross Island.

"Lieutenant Commander Johnson, that's one fat transport," said Stansfield to his Executive Officer.

"It's riding low in the water, Sir. She's probably pregnant with over 800 troops. They can't be going to Mischief Island."

"I figure they're moving towards the southern Philippines, Johnson. There have been two PLA landings on Palawan in the past 24 hours. They massacred forty US Marines on a small outpost there last night.

"We've caught these bastards by chance."

"What do you want to do, Captain?

"Our mission plans entail only protecting against moves towards Mischief."

"As far as I'm concerned, Johnson, the SOBs are moving on our position. In an hour, they'll be over my ass. I'm not going to sit here and wait for them.

"Before then, much before, I'm going to split the fat momma in half and send her human cargo to the bottom of the South China Sea. Her boyfriend escorts are going down too."

The *Oregon* had left Pearl Harbor in early April on a surveillance and intelligence collection mission to the South China Sea. Because of her proximity to the Spratly Islands, she was ordered to rendezvous with the other submarines when *Operation Climb Mount Olympus* went active on May 12.

Captain Stansfield was the oldest son of Admiral Julian Stansfield. He had graduated from Annapolis in 2002, shortly after the 9/11 attacks and the start of the Global War on Terror (GWOT). This was his fourth command on an attack submarine in the western Pacific and adjacent seas, but his first on the latest generation of the Virginia class.

The *Oregon* was 377 feet long, 34 feet wide, and three stories tall. It had been designed with quiet stealth technology and was considered the most efficient killer in the United States Navy. It carried a complement of 121 enlisted sailors and 13 officers. All were expertly trained in the pursuit and attack of enemy submarines and surface ships, using torpedoes and conventional cruise missiles.

The *Oregon* cruised at 25 knots (29mph) and could dive to a depth of 1000 feet. It had four 21 inch torpedo tubes aft of bow and 12 vertical launch systems for her Tomahawk cruise missiles. The MK-48 advanced capability torpedoes ran at 55 knots and carried a 640 pound warhead with wire guidance precision and search control to the target. The Tomahawks cruised at 600 mph and had a range up to 1400 nautical miles. They carried a 1000 pound conventional warhead and could be launched either horizontally from the torpedo tubes or vertically. They were extremely accurate against ships and land targets at significant distances. Additionally, the *Oregon* carried several Harpoon anti-ship missiles for use at short distances.

Unique to the Virginia class were a pair of AN/BUS-1 extendable photonic masts outside the pressure hull, which provided an electronic 360° panoramic image as far as the horizon in 5 seconds. There was no conventional periscope. The imaging systems carried signals to two workstations in the control room, where the captain and his executive staff could study the color, black and white, and infrared images in real time. A laser range finder provided accurate ranges to targets and aided in navigation. Sonar information was analyzed and projected on the same screens.

The three American submarines had coordinated their arrivals near Mischief Reef for 0200 hours. At 0230, two submersible delivery vehicles departed the Los Angeles class submarines en route to shallow water off the Chinese base. Each carried 10 SEAL commandos. Undetected, the SEALs expected complete surprise as they left their submersibles and swam ashore.

Captain Julius Stansfield looked at the sonar blips on the screens in front of him. He carefully measured in his head - times, distances, and angles of attack. He mentally matched power of ordnance with size of target. He calculated wind speeds and directions. He reviewed the underwater and surface sea conditions. The captain quickly completed all his mental mathematical analyses. He correlated his numbers with those on the screens. They needed to be the same. Both man and machine had to be perfect....They were.....

Stansfield stared over at his XO. Johnson waited patiently for his captain's order. Small beads of sweat had formed on their brows. All talk stopped in the control room. The only sounds were the pings and pangs coming from the display screens. Both men were caught in an intense eye contact which would signal the end for many hundreds of PLA soldiers and sailors.

Stansfield finally signalled with the quick drop of his right hand. The silent command was given to unleash fury on the enemy.

"Chief of Watch, man your battle stations! All sailors to battle stations!" The alarm sounded.

The XO shouted, "Make torpedo tubes one, two, three, and four ready for deployment."

Frenetic activity filled the command and control room of the *Oregon*. Captain Stansfield brought his sub up to a depth of 25 feet to get a GPS fix. As the PLA ships appeared over the horizon, the photonic system projected all visual information onto the display screens. Ten crew members crammed into the control room and analyzed the data as it presented. Eight sailors jammed into the adjacent sonar room.

Captain Stansfield carefully inspected the final visual and sonar data. He re-confirmed calculations and targeted the destroyer at 10 nautical miles.

"Fire tubes one and two!"

A thud and a whoosh could be heard as torpedoes one and two left the ship.

The captain then quickly targeted the lead frigate and ordered, "Fire tubes three and four!"

All four torpedoes sped to their targets under wired guidance from the *Oregon*. Arrival time was estimated at 10 minutes.

From further away and concurrently, the LA class submarines each fired three Harpoon anti-ship missiles at the troop transport and the trailing frigate. The six Harpoons were under radar control and carried 800 pound warheads. They travelled at 560 mph above the waterline in a sea skimming trajectory to their targets, 30 nautical miles away.

The American missiles found the PLA warships within 3 minutes of launch. The troop transport was pulverized by three rockets and sank within 5 minutes with all 800 Chinese marines still on board. The frigate was hit by one Harpoon and became disabled in the water. Some Chinese sailors frantically attempted to contain the damage while others jumped overboard into the sea to escape the raging fires. The sea quickly filled with dead and dying PLA sailors.

Moments later, torpedoes one and two from the *Oregon* slammed into the Chinese destroyer. They ignited munitions, creating a massive explosion. It rolled to its starboard side and sank into the South China Sea.

The lead frigate evaded torpedo three by making a rapid movement to port. Torpedo four, however, caught it at midsection and set the ship ablaze.

The LA class submarines launched two more Harpoons at the burning warships, both sitting motionless on the water. Within 7 minutes, they sank into the blackness.

In less than a half-hour, the convoy of four PLA ships and more than 1700 men had been attacked and destroyed without any retaliatory fire. The stealth of the American approach and assault had been the decisive factor.

It was 0430 hours. The Navy SEALs on the beach had watched the lights of the Chinese ship fires over the horizon. They had heard the thunder of the explosions. Now, the horizon was dark and quiet. The sea was calm and settled.

The Americans had encountered light resistance on the island. Yet, more than 50 Chinese marines were killed after being taken by surprise. It was payback for Palawan.

All of the communication center's equipment was destroyed. Explosives were placed on the heavy structures of the seaport and airport for remote detonation from the submersibles, offshore in shallow waters. Four SEALs had died in action and three were wounded.

The first combat naval encounter with the PLA had been successful for the Americans. The operations at Fiery Cross also achieved their mission goals. Chinese naval communications, command-and-control structures, and port facilities were disrupted in the southern area of the South China Sea.

Captain Stansfield and the *Oregon* were commanded to sail towards Singapore and the Malacca Strait. The other submarines were ordered to Subic Bay Naval Base, which had again been placed under US control by the Philippine government.

To the north, the *Carl Vinson* Carrier Strike Group prepared to leave Subic Bay and navigate toward Woody Island and the Paracels. A large scale naval engagement was in development and expected within the next 24 hours. The First Marine Regiment would land on Woody Island and take on a well fortified Chinese garrison of 6000 PLA marines. The operations against Woody Island were being conducted to destroy its large airfield and to draw out the Chinese Southern Fleet from nearby Hainan Island's Sayana Naval Base.

The US naval base on Guam Island was preparing a large task force for battle off of Taiwan. Three carrier strike groups, led by the *USS Ronald Reagan*, the *Abraham Lincoln*, and the *John C. Stennis,* would take on the PLA East Sea Fleet and hundreds of landing barges.

If the *Carl Vinson* Strike Group was successful in its operations to the southwest, Task Force 93 would have a protected left flank as they sailed from Guam towards the Philippine Sea. The greatest battle in naval history would take place east and west of Taiwan.

Further to the north - South Korean and Allied troops, composed of American, Japanese, Indonesian, and Australian forces, had crossed the Demilitarized Zone into North Korean territory. They were under heavy fire.

Israeli armored and mechanized forces prepared to dash into southern Lebanon and across the Golan Heights into southern Syria. Haifa and Tel Aviv had come under high density rocket attack by Hezbollah, Iranian Revolutionary Guard, and Syrian Army units. Chemical weapons were expected at any moment.

The warships of the combined British-French Expeditionary Force in the eastern Mediterranean Sea began bombarding the coastlines of Lebanon and southern Syria. The skies of the Levant filled with jets in combat. Allied troops prepared to land on the heavily defended beaches.

It was 0100 hours on May 13 in the Persian Gulf. US and allied British, French, Canadian, and German aviators pounded Iranian military targets in the Middle East. Iranian missile retaliation against hundreds of oil fields in US-allied Gulf states set the region ablaze. Fires raged everywhere. An ominous, toxic, black smoke obscured the stars from the night sky.

Hell had come to the Earth. No one would be safe, anywhere or at any time. The angry demonic dragons of Lucifer were free to roam and lay waste. The mad, mad world was officially at war.

CHAPTER 6

The South China Sea

What is past is prologue.

***William Shakespeare* (1564 to 1616)**

JAPAN'S VICTORY over the powerful Russian fleet at the May 1905 Battle of Tsushima Strait led to Theodore Roosevelt's mediated Treaty of Portsmouth and the end of the Russo-Japanese war. Japan gained control of the Liaodong Peninsula in present-day China, southern Manchuria, southern Sakhalin Island, and the Korean peninsula. A decade earlier, Japan annexed Taiwan after a short war with China in 1895. Japan had become one of the world's great powers. The United States and the major European countries quickly accepted her imperial expansion in East Asia.

As events unfolded, history recorded that Japan continued to expand into China and Southeast Asia - leading to the Pacific War with America and the death of millions. Intoxicated with nationalism and militarism, Japan sacrificed all her other institutions to 'patriotism'. Her systems of government, education, commerce, and industry suffered a fatal decline. Her relative lack of economic might, and America's overwhelming industrial military complex, led to Japan's total defeat in World War II.

China learned her lessons of history. Without economic power, empires collapse. The disintegration of Japan in 1945, and the Soviet Union in 1991, were associated with failed economic policies and a common adversary that had mastered, through trial and tribulation, the arts of industry and world commerce.

China's progressive development of state capitalism since 1991 allowed for phenomenal economic growth. Without the drawn out process of democracy, she moved swiftly without much internal debate. The economic invasions of foreign lands, near and far, began in earnest.

China, through the purchase of land rights and large foreign corporations, began to 'occupy' other countries. Nations in Asia, Africa, and Latin America had significant proportions of their local economies controlled by Chinese capitalism. Seaport management and mineral rights were favorite acquisitions. Money talked and foreigners walked.

Economic influence spread to involve the government structures and legal institutions of these foreign countries. The Chinese economic 'vice' began controlling 'minds' and 'bellies' of peoples all over the planet.

China's increased prosperity also led to a rapid development of her armed forces. Before the end of the twenty-first century's second decade, her military had the capacity to project power across the globe. There were PLA military 'advisors' working with China's 'new friends' everywhere, even in Mexico. With seaport access privileges on all continents, China's navy became blue-water. They had become a significant counter-force to America's international military presence.

The Chinese were strongly intent on continuing to grow their economy and military power internationally. This demanded access to all of the world's energy supplies. They had committed themselves to gaining influence in critical regions in Latin America, Africa, the Middle East, Central Asia, and Southeast Asia. China's sea lines of communication with these regions had become of paramount importance. Naval power was essential to defend their access to vital sea lanes.

China considered the South China Sea to be within her exclusive economic zone. Similarly, the East China Sea was theirs. Both seas were sacred and sovereign maritime territories. The areas had rich oil and natural gas reserves, making them highly contestable.

After brewing for several years, Japan and China were at war over energy rights in the Senkaku Islands. The East China Sea was becoming a graveyard for ships of both sides. Conventional missile attacks on cities had begun.

Territorial disputes with Vietnam, Taiwan, Singapore, Malaysia, Brunei, and the Philippines had developed in the South China Sea over the past 40 years. China had seized islands in the South China Sea and fought naval engagements with neighboring countries. Vietnam was a particular nemesis.

The PLA had built strong military fortifications and airfields on several Paracel and Spratly Islands. Military bases on Woody, Pattle, Duncan, and Drummond Islands in the Paracel archipelago, as well as on Mischief Reef and Fiery Cross on the Spratly Islands, had been upgraded with advanced radar and GPS communication systems. This allowed for pinpoint accuracy of Chinese missiles, and the detection and identification of US ships in the South China Sea. Missile systems and anti-aircraft batteries were found on all the islands. Airfields could project air power throughout the region. All of the South China Sea island bases were networked with major naval and air bases on Hainan Island - off the southern coast of China, and South Fleet headquarters in Guangzhou - west of Hong Kong.

Like America's Pearl Harbor, Hainan Island's massive base - northwest of the Paracel Islands - could accommodate aircraft carriers, nuclear submarines, and advanced jet fighter bombers. It allowed for power projection throughout the South China Sea, the Strait of Malacca, and into the Indian Ocean. It was also a strong deterrent against the United States sailing to the aid of Taiwan, if invaded.

For several years, the United States had been involved in a covert war with North Korea and China on the high seas. America's decision in 2009 to neutralize North Korean vessels carrying nuclear and ballistic missile technology to Iran had led to multiple sinkings by US nuclear attack submarines in the South China Sea and Indian Ocean.

Contraband ships would be confirmed and marked by covert operatives in North Korea and China. When alone in open ocean, they would be tracked by US submarines and sunk.

North Korea was not able to make public accusations, due to the fact that America would simply deny them or raise the contraband ships with the evidence from the ocean bottom. The North Korean government did retaliate initially by sinking a South Korean naval frigate in the Yellow Sea in early 2010. A month later, they attacked an American oil platform in the Gulf of Mexico. Both assaults were conducted by North Korean submarines. The Gulf of Mexico attack was assisted by the government of Venezuela. To not alarm the American public, the oil platform explosion had been blamed on human error.

In a carefully considered retaliation a few months later, a US submarine-launched Tomahawk land attack missile caused a large explosion at China's strategic oil reserves in Dalian, China. Several oil workers were killed. It led to a shutdown of critical operations for two weeks. The American attack was also blamed on 'human error'. There were many more 'secret and undocumented' threats of further attacks made by both sides.

In May 2013, North Korea stopped shipping ballistic missile materials to Iran on the open seas and began to transport them over land through China and Pakistan. US Special Forces were eventually able to eliminate the routes through Pakistan. A short time later, Chinese naval vessels began to escort North Korean freighters through the South China Sea and Indian Ocean. To not escalate tensions further, America stopped intercepting the transports.

Because of China's unlawful claims and activities in the East and South China Seas, and her military occupation of several islands, the United States began to build up their presence in the regions. South Korea and Japan were urged to increase their defensive forces. The Japanese constitution was changed to accommodate a more aggressive army, navy, and air force. American military bases on Guam, Singapore, and Diego Garcia Island were progressively upgraded. The Subic Bay Naval Base and Clark Airfield on Luzon were reopened with permission of the local Philippine government. Carrier strike groups were placed in forward deployments on Guam and Subic Bay. A heavy US nuclear attack submarine deterrence force was also activated in both the South China Sea and the Indian Ocean.

China's strategy was to support terror regimes in the Middle East, economically and militarily, and tie up

America's armed forces in the Persian Gulf and Central Asia. In the meantime, China would extend her control and domination over the South China Sea and its energy resources. The PLA hoped the United States would refrain from direct involvement in this region.

In the event of war between the US and Iran, China would invade and subjugate Taiwan. If confronted by America over Taiwan, a quick and bloody fight would possibly decrease American appetite for sustained involvement in the area. China's influence over South Korea and Japan would increase by default, leading to a new Chinese commanded 'Asian Co-prosperity Sphere'.

The United States considered a Chinese managed co-prosperity arrangement in Asia unacceptable to its free global trade policies, similar to their position with Japan prior to World War II. America was prepared to concurrently confront Persian aggression in the Middle East and China's moves in Asia. The US felt a coalition of willing democracies, such as Britain, France, Japan, South Korea, Australia, and India, would deter China's plans. Vietnam also made public statements in defiance of China's hegemonic moves and joined the coalition of allied democratic nations.

US combat operations would begin in a synchronized manner in the Middle East and South China Sea areas. America hoped China would quickly abandon her expansionist plans and not proceed with attacks on Taiwan and South Korea. Nevertheless, US forces were prepared and positioned to deter such attacks.

At 0800 hours on May 13, the *Carl Vinson* Carrier Strike Group left Subic Bay en route to an amphibious landing of

US Marines on Woody Island in the Paracel archipelago. The *Ronald Reagan* Carrier Strike Group sailed out of Guam and into the Philippine Sea, positioning to support the landings on Woody Island. The *Reagan* was to contain Chinese naval elements out of Hainan Island to the northwest.

To the southwest in the South China Sea, the *USS Oregon* cruised at 25 knots toward Singapore and the Strait of Malacca. It had been ordered to rendezvous with three other US nuclear attack submarines and intercept the PLA convoy coming from the Indian Ocean after their sinking of the *USS Spokane*.

After observing a moment of reflection aboard the *Oregon* for the four Navy SEALs killed in action at Mischief Reef, and the five lost at Fiery Cross, Captain Stansfield retired to his state room for a rest. He was feeling a long way from home. Julius hadn't seen his wife Sandra and two young daughters in over six months, when he had enjoyed their company for a short period of time at Pearl Harbor. He had been on dry land for only a few days in the past year.

Because nuclear submarines don't need to surface, except for resupplying of food and other essentials, sun and moon are rarely seen. There aren't opportunities to appreciate the hazy blue sky in day or the starry heavens at night. You can't breathe in the salty sea air or the rich scent of nearby land. There is no nature's wind or ocean spray on your face inside a submarine. Nature is nowhere to be found. One's internal clock becomes disturbed..... There is loneliness on occasion, particularly after the loss of comrades..... The submarine's captain is always guarding against this in himself and his crew.

Captain Julius Stansfield sat at his desk and slowly pulled Thucydides' *History of the Peloponnesian War* from his bookshelf. This timeless account of the war between Athens and Sparta in the fifth century BC had been required reading at Annapolis. But this particular book had belonged to his mother, Olivia. She had given it to him as a gift on his 15th birthday.

Olivia had been a Classical Studies major at Dartmouth College. She had a special appreciation for ancient Greece and the origins of democracy.

Olivia was exiled to America from her native Cuba as a young child. Her father had been a Cuban CIA operative, captured near the Bay of Pigs invasion beaches in 1961. His execution a month later was a very traumatic blow to an intelligent and sensitive little girl.

Growing up, she had spent much time reading and re-reading her father's letters to her mother. Her father had recognized the lack of true republican freedom in his country before Castro's Revolution. He wanted his counter-revolutionary activities to metamorphose into true democracy for his people. He felt they could be the seeds for a better future. His passion for justice had been extinguished with his death. But his desires passed to his daughter.

Olivia understood the essence of freedom and believed democracy was the only form of government that dignified each and every citizen. She instilled in her four children the same love for America that she maintained until her death.

His mother had always impressed Julius with her deep visceral faith in the United States. For Olivia, democracy was the only true hope for long-term world peace. She saw American warriors as fighters for justice, freedom, and an eventual eternal peace on Earth.

Julius opened Thucydides' classic to his description of Pericles' *Funeral Oration*. He looked at the book's yellowed pages and brought them close to his nose. Julius could smell his mother's memory in the aged paper. The scent of her perfume had become part of the story.

Pericles, the eminent Athenian general and politician, had delivered a speech at the end of the first year of war with Sparta as part of the annual public funeral for the war dead. It is considered by most authorities as the greatest testament to democracy, and those who defend it, ever spoken.

Olivia Stansfield had a unique affection for Pericles' words, as recounted in Thucydides' history, and would occasionally recite the oration aloud to her children in its entirety. From memory, and always in a remarkably noble tone of voice, she would stress and emphasize the following passage:

> "So died these men as became Athenians. You, their survivors, must determine to have as unfaltering a resolution in the field, though you may pray that it may have a happier issue. And not contented with ideas derived only from words of the advantages which are bound up with the defense of your country, though these would furnish a valuable text to a speaker even before an audience so alive to them as the present, you must yourselves realize the power of Athens, and feed your eyes upon her from day to day, till love of her

fills your hearts; and then, when all her greatness shall break upon you, you must reflect that it was by courage, sense of duty, and a keen feeling of honor in action that men were enabled to win all this, and that no personal failure in an enterprise could make them consent to deprive their country of their valor, but they laid it at her feet as the most glorious contribution that they could offer. For this offering of their lives made in common by them all, they each of them individually received that renown which never grows old, and for a sepulchre, not so much that in which their bones have been deposited, but that noblest of shrines wherein their glory is laid up to be eternally remembered upon every occasion on which deed or story shall call for its commemoration. For heroes have the whole earth for their tomb; and in lands far from their own, where the column with its epitaph declares it, there is enshrined in every breast a record unwritten with no tablet to preserve it, except that of the heart."

With his mother's gift, Julius had also received a large laminated bookmark with the following inscription:

"Love of a just, honorable, and hopeful democracy can be likened to a mother's love for her son. It must be cherished, nurtured, and protected for all of time. Happy birthday, Julius. Love, Mom."

Deeply recessed between perfumed pages of Thucydides' account of war and the words of Pericles, lying next to Olivia's inscribed dedication, was a single preserved red globe amaranth flower.

CHAPTER 7

The Battle of Woody Island

But the bravest are surely those who have the clearest vision of what is before them, glory and danger alike, and yet notwithstanding, go out to meet it.

Thucydides (460 BC to 395 BC)

I ARRIVED BACK AT the Pentagon and found Lieutenant Commander Louis Stevens waiting for me at the entrance. "Admiral, Task Force 94 leaves Subic Bay shortly..... Satellite images show Woody Island is fully defended with at least a garrison of 6000 Chinese marines. There are multiple missile and gun emplacements, all behind heavy concrete fortifications. They're well dug in. We believe there is a deep underground bunker lattice network throughout the island - full of munitions, supplies, and reserve troops..... The PLA Navy has concentrated several ships, including a carrier, 150 miles northwest of the island. They also have a heavy submarine presence for a 200 mile radius. We can expect to pick up some enemy submarine activity in the next six hours..... B2 bombers from Guam have been hitting Woody and Hainan Islands over the past two hours. We have confirmed heavy damage at airfields and the Yulin Naval Base..... The B-52s start their runs in 90 minutes, followed by unmanned attack drones from the *USS Ronald Reagan* in the Philippine Sea. The drone assaults will continue into tomorrow morning's planned landings on Woody..... In eight hours, F-35s from Clark Airbase in the Philippines, and F-18 Super Hornets from the *USS Carl Vinson* in the South China Sea, begin to hit the islands and the naval surface ship concentrations northwest of them..... Our amphibious landings are set for 0600 hours May 14, Subic Bay time."

"Much is happening. The pace will be speedy and merciless," I said. "For every action we take, there'll be a reaction by the enemy. After every bolt of lightning we throw at them, they'll clap back with increasing thunder. Our job is to constantly analyze the shock from both sides of the equation and devise even better plans for our future operations."

Stevens walked with me down an empty corridor. He waited for the perfect moment and added, "Our mission in the Spratly Islands was successful, Admiral. Julius was involved. The *Oregon* dropped two ships and is now on her way to the Strait of Malacca."

"Thank you, Louis," I said in low voice.

Although I would never ask directly, Lieut. Cmdr. Stevens kept me updated on any activities involving my sons. He had a subtle manner with the personal aspects of strategic information. Louis was clever with his deliveries, and I appreciated that.

"Director Mitrano is waiting in your office, Sir. He said it was an unscheduled visit."

"The Director of the CIA only has unscheduled visits, Louis," I laughed.

I had seen Joe a few hours earlier at the White House. I wondered why he had stopped by.....

"This is a masterpiece, Julian," said Joseph Mitrano as I closed the door to my office behind me.

The director looked through his reading glasses at the delicate details of a marble sculpture on a pedestal in the corner of my office.

"It's been there for years, Joe."

"Perhaps, but I hadn't really seen it until today.

"It's remarkable.

"The artist was talented. He captured both of you in full youthful splendor."

The significantly sized creation depicted Olivia and I as young lovers, walking down a shoreline hand-in-hand.

Joseph continued to enjoy the art. "The sculptor recorded every feature of Olivia's face perfectly. Also the gesture of her other hand on your lips, and her expressive smile as she prepares to kiss you, are exemplary of what I remember. She's flawless.

"Both your figures are realistic. It's extraordinary work.

"She's extraordinary....."

"She was," I said softly.

Joseph gazed at me over his readers and smiled with affection.

"She was," he agreed.

"Sit down, Joe. Let me get you a cup of coffee."

"I was in the neighborhood, Julian. I just finished a short meeting with the Secretary. I hope you don't mind my visit."

"A visit by an old friend is always welcome, even more so in wartime."

I gave the director his coffee and sat across from him by the window. The late afternoon sun was visible through the blast-resistant plate glass.

"They did a great job with the reconstruction of the west block of the Pentagon. You'd never know of the previous damage," said Mitrano.

"This area was wiped out on 9/11, Joe."

"You've been here for a long time, I recall," remembered the director.

"This is my original office location. I've had it since my lieutenant commander days. The Navy let me keep it after becoming Director of Naval Intelligence.

"I was in Israel on 9/11. I had overstayed my visit. I would have been here on the morning of the attack if Olivia hadn't convinced me to stay a few more days by the Sea of Galilee.

"She and I saw the events unfold on television from our bed."

"So Olivia saved your life more than once."

"Unquestionably, Joe, many more times than once," I said gently.

"9/11 was certainly a dark day in American history," stated Mitrano.

"It's amazing to me, Joe, that I still haven't been shown the video recording of the Pentagon attack. It's classified even to my eyes."

"Julian, I've been at the CIA for years and I haven't seen it.

"It's not relevant to our program. Our mission for the United States is to keep her alive and prosperous. The geopolitical agenda is what it is."

"That's correct. You and I don't set the agenda, we play it out. We steer the ship through enemy waters. And all the waters are enemy, Joe....."

"Nothing has changed, Julian.

"The *Maine*, the *Lusitania*, Pearl Harbor, the Gulf of Tonkin, and 9/11 – they're all watershed events for our country and the US military. They set in motion the military-industrial complex in a process of strategic thinking, war fighting, and national defense."

I stepped over to the window. The sun's rays felt warm on my face. I squinted my green eye. The weight of the world, and the hopeful future prospect of 'Peace on Earth', felt heavy on my shoulders.

"How is the 'Directive', Julian?"

"What do you mean?" I asked for clarification, squinting even more.

"Are the members of the commission in agreement, or is there discord on the planning?

"You've been directing the commission for a long time, Julian. If you're unsure of allegiances, it tells me that *Global Directive 93* is in danger. And if it is, America is in danger.

"Being Director of the CIA, I feel entitled to your insight."

"You're the second person today, Joe, who has made me question the allegiances of respected American military officers. It's an injection of doubt for the men who are working with me in the never-ending challenge to keep our country secure and victorious.

"Earlier, Sam Powell put the germ in me also.

"When the Chairman of the Joint Chiefs of Staff and the Director of the CIA are concerned about the possibility of treason in my ranks, I become uneasy.....

"*GD-93* is intact. Our mission for the United States is intact. The other officers working with me are loyal to America's destiny. There are no traitors among us. Of that, you can be certain.

"Yet, I personally believe the political and economic arms of *GD-93* have been less than cohesive, orderly, and faithful to our cause as a nation.

"My military commission is being prodded by both socialist and fascist elements inside those arms. Some people in Washington and on Wall Street are not doing their part. Those forces are unpatriotic, and worse, they are irresponsible to the Constitution of the United States.

"We on the commission do not have a liking for these people. Their intentions, I believe, are counter-productive for America and the future prospects for peace on our planet.

"Having said all this, I will strive with all my remaining energies to keep our ship afloat. I will not pander to the politicians or the banks. I will perform my duties with honor and loyalty for America in my heart. I have a correct vision for the future of my country and the world, and Communism and Fascism do not play a part in it.

"Power is only a means to an end. My mission is to secure a peaceful and hopeful end to this war. A peace that lasts, and a world that looks to the future optimistically, with freedom and justice for all. I desire this with every fiber of my being."

I returned to my chair across from the director. I stared at him with my only eye. He could sense the loyalty.

"I hope my words have been insightful, Joe."

"They certainly have been, Julian....."

The director finished his coffee and set the empty cup on the table, next to a book he found familiar.

"I gave this book to you and Olivia on a Christmas, many years ago. 'A Backyard Guide to Astronomy', it seemed appropriate at the time, Julian."

"It was very appropriate," I said.

"You were both enchanted by the grandness of the cosmos. Olivia appeared to understand it all, the reasons for being in this infinite universe.

"Being around you both made me happy. Your love seemed to tie the stars and planets together in one cohesive energy. It was almost as if the whole show was there for you.

"I felt a little envy, I'll admit. But I admired you both for having so much love, and entrusting so much in each other. It all felt so hopeful to me," stated Joseph Mitrano.

The director opened the book to the first page. His eyes widened.....

"I think my dedication was also quite appropriate, Julian.....

"A gift for two people who have a love grander than all the light of all the suns of our immense universe."

I smiled longingly, thinking of my girl..... My old friend understood the relationship I had with Olivia. He knew what she meant to me. He was very respectful of the profound immeasurableness of it all.

Joseph could also perceive my time on Earth was nearly expired. I could sense it in his eyes.....

"Louis Stevens will walk you out, Joe. The Pentagon is a big place. I don't want you to get lost on your way to Langley. There's enough chaos already," I joked.

"Thank you, Julian, for your time and valuable insight."

After saying goodbye to my friend, I sat awhile in front of the sculpture. It truly was alive with Olivia. In my mind's vision, I could see her warmth in the stone. I saw her walking the beach with me, laughing and living her life.

She disappeared from my view after I touched the cold marble. The realization of an ugly and sad truth is cruel, no matter how many times you realize it.

I could not grasp her passing. It was impossible to adjust to her absence. Olivia had been too vital for me.

Stevens returned to the office. "Admiral, I saw Doc Wallace downstairs. He'd like to see you before he leaves the clinic this evening. He appeared worried about you, Sir."

"Worried?

"An old war horse doesn't die easily, Louis.

"A fine doctor like Wallace should know better.

"It takes more stress than this to kill a Christian, even one with a tin heart," I laughed.

Louis nodded his head in agreement. "But I promised the doctor, Sir, I'd get you down there."

"Let's not keep him waiting then. An officer's word is always to be trusted. Lead the way, son."

Daniel Wallace, a naval medical officer, had practiced at the Pentagon's medical center for years. A graduate of Duke Medical School and an internal medicine residency at Emory University, Wallace was working in South Carolina in 2003 when his young son Danny, a US Marine, was killed in the invasion of Iraq.

Soon after the loss of his only son, Dr. Wallace entered the United States Navy. He had served at base hospitals in Norfolk and San Diego, before transferring back to the East Coast. Wallace had recently been named director of the medical center at the Pentagon.

I had deep empathy for Wallace. I understood his painful sacrifice. His medical service to the Navy and the Pentagon honored Danny. I considered Doc Wallace a great man, a great doctor, and a great friend. I was lucky to be his patient.

My respect for Dan evolved into a close personal relationship. I would sometimes drop by the clinic without an appointment to chat, particularly when I wasn't feeling well. I admired the doctor's intellect, and his noble serenity after Danny's death.

Although my doctors at Bethesda Naval Hospital were extremely competent, they would make official documentation of all clinical findings. I didn't enjoy going there.

My personal friendship with Dan allowed for some laxity in record-keeping at the Pentagon's clinic. This gave me more confidence that my heart condition would stay under the radar. Hopefully, it would not force the Navy to require my retirement.

Dr. Wallace quickly attended to me.

"It's good to see you can still take an order, Julian."

"I was told you were worried about me, so I ran down," I grinned.

"I don't want your heart fading out on us, Admiral," laughed Wallace.

"I know it's still ticking, Dan. I feel it jumping all over the place. It won't fade out under all the adrenaline."

"Adrenaline for you, Julian, can be like cyanide.

"How are you feeling?"

"Quite frankly, I've been short of breath most of the day. I haven't slept much the last week. I'm sure it's just stress."

"I've been stressed also, and I'm not short of breath," said the doctor, reminding me of my poor health.

"Remember you're a heart patient, Julian. Any time you feel unusual, give me a call. Let me decide if something is significant."

Dr. Wallace reviewed my medications and performed a complete physical examination. He then ran an electrocardiogram, a heart rhythm strip, and an oxygen saturation test.

"Julian, you're having premature ventricular contractions of your heart. They're more frequent than before. They cause you to have sensations of flipping, dancing, and skipping in your chest.

"The irregular heart beats are associated with mild congestive heart failure. Fluid builds up in your lungs because of your heart's inefficiency, leading to shortness of breath.

"Look at yourself in the mirror, Julian. Your lips are more purple than pink. Look at the poor color of your fingernails. The oxygen level in the blood is decreased."

"So I'm drowning in my own circulatory fluids."

"That's right, Admiral."

"What can I do, short of hospitalization, to make this better, Dan?"

"Normally, I'd send you to Bethesda for admission. We'd get you better over a few days. Possibly a cardiac catheterization would be done. Even heart surgery wouldn't be out of the question."

"Let's get real, Dan..... I'm not dying in any hospital.

"We're in a war..... Young boys and girls are dying all around me.

"Every old man dies sooner or later, Dan. I'm not concerned about my own early exit. If I don't sleep well, it's not because of fear of dying.

"But I do have one wish..... When I go, I must go on my terms only - on my feet and in action.

"So be a pal, Doc, and tune up these problems here. Keep me going long enough to be a factor in this war. Keep me alive so I can preserve as many young American lives as possible."

"I understand the stress that you're under, Julian. I know you need to be here at the Pentagon. At this stage of your life, I'm not going to take away your thunder and lightning.

"Let's compromise. I want you to increase the dose of your digoxin and your diuretic.

"We'll draw blood today for tests.

"Come back and see me in three days. If you're not better, we'll reconsider the options."

"The options, Dan?

"America doesn't have any options, and I don't either....."

"There are always options in medicine, Julian."

"Perhaps in medicine, Doc," I smirked.

"I never imagined I'd die a cardiac cripple. As a young man - I envisioned going out like Horatio Nelson at Trafalgar, leading my men to victory.

"My hope now is simply to outlast the present predicament. I need to get my young Americans back home to their families. This is my Trafalgar."

Dan Wallace had keen senses. He was a sentient being. He could see the mercury rising and falling in my blood.

"As a physician, Julian, I don't only treat my patient's physical ailment. I'm interested in the entire human condition.

"There's a sad tone in your voice, and I know it's not because of your health. You don't give a damn if you die, as long as it's after the war.

"How are you really feeling?"

I paused and searched my mind for the right words.....

"Dan, did you have nightmares after losing your son in Iraq?"

Wallace gently sighed. He also paused, searching his mind for the right words.....

"The nightmares never end, Julian, not as long as you have life. They begin after you finally fall asleep with the sad news. Thereafter, they come every night to visit.

"At first, they were distressing. I'd awaken in the middle of the night in a panic. To not alarm my wife, I'd go downstairs and spend time with Danny's dog until sunrise.

"After several months, the dreams would ease into my sleep. Calm and loving, they'd visit me like a dear old friend.

"One dream, in particular, repeated itself over and over again.

"I was a young man, sitting on the beach behind our home in South Carolina. It was a warm and sunny morning. A mild breeze came to me from the sea. Gulls flew low over the blue water.

"I stared across the water at the horizon, where the blue sky and sea met. Everything seemed so perfect. The nature was serene, and so was I.

"I gazed to my right, and sitting next to me was Danny. A small boy, he was building a sandcastle between his legs. He turned to me and smiled. 'Father,' he said, 'you're still with me and I'm still with you. Nothing has changed. You love me and I love you. It's all in our minds.'

"In our minds? I repeated.

"'In our minds,' he affirmed. 'The sea and sky are the colors we wish them to be.'

"He pointed with his small hand to the horizon. The light blue above had become lighter, and the ocean a deeper and darker blue. Bright colorful bands of a rainbow arched as far as my eyes could see.

"Danny said to me, 'I like rainbows, Father, and you do also.'

"He kissed my cheek..... I could smell his baby breath when I awoke.

"It's all in our minds, Julian.

"The subconscious is always searching for ways to trade places with your son. But you always come back to the painful realization that you simply have to wait your turn.

"In dreams, you sense his presence is with you. You silently go to sleep every night hoping to dream of him. The dreams feel alive. You even begin to confuse your dreams with reality."

Tears welled in Dan's eyes, but not one dropped from them. He shifted the conversation back to my state of mind.

"For months after Olivia's death, I dreamed of her. Like with you, the dreams went from painful nightmares to soothing and beautiful visits with my best friend. I also found myself hoping for night time. While I slept, I was with her again...."

I stared out the window at a small flower garden by the clinic. My mind wandered off for a moment....

The vivid colors of spring attracted my eye. The flowers were beautiful to me, as Olivia had been. She had revealed the tender uniqueness of flowers to me many years ago. Appreciation of tenderness was Olivia's way. And I loved her way....

I watched a graceful blue butterfly delicately land on a blue passion vine. The magnificent shades of blue fauna and flora mixed as God intended. She stayed there for a while, fluttering her wings in the sun. I sat admiring her....

I returned to Dan and said, "Over the past two months, Olivia has left me in darkness a second time. She's been replaced by turbulent dreams of losing my sons. I'll awaken in a cold sweat and lie in the dark until morning comes.

"Olivia has let me go so that I can focus on my tasks. I can't seem to get back to her."

I stepped off the examination table and began to put on my shirt.

"Julian, these dreams are about love and loss. The love and loss of your wife; the love and potential loss of your sons and your country. These deep emotions are sometimes best dealt with in dreams. They are simply too painful to consider while your mind is awake. Let your dreams run their course."

Louis Stevens politely interrupted my meeting with Doctor Wallace.

"Admiral Stansfield, I'm sorry, Sir, but there's been a missile attack on Guam."

I nodded at young Stevens. He left the room and waited for me outside the door. I looked over at Dan and smiled.

"Do you believe in eternity?" I asked.

Doc Wallace nodded his head, yes. "One can't help but hope for the eternal nature of a soul. As a father longing to see his son again, I can only pray there's an eternity for us all. Don't worry, Julian. You'll see Olivia again. She'll return to you."

I kindly thanked Dan for his discretion and excused myself.

"Julian, do you mind if I check up on you later this evening?" asked Wallace.

"I'm not going to die today, Dan; but if you wish, you know where to find me," I answered.

I returned to the Naval Operations Center with Lieut. Cmdr. Stevens and began reviewing all incoming data. The room was abuzz with Navy personnel as real-time audio-visual communications arrived from Pearl Harbor, Guam, and Subic Bay Naval base. There were also direct hookups with the *Carl Vinson* and the *Ronald Reagan*.

I first turned my attention to Guam, the largest and southernmost of the Mariana Islands in the western Pacific Ocean. The United States had taken control of the island after their victory in the Spanish-American War and the signing of the Treaty of Paris in 1898.

Guam had been attacked and invaded by the armed forces of Japan on December 8, 1941. The United States regained the island after the Second Battle of Guam on July 21, 1944.

Because of China's growing military power and aggressive rhetoric over the past twenty years, Guam's military facilities had been upgraded and developed into the most formidable - west of Pearl Harbor. Naval Base Guam and the Andersen Air Force Base were considered centers of US operations for the South China Sea region.

The island was home for two carrier strike groups, the *Ronald Reagan* and the *John C Stennis*, as well as squadrons of B-2 stealth and B-52 bombers. A latest generation missile defense shield protected the stronghold from Chinese ballistic missiles, 2000 miles away. Guam was a bastion of US offensive and defensive capabilities.

However, in preparation for impending major combat operations in the South China Sea and East Asia, China attacked Guam with multiple conventional ballistic missiles. Each missile carried several 4400 pound warheads.

Guam's missile defense included the Patriot PAC-3 Extended Range Interceptor System, the THAAD Fire Control Radar High-Altitude System, mobile land force SAM systems, and the AEGIS Naval Weapons System. Together, the multiple systems provided redundant safety, theoretically.

In reality, no system is fail-safe. And on the morning of May 13 (Guam time), several Chinese missiles found their targets at the Naval Base Guam and Andersen Air Force Base.

A guided missile cruiser which had been preparing to leave port, the *USS Coral Sea*, received an unfortunate direct hit and sank quickly near the entrance to Apra Harbor. Most of her 360 men were lost.

Several hangars at the airfield were severely damaged with the contained fighter aircraft lost. The Marine barracks on Guam also received some minor damage. Overall, several hundred Americans had lost their lives in a few moments of fire and thunder.

The *Ronald Reagan* Strike Group had left port earlier this morning and was saved from the attack. The *John C. Stennis* was on patrol in the eastern Philippine Sea, northwest of Guam. No B-2 or B-52 bombers had been damaged, and most of the F-18, F-22, and F-35 fighters had been saved.

Hours before, the US Ballistic Missile Defense System had destroyed many of China's orbital guidance satellites. We had degraded China's capacity to accurately pinpoint US military targets with missile strikes. The missile attack on Guam had been 'old school', without fine precision.

America's Regional Space Command, consisting of land-based ballistic missiles in Alaska, Hawaii, and Guam, eliminated more than 40% of China's satellites over the western Pacific. Top secret US orbital laser satellites and US Naval AEGIS equipped ships destroyed another 30%. China's capacity to do the same damage, or to prevent these attacks, was limited and probably two decades behind the United States.

In the early hours of conflict, America had sustained a significant loss of life from a limited-guidance rocket barrage. After the attack on Guam, we proceeded to further degrade the number of Chinese satellites.

My intelligence staff and I had expected the Guam attack to occur early in the conflict. However, we did not feel the Chinese would risk losing their entire satellite system prior to their invasion of Taiwan, where they had already committed large land, air, and sea forces. An invasion of Taiwan without satellite cover would greatly increase the risks of failure and lead to greater losses of men, ships, and materials.

As I saw the data coming in from Guam and Space Command, I realized America would win this war quickly. We were certain to inflict heavy losses on the PLAN in the South China Sea and the Taiwan Strait. If China's Navy was destroyed, they would have to settle for peace rapidly before losing a land war on the Korean peninsula.

The B-2 stealth attack on Woody and Hainan Islands had been conducted at night by nine bombers from Anderson Airbase on Guam. Cruising at 630 mph at low altitude, they each dropped twenty 2000 pound JDAM smart bombs on their targets without the loss of even one plane. Damage at Woody Island was heavy, including loss of the airfield and most of the SAM sites. Hainan Island's naval base and airbase were also severely damaged.

Next came the B-52 raid. Ten bombers - each carrying 70,000 pounds of JDAM bombs and missiles - further degraded the already softened positions at Yulin Naval Base on Hainan Island, and airfields on both Hainan and Woody Islands. Much of the underground bunker network on Woody was broken apart. Satellite images showed significant damage to missile batteries on both islands.

One B-52, hit by a surface-to-air missile over Hainan Island, crashed into the South China Sea. Another bomber was hit near Woody by an HQ-9 missile fired from a PLA guided missile destroyer. Slowly losing altitude, the damaged B-52 landed safely at Clark Air Base in the Philippines. No Chinese fighter aircraft had challenged the attacks.

The *Ronald Reagan* Strike Group had left Guam and sailed into the Philippine Sea. When 1100 nautical miles from the Paracel Islands, the nuclear Nimitz class super-carrier launched her 50 unmanned X-47B fast attack drones in the direction of Woody and Hainan Islands.

The *Reagan,* and her escorts of four guided missile destroyers, two Ticonderoga class cruisers, and three Los Angeles class nuclear attack submarines, remained out of range of land-based fighter aircraft and the DF-21D carrier killer ballistic missiles. The drones, with a combat radius of 1500 nautical miles and carrying several air to surface and anti-ship cruise missiles, attacked the PLA surface ship concentration northwest of Woody Island.

The PLA task force was composed of the *Shi Lang* aircraft carrier, five guided missile destroyers, and six frigates. The *Shi Lang* launched 16 Shenyang J-15 fighters and 17 Sukhoi SU 33s to meet the drones. The PLA surface escort vessels launched their surface-to-air missiles.

In the ensuing battle, one PLAN destroyer was sunk, two PLAN frigates were damaged, 2 J-15's were downed, and 19 US drones were destroyed. The Chinese carrier was hit by a missile but only sustained minor damage below the flight deck. Several fuel tanks and port facilities were further damaged on Hainan Island.

The US drone attack had served its primary purpose. The PLA convoy defending Woody Island was diminished.

The Chinese ships regrouped. They sailed south around the western Paracels to meet the *Carl Vinson* Strike Group from Subic Bay.

At 0100 hrs. Washington time, 1300 hrs. Subic Bay time, on May 13 - three squadrons of F-18 Super Hornets, 40 planes total, were launched from the *Carl Vinson* in the South China Sea. They were approximately 400 nautical miles southeast of Woody Island and the PLA carrier task force. The Super Hornets were accompanied by four EA-18G Growlers, specialized in electronic warfare and jamming of enemy radar.

The *Carl Vinson* was accompanied by four Arleigh Burke class guided missile destroyers, two guided missile cruisers, two Virginia class and two Los Angeles class attack submarines.

The *Shi Lang* launched 20 J-15's and 18 SU 33s towards the *Carl Vinson*. At the same time, a pack of four Shang class nuclear attack submarines approached the *Ronald Reagan* Strike Group in the Philippine Sea.

Anti-submarine Seahawk helicopters from the *Reagan* had formed a defensive shield of dipping sonar and sonobuoys around the US task force for several miles. At sixty miles away and without detection, the Chinese subs launched a barrage of YJ-83 supersonic anti-ship missiles at the strike group. Each sea skimming missile carried a 350 pound conventional warhead.

I stood in front of the screen maps, showing the positions of all US warships in the western Pacific and South China Sea, and listened to the audio feeds from the *Reagan*. The *Reagan* Strike Group's radars picked up the missile barrage and directed defensive actions. F-18 Super Hornets on combat air patrols shot their AIM-120 and sidewinder air to air missiles at the inbound Chinese rockets. The AEGIS naval defense systems on the US surface ships employed their surface-to-air missiles, activated electronic countermeasures, and the Phalanx close in weapon systems.

Although most of the Chinese missiles were shot down, there were direct hits on a destroyer and a cruiser. Both were partially disabled but continued combat operations.

The Seahawks located the Chinese submarines and employed their MK torpedoes. One of the submarines was hit and destroyed. The American destroyers used their MK 46 torpedoes to blast a second submarine.

The two surviving PLA subs escaped attack and stealthily departed the area.

Fires on the disabled US destroyer ignited munitions and caused a horrible explosion. The ship sank quickly with the loss of over 100 men, including its commander.

The *Reagan* task force regrouped, picked up survivors, and began the return to Guam.

Lieut. Cmdr. Stevens and I stood in shock while we listened to the carnage which had occurred over twenty minutes. Modern warfare was brutal in its speed and ferocity.

Over the South China Sea, American F-18s faced off with Chinese J-15s and SU-33 fighters. The aviators began their death embrace. They were soon joined in battle by eight Chinese J-20 stealth fighters from Hainan Island, and 12 US F-35 Lightning stealth fighters from Clark Air Base in the Philippines.

The Chinese aircraft released their Sunburn and their C-803 long-range anti-ship missiles with 350 pound warheads. They activated their R-73M, PL-10, and PL-12 shorter range air to air missiles for deployment.

As the US F-18s and F-35s came within 100 miles of the Chinese fleet, they launched their Joint Strike Missiles with 275 pound warheads, and AGM84 Harpoons with 500 pound warheads.

Aircraft on both sides frantically attempted to shoot down incoming anti-ship missiles. The American planes simultaneously engaged the Chinese with AIM-9 sidewinders, AIM-120, and AIM-132 infrared heat seeking air to air missiles. The Chinese countered with short range rockets of their own.

Within minutes, the carriers on both sides had been hit multiple times. Two Chinese destroyers and two frigates were burning and dead in the water. One US destroyer was also hit and disabled. Aerial dogfights at distance and close range had claimed 25 Chinese and 5 US aircraft.

A second Allied convoy - composed of three Australian guided missile frigates, two Vietnamese frigates, two Indonesian Corvettes, and two US nuclear attack submarines - had sailed from Cam Ranh Bay in southern Vietnam to a position 75 miles southwest of the Chinese fleet.

A second wave of 32 F-18s and F-35s attacked the PLA ships, meeting only light resistance of 14 aircraft. Multiple hits were recorded on the ships. All 14 Chinese fighters were downed without a US loss.

Of the 11 surface ships accompanying the *Shi Lang*, seven had been sunk. The remainder were on fire and being abandoned by their crews. The *Shi Lang* had four separate large uncontrolled fires and was listing severely to its port side.

The Allied support convoy performed the *coup de grace* by firing multiple anti-ship missiles at the remaining Chinese vessels. The *Shi Lang* was the last to sink into the South China Sea, thirty minutes later. The surviving sailors in the water were taken by Allied ships as the first prisoners of war in the conflict.

In the meantime, the *Carl Vinson* Strike Group's radars and satellite communications had picked up three DF-21D ballistic missiles fired from the Guangzhou region of southern mainland China - 600 nautical miles away. Without total satellite guidance on their targets, one of the DF-21Ds split a Ticonderoga cruiser in half. It sank almost immediately. Of 400 men, there were six survivors.

In the ensuing mayhem, two Chinese attack subs penetrated the American task force's defensive perimeter and punched two torpedoes into the disabled US destroyer. She sank within five minutes, taking forty sailors with her.

Both Chinese subs were quickly stalked and sunk by Seahawk helicopters and surface vessels. The American MK torpedoes and anti-submarine mines were accurate and unforgiving.

The US task force regrouped and was joined by the Allied convoy from the southwest. They were soon met up by an amphibious Marine landing force from Subic Bay.

The Marine task force consisted of two WASP class amphibious assault ships carrying 4000 US Marines of the First Marine Regiment. They brought their supporting Harrier attack aircraft, Super Cobra attack helicopters, Sea Knight, and Sea Stallion transport helicopters.

The WASP assault ships were accompanied by a San Antonio class amphibious transport dock with 800 Marines and Osprey tilt rotor aircraft, and a Harpers Ferry class dock landing ship with 600 more Marines of the First Marine Regiment. Four destroyers provided escort service.

The combined US carrier strike group now consisted of the *Carl Vinson*, one cruiser, seven destroyers, five frigates, two Corvettes, six attack submarines, and four Marine landing ships with 5400 assault troops.

The First Marine Regiment, which had distinguished itself at Guadalcanal, Peleliu, Okinawa, Inchon, and the invasion of Iraq, was now prepared to fight on little Woody Island in the South China Sea. Their objective was to secure the 8000 foot runway on the island and destroy the communication center atop the adjacent Rocky Island.

Woody and Rocky were connected by a 2500 foot-long cement bank. Defending the islands were the remains of an original Chinese marine garrison of 6000 men. Intelligence estimated that at least 1500 troops had been killed or severely injured by the massive B2 and B-52 raids from Guam, and the air strikes from the *Carl Vinson*.

The capture of the islands would help contain Hainan's naval forces to the northwest. It would also protect the U.S. Navy's left flank in the event of a Chinese invasion of Taiwan.

In the preceding 12 hours of combat operations on Guam, the Philippine Sea, and the South China Sea - America had lost two cruisers, two destroyers, five F-18 Super Hornets, one B-52 bomber, and 19 drones. Over 1000 US fighting men and women had lost their lives.

The Chinese had lost a carrier and its accompaniment of 11 surface vessels. Four attack submarines had been destroyed. Their aerial forces were thinned with 41 fighters downed, and probably twice that number crippled on the ground. Over 5000 aviators, seamen, and marine troops had lost their lives.

The naval Battle of Woody Island had been costly for both sides. Its speed and brutality were dictated by the high-technology of offensive weapons. Modern defensive systems were not fail-safe. In modern warfare, offense tended to beat defense.

Back at the Pentagon, my staff and I reviewed real time satellite images of Woody and Hainan Islands. In our estimation, most of the missile batteries, heavy gun emplacements, and fortifications on Woody Island had been destroyed. Hundreds of dead Chinese marine troops were clearly visible on the satellite images. Hainan Island's seaport and harbor, fuel storage facilities, airfield, and military barracks were unrecognizable. Several warships were seen to be on fire and at least 80 aircraft appeared destroyed on the ground.

I did not expect the Chinese marines left on Woody Island to put up much of a fight, especially after four hours of pre-landing naval bombardment from the US surface fleet. Air cover from the task force would help defend the landings against attacks from Hainan Island and the Chinese mainland. B-2 and B-52 bombers from Guam raided missile sites and airfields along the southern coast of the mainland - a few hours prior to the Marine landings at 0600 May 14 South China Sea time, 1800 May 13 Washington time.....

Eight minutes before sunrise, with an orange glow in the eastern horizon, the First Marine Regiment began landing by hovercraft and conventional landing crafts along the northwestern beaches of Woody Island. One thousand Marines faced very little defensive fire as they moved inland along a main road. Several pockets of resistance were eliminated with the aid of five M1 Abrams battle tanks. Harrier ground attack aircraft and SuperCobra helicopters provided close air support over the island.

At the same time, Sea Knight and Sea Stallion helicopters landed troops at the airport on the southeastern side of Woody Island. Here, resistance from Chinese marines was heavier. The Americans suffered 18 dead and 46 wounded in the first hour of combat.

As US Marines moved towards the center of the island, even stronger fighting broke out. The Chinese, using their underground tunnels and the destroyed remains of buildings for cover, slowed down the US advance with heavy machine-guns and sniper fire.

By late evening, the airport and main building centers were controlled by the US. American tunnel teams went underground and placed demolitions at key sites of the network. The three main roads on the island had been secured.

By 1600 hours May 15, all Chinese resistance had ended. Woody Island went quiet. America had suffered 168 US Marines killed in action and 780 wounded.

Of 6000 Chinese marines originally on the island, only 560 had been taken prisoner. The remainder had been killed by bombardment from the air or ground combat.

Naval construction teams began repairing the airfield for use by the United States. Three squadrons of American fighter aircraft would begin landing shortly in preparation for the defense of Taiwan - 700 miles to the northeast.

The US planes would be responsible for negating the sea and sky to Chinese naval and air forces along the southern coast of China, as far as 400 miles east to Hong Kong. The *Carl Vinson* Strike Group would remain in the area and provide deterrent force.

Just ten hours after the landings on Woody Island, Captain Julius Stansfield and the *USS Oregon* had arrived at their rendezvous point - fifty miles east of Singapore, the southern gateway to the Strait of Malacca. The *Oregon* joined three other US nuclear attack submarines and waited for her prey.

Chinese convoy HP666, responsible for the sinking of the *Spokane* in the Indian Ocean two days prior, had navigated south along the Strait of Malacca. The PLA would soon enter the Strait of Singapore and head east into the South China Sea. Up to now, they had not met any US forces along their path.

Captain Stansfield stood tall in the *Oregon*'s control room and read aloud his final orders from Pacific Command at Pearl Harbor: "Gentlemen, in short time you will meet and engage the enemy forces responsible for the sinking of the *USS Spokane* and the death of 134 of your comrades..... Overcome them and ensure they never see open ocean again."

CHAPTER 8

Men of War in The Land of Shangri-La

Upon the conduct of each depends the fate of all

***Alexander the Great* (356 BC to 323 BC)**

CAPTAIN MARK STANSFIELD led his rope team of four Marines across the large snow drift. Three more teams followed. A persistent heavy snowfall in the Sierra Nevada Mountains had created white-out conditions. The sky and the mountain, and everything in between, was white. On the high slope where they trekked, there was no visible horizon. They could see no reference points in their distorted orientation.

Mark was the third and youngest son of Admiral Julian Stansfield. A Marine Special Forces combat veteran from campaigns in Afghanistan, Pakistan, and Venezuela, he was known for his true grit. Young Stansfield had been awarded a Navy Cross for his actions in the clandestine US raid on the Iranian missile base on Paraguana Peninsula in northwestern Venezuela. His company's heroic parachute drop had initiated the Amazon War between Colombia and Venezuela a few years ago.

Since September of last year, Captain Stansfield and 83 other Marines had been training at the Mountain Warfare Special Ops Marine Center at Pickel Meadows in the Sierra Nevada Mountains - south of Lake Tahoe. The all-weather top-secret preparations had been conducted at 8000 to 11,000 foot elevations.

In February of this year, the men were divided into six teams of 14 Marines each and proceeded with more defined specialized training. High altitude combat was arduous. The climate and terrain, however, were more dangerous than the enemy.

This morning, Stansfield's team had begun a fifty-mile hike through northeastern California into Nevada. The men carried an assortment of weapons, many of them heavy. They were equipped with protective winter-thermal gear and snowshoes. Each man was allowed a canteen of water and two packets of high energy dry food. The four day mission would require them to subsist off the land for additional hydration and nourishment.

A heavy snowstorm had moved into the mountain range. It was expected to last at least two days. The hike was coordinated for the special demand impacts of unstable weather.

"I can't see a fucking thing through this storm!" shouted Stansfield into the howling wind.

"I signed up for the Marines, thinking of sunny beaches and palm trees, not this crap!" yelled Lieutenant Jimmy Thomas, second on the rope behind Stansfield.

"You must've seen too many John Wayne movies as a boy. We're not old-school anymore, Jimmy!

"Be all you can be!" laughed Mark.

Stansfield looked back through his goggles at Tommy Presley. The giant red-bearded red-neck from Arkansas was the tail-man on the rope. He weighed 280 pounds and was stronger than a gorilla.

"If we slide, Big Man, use your ice axe to arrest the fall!

"Use all your strength to prevent us going over the ridge!

"It's a tall fall into the valley, Tommy!

"You copy me, Big Man?"

"Yes Sirrrr, Captain!" shouted back Corporal Presley in southern twang.

Sergeant Javier Sanchez, third in line, turned and stuck the spike of his ice axe into Presley's belly.

"I weigh 145 pounds, Tommy. I'm relying on you to be the man. I don't want to pancake 5000 feet into that valley, especially if you're falling behind me.

"Stick your axe and your big dick into the snow if we start sliding!" yelled Sanchez.

"All you Puerto Ricans are chicken shit!

"I'll stick my prick into the snow bank, Javi, if you give me those ham *croquetas* you're hiding!

"You mother-fucker!

"I saw you throw that bag into your back-pack, Javi!"

"You good for nothing fat hillbilly! You didn't see shit!"

"If that big gorilla saves our asses, Javi, your *croquetas* are his!" shouted Stansfield.

Sergeant Sanchez prodded Presley again in the belly. The red-neck kicked the Puerto Rican in the ass.

Captain Stansfield stopped for a moment. He had lost sight of the other rope teams behind the snow drift. He checked his compass.

"We're lying low for a few minutes, Jimmy!

"I don't know where to go in this storm. I don't want to walk us over the edge of the mountain!

"Radio the other teams and tell them to stop. We'll wait for a short break in the snowfall. At least until I can get my bearings for the ridge line. It's too close for us to risk it!"

"All right, Captain!

"Let's hope we don't get covered up into this snow drift."

The four men huddled together in a shallow cave-out of the snow bank. They were protected from the icy cold winds.

After an hour and a foot of white snow, the storm began to break. A blue sky became visible.

Stansfield climbed up the bank and looked over the drift. He could make out the other teams on the far side.

"Radio the other teams, Jimmy, and order them to move out. We need to cross this mountain pass before the storm redevelops."

"It appears you're not getting the *croquetas*, Tommy!" laughed Javi Sanchez.

Five minutes into their restart, the men heard a rumble above them. A powder snow avalanche was coming their way from a thousand feet above.

"What the fuck!" shouted Stansfield.

"Everyone use your axe to arrest the fall!

"I need your weight to hold, hillbilly!"

"You got it, Captain!"

The rapid flow of snow came down the slope. The men lost their footing and began to slide downhill. All ice axes went into battle.

Presley used his strength to get a secure hold. Stansfield and Thomas slid past him over the edge of the ridge.

With the captain and lieutenant hanging helplessly in thin air, the red-bearded giant from Arkansas pressed his 280 pounds of muscle into the mountain. Sanchez also had a secure hold.

"Javi, use your left arm to pull the rope with all your might!" yelled Presley.

Sergeant Sanchez's eyes popped from his head as he pulled Lieutenant Thomas onto safe landing. With

Presley still pressing against the mountain, the other two men pulled Stansfield to safety.

The captain sat back against fallen snow and took off his goggles. He stared over at Tommy Presley, who had let go of his precious axe.

"Jimmy, look over the bank and tell me if you can see the other teams!" yelled Stansfield with a cracking voice.

"Yeah, Captain! I see everyone on their feet, dusting off."

"Should I thank your axe or your big dick, Tommy?" laughed Mark Stansfield.

"Both, Sirrrr!"

Sanchez pulled his secret hidden bag of *croquetas* from his backpack and tossed it to the red-neck.

"Thank Ya, Puerto Rican!" twanged a smiling Presley.....

On April 26, Captain Stansfield's team boarded a transport plane and took a long sixteen-hour flight to destination unknown. On arrival, the 14 men were rushed into a small briefing room. They sat alone in silence, knowing the time for action had arrived.

The Special Forces commandos had spent nearly eight months in gruelling training. It was understood by all that the object of their preparations would be a critical target. America didn't spend that kind of effort and money to police riots in third world countries. Their target would be 'big-time' in every sense of the word.

The team members were a diverse and eclectic group from a variety of racial and religious backgrounds. Their home towns were scattered across the United States. Many of them had special weapons expertise in anti-tank, anti-aircraft, and demolition tactics. Their only commonalities were extreme loyalty to America, a general fluid and crystallized intelligence of the mind, front-line combat experience, and a willful and deliberate acceptance of self-sacrifice. These were men of their times. They knew and understood America's enemies, and their attempts to destroy freedom in the world. They would not allow a reset of the globe's economic, social, and political order, disadvantageous to their country.

The men had also become close friends over the past months. They had worked together under duress, believing their lives would depend on each other at the ultimate moments of do or die.

Mark Stansfield sat back in his chair with his feet on the table as he read a weekly baseball magazine. The other men scattered around the room, napping, listening to music with earphones, or daydreaming. It had been a long trip, and everyone was tired.

"Mark, what do you think?" asked Jimmy Thomas.

"I think the Miami ball club is going to kick ass this year. They have a tremendous starting pitching staff and bullpen."

"No, bitch!

"Where the hell do you think we are?"

"Well," said Stansfield without taking his eyes off the magazine, "with 16 hours of flight time, unless we flew in circles, we're likely in Asia somewhere.

"I can tell you one thing for sure, Jimmy. We're not in your home town of Buffalo, New York."

"Those big mountains outside aren't the Ozarks either," tuned in Tommy Presley.

"Those mountains you see outside, boys, are the tallest in the world," said Stansfield, still reading his baseball reports.

"The Himalayas, Captain?" asked Sanchez.

"I guess they still teach basic geography in Puerto Rico, Sergeant," laughed Stansfield.

Lieutenant Thomas walked over to a small window near the room's entrance. The captain followed him.

"Jimmy, those are some big-ass mountains..... Over 18,000 feet for sure. It must be the Himalayas.

"The MiG-29s parked out front have orange roundels with green spot centers. It's no secret we're in Indian held territory."

"Why India, Mark?"

"Come on Jimmy! We've been training for icy peak combat. Were you expecting Indochina, the Congo, or North Africa?

"These are the tallest and iciest peaks in the world.

"I always figured we'd be coming here.

"We're going to be scaling those mountains soon. I just don't know the objectives or the 'bad guys' defending those rocks. I'll give you two-to-one, though, it's the Chinese.

"Our level of preparation is not to go up against a bunch of renegade terrorists, herding goats in the mountains of Central Asia.

"We're going against an organized field army in those mountains - likely PLA."

A heavily armed US Army captain entered the room through a back door.

"Attention!" shouted the officer.

Stansfield and his men came to attention.

Three plain-clothed security agents with machine guns went to the windows and pulled down black-out shades. They turned on the overhead lights.

A US Army colonel and an associate briskly walked past Stansfield and Thomas towards the podium at the front.

"At ease, gentlemen!" barked the colonel.

"Good morning.

"I'm Colonel Steven Forster from Army Intelligence. Welcome to Avantipur Air Force Base in India controlled Kashmir.

"Your presence here and your mission are top secret, and I want it to remain that way. Keep your mouths shut. Leaks of information may cost you your lives.

"Your months of rigorous training come down to this one operation. It is an all-important mission, which quite likely could decide the future of America in the twenty-first century. The lives of over three hundred thousand Americans and Allies depend on your success. Failure is not an option, at least not one I can live with. If you don't succeed, don't come back.

"Within days, America will be at war around the world. It's unfortunate, but it's reality. Our enemies in China, Pakistan, North Korea, and Iran want it that way.

"The AFPAK region of Central Asia will be a major one in this war. Your secret operation in northern Pakistan will be the 'tip of the spear'. Success will give us a head start in the conflict.

"Let me introduce to you - Mr. Henry King from the CIA. He will give you a synopsis of the situation and our mission."

King, a wiry man of short stature, appeared to be in his late thirties. He had dark penetrating eyes and a strong determined face. The CIA man took the podium, dimmed the room lights, and projected a slide on the front wall.

"The slide, gentlemen, depicts a topographical map of northern Pakistan and its border regions with Kashmir, China, and Afghanistan. Multiple sites are labelled in red, including the Avantipur Airbase in northwestern Kashmir, near the city of Srinagar.

"Last year, as tensions grew between the United States and Pakistan, we began to openly support the insurgency in Balochistan - a southwestern province of Pakistan which is rich in minerals and energy resources.

"The Balochis have been fighting for their independence from Pakistan since 1948. Their tribal region bleeds into southeastern Iran and southern Afghanistan. Their secular culture has been discriminated against by these federal governments for years.

"The CIA began to secretly support the rebellion in 2008, just prior to the Chinese opening a naval base at Gwadar. The port city along the Balochi coast on the Arabian Sea is 30 miles east of the Strait of Hormuz. Pakistan has allowed the Chinese to base several warships and submarines at this naval base.

"These PLA ships have provided escort to North Korean freighters transporting military contraband to Iran. Obviously, it is of strategic importance that the United States eliminate the Chinese presence at Gwadar as soon as possible.

"As our support of the Balochi insurgency grew, open hostilities with the Pakistani army developed. We have approximately 20,000 troops presently in Balochistan engaged in combat with Pakistani army elements.

Neither the Pakistani nor Western media are reporting on these hostilities. There's a veil of secrecy over most of it.

"The Chinese have transported 30,000 PLA troopers by sea to Gwadar in the past six weeks and are concentrating several divisions along their border with northern Pakistan in Xinjiang province. We believe these PLA troops will begin to move south into Pakistan in the next two weeks to help support the Pakistani army operations against the United States. Things are heating up, gentlemen.

"When war comes, the US Navy will prevent further PLA troop transfers to the region by sea. China's only lifeline to support Pakistan and Iran in the conflict will run through northern Pakistan. We need to destroy that lifeline before it's activated.

"In 2006, the Chinese began to modernize and enlarge the Karakoram Highway (KKH) to allow the movement of heavy equipment. The ancient Karakoram Highway - an old Silk Road - had existed for more than 2000 years as an unpaved, 800 mile long, primitive caravan road from the town of Kashgar in Xinjiang province, China, south through the beautiful northern provinces of Pakistan to the capital city of Islamabad.

"The Chinese, as a 'gift of friendship' to Pakistan, paved the entire stretch of road, enlarged it to three lanes, and extended it to Gwadar on the Arabian Sea. They also built an adjacent railway and oil/gas pipeline. This tri-rail system is connected to the PLA port facilities at Gwadar, and China's pipeline connections with Iranian oil and gas fields in southern Iran.

"The PLA is committed to protect this transportation system with Gwadar at any cost. The Balochi insurgency and American hostilities with Pakistan have jeopardized this corridor.

"In 2010, the KKH was submerged after a severe landslide in the Hunza Valley of northern Pakistan's Gilgit-Baltistan area. The massive earth slides resulted in the damming of the cold and rapid flowing Hunza River. A 12 mile-long lake formed over the highway.

"Over the past few years, Chinese army engineers created spillways to reconstruct the highway. They built several bridges at key points.

"Because of the tri-rail's meandering through narrow mountain passes and valleys, and the presence of several bridges, China's lifeline is susceptible to sabotage. If the Karakoram Highway is cut off, the PLA cannot move south into Pakistan, nor can they move oil and gas northward from Gwadar's port and oil facilities.

"When war with China comes, the Karakoram Highway tri-rail system must be non-functional. We will create a naval blockade of Gwadar and disrupt all Chinese lines of communication to and from the Persian Gulf and Red Sea.

"The Chinese military must not have any impact in Central Asia, Iran, and the Middle East. Their oil and gas connections from this region must be out of service.

"We have created 16 teams of 14 men each. All the commando squads are superbly trained for the actions required. You and your colleagues are combat experienced and highly decorated veterans of the struggle.

"The teams will be dropped along the Karakoram Highway over a 150 mile stretch. The landing zones extend from the Khunjerab Pass on the Chinese border, south to Chilas - halfway to Islamabad. All the drop zones are in high mountain ranges and are difficult to access. Long hikes through difficult terrain will be demanded.

"All team members will be heavily armed for combat. Each will carry an AK-47 rifle and a Glock 40 caliber pistol. M870 Remington shotguns, M40A3 sniper rifles, M249 light machine guns, MK 47 grenade launchers, M67 high explosive fragmentation grenades, M3 Carl Gustav antitank guns, and FIM-92 Stinger anti-aircraft missiles will be deployed as well. PETN demolition kits will be carried by your explosive experts to sabotage bridges.

"Near the landing zone - you will meet up with a local guide, recruited by the CIA to help you navigate the treacherous terrain. There will be no safe houses. There are scattered, abandoned, old mine shafts and caves available as resting places. Your guides will know the locations of these available sites. Stay in these at night when it gets cold and windy. Weather conditions can change abruptly at high altitudes in April.

"If the Chinese army moves south, you can expect PLA scout squads along the mountain passes. Try to avoid engagement as much as possible, unless circumstances dictate otherwise. This would likely give away your position and lead to your demise.

"Your mission is to reconnoiter the designated area and pass on information on troop movements along the highway. If the order to engage is given, each team has a specific target to sabotage. It is vitally important to prevent the movement of Chinese heavy armor down the Karakoram Highway into southern Pakistan.

"Of the 16 teams, eight are U.S. Army Green Beret Special Forces. They are assigned to the southern half of the sector. The northern half will be covered by six US Marine Special Forces teams and two CIA teams. Each team has been given a number codename.

"Captain Stansfield's team is number 35. Your landing zone is 10 miles northeast of Karimabad in the Hunza Valley. Your guide will be Marcus Callanan and his two sons.

"Callanan is an ex-US military Tenth Mountain Division veteran who has lived in the Hunza Valley for many years. He's middle-aged, but very fit and tough. I'd describe him as having an adventurer mentality and a lion's temper. He's been working for us the past three years and has already inflicted a great deal of damage on Chinese military personnel in this region.

"Your strategic demolition target is Shishkat Bridge. It connects the village of Gulmit to Shishkat - just northeast of Karimabad along the Karakoram Highway in the northern sector. It's the most critical bridge in the network.

"For those of you who don't know, the Hunzakut people and the Hunza Valley were the inspiration for Shangri-La in James Hilton's famous 1933 novel, *Lost Horizon*. It may be the most beautiful place on Earth. The valley has endless terraces of apricot orchards, maize, tomatoes, and pumpkins, irrigated by meltwater of glaciers that crowd the sides of the Karakoram mountain range above the Hunza River. You'll wake up every morning to stunning natural beauty. But remember, gentlemen, this is not a vacation. The enemy will likely be trying to kill most of you. Keep your focus on the mission.

"The Hunzakuts are kind and loving people who have lived a peaceful idyllic life in this remote region for hundreds of years. They generally have light-colored eyes and Caucasian features, and claim to be descendents of soldiers from Alexander the Great's army as they passed this area on their way to India over 2300 years ago. They are not very liked by the Chinese troops already in the valley. PLA soldiers have frequently abused the villagers. Murders and rapes have been reported.

"You are all probably asking yourselves the following question: How can the world bring war to this place and to these people?

"Well, gentlemen, war does not often discriminate. It is a sad fact that innocent lands and peoples suffer in major conflicts. America tries to mitigate that reality but we cannot eliminate it.

"You will leave by helicopter for the Hunza Valley at 0100 hours tomorrow morning. Your landing zone is 150 miles to the northwest and will take less than one hour flight time.

"Four other teams will leave at the same time from this air base. The rest will fly out of Bagram Airfield in Afghanistan.

"The Avantipur Air Base will be the center for communications with all 16 teams. Each team will carry a high frequency FM radio and a broadband satellite phone for communication with air support and the central base respectively.

"Study the mission plans today. Learn the geography. Acquaint yourselves with the names of villages and mountain passes, and remember their strategic positions. Your military packs will contain a map of your sector, as well as surrounding sectors - in the event a strategic retreat is required.

"Finally, we expect the teams to be in the theater of operations for two weeks. Living off the land may be needed. The valley is an abundant land with plenty of available food stock.

"Good luck to all."

Henry King and Colonel Forster ended the meeting. Stansfield and his men began making their way to the barracks for rest. They were surrounded by American intelligence personnel, who would provide them with more detailed data.

"Wait up, Stansfield!" shouted King.

The two men shook hands.

"I'll be going along with your team, Captain. I hope you don't mind dragging me with you. I think I can be of assistance. I've been studying Shishkat Bridge for a long time. I'd like to help you blow it up. It's the most critical bridge in the network. If we eliminate it, the PLA will be unable to send tanks down south for a good while. That alone could be the difference between victory and defeat in the whole region."

"I have no problem with you tagging with us, as long as I remain in charge. I know these men like family. I've been living with them for eight months. They trust me with their lives."

"We know all this, Stansfield. Your team is key in the operation. Your command skills are well reported. The Pentagon and Langley have picked you specifically for this mission. I'll be just one more member of your elite team of marauders."

"So I'll see you in a few hours, King. The Marines are happy to have you aboard....."

After eating a large late afternoon breakfast, Mark Stansfield lay in bed to rest and review the maps and other pertinent information provided in his pack. He saw the Hunza Valley was situated at an elevation of 8000 feet. It was surrounded by a spectacular scenery of massive glaciers and several mountains taller than 20,000 feet. The Rakaposhi, the Ultar Sar, and the Bojahagur peaks, each dominated at more than 24,000 feet.

The 30,000 Hunzakuts had been ruled by the same family for almost 2000 years. In Stansfield's sector, they spoke Burushaski - a language of ancient Celtic origin, similar to the Basque language. Historically, they had interacted with European cultures only twice in the past. Alexander's army had passed through this region around 325 BC, and the British in the late 1880s. The Hunzakuts had retained their isolated independence until becoming part of Pakistan in 1974. Their valley had been a land of peace and contentment - where the people lived a cooperative existence, free from social stresses.

Jimmy Thomas pulled a chair next to Captain Stansfield.

"What do you think, Mark?"

"I think it's god-damned ironic that we're coming into Shangri-La to kill Chinese. These poor Hunzakuts happen to live in the wrong place, at the wrong time. Two modern fighting armies are coming down their throats to disturb this beautiful peace they have. No matter how surgical we are, Jimmy, you know as well as I that collateral damage is inevitable. War is ugly anywhere, but especially in a land of peace. This valley won't be Shangri-La much longer. It's a shame."

"You're right, Mark," said Jimmy, while looking at photographs of the Hunza people in their colorful tribal dress.

"God damn it!" shouted the lieutenant. "Why do they give us these frickin travel pamphlets?

"I don't want to see these people living their lives. I don't want to see Ma and Pa and the kids with smiles on their faces.

"They did the same before we went into Pakistan two years ago, and Syria last year. Both were in-and-out missions at night. They didn't have to show us pictures of the kids there. We just needed to know who we had to kill and where. That's all. I don't want to know anything about these village friendlies. It makes me sick to my stomach how we impact these poor people."

"Oh! So if you don't see it, you don't think about it, Jimmy?

"Who are you kidding, Jimmy?

"You do need to know. And you need to think about how we impact the friendlies with our actions. You need to see their faces and their joy of life. We're fighting for them as much as we are for ourselves and our country.

"How long do you think their little 'Heaven' will last at the hands of the Chinese?

"Ask the Tibetan children about their Shangri-La.

"They survive, if we survive.

"Some of them may die unnecessarily. Hopefully, not many.

"But more will live.

"Their culture and way of life will continue, if we are successful.

"So let's make god-damned sure we succeed."

Lieutenant Thomas smiled at the captain.

"You're one smart son of a bitch, Mark. What makes you think the way you do?"

"Isn't it obvious, Jimmy?

"Don't ever allow this ugliness to extinguish any good thoughts you may have of the world. Don't let it make you forget the beauty. Remember always the unique qualities of human beings. It's not easy to do, but do it. Use your force of mind, Jimmy.

"Those children in the photos are about as beautiful as anything you can find on this planet. Look at their faces. There isn't any better reason than that to get the Chinese out of here. Let's go kick their asses all the way to Shanghai!"

Thomas shook Stansfield's hand and returned to his bunk. The captain stayed in bed and closed his eyes. The lights went out. There was dark silence in the room as the men settled for rest.

Mark thought of a sad reality. America was coming to this region because of its strategic military value, not for its cultural depth. Men of war were going to march across Shangri-La and likely turn it into a burning inferno.

How could we explain to the Hunzakuts their valley's critical importance in the battle for control of the world's energy reserves? What would they think of us if we killed their children?

These precious people didn't care about our needs for oil or our desire to dominate the world structure. They didn't much care about physical wealth and 'quality of life'. They weren't interested in mining for gold and uranium, or selling stocks and bonds. They didn't care about power of arms and nuclear energy. 'Advanced' society didn't play into their thinking.

The Hunza people only cared about being happy with their families. They wanted clean water and food for their children. They wanted their natural landscape intact. The Hunzakuts wanted their children to live.

Blood would be spilled on their mountain flowers. The clear meltwaters of the lost horizon would turn red. Pathetically, the Hunza Valley would never be the same again.

In the quiet darkness, Captain Stansfield reached into his backpack for a flashlight. He stared at the photographs of the Hunzakut children. He observed their smiles..... Their joy was revealing.....

He thought of his mother, Olivia. All her life, she had been both a patriot and a humanist. She was proud of his defense of America; but also, Olivia had been deeply pained by the unwanted collateral consequences of 'noble' actions on the innocents of the world.

No Stansfield could ever allow the harming of children. Innocent blood could not be spilled in the Hunza Valley.

With these thoughts in his mind, Mark turned over in bed and fell asleep.....

CHAPTER 9

Inferno in Heaven

Vengeance has no foresight

Napoleon Bonaparte **(1769 to 1821)**

UNDER A DARK MOONLESS SKY, the Sikorsky UH-60 stealth helicopter whispered at 175 mph towards a landing zone destination in the Hunza Valley. Captain Mark Stansfield and his team of 13 specially trained Marine warriors were accompanied by CIA operative Henry King. All were saddled with heavy gear and supplies as they put on their night vision goggles. The short trip had been uneventful, and Pakistani air defenses had not picked up their reduced radar signature. The helicopter landed silently in a small patch of flat terrain surrounded by tall mountain peaks, approximately 10 miles to the northeast of Karimabad. The men quickly exited the UH-60 and ran towards a thicket of tall poplar trees at the base of the mountains. Ten minutes later, from 200 feet away, three short red light flashes alerted the men to the arrival of Marcus Callanan and his teenage sons Martin and Gilbert.

The Callanans appeared slowly out of the darkness and walked into the group of Marines. They were armed with Kalashnikov rifles and carried US-issue military backpacks.

"Welcome to Shangri-La, Captain," said the tall and rugged Marcus Callanan, shaking Stansfield's hand. "My boys and I are here to make your stay worthwhile. But before getting acquainted, let's get out of infrared sight of the Chinese spotters in the mountains."

The men walked in single file through the small forest and up a short distance to an old mine shaft. They went deep into it before dropping their gear and supplies.

Two oil lamps lit an alcove carved from the rock. Marcus Callanan had built up supplies of ammunition and food to last the duration of a long war.

"It seems you're prepared for World War Three, Callanan," said Stanfield as he leaned his rifle against the wall and dropped his backpack to the ground.

"I've been fighting here for a good while already, Captain."

"I see," smiled Stansfield.

A deep howling wind blew through the shaft. The sound was strange and mysterious.

"There's a hole in the roof of the shaft. It must be connected to the outside somewhere. The noise spooks the yellow patrols," laughed Callanan. "The shit-ass bastards don't dare coming in here. The ghostly wind is worth a hundred troops."

"I hope they're as scared of us as they are of that wind," grinned the captain.

"I wouldn't function on that premise," murmured the CIA guide, opening his sleeping bag. "Get some rest before dawn."

Mark Stansfield slept two hours next to a small poplar wood fire made by Martin Callanan. The other men rested nearby.

As morning approached, Captain Stansfield was awakened with a cup of hot coffee. "Wake up, fearless leader," said Marcus Callanan as he shoved the coffee in front of him. "Drink it and let's get moving. It's a long trek to your bridge, and there's PLA aerial recon all over the place. There are better shadows to hide into in the early morning."

Callanan sat with his back against the rock wall. He finished cleaning his rifle while Stansfield drank his coffee.

"Where are your sons?"

"They took watch with your Corporal Presley at the entrance to the shaft," answered Callanan dryly without making eye contact. "The only American they know is their father."

"I'm sure Presley kept them entertained with stories from America. He's a talker if given the chance."

"He seems to be a gentle giant," laughed Callanan, still not making eye contact.

"He is but he can also be a mean mother-fucker," added Stansfield.

"I reckon all of you are, just as I am," said Callanan, finally looking up as he stood. "We wouldn't be here if we weren't."

Callanan wore a colorful woolen head cap with a rolled edge, and a long tan-colored tunic shirt with dark baggy pants. His wiry 6'4" frame appeared too tall for the shaft. He gave the captain some dried apricots from his backpack and led him towards the shaft entrance.

Callanan looked out over the valley and said, "Captain, pick three men to come with us on our walk to see your bridge. My sons will stay here with the rest of your men."

Stansfield ordered Lieut. Jimmy Thomas to stay put. He asked Presley and Sergeant Javi Sanchez to come along with him and Callanan. CIA man, Henry King, joined the group.

The early morning was unseasonably warm for spring. Shadows filled the valley. A glimpse of the rising sun was visible low in the sky between two mountains.

Mark Stansfield could see for the first time the awe-inspiring natural wonder of the Hunza Valley. He stood spellbound at the entrance to the shaft.

"You aren't going to find anything like this anywhere else in the world, Captain," said Callanan, not breaking stride as he walked past Stansfield. "I suggest you take a memory snapshot to tell your kids and wife later. It's a walk through Heaven, my friend. Don't forget it."

The panorama was of majestic snow-capped peaks touching the sky, a tree line of tall evergreen Alpine junipers, and endless orchards of apple, apricot, and cherry blossoms. The fruit blossoms gave the air a sweet fragrance. Two 400 foot waterfalls sprinkled into the valley clearing, forming large blue-green pools at the base of the mountains. The beauty of the place literally took Stansfield's breath away.

The men followed Callanan along the edge of the valley, east towards the Hunza River. After walking a mile, they climbed rocky outcroppings to a higher elevation. They passed two hanging passageways along the cliff face. Stansfield saw centuries-old inscriptions on the rock walls from travelers that had passed this way on the ancient Silk Road. There were names and dates tracing back nearly two thousand years. Finally, the men came to a clearing with an overlook onto the Hunza River.

Over one thousand feet below them was Shishkat Bridge. The Chinese had built the 600 foot-long concrete structure in late 2013. It spanned a small residual lake, originally formed by landslides damming the Hunza River in 2010. The vital bridge connected the village of Gulmit to Shishkat in the south, approximately 12 miles northeast of Karimabad - the largest town in the Hunza Valley.

Lying on his belly next to Callanan, Stansfield looked through his binoculars at the Chinese heavy machine gun emplacements at the north and south ends of the bridge. There was another fortified pillbox at the center of the structure. He counted at least 20 PLA troopers along the span. There were bunker houses at both ends filled with more Chinese soldiers.

From Stansfield's overlook position, his men would only have access to the south end of the bridge. The only way to destroy the objective would be with underwater demolitions, concentrated at the center of the structure.

Convinced the PLA's heavy armor would move south down the Karakoram Highway in days, the US commando squads had been ordered to attack their targets at 0300 hours on May 6.

"What do you think, Callanan?" asked Stansfield, still looking down on Shishkat Bridge.

"About what, Captain?"

"Waiting so long to blow the bridge. If we know they're coming, why not blow it to smithereens tomorrow?"

Callanan snickered. "You know the answer to your own question. You're a hotshot captain in the US Marines; you wouldn't be if you were stupid, Stansfield. America is waiting for a public provocation from the Chinese. If the slants fuck up before then, you'll be commanded to screw the bridge earlier. America will wait as long as May 6. If the PLA hasn't downed an American plane or sunk one of our ships by then, we'll act and secretly provoke them ourselves. Either way, the slants are getting a pole up their asses as bad guys."

"Well, aren't they bad guys?"

"I have a personal war against these SOBs, Stansfield. I have my own good reasons to have one. If left up to me, I'd kill every last one of them.

"But don't ask me if they're bad guys. To me, most of the world is bad. That's how I came to live in the Hunza Valley in the first place.

"I don't like the fake politics of it all. You people are fighting for God, country, and resources. This is all a game in Beijing and Washington.

"I'm fighting for love. I need revenge more than I need air to breathe....."

Mark Stansfield glanced over at Callanan before returning to his field glasses. "What are you talking about?"

Marcus Callanan remained silent. The captain reciprocated by changing the focus of his questions......

"Do you think we can knock out the bridge without first wiping out the bunker houses at both ends?" asked Stansfield, handing the binoculars to Callanan.

"Destroying the bridge without killing all the Chinese would be an incomplete mission, Captain," said Callanan, smacking his lips. "You don't come all the way out here to leave these PLA flunkies hanging around getting suntans. I say we wipe out the bridge and kill every last one of these scum-bags."

"Do you think we have the time, Callanan?"

"I say we make the time. It's time well spent," said Callanan, passing back the binoculars.

"Each and every PLA trooper you leave standing, Captain, will want to go out and kill himself some red-blooded American boys. I suggest we leave as much yellow blood spilled as possible. Let it serve as an example to the rest of the PLA. If they're going to come into this valley and rape it like they have, let them understand the consequences of doing business with America. Fuck them and all their leaders. If you allow me, I'll leave their heads on pikes along this lake."

Marcus Callanan stared into Captain Stansfield to make his point clear. He passed his right index finger across the base of his neck, indicating what he'd do to the PLA troopers, and then rolled away from the edge of the cliff. The CIA guide had made his opinions clearly understood. His bottom line was – no bridge, no Chinese, no prisoners.

Stansfield spent the next hour taking distance measurements. He studied angles of fire onto the bridge. He carefully examined the surrounding thickets of trees near their end of the concrete structure. The captain made numerical notations on his map. After a while, the squad began their return descent to base camp.

The guide led the way down to the valley. Stansfield walked right behind him. Mark pondered the possible reasons behind Callanan's assistance. Sure he was an American veteran, and perhaps he still loved his country; but there was something else driving Callanan. There was hard and cruel vengeance in his blue eyes. Hatred of the Chinese raged from him like a red fire storm.

As the men entered an apple orchard on the edge of the valley, Callanan silently signaled them to get down into the brush. He turned and hushed Stansfield with two fingers to his lips.

A moment later, a small patrol of three Chinese soldiers passed into Callanan's line of sight. Stansfield saw the ex-US mountain trooper pull out a Pakistani Damascus knife with a 12 inch blade from a sheath on his waist.

Like a tiger in a crouch, Callanan steadied his legs and positioned his upper body for attack. He sprung forward and decapitated the lead PLA soldier with one pass of his right arm. The trooper's head rolled into a shallow ditch next to the Americans.

Callanan stood upright in front of the other two PLA troopers, aiming a pistol with silencer in his left hand at arm's length. Blood dripped from the blade in his right hand at his side. The two young Chinese soldiers stopped in their tracks and stared at Callanan in disbelief.

Callanan motioned for them to drop their carbines. They nervously did. He then shot each of them in the head at point blank range. Within a few seconds, all three of the Chinese soldiers had been disposed of.

Stansfield had never seen anything like it. The PLA trooper's head had landed next to his foot like a soccer ball. The dead man's face had an astonished look, not believing his own violent decapitation.

The Americans quickly hid the bodies in a ravine and covered them with large stones. They continued toward the mine shaft, stopping only once for Callanan to wash blood splatter off his right hand and arm in a pool of clear blue mountain water.

In the afternoon, Captain Stansfield spoke with Presley and Sanchez - underwater demolition experts - about how to approach the bridge. Both men felt they had the expertise and materials to destroy the target with certainty.

"You'll be swimming in the dark, upstream against the current, and likely face an anti-swimmer net as you approach. It won't be easy," said Stansfield.

"We understand, Sir, but we think it's doable," commented Presley.

The Marine unit leader agreed, but worried about detection during the process. "If you guys are discovered, the element of surprise is lost. We'll be forced to take out the bridge from up top. That drastically changes the odds of success. Let's review the options in our heads for the next couple of days and discuss our ideas as need be."

The captain saw Callanan standing just outside the shaft. He walked out to him. The Marine had been left open mouthed by Callanan's fit of fury hours before.

"Getting fresh air, Marcus?"

"You could say that."

"Do you mind if I join you?"

"Be my guest."

"How did you ever come to live in this place, Marcus?"

"It's a long story, Captain.....

"I entered the U.S. Army in 1985, after graduating from high school in Colorado. I was a young and strong kid without much direction, I guess. But slowly, I left my troubles behind and found a good path in my life.

"Because I had always loved mountain climbing, I worked my way into the 10th Mountain Division. I saw some combat during the First Iraq War in 1991. I even won myself some medals. But the army wasn't for me, Mark. I didn't see it as a long-term career. I was discharged the next year.

"After junior college, I came here in the summer of 1995 on a mountain climbing expedition to the Ultar Sar. I was a good mountain-climber, but I wanted to get better. I thought this place would push me to my limits.

"I soon realized the Hunzakuts and their valley were unique on earth, and I stayed a while. Alexander's army did the same, over two thousand years ago. I understand why.

"In short time, I met my beautiful Amara. She had emerald green eyes, porcelain white skin, and light brown hair. Amara was exotic and captivating. Her joy for life illuminated me. She made me appreciate the true reasons for our existence. Her interests were only in thoughts and emotions and simple pleasures. I came to realize with her that all the great things of life were free of financial cost. Money could not buy happiness. It was free for the taking if you only looked.

"We had a traditional Hunza wedding. She became my reason to live. It was the first time in my life I had felt emotional love for a woman.

"Imagine? I had to cross the globe to find my dreams....

"We had two sons – Martin, now 17 years old, and Gilbert, 16. We were a loving family. I learned the local language and customs, and became a Hunzakut myself.

"The Chinese came here in 2006 to develop the Karakoram Highway. At first, they sent civilian engineers and construction workers; but the situation changed completely in 2010. After the landslides and floods, I saw plain-clothed PLA in the valley. You can't hide a soldier from a soldier, Mark. Their military behavior was easily apparent. Over the years, more of them came. The PLA increasingly controlled the local government and abused the people by taking their land and food. They took what they wanted, whenever they wanted. Last year, they all changed into uniforms.

"Three years ago, on a warm and lazy summer afternoon, I walked with my sons to the village store for supplies. We were gone for less than two hours. While away, Chinese soldiers came to our farm to steal dried food from the barn. My brave Amara confronted them and asked them to leave. They raped and beat her to death.

"When I returned with my boys, we found her dead in our home. She clutched a photograph of our family in her hand. I held her in my arms for hours.....

"The next day, we buried Amara in the apricot orchard. It was the perfect place on our farm for her to rest. It was where we spent much of our time together - laughing, loving, and enjoying our lives.

"Soon after, I returned to my warrior instincts. I spent two months studying the PLA work detachment in my region. I found out where they ate and slept. I learned their schedules. I even discovered the identities of the four men responsible for Amara's murder.

"In one evening, I silently killed 32 yellow-bellied PLA pigs. The only ones allowed to see my face before killing them were Amara's murderers. I looked into their eyes as I cut out their hearts.

"Now I kill Chinese professionally for the CIA. I've grown to like my work."

Stansfield understood the fury he saw in Callanan that morning. Vengeance would not be denied.

"Think of your sons, Marcus.....

"Don't you want them to live safely?

"Wouldn't their mother wish for them to be in the United States, waiting out this conflict?

"Do you want them to see the death and destruction of war?"

"Listen to me, Captain! You can't have more concern for my sons than I do. But these boys saw their mother murdered. They cleaned her blood off the floor.

"I love them! I wish for their safety and good fortune. Yet, I must allow for their vengeance as well. I will protect them as much as I possibly can, but I cannot suffocate their spirit. When the time is right, I will get them out of harms way."

Callanan fixed his gaze intensely at Stansfield, like a man who knows his fate is decided and time is running out.

As darkness fell on May 5, the Americans prepared to leave the safety of the mine shaft for the last time. Dressed in dark mountain camouflage uniforms - they applied black face paint, and checked weapons and gear. The Callanans remained in their traditional Hunza clothing.

Sergeant Sanchez and Corporal Presley packed their explosives, and reviewed their plan of action with Captain Stansfield. The men sat on a ledge near the entrance to the shaft. Marcus Callanan came and joined them.

"Have you ever seen that many stars in your life, Marine?" Callanan asked the Captain. "Every star in the Milky Way is out tonight."

The black moonless evening was crisp and clear. The white haze of the Milky Way seemed like a cloud above them, speckled by countless bright stars.

"They're close enough to touch," said Mark Stansfield. "I've never seen anything like it."

"Stars seem closer when you're on top of the world, Mark....."

"Are your sons ready?"

"They're ready, but the important question is whether your Marines are ready for the fight of their life?"

"My boys have been fighting for a long time, Marcus. We've all had many dangerous missions in the past. I'm sad to say that war for us has become routine. I hope it doesn't become that way for your sons."

"My sons and I will stop fighting when the Chinese bastards leave the Hunza Valley. When peace comes, we'll return to the farm and restart our lives."

"I'm happy to hear that, Marcus. The US Marines are here to help you get back home to till the soil. Maybe you can still give those boys of yours a chance at a special life in this place. It'll never be Shangri-La for you ever again, but perhaps your sons can relive the magic....."

Callanan and Stansfield shook hands.

"Let's start this gig, Hunza Warrior," smiled the Marine.

"Time to fire up your bridge, Captain."

Carrying all of their heavy equipment on their backs, the men hiked across the valley and up to the overlook above Shishkat Bridge. The night sky over the plateau was spectacular. Like a stairway to Heaven, the stars became bigger, brighter, and more awe-inspiring.

The assault plans had been discussed, and decisions had been made. Operational headquarters at Avantipur Air Base in India-controlled Kashmir had approved Stansfield's recommendations. Now it was time for Team 35 to put their plan into effect.

On the overlook, Captain Stansfield positioned two men with night-scoped M40 A3 sniper rifles. Grenade launchers and a Carl Gustav anti-bunker gun were aligned for accuracy. He also directed Martin and Gilbert Callanan to provide cover fire with their AK-47s.

"Your father is coming down with me to the bridge. You boys have a very important function to serve from up here. Keep your heads down when the firefight starts."

"We never leave our father," said Martin.

"He needs us," added Gilbert.

"He does need you, and you're going to help him from this overlook," assured Mark Stansfield.

"Both your father and I need your bravery. We also want you to survive this hell. So keep your heads down when the shit hits the fan.

"Do you understand me?" shouted the Marine.

"We understand, Captain," said the boys.

"Good! I like my men to follow orders."

The remainder of the squad silently hiked down the mountain to the edge of the forest near the south end of the bridge. They set up four light machine gun positions in the darkness.

Stansfield, Callanan, Henry King, Jimmy Thomas, and two other men came along the southeastern sector of the lakefront to provide cross fire. They hid themselves behind the tree line.

Presley and Sanchez entered the water in black wet suits, and swam against the current towards the center of the bridge. Only starlight shined above them.

The demolition boys discovered there was no anti-swimmer net protection. Within ten minutes, they arrived at their target and began to place multiple PETN charges along the central support pillars of Shishkat Bridge. Electrical detonators were placed with timers set to 20 minutes. Presley and Sanchez quickly swam back to shore.

All had remained quiet. Posted Chinese guards on the bridge smoked their cigarettes and listened to music. Two more troopers played cards.

Sanchez left the water and sprinted toward Mark Stansfield's position. Presley followed him.

Suddenly, a searchlight turned in the direction of the men. Two flares went up. Within seconds, all hell broke loose.

Chinese machine guns cut down Presley and Sanchez near the tree line. An RPG round instantly killed Henry King. Mortar fire came raining down on the Marines.

The Americans returned fire. Machine guns rattled from the forest at the south end of the bridge. Snipers shot down from the overlook. The Gustav anti-bunker gun demolished the bunker house on the south side. Stansfield and his men shot their guns from the woods across the lake. Grenade launchers hit the north side bunker with devastating effect.

Red tracers of hot metal flew in all directions. Explosions tore through the forest, starting timber fires.

The Marine captain looked at his watch and ordered his men to the ground. A powerful bomb blast blew off the central 200 feet of the bridge. Flying concrete and steel debris fell into the woods and lake. The pressure shock wave of the explosion stamped out many of the forest fires behind Stansfield.

Seconds after the deafening sound, there was total silence. All Chinese combat had ceased.

Mark Stansfield collected his men by the lake. He stared across at the decimated PLA positions. Dozens of Chinese floated dead in the water. Shishkat Bridge was no longer.

Marcus Callanan sat next to Tommy Presley's body. He gently cleaned his bloody face and beard with his hands.

Captain Stansfield turned to Lieutenant Thomas and two other Marines. "Get Javi and King ready to go. They're coming home with us. Callanan and I will carry Tommy."

With their war dead, Team 35 struggled up the mountain. The trek was long and difficult in the darkness. From the plateau overlook, the Marines could see other fires raging across the Karakoram Highway to the north and south.

"Mission accomplished, Mark," whispered Jimmy Thomas.

"Yeah, Jimmy..... mission accomplished....."

Two trucks filled with Pakistani troops arrived at the south end of the lake. They fired up at the raiders. Marine snipers on the overlook shot out the Pakistani searchlights, ending the enemy's attempt to stop Team 35.

Quiet blackness covered the Americans on their return descent into the Hunza Valley. The squad had suffered three men killed in action, and two lightly wounded.

With sunrise, they again walked through the apricot orchards and pumpkin patches. The cool spray of waterfalls wet their tired faces. The Marines were back in Shangri-La.

"Take five!" shouted the captain.

The men settled by a stream for a short break. Mark Stansfield dropped his backpack and sat against a large stone by the water. The sound of the rushing glacial melt was soothing.

He looked across at Marcus Callanan and his sons as they picked violet-blue mountains flowers in a field. With their hands full, they lay down together for a rest. The father was happy his boys were alive. The scene brought a smile to Mark.

Jimmy Thomas called for extraction on his broadband satellite radio. The Americans were commanded to stay near the landing zone. They could expect help within the hour.

"Let's get back on our mules, jarheads!" yelled the Marine captain.

Callanan and his sons hiked ahead of the team. They went west of the landing zone, scouting for enemy troops on the far side of the valley.

Stansfield and his Marines arrived at their extraction location. They set up a defensive perimeter.

"We're almost home, Jimmy."

"Yes Sir, Mark!

"I can already smell a big steak and a mound of French fries....."

Gunshots rang out west of their position. Knowing Callanan and his sons were in trouble, Stansfield and Thomas rushed towards them.

The captain and lieutenant ran fast through the poplar forest. Ahead, Mark saw several hundred Chinese troops attacking into the valley from the west. He fired several bursts from his M249 machine gun, providing cover for

Callanan and his boys as they tried to withdraw towards the landing zone.

Callanan was shot in the right hip and stumbled to the ground. His sons rushed back to protect him.

Stansfield handed the machine gun to Thomas. He ran another 300 feet before reaching Callanan and his boys.

Two American helicopters arrived overhead and fired rockets into the onrushing PLA infantry formations. The enemy was held up long enough to allow the Marine room for action.

"Get moving!" shouted Stansfield at Martin and Gilbert. "Run to the landing zone! I'll take your father."

He tossed Callanan over his shoulder and carried his long frame back toward Jimmy Thomas' machine gun position. The captain would occasionally turn and fire the Hunza Warrior's AK-47 with one arm. The Chinese kept coming.

On reaching Thomas, Stansfield handed Callanan off.

"Get out of here!

"Don't stop or look back, Jimmy.

"Take Marcus back to his sons!"

The Marine captain grabbed the M249 and charged the oncoming Chinese with heavy fire.

Thomas turned once, as he carried away Callanan, and saw dozens of Chinese soldiers falling to the ground behind them. Stansfield created a wake of dead PLA troopers with his counter-assault.

At that moment, Callanan was shot a second time in his right chest. The force of the impact threw both men to the ground.

The helicopters landed in a valley clearing under mortar fire. They took on the raiders as quickly as they could.

Stansfield turned back, firing the machine gun as he retreated towards the landing zone. Upon again reaching Callanan and Thomas, a short distance from the helicopters, the captain received a rifle round in his back. He fell to the ground next to the Hunza Warrior.

Callanan, bleeding profusely from his right chest, picked up the light machine gun to provide suppressive fire. Rescuers came to the aid of Thomas and Stansfield.

"Take them away!" yelled Callanan. "I'll hold these bastards back!"

Marcus grabbed Stansfield's hand..... "It's time..... Take my sons home..... I can not leave this land. My Amara is here, and I will be here..... Return my children to freedom....."

He took off his pakol hat and put it on Stansfield's head. He turned and shouted at the rescuers, "Leave now!"

The helicopters lifted up with the brave members of Team 35. Martin and Gilbert helplessly watched the Chinese cut down their beloved father. Mark Stansfield put his arms around the Callanan boys and passed into unconsciousness. The Americans departed the Hunza Valley and left behind Shangri-La's heaven on earth.

CHAPTER 10

The Seduction of Beauty

Beauty is not caused. It is.

***Emily Dickinson* (1830 to 1886)**

MICHAEL STANSFIELD looked up from his book at the attractive waitress. He had eaten breakfast at the *Trattoria Raffaello* the last several mornings, but this was the first time he'd seen the sexy redhead. The *Piazza del Duomo* in Florence, Italy, was active. Shopkeepers opened and prepared their storefronts, and schoolchildren in uniform arrived for their cultural field trips. The *Basilica di Santa Maria del Fiore*, with its famous red-brick *Cupola del Brunelleschi,* was the architectural centerpiece of the plazza. Across the way from the *Raffaello* was the octagonal *Florence Baptistery*, with its polychromatic marble facade and relief bronze doors. The *Giotto Campanile*'s seven bells tolled; their slow and repetitive sounds created a musical accompaniment to the most beautiful place on earth.

"*Buon giorno,*" pleasantly greeted the girl.

"*Buon giorno,*" smiled Michael Stansfield. "*Caffe Espresso, succhi di frutta e un cesto di pane, per favore*."

The American couldn't help but stare at the tall redhead's figure as she walked away from his outdoor table at the trattoria. She was showing a lot of bursting white skin. Michael always enjoyed the cultures and traditions of the lands to which he was sent. He particularly delighted in the beautiful exotic women that foreign assignments had to offer. Danger and pleasure made a curious and intriguing mixture. Michael was going to amuse himself as much as possible, while he could.

He understood this mission would be his most complex and perilous. The world was quickly evolving towards total war. Few civilized countries would be spared. Stansfield's actions over the next several months could decide the fate of people everywhere. Nevertheless, he could still enjoy the graceful and sexy moves of a beautiful Italian woman.

"You speak my language well for an American," said the waitress as she placed a cup of strong Italian coffee, a tall glass of blood orange juice, and a plate of warm, freshly baked, hard-crusted bread in front of Stansfield.

"How are you sure I'm American?"

"Your accent!

"You may be tall, dark, and handsome, but your accent gives you away."

"I'll have to work on that," grinned Michael.

"Why is an American in Florence reading a book on the *Spanish Reconquista*?"

"I'm interested in the Christian-Muslim wars. These religious crusades have been happening for over 1300 years. I don't see any end in sight. Do you?"

"I'm not interested in wars, American. I'm twenty-three years-old and single, and live in the most beautiful city in the world. I'm into art and music, and making love."

"I like those pleasures also; but if the Spanish had not turned back the Moors in Iberia, perhaps we'd be speaking Arabic this morning. There'd be a mosque across the plaza, not a church. Maybe, there wouldn't have been a *Renaissance*.

"Your art and music would be different, although the love-making would be the same," smiled Stansfield.

The pretty Italian redhead laughed.

"You American playboys are the same. War and sex are all you think about."

"Is there anything else?" said Michael before the young woman strutted her stuff back into the restaurant.

The American laughed to himself and closed his book of war. He waited for the Italian girl to return.

Stansfield noticed an old white van parked across the street. Two dark-skinned men worked on a flat tire. The scene was curiously out of place.

The waitress brought Michael another cup of coffee.

"Targum," whispered the American.

"Ishtar," said the redhead.

"Inanna....."

"Astarte," finally responded the Italian beauty.

Michael Stansfield nodded his head and opened his book again. The girl walked away.

Moments later, the waitress placed a postcard of Michelangelo's *David* on the table next to the American's bill.

"A trip to Florence is made complete only after visiting the *David*. Make sure you see him this morning within the hour."

"I wouldn't miss it for the world," said Stansfield. "Would you like to accompany me?"

"They expect you alone.

"But perhaps later, I can show you some art and music," smiled the Italian goddess.

"That would be very nice of you," slowly responded the American.....

A rat-tat-tat-tat-tat sounded in the piazza. The men by the white van had shot down someone walking by them. The unfortunate target had been blown by the machine guns through a plate-glass window into a fine woman's shoe store. His body bled red on expensive Italian black leather.

Stansfield rose from his chair and went for his guns. The redhead grabbed his arms.

"Don't do that," she said quietly. "Stick to your mission. Your job is much greater than retaliating for another dead Western agent. This is an everyday occurrence here. Sometimes we get them; other times, they get lucky. You don't want exposure in this town, American."

Stansfield retracted his hands from underneath his jacket. He sat back down.

"I'll see you later," he whispered to the girl.

Michael slowly drank his coffee while watching police motorcycles and cars speed to the scene of the assassination. He wondered if the target of the hit had been American. Maybe he was someone known to him. On the other hand, Western agents may have been the assassins. It was a complicated world, and one never knew for sure. Regardless, he was sickened by what he'd seen. It just didn't go with the beauty of Florence.

Stansfield looked at his watch and saw it was time to move. He had responsibilities nearby. The central focus of his mission was only a ten minute stroll away.....

He merged imperceptibly into a throng of tourists in the *Tribuna* of the *Galleria dell Academia*. Everyone, except him, had come to view Michelangelo's Renaissance sculpture masterpiece. As a CIA operative, Michael had learned to easily mix and melt into a crowd. He appeared completely inconspicuous.

Listening to Coldplay's "Fix You" on his music earphones, he slowly scanned around the hall looking for his mark. His eyes searched for Dr. Nasrin Jahanpur, the Iranian-born nuclear scientist from Cambridge University in England. Unbeknown to her, Stansfield had come to Florence simply to see her and commit to memory all of her physical characteristics. He was also to detail any possible VEVAK (Iranian intelligence service), Chinese, or North Korean agents trailing her in secret.

The CIA spy had become an expert in spotting foreign service agents. Survival on his previous clandestine missions in the Middle East had demanded this talent. While American agents could be male or female, of all ages, races, and sizes - Stansfield's time spent in Syria, Iraq, Iran, and Pakistan had taught him that enemy services used young physically fit men to trail their marks. They usually worked in pairs.

Dr. Jahanpur was known around the world as a dynamic and brilliant scientist. Her uncommon physical beauty was also legendary. She had been a child mathematical prodigy by the age of ten. She had graduated with a Bachelors of Science degree from Sharif University of Technology in Tehran at age nineteen and gone on to earn a doctorate in nuclear physics from Cambridge University.

While at Sharif University, she was mentored by Dr. Jalil Kazmi - now the nuclear scientific director at the secret Khojir nuclear ballistic missile research base, just east of Tehran. Kazmi, recently widowed and twenty years her senior, had developed a unique love interest in the famously attractive Nasrin. He had been persistently trying for years to recruit her back from England.

Impeccable and selective in her taste, Nasrin had remained unmarried and independent. She was a frequent visitor at the finest restaurants and nightclubs in London. High society parties always had her name at the door. But even with all her fame and exotic beauty, Nasrin had been unlucky in love. No man had been quite enough for her.

Dr. Jahanpur was discreet in her public opinions. She never expressed her political views or thoughts on the present state of the world. Her parents and brother still lived in Tehran and would often indirectly tell her of their unhappiness with the Iranian Islamic regime. She did not want to jeopardize them.....

The scientist's introduction to the spy business had come months before. During a fund-raising event last spring for Cambridge University's Physics Department, Dr. Jahanpur had sauntered up to the wine bar by herself.

"What would you like, young lady?" asked the elderly tender.

"Do you have any southern Rhone Valley reds?" asked Nasrin.

"I have a very fine *Chateauneuf-du-Pape* which is rich and spicy. I'd like to open it for you."

"I'd enjoy that very much, thank you," said Nasrin, sitting alone on a corner stool.

The polite bartender slowly poured her offering into an ornate golden chalice. Nasrin tasted the wine and approved of its taste.

"I think the goblet is even more interesting than the wine," remarked Nasrin while the tender filled her drinking vessel.

"It should be," answered the man. "It was Sir Isaac Newton's ceremonial chalice. Legend says he drank from it to celebrate his 'discovery' of gravity and its mathematical elucidation. Quite a feat for quite an intellect, I'd say.

"I don't frequently remove it from its hold, but I thought your honor was deserving. As I understand it, you have done much for this university, Dr Jahanpur. Perhaps the chalice will be an inspirational source for further scientific discovery," smiled the old man.

Dr. Nasrin Jahanpur returned the smile and continued enjoying her glass of wine. "I wonder what Sir Isaac would have said of a young Persian girl drinking out of his chalice?"

"I don't think he would have been moved at all, not even by a girl with as beautiful a smile as yours. Apparently, he had neither passion nor weakness for anything but numbers, Dr. Jahanpur. His loss, I suppose," said the old man, slightly laughing before walking away.

The prior month had been a poor personal one for Nasrin. She had broken from a boyfriend who seemed, at first, to have promise. Also, she had been unable to communicate with her family in Tehran for over five weeks. She was alone again, and the world was inching closer to war.

Nasrin drank her wine from the golden chalice. Although professional stardom followed her, happiness did not. She needed more in her life than just atoms. Where was the man for her? Where was the true energy she had searched for in her life?

A short time later, the tender came back. "Would you like anything else, Doctor?"

He passed a handwritten note to Nasrin. In a hushed voice he said, "We understand you have a deep interest in changing your country. We are aware of the delicate situation regarding the safety of your family in Tehran. We appreciate your desires for a terminal resolution to your home country's problems. We know of Kazmi's overtures and desires for you to return to Iran. The CIA would like to discuss this further with you. We believe there is opportunity in the situation. Through scientific discovery, we can all benefit. Don't discount the dangers involved. They are great. But in all greatness, there is risk. Let inspiration guide you."

A shocked Nasrin stayed sitting at the bar. The bartender stepped away and provided service to another guest.

She slowly looked down at the note. It said, "For country, for freedom, for justice and dignity - if you choose to involve yourself in an important attempt to pacify the world, be available at your office tomorrow at 2 PM."

The next day, Dr. Jahanpur secretly met in her office with a CIA official from the American Embassy in London. She told him about Dr. Kazmi's desires for her to return to Iran and work with him. She explained that Khojir was a secret research base staffed by Iranian, Chinese, and North Korean scientists. She said it was dedicated to developing and mass-producing compact nuclear warheads, adaptable to medium and long-range ballistic missiles. Recently, Nasrin had received threats against her family from Iranian VEVAK agents in London.

Nasrin offered the United States a unique opportunity. She would return to Iran for the CIA and pass on information regarding the progress of weapons development at Khojir. The CIA official did not commit to any deal. Her case would be passed on to his superiors. Someone would contact her again within the next few days.

After thorough discussions at the highest levels of the CIA, it was decided to further investigate Dr. Jahanpur. The US followed her everywhere for several weeks. They excluded the possibility of her being an Iranian double agent. The CIA finally accepted her offer and assigned an experienced team to the case.

The United States had already confirmed the presence of Khojir in 2013, but the Pentagon had no detailed information on the research and development being performed there.

The worsening crisis in Pakistan and East Asia had forced China's direct involvement in the transport of missile technology to Iran. The United States also suspected China had become directly involved in the nuclear arms scientific development program. Dr. Jahanpur's brave willingness to risk her life offered an opportunity for the CIA to get inside Khojir and verify its level of sophistication.

Operation Esther was formulated by early August. The risky mission was named for the beautiful biblical Jewish Persian queen who had prevented the slaughter of her people in ancient times.

Michael Stansfield was assigned to lead the CIA team. A graduate of Annapolis and ex-U.S. Navy SEAL, he had been recruited by the Special Activities Division of the CIA for paramilitary special operations work several years before. He had performed brilliantly on several prior missions in the Middle East and Central Asia. Stansfield was fluent in Spanish, French, Italian, Russian, and Farsi (Persian). He was well educated in the culture and history of Iran, and could read and write Perso-Arabic script. He was a martial arts expert, having won the NCAA Judo National Championship while attending Annapolis.

Michael Stansfield, the second-oldest son of the admiral, was the proverbial tall, dark, and handsome type. He had been nicknamed "Cuba" at the Naval Academy because of his Latin American physical features. He often joked that his mother had provided him with all the genetic qualities to make him the ultimate ladies man.

Stansfield would be inserted into Tehran. The American was to be "Iranian" for all intents and purposes. He would work closely with Professor Jahanpur and report back to the CIA on all important activities at Khojir.

The Iranians organized Nasrin's late summer tour of Europe's great art museums. She would first go to Madrid, Paris, Milan, and Florence. After her last stop in Rome, she would travel to Cairo and Tehran without telling anyone at Cambridge of her plans to leave England forever.

On the morning of August 10, Nasrin and Michael found themselves in Florence. Fate had touched them in a peculiar way, as it usually does. Both were young, attractive, intelligent, and courageous. Both were also alone.

The American was already thinking of the next day. He was to depart from Vienna in the cargo bay of a commercial flight. At the appropriate time, he would free fall into Iran using HALO stealth parachute insertion.....

Michael Stansfield listened to Coldplay while he slowly walked around the *David*. He continued to search for Nasrin. The spy had seen several photographs of the professor and thought he was familiar with her physical appearance.

The *Tribuna* was crowded with European tourists. As Stansfield walked past the *David's* dramatic right hand towards the entrance vestibule, he set his eyes on the most beautiful woman he had ever seen. Nasrin stood ten feet away facing the *David*. She appeared to be admiring the sculpture less than Michael was admiring her.

She was tall and elegant. Her fit body was firm in all the right places. She had smooth and flawless white skin. Her face seemed painted by a Renaissance master, with a perfect nose and mouth. Her big hazel green eyes beamed light. Long brown hair fell to the middle of her back.

Michael was the only person in the room not looking at the *David*. And she had a brilliant mind as well, he thought.

As he approached more closely, Nasrin dropped her travel guide to the floor. Michael took the opportunity and quickly picked it up. Returning it to her, he slipped along a small note.

"Burn it," he whispered.

Michael gazed into Nasrin's eyes like a boy stares at forbidden candy. He smiled, as his mother had always taught him, and continued on his way.

The American rapidly scanned the area for enemies and saw none. He went around to the posterior rotunda and put on his sunglasses. He stood another 5 minutes admiring Nasrin from afar until she walked away.

Michael walked around the statue one more time. He faced the front of the 17 foot tall biblical hero, defender of civil liberties, depicted before his battle with Goliath. He stared at the *David's* confidently tense face and his eyes with their warning glare. Enigmatically, the hero's body was in a relaxed position with his sling casually over his left shoulder.

The great genius of Michelangelo had caught the calm before the storm - the time between *David's* decision to attack and the actual action. In a sudden moment of ironic epiphany, Michael Stansfield felt like he was the living embodiment of Michelangelo's iconic figure.

CHAPTER 11

Insertion

Circumstances rule men; men do not rule circumstances.

***Herodotus* (484 BC to 425 BC)**

GEOPOLITICALLY, there is no argument that Iran sits in possibly the most strategic location in the world. To its north lies the energy rich Central Asian Caspian Sea region, and to the south - the Persian Gulf. It centrally straddles most lines of communication between Europe and Asia. Since before World War II, all major world powers have lined up for preference with the Iranian government. The new Eurasian "Great Game" had heated up in the past twenty years. The United States, Russia, and China needed a favorable position in this critically important energy wonderland.

With the American invasions of Afghanistan in 2001 and Iraq in 2003, along with a strong presence in Kuwait, Azerbaijan, and recent heavy involvement in the Balochistan region of Pakistan, America had effectively surrounded Iran.

As China's interest in the energy riches of the region had increased, her political, economic, technological, and military support of Iran had intensified. China had provided military assistance to the Islamic regime for over 20 years, either through their proxy, North Korea, or directly by shipments on land and sea. China had become, in effect, Iran's "Savior". This fact had brought the United States and China to the forefront of the "Great Game" and open military conflict.

Both China's capitalist oligarchy and Iran's militarized theocracy shared strong anti-American ideology. Their millenarian histories had been entwined for over 2000 years. As ancient Silk Road partners, the Parthian Empire and the Han Dynasty had their first encounter in 140 BC. The early trade of silk, porcelain, amber, jewels, ivory, and incense led to more profound cultural, political, and religious exchanges ever since. Throughout history, they had shared a common wariness for perceived Western European and American meddling and manipulation.

Iran's recent geopolitical isolation by the United States and NATO countries had induced her to open new energy corridors to China. The new Silk Road pipelines carried oil and gas from Iran to China by way of Turkmenistan in the north and Pakistan in the south, thereby assuring China her vast energy needs.

In return, China provided Iran with refining technology, modern transportation systems, telecommunications, electricity, naval construction, and modern military weaponry. This symbiotic relationship allowed both nations to grow their armed forces technologically, in defiance of the United States.

It was in China's national interests to prevent regime change in Iran. Her only open door to the Caspian Sea region and Persian Gulf energy resources sat with the Islamic government in Tehran. As Iran's influence increased in these regions, so did China's footprint.

They both believed only nuclear weapons could secure Iran's future. China's involvement at the Khojir missile base had been suspected by the United States since 2013. Now, the CIA would be able to confirm the level of weapons development directly with the help of Dr. Nasrin Jahanpur.

Since the beginning of the 21st century, America had provided support to armed Iranian opposition groups in three major geographic regions of the country. For years, the Balochis in the southeastern province of Sistan-Balochistan, the Kurds in the northwestern provinces, and the Arabs in the southwestern province of Khuzestan had fought for independence, using small unit ambushes, assassinations, abductions, and suicide bombings. Last year, after failed nuclear negotiations, the United States greatly increased their direct financial and weapons support of Iranian opposition. The CIA began to provide paramilitary special forces units to help coordinate the armed rebellions.

Earlier in 2013, with the onset of WMD talks with Iran, America had recruited her help in fighting Sunni terrorism in Syria, Iraq, Afghanistan, Yemen, and Somalia. With weakened economic sanctions and more military influence, Iran intensified her push for nuclear intercontinental ballistic missiles. America's attempts to pacify through appeasement failed. War with Iran became inevitable.

In one of history's great ironic twists of fate, al-Qaeda and the Taliban began collaborating with the United States in their assistance to Balochistan. They became allies in the fight to create a separate Balochi homeland from detached provinces in Pakistan and Iran. As Pakistan, China, and Iran fought harder to secure their interests in this region, the al-Qaeda and Taliban forces became progressively more involved.

In Iran's main oil province of Khuzestan (Arabistan), British Special Forces (SAS) aided three million ethnic Arab Shia in their attempt to regain autonomy from Persian Shia Tehran. The Arabs, target of ethnic cleansing for years by the Iranian Revolutionary Guard, wanted a separate homeland aligned with southern Iraq.

In mountainous northwestern Iran - the CIA led the seven million Iranian Kurds, and the armed wings of the PJAK (Party for Freedom and Life in Kurdistan) and the Komeleh Group, in their fight for freedom from the Shia central government. The Kurds had fought for decades to form their own homeland from provinces in Iran, Iraq, and Turkey.

Over the past months, Iran had similarly intensified their decade-long campaign of clandestine attacks on American and NATO forces in the Middle East. With Syrian support, Iranian-trained Hezbollah and Hamas terror groups increased their activity inside of Israel as well. Casualties mounted on all sides.

Tehran was a hornet's nest of spies and trained assassins from several countries. Russian and Turkish operatives played both sides with equal vigor. Chinese, North Korean, and Iranian agents were in constant battle with the American, British, and Israeli services. More than forty CIA field agents had been lost in Iran in the past five years. Michael Stansfield was prepared to free fall into this boiling evil cauldron of Machiavellian deception.....

The American took the elevator to the top floor of the Wilhelmina Hotel. He was escorted by three special agents to the corner penthouse where he was asked to wait patiently for his contact. The cavernous room had a twenty foot ceiling. The north wall was all glass and faced Vienna's beautiful *Stadtpark*. The furniture design was antique post-Napoleonic Austrian Empire. Michael Stansfield sat in a royal blue armchair by the giant window, looking out over the green meadows, colorful flowerbeds, and large pond.

After several minutes, CIA Director Joseph Mitrano passed into the room. Michael was surprised to see his chief so far from home.

"You like the view?" asked Mitrano.

"It's not bad."

"It's certainly peaceful."

"A green oasis in an angry world," said Stansfield.

"Stay sitting where you are, Michael. Relax awhile. I'll pull a chair next to you."

The room was full of light. The morning was bright and clear.

"The city of Vienna, with all its palaces and historic buildings, is a fine example of the power of empire," murmured the director. "A thousand years of power destroyed by little Bonaparte. Sure they rose again after Napoleon, but it was not the same. The emperors carried it for another hundred years, until after the First World War. The *Treaty of Versailles* made Austria a little country with beautiful parks and architecture, fine pastries and music, and not much more. It's sad if you're an Austrian."

"Depends on how you see it, Director. There's less responsibility in a simple life. Perhaps it's better to waltz and pick flowers than strategize."

"You don't really believe that, do you, Michael?"

Stansfield grinned at Mitrano. "No, I don't.

"It's always better to make decisions than be told what to do. If you're not the big cat in the room, then someone else will be.

"Lost empire is not good."

"I think the Romans, British, and Russians would agree with you, Michael....."

"So what am I doing here, Director?

"I already have my orders for tonight. Everything is synchronized and organized.

"I know you didn't come to Vienna on vacation, or invite me up here for the view.

"So what's the gig?"

Mitrano slowly rubbed his eyes with his index fingers. He then massaged his temples before bringing his right hand to his chin.

"Over the past week, I've come close to cancelling this mission several times. There are some of us in the Agency who believe it's a wasted cause. We know the Iranians will have nukes in short time. They have no plans to stop weapons production. War is a certainty.

"On the other side of the world, Japan and China are preparing to rip out each other's throats. The Chinese want Taiwan and Indochina. The PLA Navy wants the South China Sea for their backyard pool.

"North Korea is staging their army for an invasion of the South. They're willing to use nukes for control of the peninsula.

"Wherever you look, war is coming. So why send you into Iran? Why not bomb the shit out of them?

"On the other hand, my brain tells me that inside information from Khojir can better target our commitment with respect to time and place. The war effort against Iran may be better directed.

"After a full review in my mind, I've decided to insert you as planned. The extra effort could be advantageous.

But it is also very dangerous for you, Michael. The reality of your situation has me down, I must admit."

The director pulled a small steel case from his jacket pocket. He gave it to Michael.

"There are four cyanide capsules in that box," said Mitrano in a low voice. "The poison is encased in a thin glass oval, covered by soft brown plastic. If you find yourself under assault, with the risk of injury and capture absolute, place two capsules by your molars and bite down. Within seconds, you will be dead.

"You mustn't fall into Iranian captivity. Their torture techniques are medieval. I do not want cruel suffering for any of my agents.

"You are the son of my dearest friend. I wanted to pass this to you personally."

Stansfield opened the case and stared at the pea-sized brown capsules. After nearly a minute, he placed the case in his pocket.

"I'd rather die fighting, Director."

"I understand this. But in a fight, you may lose your weapon, or become incapacitated to an extreme. You may be neither capable to kill your enemy nor put a bullet in your own brain. The tiny capsules are a security blanket, Michael."

"They don't make me feel all warm and fuzzy, Director Mitrano."

"Let's hope you don't need them."

"Yeah..... Let's hope," whispered Michael.....

Aboard a late summer commercial flight from Vienna to Tehran, by way of Dubai, the American sat in the cold cargo bay of a wide-body twin-engine jet airliner. He was dressed in black protective gear, pre-breathing 100% oxygen.

As the plane began its descent into Tehran, he checked his helmet, altimeter, and GPS device. He reset his oxygen. Michael felt his leg pocket for Mitrano's cyanide case.

The American carefully opened an external door and rapidly deployed out into the moonless dark sub-freezing night. His free fall into Iran from 35,000 feet had begun.

The CIA specialist had made dozens of similar jumps in the past, but only once before into enemy territory. As usual, he hummed songs in his head while on the long descent.

Initially diving through the night on his back, he stared up at the blackness above him. All the constellations of stars were clearly defined. They seemed close. It was as if he had dropped from them. Michael was a "starman" in a great plunge.

Stansfield maneuvered his body for speed. Free-flying head-first with his limbs close to his body, like a peregrine falcon diving down on his prey, he achieved a terminal velocity of 280 mph. Constantly checking his altimeter and GPS device, he positioned himself for a landing after 90 seconds. He would fall into a dark area, unlit by city lights.

At the last possible moment, the American opened his dark grey square parachute with an audible crack and moved himself to coordinates just north of the town of Kashan in open desert, approximately 75 miles south of Tehran. His two plus minutes of HALO free fall avoided radar detection and allowed him to land safely in soft sand in uninhabited desert.

He quickly buried his parachute and all unnecessary gear and protective outerwear. In street civilian clothes, and carrying identification papers with his new alias - Mr. Majid Abassi, Stansfield walked toward his rendezvous coordinates.

The American found his means of motorized locomotion hidden behind sagebrush - a motorcycle. He sped through the sand towards the gravel road three miles away. It would connect him to the highway north to Tehran.....

Michael entered the capital shortly after 5 AM. He found the city of fifteen million people already awake and bustling with early morning traffic.

He motorbiked onto Valiasr Street, a main thoroughfare in Tehran, and headed north towards the Alborz Mountains. The tree-lined road, built by the Shah, was the largest boulevard in the Middle East. It was full of shops, restaurants, cultural centers, and parks.

After a few miles, he passed Mellat Park on his left and saw the Azadi Restaurant to his right, where he would be working as a waiter. A short two blocks further north, he turned east. One block later, Stansfield arrived at the apartment building where he would be staying.

The American had a photographic memory. He usually needed only a few seconds to commit information or images to his brain's data bank. For several days prior to beginning his mission, he had studied all pertinent materials - including maps, photographs, addresses, and contact names. He made himself an expert on Iranian cuisine and practiced his Farsi. He would not speak in English for the remainder of his mission.

Stansfield parked his bike and made his way towards the building entrance. He looked down the street in both directions and memorized the cars of his neighbors in the vicinity. He needed to differentiate strangers and potential enemies in the future.

Michael dislodged a loose wooden floor panel in front of his apartment on the second floor and found his door key. The simple studio had windows facing Valiasr Street and Mellat Park.

The accommodations had been arranged by the owner of the Azadi Restaurant, Adel Zia. The middle-aged Iranian man, with maternal Saudi blood, had been working with the CIA for several years. Zia had helped many American agents get in and out of Tehran over the previous decade. None had died under his watch.

In the apartment closet, hidden above a false ceiling, Stansfield recovered a box with more information regarding Nasrin Jahanpur and her mentor, Dr. Jalil Kazmi. He also found two 9 mm pistols with silencers, five boxes of ammunition, and a six-inch Italian bayonet stiletto knife.

The game of espionage was one of hide and seek. The CIA knew, that given time, Iranian agents would discover Jahanpur and Stansfield. The American's job was to quickly collect information from Nasrin and communicate it to Langley, while keeping the heat off the CIA's intricate network as long as possible. Escape out of Iran was a last step along a difficult and hazardous path. In the end, both Nasrin and Michael were expendable. Life was cheap in the world of cloak and dagger. To survive, a spy needed to be clever and lucky.

Stansfield read all the information provided and then burned it in the bathtub. He showered and took a long rest.

In the evening, Stansfield reported to the restaurant. He met with Adel Zia and was introduced to the Azadi's staff. The Azadi was a small ethnic Iranian restaurant. It served expensive cuisine to mainly upscale patrons who lived in the northern posh neighborhoods of Tehran.

Stansfield stepped into his character, Majid Abassi, instantly. He made friendly conversation with employees and customers alike. He soon became the restaurant's most popular waiter and took home big tips on a daily basis.

Weeks earlier, the CIA had learned of Jalil Kazmi's plan to place Dr. Jahanpur in an apartment on Valiasr Street, close to Kazmi's family home in the Zafaraniyeh district of northern Tehran. Nasrin's new residence was only two blocks south of the restaurant.

As instructed in the note given to her in Florence, the glamorous Jahanpur visited the Azadi for breakfast shortly after sunrise on August 31. Without any facial cosmetics or lipstick, her natural beauty radiated in the early light of day. Her hair was gathered into a thick long ponytail with a ruby-jewelled clip. She wore a white silk blouse, decorated with blue, pink, and red lotus flowers.

Stansfield trotted to Nasrin's isolated table in a nearly empty restaurant. He greeted her with a smile and handed her a menu.

Michael couldn't avoid staring at her beauty. By changing his position ever so slightly, the rays of daylight caught her eyes in different ways. Their color would change from light to dark green, and back again. Bursts of bright yellow would occasionally emanate from them, like solar flares from the corona of the sun. Nasrin's eyes were hypnotic.

Her lips were pink and full. Every sensuous curve attracted you to kiss them. Nasrin's mouth was magnetic.

The lotus flowers on her blouse were bright like her face. Their forms and colors danced on her. You could sense their meanings of creation and rebirth, purity, love, spiritual awakening, and eternity.

"Do you ever have a bad day, Nasrin?"

The Persian princess looked up from her menu and smiled.

"What do you mean?"

"Are you always so beautiful?"

"I just woke up," she said.

"I know.... Every day you do, you grace the world," whispered Michael.

"You're too kind," said Nasrin in a gentle low voice.

"No..... I'm simply honest and unshy."

Stansfield was tranced. His heart raced and his mind fogged, while forgetting to breathe. He closed his eyes and collected his senses.

"I'm Majid. I bumped into you at the *Galleria* in Florence."

"Yes, I know..... I didn't forget your face either..... Do you think you're the only one who can appreciate beauty?"

The two young people stared into each other. Both wanted more. A short silent pause ensued.

"Let me be brief," said Michael. "I'm your only contact in Tehran. All information you feel may be important to the United States should be given to me at this restaurant.

"If the place is empty like today, you can place the data into the menu as you return it to me.

"If the restaurant is full of people, and the information cannot wait for transfer, go to the ladies room and drop the materials into the trash deposit. I am the only person responsible for keeping the washroom clean. I'll remove the waste deposit after you leave.

"I recommend you visit the Azadi on occasion, even if you have nothing vital to transfer.

"I'll be observing your every move.

"If you ever feel danger encroaching on you, come to me here or call Zia, the owner. He will get me.

"I will protect you.

"I know where you live. At times, you may see me jogging past your apartment. It will be part of my early morning routine. Do not make conversation with me on the street. Ignore me.

"I have access into your apartment, and I can be there in less than five minutes - if the situation warrants."

Nasrin nodded and smiled again.....

"So you are my young 'David'. I see the resemblance. You are both tall and strong. You both have handsome faces. Perhaps, your eyes are deeper and more fiery. I see the passion in them.

"I sense both of you are equally dedicated to your cause. Your look seems unwilling to accept failure. The confident stare is in you also.

"You certainly remind me of him, Majid," said Nasrin, gazing into Michael's eyes.....

"What would you recommend a Persian princess have for breakfast before battle, my 'David'?"

Stansfield answered in perfect Farsi, "A Persian princess has anything she wishes before battle, my lady. I'm here to serve and protect. Your wish is my command," said Michael in a noble tone.

"I'll keep that in mind, my dear Prince 'David'. But for now, my wish is purely alimentary," answered Nasrin, laughing.

"The Nan-e lavash flatbread with sweet butter, tabrizi white cheese, and our summer variety of fruit jams - all privately delivered by the most handsome waiter in Tehran," retorted Michael.

"Your eyes betray you, Prince 'David'. They tell me much about you. They are truthful. Isn't that dangerous in a spy?"

"You are not my enemy, Princess. If you were - truth, admiration, and lust would be replaced by cunning and violent craftmanship. You would see a different side of me."

"Your soul must be a complicated one, 'David'.

"You are interesting to me. I'd like to know you better."

"You will. The times will demand it, Princess."

"I am in very good hands," said Nasrin in a sweet voice.

Stansfield nodded politely. He began to depart when Nasrin stopped him.

"By the way, you are the most handsome waiter in Tehran. My eyes are very truthful as well," she said.

Their eye contact had spoken a thousand words. Their meeting revealed immediate trust and sexual attraction. Nasrin and Michael perceived something special. Spiritually and physically, there was an instant bond between them.

As the American turned and walked towards the kitchen, he sensed an incredible lightness of being. Even with all the grave dangers lurking around him, he felt freer than ever before. His mind and heart had been unchained at the same time. There was no longer any fear in his adventure. He had reached the promised land.....

The next day, Stansfield awoke before dawn and jogged to Mellat Park. The spot was a popular family area with jogging and walking trails, snack and coffee shops, musical fountains, and a small aviary. It also had a large cineplex, open 24 hours a day. It was an easy place to not be noticed, even at such early hours of the morning.

The park had the spectacular Alborz Mountains in the background, giving it incomparable scenery. Mount Damavand, an 18,000 foot volcanic peak - the 'Mount Olympus' of Persian mythology - was visible forty miles to the northeast.

Stansfield jogged into the aviary as the sun began to ascend. He stopped to catch his breath in front of the American Eagle exhibition.

Moments later, Pedro Salazar - a CIA operative at the nearby Spanish Embassy - came sprinting into the area. The two men spoke to each other in Spanish while they rested alone against the guardrail in front of the display.

"I'm your contact here in Tehran, Stansfield," said Salazar, catching his breath.

The Spaniard did not make eye contact with the American. He turned and looked into the eagle's cage.

"Come every morning at this time and communicate to me anything you need relayed. Do not visit me at the Spanish Embassy.

"I'll also pass any information for you from Langley."

Salazar glanced slightly at Michael and added, "Always come armed. I think there may be an Iranian mole working at the embassy."

Salazar unzipped his windbreaker and continued on his jog, leaving Stansfield to appreciate the American Eagle as he awoke from his slumber.

Pedro Salazar was an intriguing character. A former championship futbol player on Spain's World Cup team, he had studied archeology at Oxford and explored the ruins of ancient civilizations in the Levant region of Israel, the Palestinian territories, Jordan, Lebanon, Syria, and Turkey.

He retired from futbol after his World Cup victory because of nagging knee injuries. His only brother had been killed in the Madrid terrorist train bombings in 2004.

The stoic Spaniard harbored deep anti-Muslim sentiment. Recruited by the CIA in 2011, Salazar entered Spain's Foreign Service. He functioned as a spy for the United States in the Middle East. Prior to joining the embassy staff in Tehran, he had worked at the Spanish embassies in Damascus and Ankara.

Intelligent and resourceful, Salazar was characterized by his independent attitude and ferociously bad temperament. He had been a very productive agent for the United States.

Through the autumn, Nasrin would breakfast at the Azadi almost daily. Although not yet in Kazmi's inner circle of scientists, she had risen within the nuclear payload team to one of three deputy directorships. Only the directors of payload, each rocket stage, and guidance system teams received Kazmi's total confidence and highest security clearance.

However, if American-educated Dr. Jalil Kazmi had an Achilles' heel, it certainly was his obsessive interest in Nasrin Jahanpur. He had begun to visit her during the evenings after work, always accompanied by two intelligence service agents who would stay outside the apartment. She used her beauty and body, along with her mind, to get information directly from the Khojir missile research site director.

Certain facts were now known. Khojir, located twenty miles east of Stansfield's apartment, was a deep underground research facility built by the North Koreans and Chinese. Iranian, North Korean, and several hundred Chinese engineers and nuclear physicists had developed a compact nuclear warhead, which could be adapted to short, intermediate, and long range ballistic missiles.

The Shahab 3, with a range of 1300 miles, and the Shahab 5, with a range of 3300 miles, had been in development for a few years. The Shahab 6, with a range of greater than 6000 miles, was close to being operational. The "6" would reach all of Europe, Asia, Africa, and the east coast of the United States from Iran, and the west coast of the United States from North Korea.

The Shahab 6 was a three stage rocket with two stored propellant liquid fuel stages. Khojir was still having engineering difficulties with the guidance system and the structurally heavy second stage. Only the Shahab 3 and 5 were being mass-produced at Khojir.

The Iranians were also working on adapting compact nuclear warheads to their two stage, solid propellant Sajjil ballistic missiles. Although newer than the Shahab missiles, with better navigation and targeting systems, more payload, longer storage time, quicker launch capacity, and lower detection profile, the Sajjil missiles had a range of only 2000 miles.

After the Russians dropped out of Khojir five years ago, the Chinese became progressively more involved in all aspects. PLA naval convoys escorted freighter shipments of missile parts and technology from North Korea.

For several months, beginning early last year, critical materials were delivered to the Chinese naval base in Gwadar, Pakistan, and transported overland into Iran. CIA special operation teams, supported by Balochi insurgents, destroyed many of the overland convoys.

Last summer, naval deliveries began docking at the Bandar-Abbas Iranian naval base in the Persian Gulf. There were now safe lines of transit into Tehran.

The world wobbled while it spun faster. The axis of the Earth began to tilt. Laws of gravity took their toll on humankind – again.

CHAPTER 12

Escape

The die has been cast.

***Julius Caesar* (100 BC to 44 BC)**

WITH THE NEW YEAR, Stansfield's contacts with Salazar were moved to the museum district in central Tehran. On Tuesday, February 16, the American arrived at the National Museum of Iran in the late morning - disguised as an old man with a limp. He wore a ragged brown suit and tie. His hair was white. Stansfield slowly walked with his cane into the Pre-Islamic Archaeological and Historical Museum Building and sat in front of the giant panel displaying a chronology of the ancient Persian Empire..... Cyrus the Great - ruler from 557 BC to 530 BC - began a long period of conquest and consolidation. During the reign of Darius I (522 BC to 486 BC), the empire reached its peak and spanned from Central Asia in the east, to Libya in the west, and north into the Danube basin of Europe. In 490 BC, Darius and the Persians were defeated by the Athenians at the Battle of Marathon in the First Persian War. In 480 BC, Xerxes (486 BC to 465 BC) led his army by land across the Hellespont, conquering Thrace and Macedonia on the way back to Greece. At the narrow pass of Thermopylae, 300 brave Spartans and their King Leonidas held off the Persian army for three days - long enough to allow the remainder of the allied Greek Army to strategically retreat south. As the Persians advanced on Athens, the city was abandoned. Soon after, it was sacked and burned. The Athenians baited the Persians into attacking them near the island of Salamis. The total defeat of the Persians at the naval battle of Salamis, followed a few months later by the defeat of their land army at Plataea, ended the Second Persian War.

The Greek victories in the Persian Wars are believed to be the ideological basis for the birth of modern Western civilization. They are the birthstones of Western democracy. The Athenian values of freedom and equality were seen as the cause of their victory, and have been sanctified and glorified by Western societies ever since.

From 479 BC to the reign of Darius III (336 BC to 330 BC), the empire was slowly weakened by dynastic disputes and rebellions of the subjected peoples.

Alexander the Great and the Macedonian Army began their conquest of the Persians in the spring of 334 BC at the Battle of Granicus. Alexander followed with further victories at Issus in November 333 BC, and Gaugemela in October 331 BC. The Macedonian general entered the capital, Persepolis, in 330 BC and ended the Persian Empire. After Alexander's death in 323 BC, his successors divided the lands into competing and hostile kingdoms (the Hellenistic kingdoms).

Pedro Salazar sat next to Stansfield. He opened his guide book and pretended to read.

"Quite a story," said the Spaniard in Farsi. "I come here often. I never lose interest in the history and passion of it all. The Greeks and the Persians..... Athens and Alexander..... Darius and Xerxes..... 'Good' dictators and 'bad' dictators..... Democracy and totalitarianism..... Hellenism..... Expansionism.....

"We were born out of all this. You sometimes wonder how?

"The names of people and places may change. The 'gods' change. But the 'story of man' remains the same. The never-ending cycle of conquest, subjugation and rebellion, and eventually, overthrow, defeat, and reconstruction - followed later by conquest and expansion again. The cycle never ends. What a waste of time, money, and life," said Salazar wistfully.....

"Instruct Nasrin to expeditiously provide more details on *Operation Arash*," said the Spaniard in his native tongue. "She must also get us a timeline for the Shahab 6 program. We need to know when it's expected to become fully operational. This data must come directly from Kazmi's mouth. He has the information. We believe Nasrin's charms can extract his secrets.

"One Shahab 6 missile can wipe out an entire American or European city. We need to hit them hard before they can achieve their goals. The nuclear meeting in Zurich, Switzerland, is set for mid-April. We need the information before then.

"This *Operation Arash* business is also of great concern to Langley. In ancient Persian mythology, *Arash* was the legendary archer who fired his arrow from Mount Damavand to mark the Iranian border. This symbolism is worrying us. It sounds pre-emptive. We need you to impress on Nasrin the urgency involved."

Salazar slowly moved away, still pretending to read his guide book. He strolled down one of the exhibit halls.

Stansfield limped in the opposite direction. As he did, he glanced at the display next to him. Reflected off the thick glass, the American saw the image of someone trailing him. When he'd stop, the man would stop. He'd go, and the man would go. There was no doubt of the stalker's intentions.

The American passed into the elevator with several other people. At the last moment, the Iranian agent also entered. He looked at Stansfield and stepped to the back of the elevator.

The doors opened on the second floor and Michael limped out. The Iranian followed at a short distance. Michael passed into the stairwell and waited for the enemy.

The Persian entered the stairwell with his weapon drawn. Hidden in the shadows, Michael raised his cane and fired a silent dissolvable micro-puncturing poison dart with 200 milliequivalents of potassium chloride into the Iranian's neck. Immediate cardiac arrhythmia dropped the enemy to the concrete floor. He seized, urinated and defecated into his pants, and died.

The American confirmed his foe was dead. The dart had left an invisible wound.....

Late that evening, Stansfield rode by Nasrin's home on his motorcycle. He circled the block twice and didn't see the usual VEVAK agents parked outside. From the back alley, he dashed up the fire escape to the third floor and Nasrin's apartment.

The hallway was quiet and dark. Michael placed his ear to the door and heard only silence inside. He used his key to enter. With a small hand-held device, the spy electronically swept the rooms for audio and video surveillance bugs.

The American found the bedroom door ajar. He couldn't prevent himself from looking in.

Nasrin had left the window slightly open. A cold winter mountain breeze floated the white chiffon shades away from the windowsill. Moonlight passed into the room and fell gently on the sleeping Persian princess. Her body was uncovered and naked on the bed. She lay on her right side with her back to the moon's glow. Nasrin's left thigh was lifted over a pillow, holding it tightly between her legs. All her shapes and forms were exposed to Michael's eyes.

The American could not pull himself away from the door's crack. Nasrin was too beautiful to justify his leaving. His mind was caught in a no-man's land. He could neither depart nor invite himself into her bed. Michael stayed there for a while, staring at her.

Nasrin softly turned her head in Michael's direction. Sleeping beauty and her desires had awakened. She held out her hand and called for her 'David' to join her.

Morning came slowly and reluctantly. The window was closed and the bedroom was warm. The musk of love was in the air.

Nasrin's eyes opened calmly and found the prince sitting at her desk, observing photographs. She sat up in the bed, uncovered, and pulled her thick brown hair behind her ears. Bright sunlight illuminated her eyes green like emeralds.

Nasrin's face was exotic and unique. Her features were fine and unblemished. Her nose, lips, and cheeks seemed conceived by angels and drawn by Botticelli. She truly was a Persian princess.

"Is it alright to call you, Michael?

"I don't like the name, Majid."

"Call me what you wish in private, but pay me no attention outside this room. To the rest of the world, we don't know each other," answered Stansfield as he continued staring at the photos.

Nasrin's travels had taken her to all the major capitals and academic institutions of the 'Free World'. She had met and worked with Nobel Prize winners, and had socialized with world leaders.

Looking at a photograph of Nasrin with the Prime Minister of England, the American closed his eyes.

"What caused you to give up this life, Nasrin, and return to Iran under these circumstances? Why would you take on the risks?

"You're young, beautiful, and brilliant. The world is your stage. Why not stay in your free life and reap the benefits afforded to you?

"There is much danger in what you're doing, Nasrin."

The princess slipped out of bed and threw on a Cambridge University t-shirt. It barely covered her hips. Her shapely thighs in motion drew Michael's attention. Everything about this woman aroused his senses.

Nasrin walked barefoot over to Stansfield and sat on his naked lap. She kissed his lips.

"Do you understand the infinity of the universe, Michael? Do you realize that even with all the advancements in our knowledge over the centuries, we still don't comprehend our own presence in the cosmos?

"People speak of the 'Big Bang' origins of the universe. They point to the data showing rapidly increasing expansion from the 'Singularity'. They study the interplay between cohesive 'Dark Matter' and the divisive 'Dark Energy'. Some say the universe will expand into oblivion, others believe it'll contract on itself in a 'Big Crunch'. Some of my colleagues say 'Black Holes' are portals to other universes, that we exist in a multiverse cosmos. Our thinking has gone from one mysterious universe to even more unknown parallel universes. Space and time are being better understood scientifically, but less comprehended philosophically. In its totality, our reality may be less discernible today than it was a thousand years ago. In a strange way, we are more confused by the objective data.

"As human beings on a little blue planet in a corner of the Milky Way Galaxy, among hundreds of billions of stars and even more galaxies, we don't know where we stand. We don't know why we are here, nor where we're going. In essence, we are vexed by it all.

"Considering the grandness of nature's spectacle, and our helpless present position to understand it, it is inconceivable to me that nations go to war over differences in gods, prophets, fiat money, or color of skin. Differences in religions and cultures on Earth don't amount to anything except diversity. These man-made creations are figments of imagination. They are contrived ideas, having no standing of importance in the natural cosmos. It is wrong to decapitate someone because of differences of opinion on immaterial themes.

"I believe free minds, those that accept cultural differences, are necessary to advance the world to a higher plane of consciousness. Perhaps with time, we can arrive at a better understanding of why humankind exists, and why our universe exists. As a species, man may never achieve that spiritual height, but without free minds to think – we'll never know.

"Instead of wasting man's intelligence and the Earth's natural resources for war and conquest, we should use our gifted powers to explore the secret vastness of the cosmos, cure disease, eliminate famine, and conserve our natural ecosystems. It is insane for us to choose unwisely."

Nasrin pointed to two photographs. The smaller one was of Nasrin as a teenager on a holiday ski trip in the Alborz Mountains with her parents and brother. The larger photo showed Nasrin standing in front of the Lincoln Memorial in Washington while on a summer trip from Cambridge.

"I believe my homeland of Iran is on the wrong course. My country has a vibrant and intelligent culture. It's capable of great achievements in science, art, music, and literature. It could have a prosperous economic future with its natural resources and industrious people. However, our government has chosen to invest most in weapons of war and project a defiant stance to the rest of the world. I don't wish for my parents and younger brother to live in constant danger of being destroyed. I want their hearts and minds free to love and enjoy life. I wish them liberty, and the freedom to express their individualism and various points of view. I want their honor back.

"Michael, do you believe in American exceptionalism? Do you feel the United States is qualitatively different from other nations?

"The French writer Alexis de Tocqueville, in his 1831 work - *Democracy in America*, keenly described your country as exceptional in its ability to navigate through geopolitical peril while maintaining its practical democratic ideology.

"I sense America's puritanical roots, and its historical absence of feudalism, allowed it to be molded and tempered by revolution and civil war into an ideal republic. Americans paid a heavy cost for freedom, but they achieved it. Their only scourge - slavery - was abolished through deep sacrifice. Lessons were learned. Strength of character was gained through loss of blood. As Lincoln said in his *Gettysburg Address: 'America is a nation conceived in liberty, and dedicated to the proposition that all men are created equal.'*

"America's federalism and system of checks and balances, along with a limit on ecclesiastical powers, and a profound depth of the institutions of law and order, are all designed to prevent any person or group from becoming too powerful. This balance, envied by all other countries of the world, makes America exceptional. She is an irrepressible model to be supported and maintained for all time.

"Yes, I am scared. There are many dangers. But Iran is my birthplace. It's home for my mother, father, and brother. I have many friends living here.

"Why not make it better? Why not invest our energies in promoting peace instead of war? Why not use our collective intelligence to advance society? Why not stop the madness?

"Our world can be better, Michael. I know it. I will do everything I can to make it so....."

Michael's eyes welled with tears as Nasrin spoke.

"Your words remind me of my mother. She died young, not too long ago. Her name was Olivia.

"She was smart and beautiful like you, Nasrin. She also had rare and exotic uniqueness.

"Olivia studied Classical Greek history at Dartmouth. She used the amaranth flower as a symbol to represent the American identity. My mother preferred it to the term 'American Exceptionalism', which she found arrogant. In Greek mythology, the amaranth flower represented eternity and everlasting immortality.

"A refugee and orphan of communist repression on the island of Cuba, Olivia emigrated to the United States as a young girl. Her love of America was exemplary in our home. She'd often say that 'American Amaranth', the limitless and never-ending spirit of the American people, would eventually settle our turbulent world. I hope my mother's faith in democracy for all peoples comes true, and that the hopes and dreams of your family are realized."

Michael kissed Nasrin's lips. The prince and princess embraced.

"I believe in your mother's 'American Amaranth'. I saw it in your eyes the moment we met," whispered Nasrin.

"There's a fire in you, Michael, which I've never seen before. You project to me a simple, noble sense of justice and honor. It's both exhilarating and calming at the same time. You make me hopeful. You captivate me."

Nasrin made love to Michael on the chair.

Later in the morning, the American lay awake in bed next to his woman. Nasrin was asleep. Bright sunlight edged around the window drape and landed on Michael's face.

He thought about how much he liked this woman. She was kind, loving, and spiritual. And very sensuous. She was attractive in body and soul. The sunshine made him squint as he sat up in bed. The American was restless.

Stansfield pondered the perils of the mission. He was uncomfortable for Nasrin. It was not easy to run an operation while falling in love with your partner.

They urgently needed to get the information demanded by Langley. And they needed to get out of Iran quickly. He did not want to risk Nasrin's life any longer. Michael softly nudged Nasrin awake.

"Nasrin, do you know anything about *Operation Arash*?

"Does it involve the Shahab 6 program?"

Nasrin edged over and went face to face with Michael.

"I've only heard whispers on *Arash* from Kazmi.

"The man is an idiot. He sickens me. He spends all his time talking about our 'affair', and how he will be perceived in the government if discovered. He's more concerned of our relationship's policy repercussions than Khojir's scientific programs.

"I know the Shahab 6 program is close to completion and that *Arash* is big. I don't know details yet, but I'll get there," answered Nasrin confidently.

A nude Stansfield walked over to the window. He pulled the shades slightly to the side and looked down onto the street. He saw no suspicious cars or people.

The American quickly dressed. He kissed Nasrin goodbye, stepped out of the apartment house quietly, and biked two blocks to the Azadi.

On Tuesday morning, April 19, Pedro Salazar waited for Michael Stansfield at the Treasury Museum of the National Jewels. He stood observing the Darya-ye-Nur (Sea of Light). At 182 carats, it was the world's largest pink diamond. As the hall cleared of people, Stansfield walked in and stood six feet away from Salazar without making eye contact.

"Michael, the Zurich talks have broken down. Because of Nasrin's work, we know the Shahab 6 is operational. The United States believes that war with Iran, North Korea, and China is now inevitable. We're just picking our time. We still need to find out about *Operation Arash*.

"Chinese naval activity has increased recently in the Taiwan Strait and the South China Sea. Several near-incidents have occurred with US naval forces.

"In the past twenty-four hours, there have been two naval engagements between the PLA Navy and Japan in the East China Sea. Two Japanese destroyers and three PLA frigates have been sunk. There has been much loss of life. Tensions are rising rapidly in the region. Japan wants war.

"There have been several artillery exchanges between North and South Korea along the DMZ. Although there have been no American casualties, over forty South Korean soldiers and civilians have been killed. Pressure is mounting on both sides for more definitive action.

"Ten PLA divisions are preparing to come south from Xinjiang into Pakistan along the Karakoram Highway to reinforce the Pakistani army offensive in Balochistan. The Chinese will come up directly against US forces in battle there.

"The U.S. Navy has established an interceptor missile defense shield with Aegis guided missile cruisers and destroyers in the eastern Mediterranean, the Black Sea, the Red Sea, and the Persian Gulf. We have three US carrier strike groups in the region, along with a British and a French carrier strike group. The Missile Defense Agency has land-based interceptor missile batteries throughout the Middle East. All our forces have been put on high alert.

"The United States is planning a naval blockade of Gwadar, and with the British and French navies - a blockade of the Syrian and Lebanese Mediterranean ports. Military action is forthcoming, Michael; it's going to get very dangerous around here. Be careful and prepare an escape plan.

"I expect the Iranian authorities will soon close the museums and begin to place their contents into underground storage. We will have to meet at Mellat Park, as we did last autumn. The name of the game now is survival, Michael. Stay safe. I'll meet you at Mellat Park around sunrise in two days. Take care of yourself."

The men exited the area separate ways.

Stansfield rode back to his apartment. He loved Nasrin. He was with her as frequently as circumstances allowed. She loved him equally. An escape plan would undoubtedly have to include her. Michael was not leaving Tehran without Nasrin.

On May 5 at the restaurant, the American asked to speak with Adel Zia in private. The two men had become friends in the past eight months.

"Adel, why do you do this work?" asked Stansfield.

"During the street protests in 2009, Majid, my twenty year-old niece was killed by a rooftop Revolutionary Guard sniper. She bled to death in my arms from a chest wound as big as my fist. I tried to tamponade the bleeding, but the injury was too grave. I looked into her eyes while life abandoned her. I pleaded with God for her not to leave us. God was not listening. The All-Powerful did not help her or me.

"I realized if a government could murder a beautiful innocent creature like her, it could not be my government any longer. It was not worthy of my support.

"It was not a matter of supporting America over Iran. It was simply a matter of me against them.

"Since that day, I have done everything in my power to rid my country of this regime. I love the Persian people. I know this government will lead to our destruction. If I lose my life in this struggle, let it be my end. I accept my fate," answered Zia.

"If America attacks your country, Adel, what are your plans?"

"I will take to the streets with thousands of others and topple our government before the Americans arrive. The United States will help us establish a democratic republic with equal rights for all. That is my hope for our country."

"Adel, I love the girl, Nasrin.

"How can I get her out of Iran?"

Zia excused himself for a moment and went to a back room where he had a safe. He returned with two keys and an address.

"When the time comes, Majid, run away with your woman. This is not your country. You should not die in Iran. Let me die in Iran.

"Save the girl. The real Iranian men will fight for her. I wish her to be free with you. Her love will take you far in this world.

"Head north on Highway Road 59 through the Alborz Mountains to the Caspian seaside town of Chalus. Go to this address. It is the villa of a close friend who is with us in the underground resistance movement. The home is safe. It has a high privacy wall around the entire property.

Behind the house, there is a pier and a boat dock with a speedy Australian motor yacht. Take the boat northwest to Lankaran on the Azerbaijani coast. It is two hundred kilometers away. The boat is always full of petrol, ready to be used for escape. The trip to safety will take four hours at full speed.

"There are automatic weapons hidden in the house's cellar. Look also behind the cushions on the boat and you will find AK-47s.

"Majid, go with God and be safe. Take Nasrin and give her children free from birth. Have many boys and girls. Enjoy your family for all of life and never worry about war taking them away."

With tears running down his face, Adel Zia kissed Michael on both cheeks.

"It is time for me to prepare for war, Majid. It is my moment of truth. My eternal soul will depend on the nobility and bravery of my actions. It is as it should be. Like you Americans say, actions speak louder than words."

On Thursday, May 12, Stansfield arranged with Adel Zia to get Nasrin's parents and brother out of Iran by car through the northwestern Kurdish territories into Azerbaijan. It was a dangerous escape, but they had no other choice.

Michael took the day off from work and met Nasrin at Tehran's Grand Bazaar. They threw off her usual tail of two Iranian intelligence agents in the melange of the Bazaar and escaped to privacy at his apartment. According to plans, the couple landed in bed by early afternoon.

After lovemaking, Nasrin turned to Michael and said, "I now know the details of *Operation Arash*.

"The Chinese and North Koreans have helped Iran build several freighters with intermediate range missiles in their hulls. The missiles have sophisticated nuclear warheads.

"If attacked by the United States, or possibly even pre-emptively, Iran will order the freighters to fire their missiles from international waters - a thousand miles from their intended targets inside the United States. Each missile can destroy an American city with ease.

"Some rockets are programmed to explode 300 miles over middle America, creating a disruptive electromagnetic pulse radiation. The blasts will disable most of the electronic power networks in the United States. The American infrastructure will be pushed back to the 19th century. It will lead to the probable death of millions through food and water shortages, and general chaos.

"Kazmi told me this last night in a state of panic and disbelief. He said the Iranian Revolutionary Guard had hijacked all of the government's decision-making. He swore they were on a suicide march. Nothing could stop them now.

"The idiot kept saying how all his work for defensive purposes was now going to be used offensively on the United States in a final glorious assault. He kept screaming that he had been betrayed.

"Michael, these freighters are operational. They are mostly still in ports along the Iranian Persian Gulf, the Syrian and Lebanese Mediterranean coasts, and at the Port of Sudan in the Red Sea. They are all carrying false flags. Only one freighter has left port from Tartus, Syria, and is heading west in the Mediterranean Sea. It has to be stopped.

"There's more bad news. Iranian and Hezbollah agents have smuggled disassembled nuclear bomb parts through Central America and Mexico, across the southern US border, and scattered throughout the United States. The agents are commanded to deliver their precious cargo at safe houses for assemblage into working bombs. The bombs will then be placed in key American cities, programmed for destruction by the Iranian regime.

"Michael, this truly is a national death march. It seems the Iranian Revolutionary Guard has decided that before they are removed by the United States, they will take out as much of the United States as possible. It is essentially a multi-pronged nuclear Kamikaze attack."

Nasrin sat in bed with her legs crossed. She stared at Michael's face as his mind worked through all the possible options. Beads of sweat formed on his forehead. He sprung to attention and began pacing in the room.

"Get dressed and be ready to leave when I return," said the American. "We're heading out before the bombs fall."

Stansfield went to the Azadi and ordered Zia to the Spanish Embassy.

"Tell Salazar to meet me at Mellat Park immediately. There can be no excuses. Say it's do or die."

One hour later, Stansfield and Salazar stood a few feet apart at the American Eagle exhibit at Mellat Park. The eagle had been removed from his exhibit cage.

In Spanish, Stansfield told Salazar of the recent revelations.

"War has come, Spaniard. I regret to say Iran will be changed forever. We will be changed forever as well.

Many people will die. Women and children will pay a big price for the ideas of mad men.

"For all the years of insincere negotiations, the world will crumble at their feet. They have built their own tombs.

"Transmit the information to Langley. The waiting game has ended.

"Take care of yourself, my brother. Don't wait for them to come searching for you. Get out of Tehran now."

The men said their final goodbyes and separated for the last time. Salazar walked to a waiting taxi and drove off.

As he mounted his bike, Stansfield saw two men running towards him from across the street. He pretended to not notice and slowly rode off.

The American circled the park and allowed the pursuing car to close in on him. He turned into the alley behind his apartment and quickly dismounted. He stayed silent behind a structural cement barrier and waited for the men to leave their car.

Stansfield stepped out from behind the wall and fired, *Pop-Pop.....* Perfectly placed 9 mm rounds went into the back of the heads of both Iranian agents. They dropped like flies. The American stripped the enemy of their identification papers and cell phones, and dragged them back into their car.

Michael raced up to his apartment. Nasrin was frozen by the window.

"Grab a few things and let's go," said Michael, before throwing ammunition into a backpack. He put two extra magazine clips in his pants pocket.

"Nasrin, take the map on the kitchen table," he ordered.

"I saw you kill those men," cried Nasrin.

"It's either them or us, Baby. And I'm not letting anyone take us down. I'll kill any living thing that gets in our way.

"Now let's move!"

The couple escaped on the motorcycle. Nasrin squeezed Michael from behind and kissed the back of his neck. Both realized the tremendous danger facing them; yet, they were comforted by running the gauntlet together.

Salazar returned to the Spanish Embassy and relayed the critical information to Langley by secret cable. Ten minutes later, he received a coded reply. The stoic Spaniard whispered, "GET OUT OF TEHRAN."

Salazar understood his relay had started World War III.

CHAPTER 13

World War

Never think that war, no matter how necessary, nor how justified, is not a crime.

***Ernest Hemingway* (1899 to 1961)**

AFTER LESS THAN two hours of sleep, I was awakened by my aide, Lieutenant Commander Louis Stevens. I had slept on a small cot in my office at the Pentagon. The room was not like the typical clean and spartan work space most officers maintained. It looked lived in. There were ashtrays with burnt out cigarettes scattered everywhere. Papers covered the desk. One wall contained a shelf case filled with remembrances from my world travels, and photographs with military friends from more than forty years in the US Navy. Another wall was dedicated to my children. A third wall was reserved only for Olivia, with many photographs of us together on our sailboat in South Florida.

I sat on the edge of my cot and adjusted the black patch over my left eye. It was nearly 6 AM Washington time, on May 14. Stevens brought me a hot cup of dark coffee and fresh data from naval theaters of operation around the world.

Twelve hours earlier, the US Navy had landed Marines on Woody Island – after a dramatic engagement in the South China Sea against the PLA Southern Fleet. Although the island battle still raged, we'd have total control by this time tomorrow.

My plans for the defense of Taiwan had been completed and would go operational in 24 hours. Satellite images and intelligence predicted the

Chinese would delay their invasion until June. They had suffered heavy ship losses in the South China Sea; and their developing land engagement with over 300,000 Vietnamese troops was drawing away valuable resources from their Taiwan appropriations. In addition, the Korean Peninsula was getting hot. The PLA was reinforcing her 340,000 troops already fighting with the North Koreans against the combined Allied force of 700,000 American, South Korean, Australian, Indonesian, and Japanese soldiers.

Three carrier strike groups were assigned to the Taiwan operation - the *Ronald Reagan*, the *Lincoln*, and the *John C Stennis*. Over 30,000 US Marines were in fortified defensive positions on Taiwan, and another 10,000 were held in reserve at Subic Bay.

Allied operations in Korea were directed by the U.S. Army. Our navy had two strike groups providing support from the Sea of Japan, led by the brand-new carriers *John F. Kennedy* and *Gerald R Ford*.

The *Carl Vinson* Strike Group remained in the South China Sea. It protected the left flank in our approaches to Taiwan. It also provided air cover for Vietnamese Army operations along the coastal border with China. Our submarines prevented oil tankers from getting through to the enemy mainland from the south.

The *Nimitz* Strike Group was east of Pearl Harbor. Coupled with the *Eisenhower* out of San Diego, there was adequate naval protection for Hawaii and the western United States from Chinese ballistic missile submarines.

In all, Pacific Command controlled eight carrier strike groups in the Pacific Ocean. They provided awesome offense and defense.

Although America did not have a significant number of surface vessels in the Indian Ocean, thirty nuclear attack submarines were active in the area. They had been ordered to sink all Chinese and North Korean vessels identified. Six US submarines blockaded Gwadar, Pakistan, and had attacked all ships in port.

On the evening of May 12, the United States had begun an aerial and naval bombardment of Iranian targets - including military bases and airfields, naval and oil ports, oil depots, pipelines and refineries, government buildings, and nuclear facilities. Several atomic centers, including Khojir, had been destroyed with tactical nuclear bunker-buster bombs which would detonate more than 90 feet below ground level.

The Strait of Hormuz was open for oil traffic. However, several oil facilities in Iraq, Kuwait, and Saudi Arabia had been destroyed by Iranian missiles. The amount of oil leaving the Persian Gulf had been reduced 70%. Russia, the United States, Canada, Mexico, United Arab Emirates, Brazil, and Venezuela had all recently increased production to help stabilize the oil markets over the next several months.

Early on May 14, US Army infantry and mechanized armor had invaded the oil-rich province of Khuzestan in southwestern Iran. They originated from bordering bases in Iraq, reclaimed by the US during the Iraqi Civil War turmoil several months earlier.

Coordinated US invasions into the southeastern Sistan-Balochistan province from Pakistani Balochistan and Afghanistan, and into the northwestern Iranian provinces from Kurdish Iraq and Azerbaijan, had all been heavily contested by Iranian Revolutionary Guard troops. America's objective was to swiftly control Iran's oil-rich regions and hold Tehran economically hostage. By undermining the ruling government and clerics economically, the United States could dictate peace terms and allow reformers to take over.

The United States Navy had the *George Washington* and *George HW Bush* carrier strike groups in the Persian Gulf. The *Harry S Truman* was in the Arabian Sea, near the Gulf of Oman and the eastern approaches to the Strait of Hormuz. From there, the *Truman* could support the Persian Gulf operations, blockade Gwadar, and provide air cover for American forces battling in Balochistan. US Marines had landed near Bushehr and Jask on Iran's southern coastline, meeting heavy resistance.

The Saudi Air Force was charged with securing the airspace over the Red Sea and not allowing any freighters to exit through the Gulf of Aden, unless specifically screened by US naval surface forces. Any Iranian vessels were to be immediately sunk.

The eastern Mediterranean Sea off the coast of Syria and Lebanon was assigned the British carrier *HMS Queen Elizabeth,* and the French carrier *Charles de Gaulle*. They and their escort ships supported the combined British-French Expeditionary Force landings. The United States had four Aegis class destroyers in this region, two in the Red Sea, and one Aegis cruiser in the Black Sea. The American ships supported the Turkish Army invasion of northern Syria, and the Israeli invasions of Lebanon and southern Syria.

The Iranians had airlifted over 40,000 additional Al-Quds troops (foreign expeditionary Iranian Revolutionary Guard Corps Special Forces) to join the 10,000 already stationed in Syria and Lebanon. They supported the Hezbollah fighters and Syrian regular army.

The US Missile Defense Agency was on high alert. Space and land-based interceptors were prepared to destroy any incoming ballistic missiles fired from submarines or disguised surface vessels in international waters near the mainland United States.

FBI and Department of Homeland Security agents were tracking several Iranian targets inside the US. Heavily armed SWAT teams were in position outside two known nuclear safe houses. The FBI and US Southern Command forces were in Mexico and Central America, shutting down terrorist lines of communications into our country.

Louis Stevens appeared to finish his morning review. I sipped black coffee.

"It seems we have our hands full, Lieutenant Commander. They may need this old war horse to get back on a ship after all.....

"Can you imagine?

"A one-eyed pirate directing a US ship of war.

"With all the pills I take, I probably wouldn't have time to direct battle operations."

I cocked my head, drank more coffee, and smiled. I thought of the irony of my situation.

"Any anecdotes, Louis?"

"Israel's Arrow-3 missile shield is having difficulty with the volume of incoming ballistic rockets. They have dozens coming in every hour. With only 75% stoppage, they have hundreds of dead. The barrage from southern Lebanon, Syria, and Iran is immense. It's much worse than the V-2 assault on London in World War Two. Luckily, no biological or chemical attacks have occurred."

"Get our ships in the Mediterranean and Red Sea to help out, Louis. Call Admiral Turner and tell him I approved their use. Get naval aviation in the Persian Gulf to wipe out the Iranian missile trucks in the mountains. We can't allow a slaughter of civilians in Tel Aviv and Jerusalem.

"Let's hope the bastards don't use WMDs. I won't be able to hold the Israelis back from using retaliatory nukes.

"As bad as it is, it can get worse. Rational minds tend to lose acuity under duress."

"I'll call Chief of Naval Operations and pass on your recommendations, Sir."

"What else, Louis?"

"Two Boeing P-8 Poseidons hunted down a Chinese sub near Vancouver. Our quantum computers had cracked the sub's encrypted orders to attack Seattle."

"Get our submarines in the East China Sea to fire a salvo of conventional Tomahawks at the PLA port near Shanghai. Tell the Navy Intelligence office in Seoul to fire a cable to Beijing saying, if provoked, we'll light up their cities."

"Do you want it worded just like that, Admiral?"

"No!..... Tell the PLA I'm going to put Chinese firecrackers up their asses if one of our civilian population centers is touched. Sign it with my name, Louis."

"Yes, Sir!"

"Any more tidbits, Lieutenant Commander?"

"Two of your personal projects at DARPA are in action for the first time, Sir.

"The attack submarine - *USS Florida*, converted to an underwater aircraft carrier, launched a small squadron of XFC drones against a PLA marine garrison on an Indonesian island in the South China Sea. The drones did significant damage.

"And more importantly, a Boeing X-37 lifted off on a Delta V rocket from Edwards Air Force Base in California. The manned Space-Shuttle-like orbital mission is ordered to attack several PLA satellites over the Chinese mainland."

"Good..... I was always sure of those two projects," I affirmed.

Stevens began to speak again.

But I interrupted and asked, "What about my boys, Louis?"

"Julius is fifty miles east of Singapore, prepared to attack the PLA convoy that sank the *USS Spokane*. We expect exchange fire at any moment.

"He's well supported, Admiral. He'll be fine. He's got the best submarine crew in the Pacific, and the sharpest survival instincts I've ever known in this man's Navy.

"Michael's whereabouts are unknown. A friend of mine at Langley indirectly implied he was inside Iran, but there's no way of getting further information, Sir."

Stevens stopped.

I looked up with my only eye. Louis' pause frightened me. It was sincere and unconscious. He had stumbled in his own thoughts, as I was now frozen solid in mine. One's mind can imagine a lot of hurt in just a few seconds.

"What about Mark?" I asked hesitatingly.

A father's intuitions are difficult to confuse or misdirect.

Louis broke eye contact with me, and my heart sank in an instant. A lightning bolt of fear shocked it to death.

"Mark was involved in a highly classified operation in northern Pakistan. He led a Marine raider unit attack on a heavily defended bridge in the Hunza Valley, attempting to destroy it and impede Chinese troop movements south into Balochistan. He was successful in his mission, Sir," said Louis Stevens, with his voice slightly cracking.

I noted Louis' burden. There was tragedy in his speech. I knew something had gone wrong.

"Is Mark alive?" I gently asked, hoping the earth would swallow me.

"Yes, Admiral, Mark is alive.....

"Unfortunately, he was shot in the back as he helped a wounded comrade.

"He fought off a frontal assault by several hundred Chinese infantry before being wounded.

"Army Intelligence sent me a written description of the battle. Mark was heroic, Sir. Witnesses say he was possessed by uncommon valor.

"His brave actions helped save his men, Admiral.....

"Shortly after getting into an extraction helicopter, Mark collapsed. He had massive internal bleeding and went into shock. His men kept him alive until arrival at the military hospital at Bagram Airbase.

"He lost his right kidney in surgery, Admiral....

"Postoperatively, the medical staff noticed he had developed paralysis of his lower extremities. He was immediately airlifted to Landstruhl Medical Center in Ramstein, Germany, where he underwent emergency spinal surgery - a laminectomy - to relieve pressure on the L2 level of his caudal spinal cord.

"He's awake and alert now, but the lower extremity paralysis has persisted. He also has bowel and bladder issues. The neurosurgeons can't say how much movement he'll regain. It's unpredictable at the present time.

"The Navy is moving him to Bethesda Naval Hospital tomorrow, so he can recover here with his family nearby...."

Stevens paused again.

"Admiral, Mark has been recommended for a Congressional Medal of Honor. They believe his actions at Shishkat Bridge were critical in the success of the overall mission. Many lives were saved by his courage. He is an American hero, Sir.

"His is the fastest recommendation ever passed down in the history of the United States Marine Corps. Admiral Turner wanted me to stress that point to you, Sir...."

I sat motionless on my old cot. I could not speak. My lips trembled. I could feel my sick irregular heartbeats in my throat. A pain gripped my chest tightly and radiated down the inside of my left arm.

My left hand became numb. I opened and closed it several times as if to beat back death with my fist. I refused to accept my son's suffering and possible demise, and fought back against my own.

I felt powerless. I was not in control of events. Bad things were happening around me, and my force of will could not impede or change them.

Fear was overtaking me. But it wasn't the fear of my own death. Although I knew the 'Grim Reaper' was waiting for me, standing in his long and dark hooded cloak, I was not afraid of his scythe. Up to now, my unconquerable will had battled well against his sharp curved blade. My urgent need to save my country and sons had kept 'Death' away.

I felt alone in a war trench, mud and vermin all around me. Night had fallen. A cold white impenetrable mist enveloped me in my hole. The enemy sounded his bugles, and I could hear them fixing bayonets. Only I stood between them and a hopeful conclusion for the world. I felt impotent to prevent the unthinkable.

The pain of losing a son assaulted my consciousness. It bled into a hurt of broken promises. Feeling overwhelmed was not a natural state for me. I fought it with all the willpower I could muster, but to no avail. I grimaced and surrendered to it.

I lowered my head and waved for Louis to leave me alone in the room. He dimmed the lights before silently shutting the door behind him.

I thought of Olivia. She would have been distressed, knowing her youngest son was gravely wounded so far from home. To a parent - the sense of possibly losing a child, without your presence next to him, is unacceptable. No matter his age or valiant duties, degree of bodily pain or painlessness, whether it be on a lonely field of battle or in a clean hospital bed - the loss of a dear beloved son, without your comfort at his side, is the 'deepest' loss. Olivia had mentioned many times that this was her greatest fear.

But Mark was still alive, I told myself. Our son would survive this and hopefully walk again soon. I would help him recover.

I remembered my dream from three nights before..... I had desperately searched for my sons in the sea but could not find them. They had slipped from my grasp, like peace on earth.

In the darkened room, my loneliness became palpable. Like a plague, it dampened my existence. The silence inside of me grew exponentially like a cancer. It was choking the little life I had left. The weight of the void crashed down on my defenses. There was no escape from the grief.

Then, as if a bright candle had been lit inside my soul, I saw through the darkness. My mind could see Olivia's beautiful face. Her warm smile spirited me. In an act of subconscious self-preservation, her apparition was life-giving. The memory of her love brought back to me happiness. Hope returned. Olivia had saved me once again, just as she had done in the past.

With Olivia in my heart, my mind regressed to earlier times. They were precise points in time before her love, but formative stages in the path that led me to find my angel. The track to Olivia had been long and difficult. It had seen much rain and snow. But like stepping off a black cloud into heaven, I finally had my warm golden sunshine.

I began to replay our life in memories.

CHAPTER 14

Anzio and The Great Lakes

I cannot think of any need in childhood as strong as the need for a father's protection.

***Sigmund Freud* (1856 to 1939)**

IT HAD BEEN a cold wintry day like all the others. I stared out through the frosted window at Lake Michigan behind our home, north of Chicago. It was white with snow as far as the eye could see. The afternoon snowstorm had blanketed the area. Ice encased the bare branches of the ash, birch, and maple trees in our yard. The one hundred year-old oak appeared petrified. Lake Forest, Illinois, was bone-chilling in winter.

Mother had started a fire in the study to keep Bobby and I warm while we did our homework. My eleven year-old brother, four years my senior, was reading at the table behind me as I daydreamed.

"Stop staring out the window, Julian! Get to work! Mom's going to light your butt when she comes back."

"Do you think we could walk across that ice on the lake all the way to Michigan, Bobby?"

"I guess. But why would you want to, Julian?"

"I've never been to Michigan."

"You haven't been to a lot of places! That doesn't mean you're going to set out in a snowstorm to all of them, Stupid!"

"Father's been to a lot of places, Bobby."

"Dad's old! Of course he's been everywhere. You're just a punk, Julian."

"Did you know he was in a war?" I asked my brother. "Mom was in the war too."

"A war?

"Where?"

"In Italy," I said, still looking out the window at the blizzard.

"That's much farther than Michigan," said Bobby.

"Yeah, Dumbo!" I shouted. "Italy is on the other side of the world."

"How do you know Dad and Mom were in a war, Julian?"

"It's all there inside that big wooden box under the bookshelves."

"But Mom keeps that box locked," said Bobby.

"Little brother knows more than big brother!" I smart-assed. "Look inside the drawer under the table where you're sitting. The key to open the box is right there."

"Mother wouldn't keep it locked if she wanted us to see what was inside, Julian."

"If she cared, Bobby, the key wouldn't be under your stupid nose!"

"Show me," said Bobby.

I opened the treasure chest for my brother. I pulled out stacks of old photographs and news clippings. We could both recognize our young father in many of the pictures. Mother was in some of the photos also.

The contents of the secret box contained a chronicle of our parents' time in Italy during World War Two. They had met and fallen in love there.

My mother Ann Nelson, a country girl from Minnesota, had served as a front-line battle surgical nurse in North Africa and Sicily before landing at Salerno on the southern Italian Mediterranean coast. She was a hardened combat veteran by the time she met my father at Anzio.

Robert Stansfield, a Harvard-trained surgeon, arrived at the Anzio beachhead in late January 1944 – one week after the Allied landings. It was his first taste of war. He met Ann a few days later in an operating tent under fire.

Bobby opened one of the old yellowed American newspapers. The headlines shouted, **US FIFTH ARMY TAKES ROME!** He began to read aloud.

"The seaborne Allied landings at Anzio were an attempt by the Americans and British to outflank and bypass the heavily defended German fortifications along the Cassino-Gustav Line south of Rome.

"Earlier in September 1943, the British 8th Army landed in the toe of Italy, and the US 5th Army attacked Salerno. The Americans met determined German resistance. The crests and peaks of the Apennine Mountains, and their surrounding rivers and valleys, created multiple ideal defensive lines for German Field Marshall Albert Kesselring's 10th and 14th Armies.

"The Benedictine abbey atop Monte Cassino and the Gustav Line proved to be almost impenetrable to the combined Allied army of American, British, French, Canadian, Polish, New Zealander, South African, and Indian troops. The four months of brutal fighting at Monte Cassino and Anzio, before the Allies broke out towards Rome in May 1944, cost them over 100,000 casualties. It's been a pyrrhic Allied victory."

"I told you so, Bobby, Mom and Dad are heroes!"

"I can't believe it. Mom and Dad were soldiers!" whispered my brother.

We spent nearly an hour looking at the evidence. We found a smaller box with two medals. My brother and I were mystified. Why hadn't our parents told us anything?

For us, it was a great revelation. Our parents had been soldiers in a war! And they had won medals!

"What are you boys doing?" asked my mother, sneaking up behind our backs.

"Oh, nothing!" I answered, quickly returning the sacred materials to the wooden chest.

My mother smiled and sat at the table.

"Show me your homework, Julian."

"Well, let me see, Mom.....

"How do I say this?

"I haven't quite started yet....."

"And you, Bobby?"

"I'm sorry, Mother.

"Julian and I were distracted by the stuff in the chest.

"You never told us you and Pop were in a war!

"Were you really soldiers?

"Did you or Dad ever kill anybody?"

Our mother stayed silent for a moment.....

"Come and sit with me," she said.

I opened the chest once more and grabbed the box of medals. I ran and sat next to my mother.

"Your father and I weren't fighting soldiers.

"I was a nurse, as I still am.

"Your father was a surgeon, as he is now.

"We both worked very hard to save lives.

"I helped Dad operate on hundreds of young boys hurt in the war. We saved many of them, but not all."

"Did some of them die, Mother?" I asked.

"Yes, Julian, boys die in wars," Mother whispered. "Doctors and nurses can't save them all. Some are too badly hurt to piece together. That is the truest and saddest reality of war, although there are many other sad realities....."

"Did you meet Father in Italy?" I asked.

"Yes..... I met and fell in love with him in Italy," she said gently.

"Who won the medals?" asked Bobby.

"I'll let your father explain it."

Mother kissed us both on the forehead, and quietly walked from the study. After a few 'long' minutes, Father entered.

At first, he didn't speak. He added wood to the fire and lit his pipe. He sat at the couch and requested we join him.

"Mother says you boys were asking about the war."

"Yeah, we know you and Mom were heroes," I said with excitement.

"I wouldn't describe it like that, Julian. We performed our duties to the best of our abilities. There were many, many injured American soldiers to help save. We tried to mend some German boys also. I hate to say we weren't as successful as I wished. I think every day of all the boys we lost."

"You saved the Germans also, Dad?" I asked in disbelief.

"Whether American or German, young boys deserve to live their lives. No one deserves to die in a field alone because of decisions others make.

"Don't you agree, Julian?"

"Yes, I do, Father."

"How about the medals, Dad?" asked Bobby.

"One is a Silver Star, the other is a Purple Heart. They were both awarded to me for reasons unrelated to my duties as a US Army Medical Corps surgeon."

"What do you mean, Father?" I inquired.

"They were given for combat actions taken at Anzio, Julian."

"So you were a soldier, Dad!" I shouted. "You were more than just a doctor!"

"Yes," Father said in a low voice. "One night, the Army asked for a volunteer surgeon to go assist badly wounded American soldiers in a farmhouse near Anzio. They were nearly surrounded by the enemy and couldn't be transferred to our field hospitals. While helping to stabilize the injured, the farm was assaulted by a company of German troops. Many more Americans were killed. The situation compelled me to grab a machine gun and join ten others in defense of the remaining wounded Americans. I killed several Germans with that machine-gun.

"The Army gave me a Silver Star for 'Conspicuous Gallantry in Action', and a Purple Heart for a slight shrapnel injury to my left arm."

"You were wounded, Father?" asked Bobby, while I sat in silence.

"Yes I was. It was my second wound received at Anzio. Earlier, I had been injured in a German air bombing raid."

"Wow, Pops," said Bobby, open-mouthed.

"Enough war talk. That was many years ago. I prefer to forget it all.

"Do your homework, and we'll have dinner in an hour," said my father, before leaving.

Bobby and I stared at each other.....

The American evacuation combat hospitals at Anzio provided surgical care at the frontlines of the battle throughout its duration. Never in the history of the US Army

Medical Corps have field hospitals been in the middle of a battlefield for such a sustained length of time. The accomplishments of these doctors and nurses during the four-month Battle of Anzio will remain legendary in the annals of US combat medicine forever.

After the capture of Rome on June 4, my parents' medical team - the 15th Evac Hospital - set up their surgical facility in a schoolhouse for two months. They were able to operate without the sounds of exploding artillery shells for the first time since arriving in Italy.

In mid-August, their combat hospital moved north towards Florence and the Po Valley, and finally to Milan. After the end of the war in May 1945, Father was assigned to a US military hospital in Naples. He worked there until early 1946. Ann accompanied him.

My parents married in a small basilica on the island of Capri on Valentine's Day 1946. In the spring, Father returned to his home town of Lake Forest, Illinois, with his beautiful wife. He established his private practice in general surgery and provided volunteer medical services at the Great Lakes Naval Station VA Hospital nearby.

My brother and I were born and raised along Lake Michigan. It was our playground. We preferred the summers to the winters.

We learned to sail before we learned to play baseball. Our father made sure of that. Perhaps my earliest memory is of sitting next to Bobby, between Father and Mother on our sailboat, and watching the sun rise over Lake Michigan. We did that often, and the memories have stayed with me for all my life.

I was very close to Bobby. He was older and wiser, but never made me feel it. He never spoke a mean word to me, even perhaps when I deserved it. He always loved me, and I returned that love. I looked up to him immensely.

Bobby was ill. He was not robust like I was. Although four years older, he could not keep up with me in our playing. He couldn't run faster, or hit the ball farther. But he didn't resent me for it. He accepted his illness and kept living as best he could. I understood and respected that, even at a young age. He was a hero to me. He taught me much about life, and about fate, and how little control we often have over both.

When Bobby was six years old, he contracted a particularly virulent case of acute rheumatic fever. Although he initially recovered, over time it became clinically apparent to Father that Bobby had suffered irreparable damage to his heart valves. This realization was difficult for Father. He suffered much with it.

As I aged, I saw my older brother's health decline to the point of incapacity. Even minor physical exertion induced severe fatigue and shortness of breath. By the age of thirteen, Bobby was unable to attend school because of his ailment. Mother would teach him the appropriate level classwork at home.

Father continued to take us out on Lake Michigan during the summers on our thirty-four foot sailboat. We would leave at dawn to catch the sunrise and sail north along the lakefront to Wisconsin. Bobby would sit with Mother and enjoyed watching me direct the sails. As we would pass the Great Lakes Naval Station, we would all stand and salute the raising of the flag and the playing of the national anthem.

Over the years, the summer weekend sailing expeditions with Father and Mother became a worshipped event. We would spend hours together, laughing, telling stories, and living. We were a family, and I will never forget it.

In the late summer of 1961, after consultations with the best pediatric heart specialists in Boston and Philadelphia, Father decided Bobby's only hope was a surgical correction of his mitral valve stenosis. Without surgery, his son would not live beyond his teenage years. Pediatric heart surgery was still in its infancy, but the risks were still less than doing nothing.

A few days before Thanksgiving 1961, we flew to Boston for Bobby's heart operation at the Peter Bent Brigham Hospital. My brother was not scared, but I was. And he could sense it.

The night before surgery, Bobby asked Mother and Father to leave the hospital room so he could speak to me in private. I was 10-years-old but perceptive. I understood his deep connection to me. He loved me and didn't want me to suffer. His concern was for me, his younger brother, not himself.

Bobby, wearing an oxygen mask, held my hand and told me how much he loved me. He appreciated the assistance and support I had always given him. I had helped him to dress in the mornings and undress in the evenings, as his fatigue worsened. I had helped as much as I could. Bobby was aware of the dangers facing him, but he did not retract away. He felt strong because of the love we had given him. In his mind, whether he lived or died, he would remain with us. We would see each other again. There could be no end where there was love. It would last forever. How could it not?

Bobby said his biggest wish was to sail again with us. If his surgery was successful, he would help me man the sails on Father's boat. We could do it together, like a team. Later, we would teach our children also. We could pass the tradition down our families. He smiled at me and expressed he could be vigorous again.

I'll remember forever the calm and fearless look in his eyes as we sat that night like two adults, discussing our hopes and aspirations together. He had dreams like we all have. We all search for happiness, even when everything around us is dark. When we look at our own fate and destiny, we are always victorious. It is the guiding light to our lives.

I slept at my brother's bedside. Perhaps we dreamed together of what could be. I know I did. I wanted to be hopeful.

The next morning, I kissed Bobby's forehead and pinned Father's Purple Heart on him. He was proud to wear it over his own sick heart. As the nurses wheeled him to surgery, I thought of fate and destiny.....

The hours slowly passed. I sat with my parents in a special private area that afforded families some peace as they waited anxiously for their children to come out of dangerous operations. I held Father's hand throughout his vigil. Every so often, I gently stroked his face to remind him that everything would be fine.

While I provided comfort to my father, Mother eased my apprehension. Mother was very strong, I thought.

Five hours into the operation, Father was called out of the room by a nurse. I sat with Mother and waited for his return. Ten minutes later, he reappeared. Without making eye contact, Father simply opened his arms as if to say, "Come to me". He embraced us both and explained Bobby's heart had been too weak to survive the operation.

We cried together and slowly passed to the floor in a grief that could not be expressed in words. I thought of how my brother's simple wish to be vigorous and strong would never come to be. We would never sail together again.

The next day, we returned home to Lake Forest with Bobby. He was buried in a lakefront cemetery, facing east towards every morning's sunrise. Although Mother and Father were strong, they were not strong enough. Neither was I.....

The years passed. I continued to sail with Father, although not as often as before. Mother no longer went. Father and I would talk about life, and particularly, my hopes to be a naval officer.

He taught me to be independent and strong. He often said the truest measure of a man was his actions under great duress. In tough times, one needed to stand alone against the odds, no matter how unfavorable they may be. Your own survival was important, but not critical. Living true to your ideals superseded even death. He frequently spoke as if he knew he would not be available to me in the future.

We shared our memories and love for Bobby, but not often enough. Father seemed to avoid talking of him. More so, I think, to not upset me. It hurt me more to not speak of my brother.

Once strong and energetic, Father's health visibly declined. I noted his faltering with sadness. He seemed to just fade away. I began to physically handle the sails by myself.

On a July morning boat trip in 1966, Father expressed to me his greatest regret. He should have decided on Bobby's operation much sooner, when his heart may have been strong enough to survive the rigors of surgery. Pale-looking, my father cried while I held him in my arms. I tried to console his sorrow.

As I told him that everything possible had been done for my brother, he stopped breathing. My crude attempts at resuscitation failed, and Father died.

I held him tightly for more than an hour. The embrace was a communion of two souls - he into me, and I into him. Our sailboat drifted on a calm Lake Michigan while I hugged my father for the last time. Once again, I had learned about fate.

On my 16th birthday, I set sail from Lake Forest on a long solo trip to New York City. Mother had allowed me to plan this trip in an attempt to ease my mind. Before departure, Mother gave me a large envelope and said not to open it until I reached the Statue of Liberty.

I sailed the lengths of Lakes Michigan and Huron. I passed Detroit into Lake Erie and entered the New York State Canal System. I found my way down the Hudson River to New York City and the Statue of Liberty.

Sitting on Father's boat at Lady Liberty's feet, on a beautiful late spring morning in 1967, I felt proud of my voyage. I looked up at the sun and thought it was strong like me. I let it burn my face to brand me with the memory.

I gently opened the envelope my mother had given me. I found an old yellowed letter from my father, Robert

Stansfield, addressed to his mother. It was dated June 5, 1944, from Rome, Italy:

Dear Mom:

We've finally reached Rome. I can't tell you how relieved I am to be out of the wet marshes of Anzio and on dry, clean ground. My previous letters did not express the true conditions under which we were working on that bottled up beachhead. The last four months have been Hell.

Our days and nights were spent operating under canvas tents on poor young American boys who had been blown apart by German shells and machine gun fire. Most of them were missing body parts, many of them vital. We tried to piece them together again the best we could.

Our staff ran ropes across the top of the surgical tent to hang the intravenous bottles of plasma and whole blood. When we would run out of blood, the medical staff would give their own on a schedule. I, myself, gave many times.

It's sad to think I lost more men than I saved. We all felt that way. Although I gave it my best, we all have our regrets. In my rare off-times, I review my decisions and actions taken on the operating tables of Anzio. I always think I could have been better.

The twelve tables in my tent were always full, day and night. I handled most of the severe abdominal wounds. Some of my patients had been eviscerated only minutes before, a few hundred feet from our hospital.

Kesselring's army in the Alban Hills dropped artillery shells on our sector twenty-four hours a day. Some days, thousands of rounds were exchanged by our boys and the Krauts.

Messerschmitt 109s and Focke-Wulf 190s would strafe our positions during the day, while Heinkel bombers would come and drop their bombs at night. Our anti-aircraft batteries were only a few feet away from the hospital, making surgery very noisy. Hospital staff placed wooden planks over the outside of the tents to help protect us from falling debris and spent anti-aircraft shell casings. It certainly wouldn't have saved us from a German bomb.

Anzio is a collection of ancient salt marshes which were drained by Mussolini to create cultivable land. The Germans stopped the drainage pumps and flooded the area, hoping to create the perfect conditions for mosquitoes and malaria. We were told that in ancient times, the Roman Legions would avoid the Pontine Marshes in fear of contracting malaria. What were we doing there? I suspect our top brass had their reasons.

We didn't sleep much, only a few minutes whenever we could. I dug a shallow foxhole in our sleeping tent into wet ground and placed wooden planks over it, topped by used plasma crates filled with sandbags. Imagine Mom, I thought it could possibly protect me from a German shell!

It hasn't been all bad. I've met the most wonderful girl in the world. She's intelligent and as dedicated to saving lives as I am. She's also the most beautiful girl I've ever seen. Ann has been my surgical nurse since late February. We've become a team, I think.

Well, I've said enough. I hope I haven't scared you, Mother. I pray you are fine back home. Maybe this war will be over soon, and no more young boys will lose their lives.

With all my love forever, Robert

I sat alone on the sailboat at the base of the Statue of Liberty. The waters were calm, and the breeze was soft and gentle. The great Lady seemed so tall and strong in front of me.

My father's letter broke my heart. He had spent a lifetime saving lives, but till the end he thought only of those he lost. I loved him dearly, and missed him even more. It was difficult to accept his absence.

I gazed up at the sun and closed my eyes. Warm and tender rays dried my tears. I could feel my father's love. I pledged to him that I would enter Annapolis and become a US naval officer. I would make a good life for myself. I would have a family and teach them about the goodness of life. Fate and destiny were complicated concepts to understand, but I would not let risk deter me from action.

I whispered a prayer for Father and Bobby. I told them that they'd remain inside of me for always. I turned our sailboat around to come home. I would begin the rest of my life believing in eternity.

CHAPTER 15

Love at First Sight

For it was not into my ear you whispered, but into my heart; it was not my lips you kissed, but my soul.
Judy Garland (1922 to 1969)

EVEN IN THE wind, her soft and passionate spoken words had been clear. The waking seashore on the key that morning had sparkled with natural sunlight. The blue sea and wet white sands glistened, as did her soulful eyes. Everything around me was rich in scent and sight. Fresh clean air rushed from the east and rustled her black hair in my hands. The rays of the rising sun illuminated her lovely face. She brought her lips to mine and kissed me. She then whispered in my ear a truth beyond doubt, "Love is energy - feel it, breathe it, be it."

Meaningful words spoken from the heart can change a life. They certainly did for me. On that crisp December day in South Florida long ago, I fell in love with a woman. I fell into a trance that never broke. An ecstasy, I'd call it, that permeated every fiber of our being. Our bodies and spirits were exalted to the highest plane, intensifying every sensation and every thought. Glory was achieved in an instant of time, and all because of a few spoken words in a whisper. This girl was mine forever.....

I had performed well at the Naval Submarine Base in New London, Connecticut, after graduating at the top of my class in Annapolis. In the summer of 1974, I was assigned to the *USS Tunny*, a Sturgeon Class nuclear attack submarine based out of Charleston, South Carolina. I spent the next eighteen months patrolling the US east coast and the Caribbean Sea.

In late December 1975, the *Tunny* made a ten day port visit to Miami, Florida. I had looked forward to the visit. Henry Graves, my roommate at Annapolis during our last two years, was a South Florida native.

Although a lieutenant on a destroyer at Pearl Harbor, Hawaii, Henry had been given leave for Christmas and the New Year holiday. He had returned to Key Biscayne to visit his parents.

When my friend learned the USS *Tunny* was making a port visit to Miami during this time, he invited me to stay at his family home. The sprawling two-acre estate villa on the Atlantic Ocean had been in the family for several decades. Jim Graves, Henry's father, was a prosperous Florida land developer with much inherited wealth and powerful political connections. He enjoyed giving fine parties during the holidays.

Henry wanted me to meet all the beautiful girls he knew in South Florida. He had spoken incessantly about them during our time at the Naval Academy.

I had grown into a handsome young man. I had my father's strong frame, and my mother's light complexion, hair, and eyes.

The *Tunny* entered the Port of Miami in the early morning of December 23. Henry Graves waited for me at the pier, reading a *Playboy* magazine while lying on the hood of his convertible 1965 sky-blue Ford Thunderbird. In full uniform, I stood on deck and smiled as we approached port.

I stepped off the *Tunny* in my dress whites and gave him a big hug. I hadn't seen Hank in over two years.

"Good to see you, Smart-ass!

"Welcome to paradise!" he shouted with a big stupid grin.

"Hawaii and California have nothing on this place, believe me. We have better weather and prettier girls. I can't control the weather, but I can the girls. So take advantage of my little playboy heaven, Julian. You may not want to leave after your visit. They may need to get the Shore Patrol after you when this is all said and done," laughed Hank.

"It's good to know I'll have you as my guide on the safari," I laughed. "You do the guiding, and I'll do the shooting. Let me man the guns!"

"Okay, Mr. Navy!

"We'll see if your green eyes can pick up more attractive women than in Maryland. I sure damn hope so."

"Are the girls here that different, Hank?"

"We have beaches year-round. The girls stay in shape to show off their bikini bodies. We have women from all over the world in South Florida, but these Cuban girls are different. They're free spirits with sexy attachments," smiled Henry.

"It's great to see you again, Hank. It's been awhile since graduation. How have you been?"

"I've been fine. I'm the gunnery officer on an old tin can Gearing Class destroyer, the *USS Orleck*, based out of Pearl Harbor. It's not exciting like submarines, or convertible Thunderbirds for that matter. Nor can it compare with safari hunting in South Florida. But it'll do for now, I guess," said Henry.

I climbed into the convertible, and threw my officer's cap and duffel bag into the backseat. It was a beautiful sunny 60° December morning in South Florida as we headed south on Brickell Avenue towards the island of Key Biscayne.

"Take these!" shouted Hank above the rushing wind and loud rock & roll music on the radio. He handed me sunglasses while we drove east on the Rickenbacker Causeway with the sun in our faces. The highway connected the mainland with the chic island village of Key Biscayne.

"How do you like the wheels?" yelled Henry.

"It's nice and purrs like a wildcat!" I shouted back.

"It's a pussy magnet! Best gift my dad ever gave me! I drove the girls crazy in high school!"

"Beautiful car, girls, sandy beaches, and blue sea – It's a boy's wonderland!" I marvelled.

We stopped at the island's first traffic light. Two smiling gorgeous women jogged across the street in their bathing suits. Henry gassed the motor. The girls turned and blew kisses at us. This was an island of plentitude, I thought. It had abundant natural resources.

"There's a big holiday party tonight at our home. I'll show you the South Florida turf. You may never want to go back to the *Tunny*.

"You've been out at sea for the past four months. Did you even remember what a woman looked like, Julian?" laughed Hank.

"With what I've seen, my memory has come back quite well. It's already a stimulating experience!" I smiled.

Another parade of nearly nude girls walked slowly in front of our car. They all seemed as interested in us as we were in them.

"We may never get home, Julian!"

We laughed, driving further onto the island. We passed Richard Nixon's winter home and entered a long palm tree-lined driveway, leading to an oceanfront Spanish

Mediterranean villa. It had spectacular terraced views of the Atlantic Ocean and Biscayne Bay. A tennis court and a large swimming pool sat next to the main house. To me, it seemed more like a resort hotel than a private residence.

"Home, sweet home," said Hank.

"This is where you grew up?" I asked in amazement.

"Yes, Lieutenant Stansfield."

"It must have been hard to leave for Annapolis," I wondered.

"Young men with shiny ideals are the only ones who can leave a place like this. Believe me, Julian, it wasn't easy. Most boys would have to be pried away."

I put on my officer's cap and grabbed the Navy duffel bag out of the backseat. We were walking past the open garage, when Hank threw me a set of keys and peeled back a protective car cover.

"This red '71 Ford Mustang convertible is for your use, Julian - compliments of my father. He wants you to explore the island in first class. Consider it a gift for your service to the country. Be a patriot and enjoy!

"Let's go inside and get cleaned up. We'll have breakfast with my parents out by the pool terrace in a half hour. Put away your Navy uniform for the next ten days."

I put on tennis clothes, which had been left for me in the guest bedroom, and went outside by the pool to wait for Henry. I introduced myself to the service staff and sat watching the surf.

Looking around, I couldn't believe people lived like this. The ocean was cobalt blue. There was a churning white surf, and sand dunes with sunflowers down the beach. The pool was bigger than the tennis court next to it. The men of the house serving staff were dressed in white suits and ties, and the ladies in light yellow dresses. I had never seen anything like it, not even on television.

"Hello, Julian," greeted Mr. Graves, accompanying Hank to breakfast.

"We met at your graduation ceremony, a couple of years ago."

"I remember clearly, Sir. You thanked me for baby-sitting your son," I grinned.

"I think you deserved more than a thank you, Julian," Jim Graves laughed back.

We all accommodated ourselves at the breakfast table. Hank's father eased me into the formal affair.

"I appreciate the kind invitation to your home, Sir."

"Consider it my belated gift for being the top graduate in the '73 class.

"Hank speaks highly of you, Julian. He says you broke all the academic records at Annapolis, and that you're a great guy also.

"Those are tremendous qualities to have in a young US Navy officer. You have a bright future ahead of you, Son. Your parents must be very proud."

"Julian's parents are dead, Father," interrupted Hank at the table.

Two servers brought fresh fruit and juice. Another poured coffee.

"I'm very sorry to hear that, Julian..... Please pardon me for not knowing."

"Of course, Sir. How could you know?"

"Do you have family?"

"No, Sir..... I had a brother, but he died many years ago. My grandparents passed before I was born. Both my parents were only children, so I don't have uncles, aunts, or cousins."

"I see, Julian.....

"I presume you're unmarried, being a submariner.

"The life of a young American naval graduate is rough at first. There's not much time for entertaining the ladies. I know first hand, I was one a long time ago.

"I assure you, it gets better, Julian."

"You're a naval graduate, Sir?"

"Class of '40.

"As a young officer on destroyers, I fought the Japanese in the Pacific. I was at the Battles of the Coral Sea, Midway, Leyte Gulf, and Okinawa. During those years, two of my ships were sunk in battle. My presence here is a miracle.....

"I didn't meet my wife until after the war. It was probably better that way."

Mrs. Graves joined us for breakfast.

"Is my husband telling old war stories?" she asked.

Hank and I smiled.

"I welcome you to South Florida, Julian," said Mrs. Graves. "I hope you enjoy your stay. It's our great pleasure to have you.

"Enjoy peacetime. You and all of America deserve it. Maybe we can keep it this way for a while."

We were served a splendid breakfast with mimosas. The Atlantic surf roared in the background. It was more refined eating than what I was used to on the *Tunny*. I didn't see any corned beef and hash on the table.

Later in the day, we Navy men played tennis and talked of old times at the Academy. We also discussed the recent fall of South Vietnam and the rising tide of Communism around the world. As night fell, the estate prepared for the dinner party.

After a shower, I sat in bed in my underwear and read Herman Wouk's *The Winds of War.* The novel followed a U.S. Navy family in the years leading up to America's entrance into World War II. I had been reading the 885 page book since late October, and was nearly finished.

The music downstairs became louder. Shortly after 9 PM, I put on a tie and dinner jacket borrowed from Henry, and stepped down towards the party.

I came off the staircase and took a glass of champagne from a passing waiter. I worked myself through the crowd towards Henry. The music seemed much louder as I reached the poolside terrace. I found Henry in conversation with an older distinguished-looking gentleman.

"Julian, let me introduce you to Raul Sierra. He's a friend and business associate of my father. Raul fought at the Bay of Pigs. He was the oldest combatant on that beach. He's still heavily involved in the 'Free Cuba Project', financing anti-Communist movements around the world. He is the ultimate freedom-fighter.

"Mr. Sierra also happens to be the grandfather of the most beautiful girl in Miami."

"A pleasure meeting you, Sir," I said politely.

"I'd like to correct your young friend, Lieutenant," said Sierra to Stansfield. "I may have been known once as the ultimate freedom-fighter, but these days people know me more as Olivia's grandfather. She's the star of the family now," laughed the Cuban patriot.

Raul Sierra shook my hand and quickly excused himself.

"I'm leaving so that you may both find more pleasant company for the evening. In my time, with your youth and vigor, I wouldn't have allowed an old man to hold me back from the beauty I see here tonight. I would've run like a Mustang through these girls, looking to see which one could keep up with me." Sierra smiled and walked away.

Henry elbowed me in the ribs and said, "That is the toughest old man I've ever met. He was 53 years old when he stormed the beach at the Bay of Pigs, twice as old as anybody else. After two days of heavy fighting, he was taken prisoner. Castro locked him up for 20 months. In December of 1962, two months after the Cuban Missile Crisis, John Kennedy negotiated his release with the rest of Brigade 2506.

"He arrived in Miami in a wheelchair with both his arms and legs broken. His only son was executed by the Communists. Raul Sierra is definitely the most hard-line anti-Communist in America."

By 1975, South Florida had received several hundred thousand Cubans in exile. Most were highly educated and hard-working. They were all staunchly anti-Communist. They transformed Miami into a dynamic and cosmopolitan city.

The Cubans were handsome people, strong and rugged, and they enjoyed living life to its fullest. Miami was converted from a sleepy southern town to a vivacious city with an interesting political life.

Cuban Communist agents and exile patriot groups were in constant battle, sometimes on the streets of Miami in plain sight. Assassinations and car bombings were part of the eternal struggle for the liberation of Cuba from Castro's Communism. Miami was a battlefield in this struggle.

With George Harrison's "Give Me Love (Give Me Peace on Earth)" playing, Henry pointed with his eyes towards a tall leggy dark-haired woman standing near a crowd by the pool ten feet away. She was dressed in a silky black pantsuit which seemed painted on her body. It accentuated her perfect figure. She had shoulder-length black hair, smooth white porcelain skin, and dark eyes you could get hopelessly swept into. Her sensuous femininity was hypnotizing.

As I stared, she turned towards Henry and smiled. Mesmerized by her beauty, I clumsily dropped my glass of champagne into the pool. I thought my heart had stopped.

Her smile was unlike any other I had ever seen. It transmitted love, peace, and joy. She had a unique, once in a lifetime, radiant beauty that projected out from her in all directions. She was completely special in body and form. She exuded sensuality like an attractive aura.

But her smile was most defining. Its incredible impact both softened and sizzled your insides. One was helplessly drawn to it, unable and reluctant to break its gravitational pull. Like a giant 'Black Hole' at the center of a galaxy, it attracted everything to it. Her smile encompassed all of her person and power.

"Hi, Henry," she said after coming up to us. "I just arrived yesterday from New Hampshire. I wouldn't have missed your party for the world. I was here last year, but you were in Hawaii. I missed you. I'm so happy to see you again."

"Julian, this is the one and only, brilliant and world-famous heartbreaker, Olivia Sierra! She's the granddaughter of Raul, whom you just met. Olivia is a Classics major at Dartmouth. We've known each other since we were children.

"Olivia, meet Lieutenant Julian Stansfield, a brave heroic submariner and my old roommate at Annapolis."

"Good evening, Lieutenant.

"Please excuse Henry's exuberant introduction. He loves to paint me like that," complained Olivia playfully.

"You punched an arrow through my heart a long time ago, Olivia," laughed Henry. "I'm entitled to the descriptive and energetic curtain-raiser!"

"I suppose you didn't like the champagne, Lieutenant," she said, looking into my eyes. "It's probably too cold for champagne anyway. A cognac would feel better tonight."

Her smile intensified, tempting me into her. I thought of speaking, but could only imagine kissing her lips. They were the most inviting lips I had ever seen. Kind and sexy at the same time.

Fleetwood Mac's "Landslide" began to play. I was swept away by this girl.

I returned her smile and asked, "Would you like a glass of cognac, Olivia?"

"Go and get two," she said, slowly winking an eye at me.

I stepped away and closed my eyes for an instant. I said under my breath, "She's beautiful, intelligent, and witty."

Olivia stood out at this party above everyone else. She made you forget there was anyone else there.....

I returned a few minutes later and handed Olivia her cognac.

She clinked my glass and said, "Salud."

Henry, feeling the developing moment, excused himself and left us alone.

"Julian, do they serve this on board your submarine?"

"No!" I laughed. "Our tours are free of spirits. There would be too many fistfights."

We enjoyed each other's company. After two more cognacs, another Fleetwood Mac song, "Rhiannon", began to play.

"I love this song," said Olivia as she pulled me onto the dance floor.

She looked at me with her dark eyes and winked again. I was done. She had bewitched me. Olivia was the hottest and most exciting woman I had ever met. Our chemistries synchronized.

By 3 AM, I had lost my coat and tie, and Olivia had misplaced her shoes. Even her feet were the most beautiful I had ever seen. We sat barefoot together on a lounge chair near the seashore with our toes in the cool sand. Olivia and I talked about our lives.

"Tell me about yourself," I said. "How did you come to live in the United States?"

"I'm a political exile. I was born in Trinidad, Cuba, in 1954. My father - Jorge Sierra - was Raul's only son, the youngest of three children. He met my mother while studying engineering at the University of Havana. She was studying philosophy. They fell in love and married young after my mother became pregnant with me.

"After finishing their studies in 1957, my parents moved to Las Villas province, where Raul had been elected governor the year before. My grandfather was a successful businessman with large land holdings in Cuba and Latin America. Papa helped run the businesses, while Raul tended to his government affairs.

"After the fall of the Batista government to Castro's forces on January 1, 1959, the Sierra family was granted asylum in the United States. We came to live at Raul's house in South Florida.

"Early in 1960, the CIA recruited Raul and my father into the counter-revolutionary movement. In January 1961, Papa infiltrated into Cuba with 11 other men to scout and survey the landing beaches at the Bay of Pigs. Eight other similar teams scattered throughout Cuba to perform sabotage on communication centers, radio towers, bridges, and military facilities. My father's team was ordered to make regular reports on Communist troop movements near the landing beaches. Just prior to the landings, they would mine the main road to the beachhead.

"Grandfather landed with the main force of Brigade 2506 at Playa Giron, shortly after midnight on April 17, 1961. At dawn that morning, Father and his comrades became involved in a rearguard firefight with an approaching column of Communist troops. Eight men in his team were killed in action. Papa and three others were taken prisoner. By April 19 - Raul's company was surrounded, and after heavy losses, surrendered to Castro's forces.

"My grandfather was imprisoned for 20 months. He was regularly beaten by his guards and starved to emaciation. When finally released in December 1962, he weighed only 107 pounds.

"He has never spoken to me of those times, and he rarely speaks of my father. It's too painful for him.

"I do know he has contributed millions of dollars to anti-Communist movements around the world, and still confers regularly with the CIA. I think his association with Mr. Graves is for more than just business. They're a team in the fight."

Olivia took a deep breath and sighed.

"I grew up on Key Biscayne. I've had a privileged life. I studied at private schools locally, and went off to Dartmouth to study Classics and the origins of democratic government. I've become an expert on the writings of Lycurgus, Solon, Cleisthenes, and Pericles. I sense Ancient Sparta and Athens have become part of my development. Somehow, I feel I owe this to my father, who died fighting for his principles of democracy....

"And you, Julian?

"Tell me about your life."

"I had a middle-class upbringing along the shores of Lake Michigan. My parents were devoted to my brother and I. But they are all gone now.

"My mother and father died a few years after my brother's death. It's all very sad. My father left us before my mother. She settled into a deep depression without him. Her health declined and she passed on also.

"Perhaps we can talk about it another day," I said.

"I understand, Julian. I feel like that myself sometimes. You can tell me about it whenever you wish," said Olivia, lowering her head.....

"Do you enjoy sailing, Olivia?"

"I do, but only when someone else does the work."

"It's not much work when you know what to do," I laughed. "It's like everything else, it takes a little practice, that's all."

"Do you sail, Julian?"

"I graduated from Annapolis! Of course, I sail!" I laughed louder.

"Could you imagine a US Navy man dead in the water without a motor?" I illustrated with body language and a smile.

"I want you to teach me how to sail, Julian. If it's so easy, I should be able to learn in a day. We'll go tomorrow. Promise me."

"Yes..... We'll do the bay tomorrow. No open ocean until you've mastered all the ropes," I told her, staring at her beauty in the moonlight.

We both laughed like children. She made me forget all the badness of the past. Olivia refreshed me.

The early morning wind off the Atlantic was cold. I placed my recovered coat over Olivia's shoulders. She gently lay next to me and held my hand. There was a long silence. I began to speak but then stopped.

"What were you going to say, Julian?"

I paused for a moment, before asking, "What happened to your father?"

Olivia curled herself into a ball and pulled me closer.

"One month after capture, my father was executed by firing squad at the Morro Castle in Havana.

"In 1967, when I was 13 years old, my mother received a letter from a man who claimed to have been present at my father's death. A former prison guard, Samuel Velasquez had become disillusioned with the revolution and escaped to Mexico. He was granted asylum in the United States and came to Miami to find Jorge Sierra's wife and daughter. He wished to see us in person. The repentant ex-Communist said he had important information for us to know.

"Raul met with him first in a downtown Miami hotel. The next day, three of my grandfather's men escorted Velasquez to our home on Key Biscayne. My mother and I waited apprehensively in the garden courtyard, surrounded by red bougainvillea.

"Velasquez looked much older than I had expected. He was beaten down by life. His eyes had seen the horrors of revolution.

"Quickly after introducing himself, Velasquez said he'd been Papa's guard at the castle. He had personally locked my father into his cell on April 18, 1961.

"As he spoke, tears rolled down his cheeks. Velasquez cried he had never met another spirit so morally pure. Jorge Sierra had left an indelible mark on his soul. The guard was haunted by what he'd seen.

"He was one of three guards assigned to the cellblock where my father was imprisoned. Papa was in a cell with a younger 19-year-old boy who had been shot in the leg on the first day of the landings at Bay of Pigs. Without medical attention, the boy's leg became gangrenous, and he stopped eating on his own.

"Velasquez provided the once-daily meager rations of water, bread, and soup to my father's cell. He watched as my father hand fed the sick boy, never himself eating after May 13.

"Knowing he would be executed the next morning, Papa fed the dying boy for the last time on the evening of May 20. On the morning of May 21, 1961, as my father exited his cell, he quietly whispered his thanks to Velasquez for providing extra bread those last days.

"At sunrise, Jorge Sierra was escorted by military guard to a grassy promontory facing the sea. He walked shirtless and barefoot. Although he also had a poorly healed gunshot wound to his right calf, visible through his ragged pants, Papa walked proudly and erect. He did not limp.

"A Cuban Communist officer led him to a pockmarked and bloody wooden post. Eight Communist riflemen presented themselves in file, twenty feet in front. The officer asked my father if he had any last requests. Jorge Sierra answered firmly that he wished only to stick his hands in the earth at his feet. He bent down on his left leg and scooped sacred soil with both hands. He rubbed it gently on his chest and face. His blue eyes were so expressive - framed by the darkness of the rich earth - said Velasquez, that the members of the firing squad turned their heads in shame.

"Papa was tied to the post. He slowly turned his head to the rising sun and shouted, 'My Cuba, my wife, my Olivia! I pray the sun never sets on the precious loves of my life. I hold faith that God will protect them as dearly as I have.' A volley of gunshot pierced his heart, and his head softly nodded downward. Jorge Sierra was dead....."

Olivia and I quietly looked up at the stars until we fell asleep on the beach. We awoke with the sun.....

"Would you like me to drive you home?" I asked.

"I'm staying at my grandfather's house just down the beach. We can walk there."

We walked barefoot, holding hands, along the shore towards the old Cape Florida Lighthouse. I escorted Olivia to the villa's beachfront gates.

She gave me a long kiss on the lips and said, "This has been the best time of my life. I mean it, Julian - the best."

"I feel the same, Olivia.....

"You're special. It's as if I've known you always. I don't know how to describe the feeling, except to say I've never felt it before.

"I would love to see you later today if possible. Get some rest and we'll have dinner."

"Yes," Olivia answered, quickly agreeing. "I don't know if I'll be able to sleep, waiting for tonight. It can't come fast enough."

She then kissed me again, and whispered those words I can't ever forget, "Love is energy – feel it, breathe it, be it....."

I returned along the beach to the Graves residence. I couldn't get Olivia out of my mind. I didn't want to. She belonged there.

As I entered the house through the poolside terrace doors, I found Henry drinking a glass of orange juice in the kitchen.

"Did you enjoy the party?" asked Henry.

I calmly shook my head, still trying to understand the feelings I had. Sometimes things feel so good that they seem unreal. In a flash, the impossible becomes truth. The imaginary and indiscernible becomes perceptible and tangible. Your mind is numbed by the goodness of it all.

"I have no words to describe how the evening with Olivia was like," I answered with a big smile. "Certain feelings are indescribable and are best left unspoken."

Henry understood. He smiled back at me and said, "The Sierra name in South Florida is spoken in holy tones. Her grandfather and father are both legendary patriots of the anti-Communist movement here in Miami. But I think Olivia's character is the biggest legend of all. Take care of that girl, Julian. Don't let her get away."

I took a deep breath and nodded in agreement. I walked upstairs to get some sleep.

It would be difficult to rest after riding a shooting star across the sky. The emotion of the moment was unmatched by anything I had ever experienced.

I now knew why people were born. The purpose of life was to feel the bliss I had in my heart. This was the glory and the essence of existence. This was the gift.

The true power of the universe became self-evident to me. Without it, there was nothing. With it, there was everything. The entire cycle of life was driven by its energy. Olivia had revealed to me the secret of happiness, the ultimate 'singularity' of life, the most eternal of all forces in the cosmos.... Love.

CHAPTER 16

Eternity

Your words are my food, your breath my wine. You are everything to me.

***Sarah Bernhardt* (1844 to 1923)**

I FELT ONE with the sea. Sailing on open water had helped save my life. As a small boy, I had watched Father sail our boat on Lake Michigan in calm and rough conditions. He had shown me that sailing on Lake Michigan, like life in general, could be unpredictable. Fine weather and easy waters could quickly turn stormy and turbulent, requiring you to make adjustments to survive. Father taught me to be confident with my skills in open water. I had learned to be independent and secure with my abilities and judgement on a sailboat. I could adapt to whatever was thrown my way. After Bobby's death, Father and I used our time together on Lake Michigan as a form of therapy to soothe our broken hearts. Even more so after losing Father, I began to look at open water as an escape from my melancholy and loneliness in the world. Sailing eased my mind. At Annapolis, I would frequently take a single-masted Bermuda sloop out on Chesapeake Bay, sailing upwind in choppy waters out to the Atlantic Ocean. I always went alone, accompanied only by my memories. I never felt fear on the water, regardless of the conditions. It was as if the spirit of my father was always protecting me. Now finally, I had found someone with whom to share my love of the sea.

Early Christmas morning, I rented a 24 foot sailing sloop from the Cape Florida Yacht Club and invited

Olivia out on Biscayne Bay. We were to share the day together on the sea.

The rising sun touched the eastern horizon. The half ball of fire shot its rays of yellow and orange up into the cloudless sky. The newness of the day was apparent. You could feel its birth.

The heavens were a light blue over the Cape. Colors darkened slowly to an indigo violet as your eyes scanned to the west.

In the indigo, the bright crescent moon's features were still clear. The light of Venus was awake. Stars twinkled in the blue-violet. The universe was alive for us, and we were alive for her.

The panorama seemed painted for me. I was in the middle of all this glory. An impressionist's brush had created the perfect paradise. It was a spiritual dreamscape. And Olivia was at the center of it.

Olivia's beauty was astonishing. Her soul absorbed you. Her physical presence aroused you. There was no escape from her charms.

Olivia's tall figure in a black string bikini atop the ship's bow was Renaissance art in full splendor. Michelangelo could not have sculpted more beauty. Her strength and elegance were shocking. She silenced all human activity around her. All eyes were on her. I requested she sit down next to me in order to avoid a crash at sea.

"Theseus," she whispered into my ear.

I looked at her and asked, "What about him?"

"Do you know who he was?" she tested.

Olivia sat indian-style next to me. Her bathing suit barely covered her. My eyes and thoughts were fixated on her sexuality, not on her beautiful mind.

Her toes and feet, legs and thighs, hips, waist, breasts, hands, arms, shoulders, and neck led me to her lips, mouth, nose, and eyes..... Her hair flowed in the wind..... I wanted to be inside of her.....

"Theseus was one of the Argonauts in the ancient Greek quest to find the Golden Fleece, a source of royal power," I said, with my eyes on Olivia's inner thighs.

"Stop devouring me with your handsome green eyes, Lieutenant," she ordered. "There's time later for all the thoughts in your mind. I'll make it worth your wait.....

"Is that all you know of Theseus?"

"What more am I supposed to know, Olivia?"

"Much, much more," she frowned.....

"I think, Julian, you should learn more about the mythical founder-king hero of Athens. His story is full of truths, and many of them pertain to you and I.

"He was the son of archaic king of Athens - Aegeus, and Poseidon - god of the sea, both of whom had slept with Theseus' mother, Aethra, in one night. Theseus was a demi-god.

"On his journey to the political unification of Athens, our hero fought and subdued many evil enemies and monsters. But his defeat of the Minotaur of Crete was the defining event of his life.

"Crete had defeated Athens in a war. The victorious King Minos demanded Athens send to him seven courageous boys and seven beautiful maidens every seven years, for sacrifice to the half-man, half-bull monster living in the Labyrinth.

"On the third occasion, Theseus volunteered to journey to Crete as one of the sacrificial boys, and slay the Minotaur. His father king, Aegeus, accepted the offer reluctantly.

"Theseus told his father he'd sail to Crete with a black sail, and if successful in defeating the monster, he'd return with a white sail.

"After his arrival to the enemy island kingdom, Theseus fell in love with Ariadne, King Minos' daughter. She passed him a ball of thread and a sword for his trip into the Labyrinth. After killing the beast with the sword, hidden inside his tunic, he was to trace back his steps by following the trail of thread.

"The next day, Theseus decapitated the Minotaur and escaped with Ariadne. On his return voyage, our hero became lost in a strange dream and abandoned his love on a beach. In his confusion, Theseus forgot to exchange the black for the white sail.

"On seeing the returning ship with the black sail, Aegeus became distressed. The loving father flung himself from a cliff into the sea, the Aegean, ending his life.

"According to Plutarch's *Life of Theseus*, the hero's ship was kept in the Athenian harbor for centuries in tribute. As old wooden oars and planks decayed, they were replaced with stronger, fresher timber. Slowly, all traces of the original were lost.

"The philosophical question of whether it was 'the same' ship arose. It was debated for centuries. The nature of 'identity' was studied by the best minds of Athens. The subject of debate became known as 'The Ship of Theseus Paradox'. There were many opinions given, none are absolute. Each and every one of us are entitled to our own interpretation.

"My view, Julian, is that life experiences change our identity with time. In the arc of life, we do not finish where we started. We are not the same people at the end. The objective in life, I think, is to use all of our experiences, good and bad, joyous and sad, to finish better than when we started.

"I believe the lessons of Theseus and the 'paradox' have much to do with you and I. We have both learned to survive with demons, always spiriting ourselves to be better. Our identities are stronger for it.....

"Now you may devour me with your eyes," she whispered into my ear.....

We sailed south from the Cape, stopping and anchoring off Elliott Key. We took a short swim in the cold aqua-marine water and later lunched with French champagne. After making love, we continued south towards Key Largo, sailing past tiny small islands not marked on the navigational maps.

The wind was strong on this particular day, and the boat ran at considerable speeds through the whitecaps. The foamy white crests of the waves contrasted against the deep cobalt blue of the sea.

Olivia and I laughed in wonder as bottle-nosed dolphins jumped high in the air, exposing their pink bellies. They followed alongside our sloop in the afternoon.

Sailing back from the Upper Keys, seabirds serenaded our return with their songs. Nature approved of our union.

Who could not?

The sloop cut across the heart of Biscayne Bay. We were exposed to its full expansive raw beauty. The warm sun and cool wind on our bare skins, the taste of salt on our tongues, the organic smells of life in the air, all stimulated our senses. We were driven together.

As we approached the Cape Florida Lighthouse, a light drizzle began, and a magnificent rainbow arched over Key Biscayne. Olivia and I held each other and kissed.

We anchored in a hidden lagoon near the Cape and had a candlelight dinner while the sun set. Afterwards, we made more love.

Olivia and I had known each other only 48 hours, but it felt like an eternity. We were completely and uncontrollably in love. Time had stopped.

Later in the evening, we lay naked on the foredeck. Her warm body pressed against me. I could feel her heart beating next to mine. We were one.....

We gazed above at the stars and thanked fate for having given us great fortune. Both of us had suffered deep emotional loss as children. We had gone on our own personal odysseys in search of greater meanings in our lives.

Olivia's studies in Classics at Dartmouth, and my education at Annapolis, were spiritual wanderings to get closer to the souls of our fathers. Pain had never conquered our spirits. Loss had never drowned our hopes for the future. Our meeting was an affirmation of the voyage. Our love was the product of the quest.

"The stars are bright tonight. They seem so close, don't they, Julian?"

"They do. I feel I'm amongst them. Perhaps I can grab a few and twinkle them on you. It would be appropriate. They seem made for you," I said.

"What do you know of stars, Julian?"

"Well, up until meeting you, I always thought they were unreachable. I guess I was wrong."

"No, Julian, what do you really know of them?"

"As a young boy, I learned to read them for navigation. My father taught me. After he died, I'd sail alone and stare at them for hours. They became my friends.

"Look at that one there," I said, pointing at the brightest one in the night sky.

"It's radiant," said Olivia. "It must be the closest."

"No, it's very far away..... *Sirius* is very, very far away.....

"As a boy, after my brother passed, I pretended he had gone there. Some nights, I'd stare at it for hours, asking why he had left me. It helped me, I think, to deal with his loss. It had been devastating for me. But I suppose it helped to place him physically somewhere. Regardless of where I was in the world, *Sirius* would be there for me..... And so would Bobby."

Olivia held my hand tightly and whispered in my ear, "I love you."

I kissed her and made more love to her. She had become my star now.....

The days passed. It became apparent to both of us that our separation on January 2 would be difficult. The *USS Tunny* was leaving that morning on a six-month cross-Atlantic cruise to the Mediterranean Sea. Olivia would return to Dartmouth to finish her last year of studies.

We both felt an urgency to spend every minute of the day together. Soon, our union would be split physically. Somehow, inexplicably, Olivia and I had developed a co-dependency. Like a supernova, the brightness of our love was both blinding and life-giving.

On New Year's Eve, I invited Olivia to dinner at Coconut Grove's finest French restaurant. *L'Amour Les*

Uns sat atop the romantic *Hotel Le Chateau Mer* on Biscayne Bay.

After dinner, we spent the evening in a suite overlooking the water. At midnight, we sat together naked on the dark terrace, looking at the fabulous fireworks over the bay. It was cold. We covered ourselves with a thick blanket from the room. Occasionally, a loud burst of fire in the sky would startle Olivia. I could sense her flinch next to me.

"Does the noise scare you?" I asked.

"Fireworks are beautiful to look at, but I don't like the booms. They remind me of war. And I don't like war. War took my father away. The idea of killing another human being sickens me," said Olivia as she curled up against me.

"You are a soldier, Julian. Have you ever killed for your country?" she asked gently.

"No..... I haven't killed for my country..... Hopefully, I'll never have to. I'm a soldier to prevent war. I want to prevent killing, Olivia. The prevention of war is more important than the conduct of it. There is peace through strength....."

Olivia looked at me with her dark eyes, quizzically, almost disbelieving I could say such a stupid thing.

"How can there be peace through strength, Julian?

"When one is strong, rarely do you not use that strength to empower yourself. You use it to advance your ideology and force it on others. If not, it entices your enemy to challenge you with more strength. The 'Good' frequently becomes the 'Bad'. History has shown us this."

"I understand your point, Olivia. But without power, there is no life."

"Eternal power, Julian, is a myth. Like eternal life, it doesn't exist. There is an end to everything, except 'Love'. Spiritual love is eternal. It's even more eternal than your star, *Sirius*. Everything else has an expiration.

"Oh, I recognize the concept of defense against those who want to destroy you. It's a necessary evil. It's like chemotherapy. You often destroy the 'Good' to kill the 'Bad'. But remember always, Julian, when you kill - a little bit of you dies also. The more you kill, the more you die.

"Prevent war, Julian..... Remember there isn't always peace through strength. There is a delicate balance which is difficult to ascertain. That is all I can say."

I looked into her eyes and sank mystically into them. The reflections of the powerful fireworks in the sky behind me drew me in.

From where had this 'Angel' arrived? I asked myself.

I was drowning in her. Overnight, she had become my world. There was nothing else, only Olivia. She was the sun, the moon, and the stars. She was my food, my wine, my life.....

Before dawn, I drove Olivia home in the convertible Mustang. The cool early morning winter air invigorated our spirits more. I only wanted to live, to make love to her. I did not want to separate. I wanted to continue to smell her, feel her, taste her. It had become existential.

I returned to the Sierra estate a few hours later, and we spent the rest of the day and evening in the hotel suite. We didn't sleep. Olivia and I simply could not get enough of each other. We made love many times. And in between, we lay naked wrapped around each other, enthralled by the feelings we shared.

Finally, in the early morning of January 2, I left Olivia at home for the final time. Without speaking, I gave her a long kiss goodbye. I wanted to remain in her forever. I could not disconnect. She expressed her good wishes for me. I did the same for her. The time we dreaded had come.

"I'll fly to Europe in May and see you when the *Tunny* stops in Greece. I have much to show and teach you," she said.

Olivia smiled, further drowning me in her unique, attractive, and mysterious charms. It would be a long time before May, I thought. I would miss her scent, her breath, her being.

"I will see you in Greece," I said in a low voice, before I turned and walked away.

Leaving Olivia was the most difficult thing I had ever done. It was painful and unusual punishment, I felt. Unjust and untimely as well. I had experienced much of that in the past. I didn't want more of it.

Sitting alone in the cold of the Mustang convertible, I reviewed my emotions for Olivia. It had been all so unexpected. It had fallen on both of us like a meteor. The pleasurable shock and awe was numbing on the mind, like wine. I knew if she came to me in Greece, she would never leave me again.

I returned to Hank's home and packed my duffel bag. I changed into my dress blue Navy uniform. Hank drove me to the *Tunny* at the Port of Miami.

Driving in the darkness of early morning, we remained quiet. Henry understood the significance of my emotions.

Nearing the port, I said, "Hank, this girl has changed my life. I don't know how I'm going to get by without her. These past ten days have been a dream."

"You're in love, brother," answered Henry, stating the obvious.

"I don't think love and six-month tours on US submarines blend well together. It's like a bad martini, Julian. It can play with your head. She's going back to college, where she'll be surrounded by hungry boys. You, on the other hand, are going underwater with 120 lonely, crazed men. It's an unfair fight," laughed Henry.

I smiled at my friend in agreement, but I wasn't thinking of fighting. My only thoughts were of loving Olivia forever.

"I want to thank you and your family again, Hank, for inviting me to your home. They truly have been the best days of my life."

We arrived at the *Tunny* just before 6 AM. Henry Graves gave me a big hug in silence. I went on board the submarine and saluted the receiving officer on the *Tunny*.

"Hey, Julian, I'll be the 'Best Man' at the wedding!" shouted Hank from shore, leaning on his sports car with a giant grin on his face.

The sailors on deck around me all laughed and whistled. I turned towards my dear friend, smiled, and saluted, before continuing to my state room.

I set my things down and reached into my jacket. I opened the letter Olivia had handed me an hour earlier.

My sweet Julian:

Up until I met you, the only men I had ever loved were my grandfather Raul and the memory of my father. Now my world has changed. All things I consider good in this life - hopes for happiness and the enrichment of my soul -

are suddenly wrapped up in you. I love you more than I can stand. I want to be with you forever.

In Greek mythology, on Mount Olympus ~ home of the deities, grew a flower that never died. It symbolized all the human emotions you wished would last an eternity ~ Love, Passion, Honor, and Loyalty. The amaranth flower was highly prized by the Greeks for its symbolic meaning of eternal life.

I want to see you in Greece and together climb Mount Olympus. I want to pick the amaranth flower with you. I suspect you feel the same as I do. The red amaranth represents my eternal love for you.

I hope and pray you think of me in every waking moment, as well as in all your dreams. I know I will always think and dream of you.

My love for an eternity, Olivia

In the envelope with the letter was a fresh red globe amaranth flower.

CHAPTER 17

Revenge and Redemption

There is no redemption from hell.

Pope Paul *III* **(1468 to 1549)**

REVENGE IN MILITARY CONFLICT is a curious emotion. If extreme in its ferocity, it may induce in its perpetrators a seeking out for redemption. The ego-syntonic psychological gratification sensed by one side's vengeful retaliation against its enemy for a perceived prior loss at their hands is often indirectly correlated with the volume of damage inflicted as relatively compared to the original loss perceived. For example, the ambush and killing of Japanese Admiral Isoroku Yamamoto on April 18, 1943, by a squadron of American P-38 fighters over Bougainville, as the master planner of the Pearl Harbor attack flew in a Mitsubishi Betty bomber over the Solomon Islands, was extremely gratifying to the United States. However, the atomic bombings of Hiroshima and Nagasaki in similar vengeance, and in an attempt to avoid the potential future catastrophic losses of American lives in an invasion of the Japanese home islands, still today create feelings of guilt and regret in the minds of many Americans. Similarly, the killing of al-Qaeda leader Osama bin Laden in Pakistan on May 2, 2011, held responsible for the attack on Americans on 9/11, brought visible gratification to most Americans. If instead, America would have dropped nuclear bombs on all states supporting terrorism against the United States, most Americans would have been disillusioned. In essence, sane human beings do not enjoy the taking of human life; they simply want fair justice. The killing of a disproportionate number of the enemy by a victor in battle, although always desirable from a military perspective, can create remorse in the minds of many of the victorious warriors. The battle cry "Fight to Win" can have its negative psychological consequences. The winning warrior usually seeks his own redemption.....

"Battle stations!

"All sailors to battle stations!" sounded the alarm on the *Oregon*.

"Give me data, Johnson!" shouted Captain Julius Stansfield.

"We're in position to strike, Sir. Data points are coordinated and fixed," confirmed the XO.

"Good, Johnson.....

"Let Poseidon and Neptune shake the earth and swallow these sons of bitches into the sea!"

It was early evening on May 14 in the South China Sea. The *USS Oregon*, along with three other American attack submarines, sat almost motionless at a depth of 25 feet - approximately 50 nautical miles east of Singapore.

Singapore had been declared a neutral city two weeks prior, forcing the movement of twenty-four US F-18 Super Hornets from the Paya Lebar and Tengah Airbases to bases in Vietnam. These planes were now involved in providing air cover for the Vietnamese Army operations along their border with China.

Fearing Chinese retaliatory strikes against their civilian populations, Malaysia and Indonesia had not allowed the presence of US planes on airbases along the Malacca Strait on the Malay Peninsula and the island of Sumatra. Singapore's neutrality in this war, along with

Malaysian and Indonesian reticence, allowed Chinese convoys to travel the Malacca Strait with more impunity. It also forced America to project her power in this region with attack submarine wolfpacks, compensating for less control of the skies over the critical waterway.

The PLA naval convoy, responsible for the sinking of the Los Angeles class attack submarine *Spokane* in the Indian Ocean more than two days ago, had passed through the Malacca Strait and into the Singapore Strait. The Chinese convoy, composed of three guided missile destroyers and three guided missile frigates, was heading east along the Singapore Strait towards the open ocean of the South China Sea. They had not yet been challenged by the US Navy.

America developed a plan to intersect and ambush the Chinese convoy before it entered the safer open waters of the South China Sea. The stealthy US attack submarines were to sneak up on their enemy and hit them, before they had time to react.

Less than sixty nautical miles now separated the opposing navies. The *Oregon* was accompanied by another Virginia class attack submarine, the *USS Wyoming*. Two Los Angeles class submarines, the *Richmond* and the *Austin*, sat five and ten nautical miles to the southeast.

Captain Julius Stansfield ordered the subs to close on the enemy. The *Oregon*'s photonic mast was extended to the surface, while Stansfield stood at attention in the control room with his executive staff. The screens projected a 360° panoramic view of the battle area with satellite and infrared images of the Chinese ships. Sonar and laser rangefinder information provided further details.

The Americans had remained undetected. When the PLA convoy was thirty nautical miles away, the *Richmond* and the *Austin* each fired three Harpoon anti-ship sea skimmer missiles. A total of nearly 4000 pounds of paymetal was hurled at 600 miles per hour. The *Oregon* and the *Wyoming* each fired two Tomahawk cruise missiles from vertical launchers, adding another 4000 pounds of explosives. All torpedo tubes were loaded with MK 48 Adcaps, ready for firing as separation range narrowed.

Defensive actions by the Chinese helped them shoot down two US missiles, but the other eight found their marks. All six PLA ships were lit on fire.

Two of the destroyers were able to fire off three CY-3 anti-submarine ballistic torpedoes. These sonar-guided and data-linked rockets were not known to be accurate under battle conditions. Two more CY-2 torpedoes were fired from the third destroyer.

The *Austin* received a direct hit near its torpedo room and exploded immediately. It broke in two and sank slowly to the ocean bottom with her 132 Americans.

Two Chinese frigates and one destroyer sank rapidly into the Singapore Strait. The surviving US submarines, led by Stansfield on the *Oregon*, closed to twelve nautical miles before firing their torpedoes at the remaining PLA ships. Eight of the twelve MK-48s hit their targets ten minutes later, sending the two remaining destroyers and one frigate quickly down.

Within one hour, six Chinese vessels had perished. More than 1300 PLA sailors and marines were sleeping with the fish.

The Americans had also suffered. The entire crew of the *USS Austin* was lost.

Modern naval warfare was brutally fast and furious. It was a high-risk adventure for all parties involved. The volume of destruction and speed of death were rapid, not allowing time for the warriors to react. It literally took one's breath away.

Stansfield and Johnson looked at the battle screens in astonishment. They showed only an empty ocean surface for miles around; when only minutes before, an enemy convoy had been exhibited.

"Ball of lightning," whispered the XO in the quiet room.

"Unbelievable," murmured another officer near the captain.

"Inform the crew of our losses, Lieutenant Commander," said Stansfield in a somber voice. "Radio Pacific Command at Pearl and tell them we've completed our mission. Give Guam the battle report and ask for further orders....."

The Americans felt emotion for their lost comrades on the *Austin, but it* was spliced with relief and unexpressed jubilation for surviving the heat of battle.

The Battle of Singapore Strait had been another victory for the United States Navy. The PLA convoy from Sri Lanka would never see open ocean again, but neither would the crews of the *USS Spokane* and *Austin*. Even worse, 264 American naval fighting men and women would never see their families again.

While the loss of the *Spokane* had required revenge, losing the *Austin* would further haunt the warriors of the US submarine wolfpack. The planners of the ambush would also feel the pain. The death of so many fighters on both sides, in such a short period of time, would require redemption in the minds of the survivors.

The sailors of the *USS Oregon* were in low mood as they received orders to return to Subic Bay for resupply of missiles and torpedoes. There would be much more killing in their futures.

Julius Stansfield retreated back to his state room. He sat on his bunk and looked across at a photograph of his wife Sandra and two daughters - Jeannie, four years old, and Jane, three.

The captain noticed he wasn't in the picture. Stansfield thought of how sad the photograph appeared to him now. He wondered why he hadn't chosen a picture of his family with him included.....

Just two days of war and the captain fully understood his chances of never returning home. 'Lost at sea' became palpable. Poseidon and Neptune were moody and unpredictable brothers; whether the gods were foes or friends depended only on their whims.

CHAPTER 18

Medal of Honor

You will never do anything in this world without courage. It is the greatest quality of the mind next to honor.

***Aristotle* (384 BC to 322 BC)**

I RODE in the backseat of my staff car along Roosevelt Drive towards *The Tomb of The Unknowns* at Arlington National Cemetery. Lieutenant Commander Louis Stevens sat in the front passenger seat next to the driver. I had requested this morning to stop at *The Tomb of The Unknowns* to lay a wreath in honor of all the Americans lost at sea in the first three days of battle. Since last speaking to my sons several weeks ago, I had been here many times at sunrise to pray for peace. I stared out the car's window at the endless rows of tombstones, each marking a unique life ended.....

"I came here often in my childhood past," I said, still staring out at the white crosses and Stars of David. "As boys, my brother and I visited many times with our father. We'd come from Illinois and pray at the *Tomb* for our grandfather, a young officer killed in the 'First War'. Blown to bits in 'No Man's Land', his body was never recovered. Father, without any memory of him, truly believed he was buried here.

"We'd usually visit once a year, sometimes more than once. I remember in the late fifties, coming on both Memorial and Veterans Days three years in a row.

"I have recollection, though, of all the seasons..... The blue-skied spring with cool air, and the color and scent of flowers..... The summer with the Virginia heat, green grass, and the bright rays of the sun..... Fall with the changing of the leaves and the multitude of hues – reds, orange, yellows, purples..... And winter with gray sky, cold white snow, and bare trees..... Regardless of season, the crosses and stars always saddened me. I knew there was a boy buried beneath each and every one of them - a boy, perhaps, just like me.....

"It never ceases to amaze me how solemnly beautiful this sacred place is at sunrise. It's as if 'Nature' has mandated this tranquility in honor of the warriors resting here, in compensation for their last living moments of violence. Even as a boy, I've always wondered if that compensation is sufficient for the grieving families..... It must be a difficult task for a father or mother to come visit their child lying in this field."

"Yes, Sir," quietly agreed Louis.

The car stopped. Louis accompanied me to the *Tomb*, always staying three steps behind me. The Honor Guard saluted as I laid my wreath, bowed my head, and prayed.....

Arlington National Cemetery held a very special place in my heart. I had visited many times over the years to honor America's fallen. In years past, I would usually come accompanied by Olivia. Her devotion to the United States was as strong as mine.

In the year since Olivia's death, I came frequently alone. Usually at sunrise, and irrelevant of the weather, I prayed at *The Tomb of the Unknowns*. I prayed for all the boys and girls who had lost their lives fighting to keep America free. I would pray for the safety of all living Americans. And more specifically, I would pray for the safety of my sons.

I would also pray for the soul of my wife. I had always believed Olivia and I would be buried together at Arlington. After Olivia's request for her ashes to be placed in Biscayne Bay, I requested the same in my Last Will and Testament.

Dressed in our formal white uniforms - Stevens and I returned to the car, and started the short trip to Andrews Air Base to receive my son Mark. He was arriving from Germany, accompanied by five other severely injured brave Marines. They were travelling on a specially equipped Boeing C-17 Globemaster medevac, staffed by a critical care air transport team. A physician intensivist, two critical care nurses, and a respiratory therapist would provide supportive care all the way home.

Dr. John McNulley, Mark's neurosurgeon at Landstruhl, had called early in the morning to inform me of my son's condition. Gunshot trauma had destroyed his right kidney, the right lobe of his liver, and a portion of his colon - requiring their removal. Spinal trauma had left him paralyzed from the waist down. He was experiencing some bladder and bowel troubles, and had a minor infection around his colostomy for which he was receiving intravenous antibiotics. Mark would be sedated for the trip home from Ramstein, Germany, and was expected to be incoherent upon arrival at Andrews.

The prognosis for the paralysis was guarded at the present time, and the neurosurgeon could not commit one way or the other. Mark's state of mind was good, and he was ready to begin his rehabilitation as soon as possible.

Louis Stevens slowly turned and handed me an envelope from the Office of the Navy Secretary. It was addressed to Admiral Julian Stansfield, FOR YOUR EYES ONLY.

Recommendation Letter
Medal of Honor
by Colonel Steven Forster
US Army Intelligence
Commanding Officer
Operation Karakoram

From: Commanding Officer, Col. Steven Forster
To: Secretary of the Navy (Navy Department Board of Decorations and Awards)

Via: 1) Commandant, US Marine Corps
2) Commanding General, US Marines Special Operations Command (MARSOC)
3) Commanding General, AFPAK Theater
4) Chief of Naval Operations

Subj: Medal of Honor; recommendation for Captain Mark Stansfield

Encl: 1) Proposed Citation
2) Statement of Lieut. James Thomas, United States Marine Corps
3) Statement of Capt. Robert Jones, United States Marine Corps
4) Statement of Sgt. Thomas Woods, United States Marine Corps

It is recommended that Captain Mark Stansfield, United States Marine Corps Special Operations Command, attached to and serving with Operation Karakoram, U.S. Army Intelligence

Division of Special Operations and AFPAK Theater of War, be awarded the Medal of Honor for conspicuous gallantry and intrepidity at the risk of his life above and beyond the call of duty.

On the late evening of this past May 5, Captain Mark Stansfield and the men under his command attacked the heavily defended Shishkat Bridge over the Hunza River in northern Pakistan.

After destroying the bridge and a large contingent of enemy forces, the US assault team escaped the next morning into an adjacent valley and waited for helicopter evacuation. As rescue helicopters began their approach, the Americans came under attack by several hundred Chinese infantry.

In defense of his men, Captain Stansfield ran into the oncoming Chinese assault, and using an AK-47 and later an M249 machine gun, killed several dozen enemy combatants. He also carried a severely wounded comrade over his back to waiting assistance near the helicopters.

In this entire process - he received an incapacitating gunshot wound to his back, leading shortly thereafter to cardiovascular shock aboard the helicopter, and requiring resuscitative efforts by his men. Only one of his men was lost in the engagement due to his efforts.

Captain Stansfield, by his willingness to expose himself to almost certain death in order to save his men, was able to thwart the Chinese enemy effort to destroy the US assault team and two rescue helicopters. In so doing, he also inflicted heavy casualties on the large enemy force.

In addition, his actions at Shishkat Bridge the night before were instrumental in making Operation Karakoram a complete success, and denying the Chinese Army access into southern Pakistan.

His actions were those of a man of uncommon bravery and ability, and were in keeping with the highest traditions of the United States Marine Corps.

The facts contained in the proposed citation are completely substantiated by the statements of eyewitnesses and contained herein as enclosures (2) through (4).

I carefully placed the letter back into the envelope and handed it to Louis. I thought of my son as our car passed through security checks at the entrance to Andrews Air Force Base.

On the tarmac, a US Marine Corps Honor Guard stood at attention, holding the American Flag and the United States Marine Corps Banner. The Marine Corps Band played Sousa's "Stars and Stripes Forever".

Mark's wife, Sarah, and two young sons, George and Robert, were waiting under the early morning sun. Rebecca, my 30-year-old daughter - classical pianist and Mark's younger sister - stood next to Sarah.

The staff car slowly rolled behind the Honor Guard, and left Lieutenant Commander Stevens and I with the rest of my attending family.

The plane came to a stop in front of us, and the band played the "Star-Spangled Banner". The large back door of the C-17 opened, allowing a view of her interior..... I thought of the tombstones of Arlington.....

A young nurse walked down the ramp and over to us. After kindly greeting everyone, she asked me to return with her back into the plane.

I made my way past four heavily bandaged unconscious Marines on stretchers, gently passing my hand across each of their faces. Finally, I reached my son Mark.

The nurse said, "Although heavily sedated, Mark kept calling for you, Admiral, the entire trip home. He kept talking about 'Father and the Amaranth'. It seemed to be the only thing in his mind.

"He's asleep, Admiral. He's unlikely to recognize you, even if awakened. Perhaps by tomorrow, he'll be aware of his surroundings.

"God bless you, Sir, and the courage of your son. We're all praying for him....."

The nurse walked away, leaving me alone with Mark.

I looked at my boy..... He was in his own world, struggling with all his might to survive. All his energies were invested in the fight. He had not died on the field of battle, and now he was refusing to leave us in the bed of the brave. Without any evidence of pain, intravenous lines ran into both his arms, and a warming blanket covered his body.

To me, Mark appeared like he had when he was ten years old. His baby face, inherited from his mother, was intact. He seemed peaceful, almost increasingly so.

But I realized nothing in him could be at peace..... Mark's body, mind, and soul were fully occupied in his perilous odyssey. For him, the great struggle had not ended in the Hunza Valley. It would continue for a long, long time.....

I took hold of Mark's right hand and kissed his forehead. I passed my hand through his curly golden locks.

As they began to transport the first patients from the C-17 to waiting ambulances, John Philip Sousa's "Semper Fidelis" began to play. Seconds later, like awakening from a long tempestuous dream, Mark opened his eyes and saw me next to him. His eyes focused on mine. He stared at my black patch.

My boy gave me a big smile, like only Olivia's son could have, and motioned with his right hand for me to get closer. He closed his eyes.

I placed my ear close to Mark's mouth and heard him whisper, "Never fade, never die, American Amaranth."

CHAPTER 19

Challenges

Accept the challenges so that you may feel the exhilaration of victory.

***General George S Patton* (1885 to 1945)**

I SPENT the first six months of 1976 in the Mediterranean on board the *USS Tunny*. It was my first transatlantic cruise. We made short goodwill port visits to Barcelona, Marseille, Naples, Malta, and Crete; and finally in late May, the *Tunny* arrived in Thessaloniki, Greece, for a longer stay.

Olivia graduated from Dartmouth in early May and met up with me in Greece. We spent five days together, travelling the area and learning about modern Greek culture. We visited ancient Greek, Roman, Byzantine, and Ottoman Turk ruins near Thessaloniki, and discussed their political systems of government. We travelled to nearby Vergina and saw the tomb of Philip II of Macedon, father of Alexander the Great. We spent a day on the beautiful beaches of Kassandra Peninsula, swimming in the Aegean Sea. Finally, on our last day together, Olivia and I climbed Mount Olympus.

We had fallen in love and wanted to spend the rest of our lives together. I planned to speak with Olivia's mother and Raul Sierra, before making arrangements for marriage. We needed to hurry. I was to be transferred to the *USS Haddo* at Submarine Group Base San Diego in late October.

On August 6, 1976, I flew on a naval transport plane from Charleston, South Carolina, to Homestead Air Force Base in South Florida. Olivia picked me up at the airfield and drove us to Raul's home on Key Biscayne.

Raul Sierra spent many of his afternoons in the orchid house behind his home. The glass enclosure, facing the Atlantic Ocean, contained at least 300 orchids from tropical areas around the world. Raul had published four classic books on orchid horticulture and was considered a world expert on the different varieties.

Olivia and I found Raul in his yard, working with his orchids. He was expecting us.....

"Abuelo, you must remember Lieutenant Julian Stansfield, whom you met at the Christmas party last year at the Graves house. He's come to visit me from Charleston, South Carolina," announced Olivia.

"Yes, certainly..... The Navy man, friend of Henry Graves, who dropped his champagne glass in the pool just prior to meeting you," laughed Raul.

Sierra looked over his reading glasses with his expressive ocean blue eyes, smiled, and shook my hand. He invited us to sit down at a nearby garden table, while continuing to work on his flowers.

"Olivia, go inside and prepare us a Daiquiri.

"Julian, do you know anything about orchids?"

"No, Sir, I don't. They don't seem to grow well up in Chicago, where I'm originally from," I answered.

"Well, you're wrong, Julian. Like freedom, orchids can grow anywhere. You just need to know how to take care of them. They're not easy. They are complicated living things," said Raul in perfect English.

Raul Sierra explained the intricate beauty of his flowers, and how they reminded him of his island home of Cuba. He worked with his flowers as we spoke.

"You know, Julian, in Cuba they grow wild and free everywhere; unlike the children living there now.

Unfortunately, human beings need more than just rainwater, sunshine, and rich soil to live and prosper.

"No..... Human beings require much more than that to survive. They need freedom, a commodity that seems to be in short supply in the world nowadays.

"And love, of course..... Freedom and love..... Both in short supply. You can't have much of one without the other, I believe."

Raul tended his orchids like a mother tends to her babies. He meticulously removed dead stems and dried leaves, keeping his flowers looking healthy and strong.

Sierra was tall and fit, at least 6 feet in height, and he appeared remarkably younger than his 68 years. He had a full head of black hair, piercing blue eyes, and absolutely no facial wrinkles. His white skin was burned by the sun. He was a handsome man. Like his granddaughter, he projected immense personal character and moral strength. Although invisible, his aura was all around you. One could sense its presence. It was impossible to not like and respect this man.

Raul Sierra had been a very successful businessman in Cuba. He was involved in the sugar industry shortly after graduating from MIT with a degree in chemical engineering. He became prosperous in short order, and quickly amassed large land holdings in Cuba, Central America, and Brazil.

In his mid-40s, he was elected Governor of Las Villas, one of Cuba's six provinces. He served his people well until 1959 and Fidel Castro's Cuban Revolution.

He was exiled to the United States with his wife Virginia, two daughters, and only son - Jorge. Jorge was Olivia's father.

Olivia returned with a large tray of pitchers, bottles, glasses, and ice. She sat next to me at the garden table. Raul Sierra looked at her, nodded, and continued to work with his orchids.

Olivia placed shaved ice into three tall chilled flute glasses. She then squeezed the juice from two limes and half a grapefruit into each of the glasses, and waited for Raul to come join us.

The governor opened a blue parasol behind Olivia and I, and finally sat across from us. Summer rain clouds offshore created a cool breeze off the Atlantic. It made its way across the orchids and onto us at the table.

"A warm sun and a cool rain, a delicious drink, and Olivia's beauty, what more can a man ask for," laughed Raul.

"I couldn't agree with you more, Governor," I said.

"I hope you like Daiquiris, Julian. I believe they are one of Cuba's greatest inventions. Perhaps second on the list, behind the Cuban woman," grinned Raul, as he poured two and a half jiggers of white rum and six drops of maraschino liqueur into each of the glasses, and stirred them with a long handled spoon.

Raul looked over at Olivia and smiled. "There is considerable distance between them on the list. Cuban women are truly alone at the top. My grand-daughter is living proof of that," he said, while passing us the drinks.

"Long ago, I would drink these with Ernest Hemingway at my beach home at Varadero and talk about politics until the early morning. Then we would go out fishing on the *Pilar* and sweat out the alcohol. He strongly agreed with my list of Cuban inventions. The man enjoyed much of what my country had to offer. Although he enjoyed many more of these than I."

Sierra wiped the sweat off his brow with his shirt sleeve.

"Poor Ernest never saw the Communism in Castro, until the summer of 1960..... Too late.....

"After the Bay of Pigs, Castro took away his beloved *Finca Vigia*. I don't think he ever got over that."

Raul sighed and poured himself another cold drink. He subtly motioned for Olivia to go inside and get him his sunhat.

Raul watched his beautiful grand-daughter all the way to the house. He then turned to me and said, "Olivia is very fond of you, Julian. She would never bring you here if she wasn't."

"Well, Sir, I am very fond of her also..... I love her..... I've never known anyone like her."

"You've never met anyone like her because none like her exist..... She is a precious jewel of a woman, unique in every way," said Raul.

"I agree with you entirely," I added. "She is a treasure, and I love her deeply. I would like your permission to marry her."

Raul looked at me with his piercing blue eyes. He took a long drink of Daiquiri.

"Julian, I think you only need her permission. That is more than enough for me."

Olivia returned with the governor's wide brimmed Panama hat. I couldn't help but notice "FREEDOM' was embroidered into the front of the hat in big crimson letters. It seemed to make Raul's aura that much stronger.

"How do you like my hat?" asked the governor.

"I believe it suits you well," I answered.

"It's a never-ending battle," said Raul, pointing to the blood-red letters. "Anywhere and everywhere I can, I'll fight for it to the best of my abilities. I'm getting a little long in the tooth to do much more than just give money for a cause; but believe me, I'd give every penny I have to rid the world of Communism. It won't be enough, but I'll give it regardless."

The governor reached across the table with his hand and caressed Olivia's face.

"It seems, my dear, Henry Graves' friend loves you even more than Henry did. My eyes tell me you feel the same. It's not easy to disguise 'young love', and it's especially difficult to hide the gift from this old man. I suggest both of you tend to this love as soon as possible."

"We will, Abuelo," smiled Olivia, looking into my eyes.....

The rain became stronger, and we raced into the orchid house for cover. We took the Daiquiris with us.

Feeling at ease after two more drinks, I asked Raul Sierra how, at age 53, he had taken on the challenge of fighting for his country? How he had survived the beatings and torture as a prisoner of war? How he had felt when released from prison, after President Kennedy paid out ransom money for his failure in not providing air support for the Bay of Pigs?

Raul put his drink down next to an old pendulum clock in the orchid house. His spirit had suddenly abandoned his body. He sat in a small wooden chair and asked me to do the same across from him. His blue eyes became bluer.....

"Julian," he paused, "when my only son became involved with the CIA operations in Cuba, I was proud of his decision. However, I soon realized I couldn't wait safely in the United States while my son fought to liberate our country. If my son was to be in harm's way, well then, I desired to be as close to him as possible. The beaches at the Bay of Pigs were closer to Jorge than those here in Key Biscayne."

Olivia ran out of the orchid house in the rain and returned to the main home. She left the door swinging in the strong wind.

"She'll be fine, Julian. Go close the door and come back."

"You don't need to continue, Governor," I said.

"You will be family soon, Julian, I must continue. If my story can bring you a perspective on freedom, unknown to most Americans, then it must be heard.....

"I was told of my son's execution while imprisoned myself. It was agonizing to realize I had failed him. I wished the prison guards would beat me to death.

"After hearing of Kennedy's deal with Castro, I began to understand how I needed to return to the United States to help my son's wife and daughter. The pain of Jorge's death would follow me forever. He was my only son. He was a brave boy. I loved him very much..... Like I do Olivia."

Raul stared out through the glass at the rain. The falling water drowned out the tick-tock of the swinging pendulum clock.

"It's peculiar how rain can somber one's mood at times," said the Cuban. "I've always enjoyed watching the rain fall. But it does make one pensive, I believe....."

"Yes, Sir..... I agree with you. It can have that effect," I said politely.

"You are a soldier, Julian..... I respect men who defend their country.....

"Did you fight in Vietnam?"

"No, Sir. I graduated from the US Naval Academy in 1973 and was transferred to New London, Connecticut. Combat operations in Southeast Asia had ended by then."

"How do you feel about America's loss in Vietnam?" Raul asked.

"I think it was a national calamity, Sir."

Raul Sierra paused again and said firmly, "Well, Julian, you and America are still free. The calamity has been for the Vietnamese people. They will not see the sunshine of freedom for a very long time. When a nation loses its freedom, it is not easily retrieved. I can certainly attest to that. I lost my country and my son many years ago. I won't recover either of them. I was fortunate only in having this great country, America, adopt me and my family. I've grown to love your country very much. It is a noble nation. But still, it is not my country. Cuba was taken away from me, and she still burns strongly inside of me.

"Remember our talk into the future. As a naval officer of the United States, protect this country from oppression. Defend your family's freedom. Provide your children every opportunity to live with dignity and honor. Life without liberty to pursue your dreams is unbearable. Take care of Olivia like her father would have wished."

The rain had stopped. Sunshine had returned. Raul Sierra stood, gently patted me on the back, and walked from the orchids towards the main house.

I went outside and sat again at the garden table under the parasol. Olivia returned to me. I grabbed her hand tightly, kissed her cheek, and whispered, "I love you."

We were married in a small Catholic church on Key Biscayne in October 1976. We moved to San Diego, California, a few days later. I was the Junior Executive Officer on the *USS Haddo* for the next two years.

On September 14, 1978, I was ordered to the Pentagon in Washington for a meeting with Vice Admiral Thomas Jones of Navy Intelligence. No reason for the order was given.

Vice Admiral Jones was a huge man from western North Carolina, 6'5" and weighing nearly 300 pounds. He smoked big cigars and spoke with a heavy southern drawl. He had been in Navy Intelligence since the 1964 Gulf of Tonkin Incident, which set the stage for the passage of a Congressional resolution giving President Lyndon Johnson legal justification for open hostilities against North Vietnam. He had a quick mind and an even quicker wit.

"Come on in, Lieutenant Stansfield. Take a seat while I review your file."

Jones motioned with his hand, inviting me to sit in front of him. He reclined back in his swivel chair with his stretched legs on the desk. The admiral chomped on a cigar for the next fifteen minutes as he turned pages in a note binder. I waited nervously.

While I sat, feeling smaller and smaller in my chair, Jones did not peer down at me once. He stayed concentrated on my personnel folder. From time to time, he would grin, nod his head, and smack his lips. I couldn't tell if he was thinking of lunch, or preparing to eat me.

At one point, I caught myself staring at the size of his legs, as the admiral crossed and uncrossed them on the desk. I thought to myself how the table had to be of the mightiest oak to support the weight of those hams. Jones was a very tall and 'BIG' man.

"How long have you been a Soviet spy?" shouted Jones.

The admiral lifted his legs off the table and leaned in his chair towards me. He put on a stern face and took a long puff on his cigar.

I froze in my seat. Unable to speak, I rapidly turned and looked behind me, as if Jones was directing his question at someone else in the room. I may have even jumped in my chair. I don't remember. Regardless, I slipped onto the floor and hit my head against a side table, causing a bloody gash on my scalp.

"Hot diggity!" yelled Jones. "Your goddam first Purple Heart working for Navy Intel is in my frickin office. You are definitely a man of action, Stansfield. I'm gonna like you real good. Yes Sir, real good!"

The admiral helped me from the floor and wiped my bloody head with a towel.

"Apply pressure, Lieutenant! I don't want you bleeding out on my carpet. I just had it cleaned. The Pentagon won't pay to clean it again, god damn it!"

Jones returned to his giant seat across from me and laughed his heart out.

"I love watching young officers' faces when I ask them that question. But I've never seen any of them go down like a quail in hunting season!"

The admiral slapped his leg and continued laughing uncontrollably. He looked over at me and blew smoke circles from his cigar in my direction.

"Consider it a rite of passage, Stansfield. It's a step in a recruitment process into my Navy Intel.

"We are now blood brothers, Lieutenant."

Jones pulled two large photographs from my folder and placed them in front of me.

"I presume you know these two men, Stansfield."

"Jim Graves and Raul Sierra," I said..... "I know them both well. Raul is my wife's grandfather."

"Both these men are critical to our anti-Communist task force. They've worked for years around the world to cripple the bastards who want to destroy us. Graves and Sierra are the best clandestine team I have. Their business front is operating in Europe, Central and South America, Africa, and Asia. They are literally everywhere America wishes to be. My job would be much harder without them."

My eyes grew in amazement. What the hell was going on here? I asked myself.

"Jim Graves has been studying your file for us over the past few years. He considers you the best intelligence prospect we've ever had. He's given you five stars across the board, a perfect 100 out of 100.....

"The *Tunny's* port visit to Miami three years ago was organized by our department. Graves needed to see you in person. The days you spent at his home over the Christmas holidays, although you spent most of the time with Olivia, were decisive in Jim's decision for your recruitment.

"Raul was not involved in the operation initially.

"By pure circumstance, you fell in love with his granddaughter. This allowed Raul to study you even more intimately.

"The consensus of Graves and Sierra was to advise this meeting today.

"It's a small world, Stansfield."

"And Olivia?" I asked hesitatingly, almost closing my ears to a response.

"Olivia has no significant knowledge of her grandfather's work," responded Jones. "She had no involvement in our adventure, other than innocently falling in love with the most brilliant graduate Annapolis has ever had.

"What you and her share, Julian, is pure. We had no influence whatsoever in that."

I was relieved. I took a deep breath and restarted my heart.....

"Now, let's get down to business, Lieutenant.

"Where do you think the next great war will be fought by the United States of America? And against whom will it be waged?"

"Against the Soviet Union in the Middle East, Sir," I answered quickly and nervously.

"Wrong!" yelled Jones..... "The next great war for the United States will be in the South China Sea and the western Pacific Ocean, against the People's Republic of China. This war will be decided by the United States Navy, Lieutenant Stansfield. America needs her smartest war planners to begin preparing it for this conflict. The Office of Naval Intelligence is where the planning begins."

Jones lit another cigar and continued to read my file. After a short while, he closed the folder and threw it on his desk.

"Julian, a split between the Soviet Union and China developed in 1959. As the Soviets began to accept coexistence on this planet with the Western democracies, the Chinese Communists under Mao became more intent on global peasant revolution and world domination. This Sino-Soviet split led the USSR to support India in their war against China in 1962. There were multiple border clashes between Soviet and Chinese troops during the 1960s. In 1971, Henry Kissinger and President Nixon opened a dialogue with Mao and Communist China in an attempt to weaken the more powerful enemy, the Soviet Union.

"This year, Soviet-supported Vietnam is planning to invade Cambodia, a key ally of the People's Republic of China. If Pol Pot and the Khmer Rouge regime in Cambodia fall to the Vietnamese, Vietnam will essentially rule over Indochina. China will have enemies along all its borders - the Soviet Union, India, and Vietnamese Indochina.

"Deng Xiaoping and the People's Republic have decided to go to war if Vietnam invades Cambodia. They will also threaten the Soviets with total war if they support the Vietnamese.....

"Navy Intelligence believes economic reforms in China will make it a world power financially and militarily by the year 2000. They will supplant the Soviet Union as our main enemy. America's next great war will be against China in the western Pacific in the twenty-first century. It will likely decide the fate of our country for the foreseeable future.....

"I need your help, Lieutenant Stansfield."

"My help, Sir? How can I help you?" I asked.

"Let me inflate your ego a bit, Julian. You were not only the top graduate of your 1973 class at Annapolis, but also still hold the highest test score average at the United States Naval Academy since 1913. That's 65 years, if my redneck math is correct. That makes you, Lieutenant

Stansfield, one smart son of a bitch. We need to collect many smart sons of bitches here at the Navy Intel office. I want you to join us at the Pentagon in preparation for the future.....

"But first, we would like to send you to China as an observer in the coming conflict with Vietnam. We don't believe the Soviets will get involved. However, we're expecting the Vietnamese to put up a strong fight. I need you to observe the Chinese in action and report your findings formally to the Office of Navy Intelligence.

"Lieutenant Stansfield, this is not a job offer. It's an order. Our department has spent much time, money, and effort in your recruitment. Your country needs you here with me. We have many other courageous officers to man the silent killers of the seas.

"You will leave for Beijing on October 17.

"We have arranged accommodations at the Swiss Embassy for you and Olivia. The United States is not opening its embassy in Beijing until early next year.

"The People's Liberation Army has assigned Captain Shang Wei to be your liaison guide upon arrival. He will explain all their ground rules.

"By the way, Lieutenant, you are now Lieutenant Commander Julian Stansfield.....

"That is all....."

I stood at attention, saluted Vice Admiral Jones while I held the bloody towel over my scalp with my other hand, and exited his office. I left the Pentagon with a headache, but fascinated and thrilled for an opportunity of a lifetime. I was beginning a new chapter in the Navy. I felt humbled that America had chosen me to begin this new book of war on China.

It would also be an adventure for Olivia, who certainly in the past had never thought of travelling to a Communist country. We would begin this new chapter together. I felt invigorated and up for the challenge.

CHAPTER 20

Book of War on China

All war is based on deception.

***Sun Tzu* (544 BC to 496 BC)**

OLIVIA AND I arrived at the Swiss Embassy in Beijing, China, on October 18, 1978. Although I had been briefed in San Diego about the mission goals, neither of us knew what to expect culturally from this adventure. Olivia had apprehension about visiting a Communist country, but realized a Navy wife didn't have many opportunities to spend time with her officer husband. She would at least have several weeks to sleep in the same bed with me, a fortunate event in the U.S. Navy.

The Swiss Embassy was a self-contained compound, with an official government business building and annexes for recreation, dining, and sleeping accommodations. The United States was planning to open their embassy in early 1979. Several Western democratic nations were using the Swiss Embassy as an intermediary in their developing relations with the People's Republic of China.

Shortly after arriving, an embassy messenger hand-delivered a sealed note to my room. It was an invitation to meet privately with Helmut Pfaeffle the next morning for breakfast. Pfaeffle was the high-ranking Swiss official at the embassy in charge of my stay. I didn't know much about him at the time, except that he had a good working relationship with Admiral Jones. I came to recognize he was a long-time CIA operative, working out of the Swiss Embassy in Beijing.

I found the time of my appointment with Pfaeffle peculiar. I arrived at his office before 6 AM and was escorted by a young woman through a large business area to a back room.

Before opening the door, the pretty Swiss secretary said to me, "Go and sit quietly on the blue couch by the rose garden. You will find it easily as you enter the room from the hall. Whatever you do, don't speak to Mr. Pfaeffle until the music is complete. He doesn't like to begin any conversation till he is ready. He will let you know. Believe me, he will let you know in good time." She smiled and allowed me to enter.

I passed through a long dark hall filled with beautiful classical music. The melody drew me into a large and well lit living area with high ceilings. I sat down on the blue sofa as directed. An elegant breakfast buffet was set up on a table in front of it. To my left was a grand piano. To my right was a dark brown leather chair against the wall. A colossal portrait photograph in color hung on the wall above the chair. Gustav Mahler's 5th Symphony played softly in the background.

The photograph attracted my eyes. The colors of the portrait were bland, as if washed out by time. But the theme was martial and historic, and this captured my attention.

At the center of the portrait was German General Erwin Rommel in conference with his staff at a desert field station. His blue eyes were big as saucers while he reviewed a map on a table in front of him. He held sharp calipers in his left hand to measure distances. Rommel's khaki-tan general's tunic and trousers were dusted with the sand of the Western Desert in North Africa. His officer's cap was slightly pulled back from his brow and held his desert goggles. The Iron Cross hung from his neck.

Rommel was surrounded by his *Afrikakorps* officer staff, all in study with him. German tanks and armored vehicles were in transit behind the field station, trailing blown sand and black smoke as they raced to war. To Rommel's right stood a tall thin man with broad shoulders, pointing to a spot on the battle map. He wore his captain's forage cap low on his brow, slightly shadowing a black patch over his right eye. He towered over Rommel. And the German general seemed interested in what he had to say. The captain was the focus of the staff meeting. The moment in time was striking to me.

I knew much about Rommel's tactics in the North African desert during World War Two. The general had nearly won his war, although outnumbered and under-supplied. He used his tanks in the sand like ships in the sea. His battle actions seemed planned by a naval strategist. We had studied his clever maneuverings at Annapolis. I always believed Rommel had been an admiral in mind and spirit.

Twenty-five feet in front of my repose, facing away from me towards the rose garden, stood a tall elderly man. He remained silent while he listened to Mahler. When the "Adagietto" finished, he stayed silent. I did the same.

A short moment later, still with his back to me in the quiet digestion of the music, the man asked in a thick German accent, "Do you enjoy Mahler, Lieutenant Commander Stansfield?"

"Yes I do, Sir..... I listened to his music as a boy with my father. He was a great admirer of the German composer."

"He was not German, Stansfield.

"He was Austrian.

"And he was Jewish.

"I love his music very much.

"It has a sad tonality to it. It's a music of farewell. It reflects an end to things. I don't particularly like the end of things, but I do like and respect the genius of Mahler....."

Helmut Pfaeffle turned slightly and lit a cigarette. He then returned his look into the rose garden. Dawn had broken, and sunlight was beginning to rise over the red and white flowers. I could see Pfaeffle wore a black patch over his right eye, like the German captain in the photograph.

I stared once more at the portrait on the wall. "Did you serve in the *Wehrmacht* during the world war, Sir?"

Pfaeffle did not respond. He continued to look at his roses, while taking a long drag on his cigarette.....

"Are you here to ask personal questions, Stansfield?"

"No, Sir..... But you resemble the dashing young officer in the photograph, that's all. I don't mean to pry, Sir."

"How could I resemble anything young and dashing, Lieutenant Commander?

"I am worn and torn by time. There is not one cell of me robust or dashing. There is very little of me in the captain you see on the wall. I knew him well. He was torn, but not yet worn, by time. There was an evolution from him to me, and it was a weary one."

"I'm sorry, Sir."

"There is no need to be, Stansfield. You simply have curiosity. I would have asked the same thing forty years ago. Today, I wouldn't care.

"But the answer to your question is - yes. I was a captain in the *Afrikakorps*, 15th Panzer Division.

"In early 1942, Rommel chose me to direct his intelligence staff. That is why you recognize me as the tall man next to the general in the photograph, Stansfield."

"You are not Swiss then?"

"Oh yes, I am Swiss," retorted Pfaeffle. "I am not a German as you may have perhaps surmised."

"How does a Swiss man end up as Rommel's intelligence attache in the Desert War of North Africa?" I asked.

"Life is full of surprises, young man. You rarely end up where you started, or where you thought you'd be. Life is not a predictable circle, Lieutenant Commander. It's more like a zig-zag line into the unknown. You can never foretell your future."

"What was your zig-zag line to Libya, Sir?"

"You are curious and persistent. I understand even more now, why Admiral Jones chose you for this mission. You keep searching for answers when things don't make sense. I like that, Stansfield. It will serve you well in life, I think.

"As a child, my father taught me to question things that didn't make sense. He always said, 'If it doesn't seem logical and rational – review the situation in your mind and come up with a better answer.' I sense your mind works similarly.

"You are asking yourself why a Swiss gentleman fought for the German Army during World War Two? And why today, this same man is working with US Navy Intelligence out of the Swiss Embassy in Beijing?

"The answers to these questions are complicated. And at the core of complicated things, one will usually find a beautiful woman. It is true in my case as well.

"Let me serve your inquisitiveness, Lieutenant Commander. Everything you and I will discuss over the next several months is considered highly classified. I don't need to remind you of that.

"I am a 65-year-old Swiss native of aristocratic German ancestry. My real name is Jurgen Schmidt. Your country took that name away from me many years ago.

"I left my home in Geneva in 1931, to attend Heidelberg University in Germany. There, I fell in love with Camilla, a German girl from Hamburg who was studying sociology. I married her shortly after graduating with my doctorate in economics. We moved to Hamburg months before war broke out. Camilla was pregnant and ready to deliver our child.

"In mid-May 1940, the RAF bombed oil installations around the port in Hamburg. They were not accurate and destroyed several city blocks of civilian apartment buildings. Camilla and my one year-old daughter were killed.

"Instead of returning to neutral Switzerland, I enlisted in the German Army. I wanted revenge. I scored very high on aptitude tests and was placed in intelligence. Attached to the 15th Panzer Division, I arrived in Italian Libya in April 1941.

"By early 1942, I was on Rommel's personal intelligence staff. Soon I was directing it. He confided in me only.

"I spent two long years in the North African desert. I fought at Tobruk and El Alamein. I saw much killing and destruction. I felt scorching heat and freezing cold. I had deprivation of food and water at times. We were not well supplied, at least not as well as Montgomery and his British 8th Army.

"The Americans landed in French North Africa in November 1942. By early 1943, we had been forced into northern Tunisia. On March 9, 1943, I left Africa with General Rommel. We both were disillusioned.

"My general asked me to go work with *Abwehr*, the German military intelligence service. I became the liaison between Rommel and Admiral Wilhelm Canaris, head of *Abwehr*. We began planning the July 20, 1944 plot to kill Adolf Hitler.

"After its failure, Rommel and Canaris were killed. I escaped to Switzerland. I was lucky, they were not. Your Admiral Jones says I was smarter than my leaders. I doubt that. They were simply more important than I. No one was watching me, and I got out."

Pfaeffle put out his cigarette and slowly walked over. He sat in the brown leather chair next to me. He pointed to his eye patch.

"This is my physical reminder of my time with the German Army, Stansfield. Young people often make mistakes of judgement. At twenty-eight years of age, I made decisions with my heart and testicles, not my brain. After losing Camilla, I felt the world war was my war. I was wrong. Camilla and my daughter had been mine, not the war. As you see, I didn't get my girls back and I lost an eye.

"In retrospect, rather than fight for a nation and a leader that were not mine, I should have returned to Switzerland and continued my life. Or perhaps, I could have volunteered my intelligence to the English in order to defeat the Nazi causes of the war. On any account, I didn't have much place in the North African desert, fighting for ideals which were foreign to me..... But naturally, I wouldn't be here today with you, if I hadn't. Isn't that right, Stansfield?

"Working intelligence for Rommel taught me to use my brain and mind in the process of decision making, not my heart and balls. True discipline in thinking was the only benefit I received from the *Afrikakorps*.

"I fought for Camilla, not for Germany. I lived in unusual and confusing times, Stansfield. When things are complicated to understand, always you shall find at the center - a beautiful woman.....

"After the war, the OSS found me in Geneva. They changed my name and paid me good money to go work clandestine in Soviet Europe. It wasn't any more dangerous than what I had done in the past - fighting the British in Africa, and later, Adolf Hitler in Germany. The Communists were dumber than the Nazis. I developed a deep understanding of the Soviet military and KGB. The Americans prized my work.

"In 1959, as the Sino-Soviet split began, I returned to Switzerland and was given an intensive course in Chinese culture, civilization, and military history. I also learned to speak Mandarin Chinese. In 1962, I went to work at the Swiss Embassy in Beijing. I have been here ever since.

"So you see, Stansfield, life is full of surprises. You rarely arrive at where you think you're going. Life is a zig-zag into the unknown, Lieutenant Commander."

Pfaeffle nodded his head and smiled. "You have intelligent eyes, Stansfield. Eyes never lie, I believe. I think I will enjoy my time with you, teaching the ways of China and its people. America will need many intelligent eyes to prevent the catastrophe I see coming at her in the next decades. Let's have breakfast and commence your tutorial."

Pfaeffle offered me a cigarette and lit another one for himself. He summoned his staff to move our breakfast to the rose garden. He said to me, "I'd rather eat among my flowers."

My sage was dressed in an immaculate dark blue three-piece suit. He had short white hair and a fine nose. His left eye was blue. On the top of his right hand, he had a tattoo in big red letters – CAMILLA.....

We sat in the center of the rose garden. The reds and whites were enveloped by subtle solar light. The perfume of the rose was in the air we breathed.

"Do you enjoy roses, Lieutenant Commander?" asked Pfaeffle, as he gestured with his head at the garden.

"Yes I do," I answered.

"You are unique then," he said. "A man of war who appreciates Mahler and enjoys the delicate beauty of the rose..... Unique indeed," he repeated.

"Not any more unique than you, Sir."

Pfaeffle smiled at me and winked his only eye.

"Keep your uniqueness, Stansfield. Maintain your humanity regardless of what spins around you. If you lose it, you will have lost all reason to live."

"I will remember that, Sir....."

"Roses are beautiful in a very formal way," slowly murmured Pfaeffle. "I will have my secretary pick and prepare my best flowers, and send them to your wife later this morning.

"You know, Lieutenant Commander, China is much like a rose. She is beautiful to look at. But you must be careful how you hold her, for she can prick you and make you bleed."

I watched Pfaeffle with intrigue. Here was a brilliant Swiss gentleman with a doctorate in economics from one of the oldest and finest universities in Europe. As a young man, he had fallen in love with a beautiful German girl. He created a family with her, and then lost them. War took his wife and daughter away forever. A romantic idealist, he changed his life for them without ever getting them back. Decades had passed, and he still loved Camilla.

"If I may ask, Sir, how did you lose your eye?"

"My eye was only one of the many sacrifices I made in that war, Stansfield. It was certainly not the most costly.

"We had taken Tobruk on the eastern Libyan Mediterranean coast in the spring of 1942. We prepared for the summer offensive into Egypt. Our plans were to race to Alexandria and Cairo. We expected to take the Suez Canal in weeks.

"Army Group South in the Soviet Union split in two after capturing the Ukraine. A double-pronged attack was made south - deep toward the Caucasus oil fields and Baku, and east - toward Stalingrad on the Volga River. The Volga River offensive would protect the left flank of the armies fighting for Baku, and eliminate the 'Persian Corridor' lines of US materials assistance to the Soviets from the Caspian Sea.

"After taking the Suez and the Sinai, we were to capture the 'Holy Land' and Mesopotamia on our sweep towards Baku from the south. By the end of 1942, Germany expected to be in control of the Middle East and the Caucasus oil fields.

"The German war machine could no longer depend on synthetic fuels and Romanian oil. It needed the energy reserves of the Muslim lands. Our entire purpose in the African campaign was to rid this area of British influence and reach Baku by the end of '42.

"Rommel's rapid progress across the Western Desert came to an end in July '42. The First Battle of El Alamein, on Egypt's Mediterranean coast – sixty miles west of Alexandria – was fought to a stalemate with Britain. Three months later, the British beat us back into Libya at the Second Battle of El Alamein. There were no more victories for Rommel in North Africa. We retreated all the way to Tunisia.

"The defeat at El Alamein - where I lost my eye to shrapnel - coupled with the annihilation of our army at Stalingrad, ended all hopes for German energy independence. The war was lost in the autumn and winter of 1942.

"In the past, great wars were fought for gold and salt, water, food, land, women, religion, and pride. From the twentieth century forward, great wars will be fought only for energy resources. The power of nations will depend on their sources of oil. As it was for me, it will be for you, Stansfield."

"Do you think it was all worth it, Sir?" I asked.

"What do you mean, Stansfield? Are you referring to my persistent dedication to a cause? A life filled with government work and little else? The loss of my eye?

"Let me put it this way..... I believe intelligence work in times of peace can help prevent war. If I can be of assistance in preventing for you and the world, Stansfield, what happened to me, then I believe it was worth it. But above all, if my experiences in war and the loss of my right eye help me better remember my Camilla as I grow old, then it was certainly worth it."

I could see the love for Camilla in his blue left eye. It penetrated through me like a sharp sword..... I could see his regrets and his sadness, the thoughts of unfulfilled desires and of what may have been if given the chance, and the wishes for a re-living which couldn't come. Helmut Pfaeffle was a good man who had been thrown into the maelstrom of the world without his permission. Fate had been unkind to him, and I was sympathetic. I could understand his love of Mahler's music, and his passion for the rose.....

"We've talked enough about me, Stansfield. Let's concentrate on your task for Admiral Jones.

"I've been asked by your government to teach you, within a few short weeks, everything you need to know about China and its people, culture, and military history. They've told me that you're a bright young man. Nevertheless, it will be a great challenge to fully appreciate the depth of this country and understand all its idiosyncrasies.

"Let us begin..... First, let me discard the myth that China is a peaceful non-expansionist nation based on Confucian philosophy, abhorring brute military force, and favoring non-belligerent political solutions. If it had not been expansionist over its long history, it would not be its present enormous size. Confucian philosophy is usually used as a cathartic, while they wash the blood off their hands.

"Millions of Chinese have been killed in population genocides throughout the history of this nation. Massacres were perpetrated by invaders - such as the Mongols in the 13th century AD, and the Japanese Imperial Forces in this century; and by domestic governments - in multiple dynastic periods, and Mao Zedong most recently. This is a violent culture, make no mistake about it."

A fine breakfast of poached eggs, fried ham, potatoes, croissants, orange juice, and coffee was brought into the garden by Pfaeffle's assistants. The men ate as the discussion continued.

"Sun Tzu's *THE ART OF WAR*, written in the fifth century BC, has influenced military thought throughout the world for the past 2500 years. I am certain you studied him thoroughly at the US Naval Academy. Sun Tzu's cornerstones of military intelligence, maneuvers, logistics, and deception - to subdue the enemy with the minimum of force - are practiced by every professional army in the world today. His emphases on maintaining military morale and national unity, and the avoidance of prolonged wars, seem like simple military logic; but these ideas were breakthrough concepts long ago.

"Recorded Chinese military history dates back to 2200 BC. Let me give you a brief outline.

"Territorial expansion began during the Shang Dynasty (1600 BC to 1046 BC). During the Period of Warring States (479 BC to 221 BC), feudalism was abolished, aristocracy was curbed, and professional armies were established. Generals were appointed on merit rather than birth. Cavalry was introduced, and military tactics were dependent on Sun Tzu's ideas of maneuver, illusion, and deception. The crossbow revolutionized tactics on the battlefield.

"In 221 BC, powerful states were unified into a centralized empire. The Imperial Era of Chinese history began with the Qin Dynasty. The origins of the Great Wall were built to keep out nomadic warriors from the north.

"By the end of the Han Dynasty (220 AD), there was massive territorial expansion north and south. The first chemical weapons were used in battle, with poisonous materials placed on crossbow ammunition.

"During the Three Kingdoms Period (184 to 304 AD), China was broken apart by agrarian uprisings into three separate states. There were many wars between northern and southern kingdoms until the late sixth century AD. The kingdoms were reunified in 589 AD, sparking a new golden era under the Sui and Tang Dynasties. There was a tremendous increase in military power through the late Tang Period, with development of gunpowder weapons in the early 10th century AD.

"In the Song Dynasty (960 to 1279 AD), gunpowder weapons - such as fire Lancers, iron bombs, and rockets - were employed in battle in large numbers with huge battlefield consequences. Repeating crossbows and flamethrowers were first introduced by Chinese troops. A standing navy was created and quickly became a regional maritime power.

"The Mongols invaded and conquered Song China in the 13th century, establishing the Yuan Dynasty (1279 to 1368 AD). Chinese cavalry began a transformation into the most powerful mobile force on the Asian continent.

"During the Ming Dynasty (1368 to 1644), the Mongols were driven out of China, and the empire expanded in all directions. Mongolia, Tibet, Xinjiang, Vietnam, and Sri Lanka came under Chinese rule. The Great Wall was completed. Although the Chinese defeated the Portuguese (1522) and the Dutch (1662) in battle, they began to lose their lead in gunpowder weapons to Western powers.

"The Qing Dynasty (1644 to 1911) started a long military decline into the 19th century. In the late 1800s, China began to modernize its military by mass producing reverse-engineered Western technology. In 1900, the Qing-supported Boxer Rebellion by Chinese peasants against Western nationals and Chinese Christians rampaged across North China. This caused an eight nation alliance of Austria-Hungary, France, Germany, Italy, Japan, Russia, United Kingdom, and the United States to intervene and suppress the anti-foreign Boxers by 1901. A long period of anti-Western national sentiment evolved in China."

Pfaeffle paused and poured a second cup of coffee. He buttered a croissant and ate it.

"Have you enjoyed your breakfast, Lieutenant Commander?"

"Yes, it was excellent," I answered.

The old soldier lit another cigarette and walked over to his roses. He clipped off a red one and placed it into a white porcelain vase on the table.

"Camilla loved red roses. Now, I do also..... It's been almost forty years without her..... It amazes me that I've been without her that long..... I don't seem to die, Stansfield. Although I wish and try to," sighed Pfaeffle, before inspiring deeply more tobacco smoke.

"It's strange really..... Sometimes I think if I die, her memory dies..... Perhaps that is the reason I am still breathing. I need her memory to live on, so I live on.....

It's paradoxical, Stansfield," lamented Pfaeffle in a low voice.

My tutor sat back down and continued his discourse.

"The first 41 centuries in China's history were certainly tumultuous, but they cannot compare to the 20th century, Lieutenant Commander. In this century, China has experienced both more destruction and construction than in all its previous history combined.

"In 1927, the Ten Years Civil War began between the Chinese Communists under Mao Zedong and Zhu De, and the Kuomintang Nationalists under Chiang Kai-shek. Mao's Red Army, the predecessor of the PLA, fought a bitter guerrilla war against the larger Nationalist Army until the Japanese invasion and the beginning of the Second Sino-Japanese War (1937 to 1945). Many millions of Chinese soldiers and civilians were killed in these wars. Mao's 'People's War' concept of military thought was born out of the Red Army's experiences in these wars. His three phases of warfare:

1) STRATEGIC DEFENSIVE WITHDRAWAL. The enemy is lured deep into one's own territory to overextend and isolate them.
2) STRATEGIC WAR OF ATTRITION. Superior numbers and high morale among the troops and local civilian population wear down the enemy in a long stalemate.
3) STRATEGIC OFFENSIVE. Transition of Red Army guerrilla warfare tactics to regular conventional warfare and defeat of a weakened demoralized enemy.

"Mao's military philosophy became Chinese military doctrine by 1945 and the defeat of Japan. During the

Chinese Civil War (1945 to 1949), the Red Army, now renamed the People's Liberation Army (PLA), defeated the Nationalists and established the People's Republic of China (PRC). Mao Zedong became the supreme leader of the Chinese people. Chiang Kai-Shek and the Nationalist government retreated to Formosa (Taiwan). The PLA began their transformation into a modern military force in 1950, after the signing of the Sino-Soviet Treaty of Friendship, Alliance and Mutual Assistance.

"In the Korean War (1950 to 1953), the PLA fought the United Nations Forces to a stalemate. However, serious deficiencies in air power, transportation, and supply logistics became evident. Also, unsupported infantry attacks against modern defensive battle positions led to thousands of Chinese dead. In 1951, the Soviets began a long program to improve PLA fighting capabilities. Homeland military industries were also started.

"After Stalin's death in 1953, the Chinese slowly became more dissatisfied with old Soviet technology and lack of access to nuclear bomb blueprints. This, coupled with Khrushchev's acceptance of coexistence with Western democracies, led Mao to withdraw his peasant revolutionary ideology from the Soviet sphere of influence.

"The Sino-Soviet split evolved. The Soviets withdrew their advisors from China in 1960, crippling the defensive industries. Mao reintroduced his doctrine of 'Men over Materials', and increased political control over the military.

"In 1962, China fought a one-month war with India over disputed territory along the Himalayan border. China's victory, despite the Soviet Union's assistance to India, led to their occupation of the Aksai-Chin area.

"In 1966, Mao set in motion his chaotic Cultural Revolution (1966 to 1976) to advance socialism and remove Capitalist influences from Chinese society. He quickly purged most of the military high command and many local government officials. It is estimated several million Chinese died during this period. Mao reasserted civilian control over the PLA by 1971, and disengaged the PLA from politics. He also shifted resources away from the military.

"Serious clashes occurred along the Sino-Soviet border in 1969, and have occasionally flared up to the present.

"In 1974, there were skirmishes between the PLA and South Vietnamese troops over the Paracel Islands. The Chinese attacked and occupied several islands. They have staked a claim over the South China Sea.

"Beginning last year in 1977, several crucial events have taken shape.

"First, Deng Xiaoping has resumed his position of PLA Chief of General Staff.

"Second, he has started a concentrated effort on military modernization, although placing more material priority on the development of agriculture, heavy industry, and science/technology. Deng Xiaoping is intent on developing China's economy first, and then financially feeding the military machine to superpower status.

"Finally, the third crucial event - and the reason for which you have been sent here, Lieutenant Commander - is impending war between China and Vietnam. Since America's departure from Indochina, both the Soviets and Chinese have positioned for control of Southeast

Asia. China supports the murderous Pol Pot and his Khmer Rouge regime in Cambodia, while the Soviets support Vietnam and their occupation of Laos.

"America considers all these nations as enemies. We prefer they annihilate each other slowly over time. At present, we may side slightly more with China because of her lack of involvement in European and Middle Eastern affairs.

"Intelligence reveals Vietnam is prepared to invade and occupy Cambodia. China is intent on teaching them a punitive lesson if this occurs, even if it risks a wider war with the Soviet Union.

"America doesn't believe the Russians will directly engage the Chinese. In fact, we suspect they'll have a difficult time simply supplying their Vietnamese allies in a war.

"We expect the PLA to have troubles with the Vietnamese Army, but they may still be able to cause them to withdraw from Cambodia. A Vietnamese withdrawal, and nothing less, would be considered a victory for the PLA. Short of that, Vietnam and Russia gain ground in a critical area for us, and the Chinese go scurrying off to get stronger.

"In the pure geopolitical short-term - America prefers a lazy, over-confidence building, satiating Chinese victory. It would slow down their military reforms. More likely, however, a bloody nose will embarrass and distress the PLA into even more aggressive changes for the future.

"The consensus for the long-term is that China will become the dominant power in Asia. They will come into conflict with the United States in the future. I presume you have been sent here to study the PLA in action. I'm sure the US Navy will be interested in your findings.

"Lieutenant Commander Stansfield, China is an extremely complex country with tremendous potential power. If they are successful in modernizing their economy, and creating wealth for their people, their military will likely become the most powerful on the planet. I don't have to explain the consequences of that to your country and the rest of the Free World."

Helmut Pfaeffle walked me to the door, and wished Olivia and I a healthy stay in Beijing. We would meet many times over the next three months to discuss Asian politics and Chinese culture. Pfaeffle would repeatedly stress the importance of America maintaining her presence in the western Pacific as the major counterweight to the growing military power of China. He predicted that by the early 21st century, China's economy would be pre-eminent in Asia, and they would begin to impose hegemonic control over Southeast Asia and the natural resources of the South China Sea. Loss of free navigation through this area would have negative consequences for America and the rest of the Free World.

He felt, that if America showed weakness in regional geopolitics, Japan would re-militarize and become another potential calamity point in the future. Japan needed to be kept within America's sphere of influence. Pfaeffle thought a reconstituted Japanese military could be more dangerous to the United States than the People's Republic of China.

On a cold night in early December, with French cognac and American cigarettes in hand, Pfaeffle expressed his nightmare scenario for the United States.

"The 1970s have not been good for America. It was forced to leave Vietnam in disgrace after a long brutal war. President Nixon resigned after the Watergate debacle. The Arab oil embargo and the presidency of Jimmy Carter have left the country in economic decline, with rising unemployment and inflation. Years may pass before America regroups and fully recovers.

"During these years of recovery, both the Soviets and Chinese will continue to strengthen and expand their influence throughout the world. America will emphasize countermeasures against the Soviet Union, the more powerful enemy. This, in turn, will catalyze China's ascent into superpower status by leaving her free to grow without effective control.

"In 25 years, the Soviets will likely be weaker and the Chinese Communists stronger. America will be riddled with the economic consequences of global military overextension. If the Chinese can form an alliance with their ancient trade partners in the Muslim Middle East, another economic pressure can be placed on the United States to weaken it beyond repair. Sun Tzu doctrine at its finest.

"Unfortunately, Julian, I believe all this will come to pass. America will see this in early evolution and create circumstances for a major conflict with China. They will first help build their economy and accustom them to a better quality of life. Then, they will try to destroy that economy in order to create internal strife and decomposition. The Chinese leaders will have read through this and will have prepared for the eventuality of war. I truly feel a major conflict with the People's Republic of China is inevitable in the not too distant future. I suspect you've been sent here as a forward scout to reconnoiter the landscape and write the book of war on China."

Like Aristotle had been to Alexander of Macedon in preparing him for war with Persia, Helmut Pfaeffle had been my sage in studies of the People's Republic of China and the PLA. By late December 1978, I had become well informed in the ways of the Chinese military.

All excursions into Beijing by Olivia and I were directed and controlled by the Chinese government. The government tour guide and two additional officials accompanied us any time we left the Swiss Embassy compound.

Olivia found the people of Beijing cold with flat affects. They seemed indifferent to practically everything in their lives. An apparent lack of passion and emotion, similar dress, and robotic behavior made them look almost plastic. The life in Beijing did not agree with Olivia's perspectives on human potential. The Chinese experience only made her anti-Communist attitudes sharper and more antagonistic. Yet, making love with me every day and night more than compensated her for being imprisoned in the Swiss Embassy of Beijing.

On Christmas Eve, a formal dinner was given at the Swiss Embassy. The diplomatic staffs of several Western nations attended the affair. The People's Republic of China sent a small delegation. Olivia and I were seated next to Helmut Pfaeffle at a table, with the French and British envoys and their wives.

Olivia wore a stunning red dress. Her entrance into the hall that evening was likely the highlight of the dinner for everyone attending. Her beauty and presence transcended all cultures, East and West.

"Let me say, Olivia, you look striking," said Helmut politely. "Your red dress must be making the Chinese Communists very happy. Red has never been more angelic! Watching your entrance this evening into the hall was one of the most regal events I have ever witnessed. People around me were initially speechless. Later, they could not stop talking about you," laughed Helmut.

"And I thought all the fuss was about me," I said.

"No, Julian. The fuss will always be about her," stated Helmut emphatically.

"Thank you, Helmut, for your kind words," said Olivia, smiling at everyone at the table.

After an elegant dinner with fine wine and song, Olivia and I retreated to a terrace overlooking the city of Beijing. Outdoor heaters kept the temperature comfortable. We sat and enjoyed a glass of Spanish Sherry.

A while later, Helmut and his secretary, Josephine, joined us for a nightcap.

"So, Helmut, do you think Julian may be able to return to the US with me next month?" asked Olivia.

"I'm not privy to the Lieutenant Commander's orders, my sweet darling. I'm not one to know the directions or desires of the American government," responded Pfaeffle innocently.

"I hope he'll be allowed to accompany me home," said Olivia. "All this war talk with Vietnam is unnerving. Do you think there'll be conflict, Helmut?"

"Although I wish for peace, I suspect there will be war between China and Vietnam," said Pfaeffle, looking at Julian. "The geopolitics of the region mandate it, I suppose."

I hushed him with my eyes and held Olivia's hand under the table. Olivia rarely asked such questions in a public setting, but she was worried for me.

Helmut Pfaeffle pulled out a small brass cylinder from his coat pocket. He handed it to Olivia.

"This is beautiful, Helmut. What is it?"

"It's a kaleidoscope. It was hand made by my father from Swiss alpine wood and centuries-old brass. It shows great craftmanship, I think. He gave it to me on my fifth birthday.

"Raise it to the light of the chandeliers, just inside of the terrace. Rotate the brass tube and wooden box. Observe the colorful patterns formed by the reflections of light off three small mirrors and loose bits of stained glass at the end. The patterns are very symmetric and geometric."

"They are gorgeous, Helmut," stated Olivia as she peered into the magic tube.

"The constantly changing patterns of colors in the kaleidoscope are much like the complicated changing circumstances in life, Olivia. It is difficult to predict what comes next. One must simply accept and enjoy the changes as much as possible.....

"One never knows when there will be war," said Helmut. "It is easier to predict the changes of weather on Jupiter....."

The old Swiss diplomat gently placed his hand on Olivia's wrist. He smiled at her and turned towards me.

"I do know, however, when there's love. And I see it in you and Julian. I wish you both the best. Enjoy the time you have remaining together in China. Think of peace, not war. Love strongly and remember these moments forever. They are fleeting....."

On Christmas Day 1978, the Vietnamese People's Army (VPA) invaded Cambodia. Within two weeks, they had taken the capital, Phnom Penh, and ousted Pol Pot's Khmer Rouge regime. Pol Pot escaped to Thailand, from where he would direct a guerrilla war against the occupying Vietnamese forces in Cambodia for ten years. Vietnam now controlled Laos and Cambodia, and had eliminated the Chinese presence in Indochina.

On January 26, 1979, Olivia returned to the Sierra family home on Key Biscayne, Florida. The next day, Captain Shang Wei arrived at the Swiss Embassy in Beijing to escort me to Guangzhou Military Regional Headquarters in Nanning - southern China, approximately 100 miles from the Vietnamese border. We had been assigned to the "East Front", 42nd Corps, 125th Infantry Division.

Five days later, Shang Wei and I were flown to an airstrip in southwestern Kwangsi province, ten miles from the Vietnamese border.

Captain Shang Wei was a humble but proud man in his late 30s, from the northwestern Chinese province of Gansu. He had studied at the Nanjing General Senior Infantry School, the predecessor of today's Nanjing Army Command College. He had fought in the Sino-Indian War in 1962. Shang Wei spoke fluent English and French, and was considered a rising star in the middle ranks of the PLA officer corps.

Much older than I, the Chinese captain quickly opened a dialogue. By the end of the third week together, we both felt comfortable with our pairing. We got to know each other well.

On the evening of February 16, 1979, Shang and I drank Chinese tea together after dinner.

"The Chinese nation is surrounded by enemies. We have the Soviets to our north, India to our southwest, the Vietnamese to our south, and the Americans in the Pacific. This will all change with time, Julian. Eventually, the Soviet Union will crumble economically; and her allies, India and Vietnam, will wither away..... But that still leaves America on our eastern shores," grimaced the PLA officer.

"There is a great difference in our approaches to war, Stansfield. Your greatest strength lies in the vast amount of military technology available to your war machine. The US has many ships and planes. Your vast inventory of missiles can destroy the world many times over.

"Yet, the American military has one major weakness – manpower. Your culture values life much more than ours, Stansfield. In battle, the Americans try to conserve manpower. We throw as much manpower at the enemy as necessary. We'll never run out of loyal and devoted soldiers. You will, Julian.....

"Numbers will dictate who inherits the earth of the future. Will your country have the stomach for that? We'll just have to wait and see what happens with America," smiled the Chinese officer.

"America fought for the right to have benevolent influence in Asia and the Pacific," I said. "We defeated the Japanese in the world war, and liberated your country and many others. If not for the United States, Japan's forces would have enslaved the entire continent and murdered many more millions of innocent people. My nation's presence in the western Pacific Ocean ensures fair and free trade across the region. We're a stabilizing force for future peace."

"Perhaps you see it that way, Julian, but the situation is sensed differently through others' eyes. America never considers the views of other nations.

"Chinese Communism evolved from poverty and the economic enslavement of my people at the hands of the West. We fought a long war of occupation against the mean-spirited and murderous Japanese. Our women and children were massacred by these animals. My country lost millions of citizens.

"China is paranoid of foreign powers. Historically, we have suffered greatly under them. Having your military forces close to our shores worries us. We do not like American influence at our doorsteps. If our submarines sailed regularly through the Bahamas and the Florida Keys, your government would be unhappy also. The time will come when we dictate who is invited near our waters.....

"But the issues dividing China and America are better left for the future. Your interests now are to observe the mighty PLA in action. My leadership wishes to allow this, so that America sees with her own eyes the power of our surging military.

"Tomorrow, we invade Vietnam and teach her a lesson that she will not forget. We will march to Hanoi and change Indochina forever. If the Soviets try to intervene, we will defeat them also. We have over two million men along the Sino-Soviet border prepared to fight the Russians. They will not get in our way."

I looked at Shang Wei quizzically and asked, "What happens if the Vietnamese defeat you? They are strong and brave, and fought the Americans valiantly for ten years. The VPA is well armed with Soviet equipment, and has a significant air force with MiG fighters. They fight to the death.

"What happens if the Soviets attack across your common border? Can China fight a modern war on two fronts against formidable enemies?"

"Julian, first let me assure you that the Soviets will not attack. We have intelligence reports indicating the Russians are likely to enter Afghanistan in force in the coming months. They do not want a costly war with China at the present time.

"As to your statements on the strength of the VPA, I agree. They are courageous fighters, but I believe we can conduct a meat grinder war that will bring them to their knees. However, there are Chinese junior officers who discreetly wish the PLA gets a bloody nose, forcing our leaders to invest more money in a modernization program and increase our strike force potential for the future."

We finished our tea and went to rest. Our viewpoints remained separate, but respectful. Chinese and American military officers were rarely in agreement on anything. Shang and I were no different. Yet, I could understand China's paranoia about the USA. If I was Chinese, and my family had lived, suffered, and died during the 19th and 20th centuries, I would be weary and wary also. I would feel uncomfortable with America's alliance with Japan, a country which had shown so much hatred towards my people in the past. It was difficult to heal such deep and crippling wounds. I certainly could see through Shang's eyes, although I hid this fact from him.....

I lay on a simple straw mattress and contemplated the next day's events. I had never seen live combat before. I was not afraid. I remembered my father's letter after Anzio, which Mother had given me to read on my sailing adventure to New York City as a young man.

Father and Mother had spent four months together in the middle of the Anzio Battlefield, patching up wounded American soldiers in a combat hospital. Their courage had become embedded in my mind. Before I fell asleep, I realized it was now my turn to perform under fire, and show the same courage they had exhibited so long ago. The love of my parents protected me into the night's rest, and escorted me into my dreams.....

The next morning, the PLA opened with a massive artillery barrage from the Chinese provinces of Yunnan and Kwangsi on key border positions inside Vietnam at Lao Cai, Muong Khuong, Cao Bang, Lang Song, and Mong Cai.

Shortly after, the Chinese Third Field Army under General Hsu Shih Yun - composed of 25 divisions and 250,000 infantry troops - crossed the Vietnamese border along a 480 mile stretch, attacking at 26 points. Columns of over 400 T59, T62, and T63 tanks, supported by dozens of MiG-19s, J-6s (Chinese copy of MiG-19), and J7s (Chinese copy of MiG-21), advanced in four major thrust lines towards the provincial capitals of Lao Cai, Cao Bang, Dong Dang, and Lang Son.

The Chinese hoped to draw the VPA's 300,000 regular troops into the invasion vortex and destroy them, forcing Vietnam to pull their 150,000 regulars from Cambodia in a desperate defense of Hanoi. Instead, the VPA ordered 100,000 local border militia into the fight, using guerrilla tactics in the difficult hilly and wooded terrain. The militia was supported by heavy artillery and squadrons of MiG-21s.

The VPA kept their regular army of 300,000 troops in a crescent-shaped defense of the Hanoi plains. The densest missile defense shield in history defended Hanoi and Haiphong. The 150,000 occupation force regulars in Cambodia were never drawn into the fight.

The numerically superior Chinese forces penetrated 30 miles into Vietnam but sustained heavy losses against the guerrilla tactics of the Vietnamese. The PLA was marred by poor mobility and communications, weak logistics, outdated weaponry, and an unclear chain of command.

In the west, the PLA soon captured Lao Cai - a railroad center of 100,000 population on the Red River which flows into Hanoi.

On February 19 in the east, Captain Shang Wei and I moved towards Lang Son, 90 miles from Hanoi. We travelled in a BJ-212, the poorly armored "Beijing Jeep". We were accompanied by 42,000 troops and over 110 T59 tanks. The Chinese captured the northern heights above Lang Son but paused for two days in front of the city, attempting to draw more Vietnamese regulars into the fight. The VPA, tipped off by Soviet satellite intelligence of the Chinese strategy, held their reserves around Hanoi. On March 1, the PLA attacked the city. After three days of bloody house to house fighting, Lang Son fell to the invaders. Cao Bang had been taken two days before.

After capturing the provincial capitals, and assessing their heavy losses, the Chinese high command judged an attack on Hanoi would be impossible. The PLA announced their punitive mission was complete.

On March 6, the invasion army began a slow retreat back into China. The withdrawal was characterized by a "scorched earth" policy, leaving a path of destruction 300 miles long.

On March 8, Shang Wei and I passed through Cao Bang. The BJ-212 ran over and detonated a TM-46 Russian antitank blast mine. The explosion destroyed the jeep, killing Shang instantly, and catapulting me thirty feet away into a clearing. I sustained a concussion, and mild periorbital trauma around my left eye. The injury eventually caused glaucoma, and years later, a central retinal vein occlusion. It led to the blindness and disfigurement of my left eye.

The seventeen-day war killed 26,000 Chinese troops and wounded another 60,000. Although never formally declared, Vietnamese casualties were similar.

The PLA felt badly mauled. They had suffered a heavy loss of men and equipment in a short war against a numerically inferior enemy composed of militia. They had not destroyed the regular Vietnamese Army. Most importantly, they had failed to draw Vietnam out of Cambodia, where they would stay until 1989.

The biggest lesson learned by the PLA in the Sino-Vietnamese War of 1979 was the need to modernize their army and battlefield tactics. Their army was large and motivated to win; but the paucity of modern military technology and lack of air power nullified their numerical advantage. Modernization would require capital expenditure. Deng Xiaoping had been correct in emphasizing economic reforms. Without money, the People's Liberation Army would never challenge the United States in Asia and the western Pacific.

The final report to Navy Intelligence at the Pentagon on my experiences with the PLA finished with the following comment:

As after the Russo-Japanese war in 1905, when American naval analysts turned their attention to the Empire of Japan, we must now begin to plan for war with the People's Republic of China. My four months spent in China and Vietnam have illuminated and underscored this probability.

The Sino-Vietnamese War was a stalemate, and not a clear victory for China. This will work in their favor eventually, by increasing their government's economic appropriations for military development.

Compared to Japan in 1905, China has much more power potential. Their communist ideology is significantly more profound and engrained in the culture than the nationalist sentiments in Japan in the early 20th century.

If they are successful in applying their ideological zeal to their economic, industrial, scientific, technological, and military reforms, it will project this heavily populated nation into the superpower category of nations in short order. Their abundance of manpower cannot be underestimated. It literally can move mountains.

I believe the Chinese will be more patient than the Japanese were in their march towards hegemony. It is in their culture and national spirit to be more patient and measured. They have studied the economic, diplomatic, and military errors committed by Japan earlier this century, and the PLA will not repeat them.

Deng Xiaoping's economic reforms are well directed and should, over time, lead to a prosperous situation for their people. Their military status will undoubtedly benefit from this financial growth.

China's power will be projected into the Pacific and will conflict with America's direct interests in this region. It is essential that America remains steadfast in her support of allied nations in the region, Japan and South Korea, and also slowly restart a dialogue with her most recent enemy, Vietnam, which can certainly provide a future counterbalance to China in South Asia.

If America's dominant military and economic presence in the region is weakened in the future, we can expect only an enhanced probability of conflict with the ever-growing power of the People's Republic of China. Any wobble in America's power base will be capitalized on by the PLA. Keeping our dominant position in the region is our only deterrent to major war.

US naval power will be the deciding factor in any conflict in this region. US naval air power and missile technology will be the greatest obstacle to Chinese expansionism.

The only scenario worse than America ruling the world, is a world ruled by anyone else.

I placed a request to the Pentagon for allowance of time at Princeton University's Center for Chinese Culture and Civilization. It was America's leading think center on all things Chinese. I also requested assignment to the Department of Defense's primary innovation engine, the Defense Advanced Research Projects Agency (DARPA). I hoped to work on offensive and defensive naval missile technology. Both requests were quickly granted.

In my last letter to Olivia from China, I wrote:

My darling Olivia, I'm finally coming home to you. I've missed you deeply. My heart and soul ache without you.

I'm returning with a clearer sense of what is in store for America in the future. I believe we will be tested more than at any other time in our history. It is my strong determination to prepare our country for an eventuality which I hope never comes.

You and I will continue to pray for 'peace on earth'. We'll hope for the better, kinder natures of man to reign over us. We'll work diligently to prevent war, so that the children of the world may escape hardship and sorrow. I wish only goodness and happiness for all.....

Like the amaranth, my love for you never dies..... I am eternally yours, Julian.

Olivia waited for me on Cape Florida, pregnant with our first child - Julius.

CHAPTER 21

Stardust

For small creatures such as we, the vastness is bearable only through love.

Carl Sagan (1934 to 1996)

IT WAS LATE AFTERNOON on May 12. Michael and Nasrin raced north from Tehran on Highway 59 towards Chalus, 130 miles away. Highway 59, known as Chalus Road, was one of the world's most scenic highways. It meandered through the Alborz Mountains towards the Caspian Sea, with dozens of mountain lakes and flower-filled valleys along the way.

Michael looked back through the side-view mirror at a black sedan, a few hundred feet behind them in traffic. Since passing the town of Karaj, he had noticed the car with its four male occupants. The four young men were of similar age, and all were bearded. Moments earlier, Michael had stopped at a highway station for petrol, and the sedan had also stopped across the street by a flower shop. The unusual thing was that the men hadn't bought any flowers.

The sedan passed cars to get closer behind the motorcycle. Stansfield sped up to 80 mph, and so did his pursuer.

"We've got company, baby!" shouted Michael at Nasrin, above the roar of the motorbike. "Hold on tight and don't let go!"

They entered a twisting section of the road, with multiple switchbacks, leading up to an elevated mountain pass. Michael slowed his speed and took the sharp turns low to the ground. The car continued to follow them intently.

As the empty road straightened for a good length, both Stansfield and his tail increased their speed. The men in the black sedan closed to within one hundred feet and accelerated alongside the motorcycle. Machine gun fire opened up from the backseat. A salvo hit Nasrin in the left upper thigh.

Nearing a sky bridge, the CIA specialist reached beneath his leather jacket and pulled a pistol from its shoulder harness. He fired multiple rounds into the car's front tires, causing it to lose control as it passed onto the bridge. The Iranian agents broke through a protective barrier and fell one thousand feet down into a ravine. Michael and Nasrin crossed safely to the other side, and took the first exit off Chalus Road.

They raced east onto a plateau, filled with red and white tulips as far as the eye could see. A bright blue sky hung overhead.

Michael stopped his motorcycle in a grassy clearing at the eastern edge of the altiplano. He placed Nasrin on her right side near a grouping of white tulips.

"How are you feeling, baby?" he asked, while stripping away her denim jeans.

"Super, considering I've been shot by a machine gun in the ass," answered Nasrin sarcastically.

Michael visually examined the wound in her lower lateral left butt cheek. He squeezed the flesh around the bullet hole.

"Shit!" screamed Nasrin. "It hurts, Michael!"

"No vital vessels have been damaged, and there's very little bleeding. It's a superficial flesh wound. Your ass still looks beautiful."

Stansfield retrieved the emergency medical kit from the bike. He poured alcohol on Nasrin's wound and on his stiletto. He put a gas lighter's flame to the knife's blade and quickly sterilized it.

"This may hurt a little," said Michael, as he dug into the wound with the sharp tip of the six-inch blade. He rapidly removed the bullet.

"It must've been a ricochet shot off the road asphalt. A direct hit from 100 feet would've nearly severed your leg. You would've bled out and died."

The CIA man carefully cleaned the wound with iodine solution. He placed antibiotic cream and a sterile dressing.

"We'll keep it clean and change the dressing every day. You'll be fine in a few days, Nasrin."

Michael retrieved a warm wool cover from the motorcycle's side compartment and laid it over his girl. The sun was setting behind the western mountains.

"I want you naked under that cover," smiled Michael, looking across the plateau and sky with his binoculars.

"Okay, macho man!"

"It's not that, Nasrin..... I want the wound to breathe."

"Sure thing, Cuba!" laughed Nasrin.

"At least you haven't lost a sense of humor, Persian princess....."

The sun lost itself behind the mountain range. The last rays of sunshine faded away in the cooling air. The blue sky darkened. Stansfield remained vigilant until nightfall.

"These bastards didn't have back-up. I wiped them out, and there's no one to pick up the pieces. There must be a lot going down for them to be sent alone. I can sense it in my bones, Nasrin. Big things are happening."

Michael sat down next to Nasrin and gently passed a white tulip across her lips. "The queen of flowers for my princess. The soft petals remind me of you. The tulip is very sexy."

"I have a second hole in my ass, Michael, and it doesn't belong there! I don't feel like making love right now!"

Both of them laughed uncontrollably for several minutes, before relaxing silently to enjoy the clear night sky. Every star was visible above them. To the south, they had a view of Tehran between two snow-capped peaks. They waited.

Michael and Nasrin lay together on the cool ground, observing the natural beauty. Occasionally, a shooting heavenly body would streak across the canvas of the gods. The white haze of the Milky Way was surreal.

"My job has taken me to many remote places. I've seen the stars from deserts, valleys, and mountaintops. They never cease to amaze me," said Michael.

"Do you believe in God?" asked Nasrin.

"I'm not a religious man..... But yes, I do believe in God."

"Why do you believe?"

"Well, because I look up into that mass of stars and interstellar gas above us, and can't conceive of how that came to be. Nor can I conceive of why it came to be. Perhaps, I don't wish to think it's all a chance occurrence. This magnificence we see around us can't be happenstance. I must believe in God.

"Furthermore, I don't fully understand man's position in the cosmos, Nasrin. I don't want to believe we're born into this greatness to eat, defecate, procreate, and die. We must be more than messengers of DNA, physical vessels to continue the life experiment on earth. Our minds are evolving for something more creative. Humankind has a purposeful destiny ahead, I reason. Having faith in God settles the spirit a bit. There must be some higher force responsible for all of this.

"I wish I could give you a more material answer, Nasrin, but I can't. I don't understand the causality of the Universe, or man's existence in it. Nor can I prove the existence of God to myself. My belief is a spiritual one. I prefer to be hopeful.

"I don't think God's intention was for mankind to spend their time on earth destroying themselves over differences of opinion. Battles of race, religious creed, and tribal political ideology have troubled us for thousands of years. I suspect the 'Creator' wants more out of us than what we've provided. God is waiting to see more humility and less pride, more compassion and less cruelty, more love and less hate.....

"I look at the beauty of the sky above us, and I sense the presence of God. It makes me hopeful mankind will evolve to a greater glory. The full creative benevolent potential of our minds should be the ultimate destiny....."

"With what I know of the Universe, I must believe in God," said Nasrin. "It is simply too grand to have come about without a plan, Michael. The cosmos is not a biophysical accident.

"Look at the Milky Way band across the sky. There are hundreds of billions of stars in our galaxy. It is 100,000 light years across. If you could travel at 186,000 miles per second, Michael, it would take you over 100,000 years to see the full extent of it. The distances are unfathomable.

"Our tiny solar system and the Earth are an insignificant speck in the Milky Way. There are hundreds of billions of more planets.

"Beyond our galaxy, there are hundreds of billions of more galaxies. Each one has billions or trillions of stars. Even more amazing, our galaxy is racing through space at 350 miles per second. All the stars and planets of the Universe are in a gravitational fast-dance through the blackness. This music could only have been composed by God.

"It was my love of the stars as a little girl that led me to study physics. The Universe is a magical place, Michael, and it's governed by the laws of physics.

"Young stars are born, composed mainly of hydrogen and helium. As they age billions of years, they begin to die. Eventually, they implode upon themselves. The massive heat releases heavier elements such as carbon, oxygen, nitrogen, phosphorus, sulfur, iron, and all the other elements required for life in the Universe. These elements disperse throughout space, and in the course of time, settle on other celestial objects such as our Earth. They begin to combine in mysterious ways and give rise to all the variations of life that we see on our planet.

"You and I, and everything else alive on Earth, are made of stardust, Michael. Our life cycles are dependent on the stars' life cycles since the beginning of time. That reality is the reason why I dedicated my life to physics."

Michael and Nasrin kissed gently.....

"What do you think will happen now, Michael?"

"An ugly, bloody war, Nasrin..... Conflict is inevitable."

"How bad will it be?"

"Very bad..... America does not conduct war softly, Nasrin. Many people will die. Many of your countrymen and mine will see their final days. Civilian losses will also be great, I regret. Iranians may have more to fear from their own government repression than American attack. Adel Zia expects this, and his resistance fighters are prepared."

"I feel somewhat responsible for this calamity," said Nasrin in a hushed voice.

"What do you mean?"

"I got the information that started this mess," she said.

"This mess began a long time ago," stated Michael. "Unimpeded, many more people would die in the future, perhaps millions more. You got me the data we needed to initiate termination of the reckless regime in your country. If war is to come, better now than later. In the end, your work will have saved lives, Nasrin."

"Will America use nuclear weapons?"

"Yes..... Ground penetrators to destroy the underground facilities in Iran. It's the only way to close down these missile factories. There will be only limited nuclear fall-out."

"How about the cities, Michael?"

"Only if our cities in America are attacked."

"Do you think civilian populations will be nuked?" she asked again.

"I don't want to think that," he answered.....

There was a sudden flash to the south. A loud explosion echoed throughout the mountain valley. Fires over Tehran became visible between the two snow capped peaks. Multiple small mushroom clouds rose into the sky, obscuring the stars. The American assault on the Iranian regime had begun.....

Briefly before 10 PM, four Ohio class submarines - the *USS Florida* in the eastern Mediterranean, the *USS*

Tennessee in the Arabian Sea, the *USS Kentucky* 300 miles south of Sri Lanka in the Indian Ocean, and the *USS Maine* in the Philippine Sea - had fired multiple "hit to kill" kinetic ballistic missiles at Iranian and Chinese military and commercial orbiting satellites. Much of the enemy's GPS capabilities had been extinguished.

Coordinated cruise missile attacks from Aegis cruisers and destroyers in the eastern Mediterranean, the Black Sea, and the Persian Gulf, delivered their 1000 pound warheads at 600 mph on Iranian government ministry buildings, military installations, airfields, and oil facilities.

Two Ohio class cruise missile submarines in the Arabian Sea each fired more than 75 Tomahawks at nuclear facilities throughout Iran. The heavy water plant at Arak, the nuclear power station at Bushehr, and the uranium conversion plant at Isfahan were each hit with dozens of cruise missiles. The uranium enrichment plants at Qom and Natanz were also targeted in the early hours of hostilities.

F-22 Raptor squadrons, based out of Iraq, Kuwait, Saudi Arabia, Bahrain, Oman, and Afghanistan, were joined by F-35 Lightnings from the *USS George Washington* and *George H.W. Bush* Carrier Strike Groups in the Persian Gulf, and the *Harry S Truman* in the Arabian Sea. Coordinated stealth assaults on nuclear facilities were conducted.

Over Tehran, ten F-22s and twenty-five F-35s, all invisible to enemy radar, slipped past the Iranian integrated air defense systems composed of mobile radar networks and surface-to-air missile batteries (SAM). A diversionary force of MQ9 Reaper unmanned combat aerial vehicles (UCAV), flying slowly at 300 mph, turned on the Iranian radars. Russian-made SA 23 rockets, travelling at over 2000 mph, destroyed most of the Reaper decoys. However, active Iranian radar positions were plotted by the F-35s, which fired a barrage of AGM 88 HARM anti-radiation missiles at the detection stations. The F-35s also jammed some remaining radars and prevented the integrated defense systems from firing more SA 23s.

As the F-35s conducted ground attacks, the F-22s provided air superiority cover. A dozen MiG-29s and eighteen SU-30 flankers approached the F-22s from the northwest. Invisible to enemy radar, the F-22s fired multiple AIM-120 D intermediate distance air to air missiles at the approaching planes. The internally radar-guided missiles with 45 pound warheads downed half of the MiG-29s and twelve of the Flankers. The surviving Iranian jets quickly retreated to the south.

Sixteen approaching MiG-35s were also engaged by the American F-22s and F-35s with AIM-120 D rockets. The MiG-35s were able to jam some of the AIM-120 Ds, and only two MiGs were shot down. The remainder got within infrared visual range and were able to fire their Archer II short-range missiles at the Americans. The heat-seeking Archers downed two F-35s and one F-22, before the American AIM-9X Sidewinder infrared seeking missiles destroyed nine of the remaining fourteen MiG-35s. The survivors also retreated south.

An Iranian computer aided low-frequency radar locked onto an F-35 Lightning and fired an SA 23 ballistic missile at it successfully.

After an hour of combat, four of the 35 American planes had been lost. Twenty-nine Iranian fighters had been destroyed. The integrated air defense systems (IADS) over Tehran had been completely disrupted.

At 11 PM, four B-2 Spirit stealth bombers flew over Tehran and dropped over three hundred 500-pound bombs on the Khojir nuclear missile research site and the Tehran Nuclear Research Center. Shortly after, five B-52 bombers from Diego Garcia dropped ground penetrating tactical nuclear bunker buster bombs into the nuclear facilities in Tehran. The sky over Tehran was lit by immense light.

Michael and Nasrin stared hypnotically at the fiery spectacle, framed by the two snowy peaks. Nasrin held Michael's hand and cried, "It is shocking the same brilliant minds that decipher the universal laws of nature, and explain the codes of life, can also create so much destruction. This schizophrenia will lead to our demise. The world is destined for extinction, Michael....."

Man and woman mounted their motorcycle, and continued on their road to Chalus. They left behind the lights over Tehran. The haze of the Milky Way had become invisible to them. Dense smoke and fallout obscured their view. An electrical storm formed in the sky over the valley. The sounds of bombs and thunder mixed in the air. Hell had come to Iran.

The Persian princess gripped her knight tightly. She was afraid of what awaited the world. She smelled the distant fires in the cold air, and wept for her country and for humanity. Nasrin rested her head on Michael's back and allowed her tears to roll down the black leather of war.

Before daybreak, the pair arrived at the Caspian seaside villa safe house. Adel Zia's offer would provide some peace for a while.

The house was surrounded by a ten foot high concrete block privacy wall. The front gate was built of reinforced iron. Michael unlocked the entrance and rolled his bike into the compound.

The two-story mansion was built in the classical Greek style with large fluted Doric columns. The roof was shingled with red clay tiles. Large lion head gargoyles stood at the corners of the roof-line, facing the entry courtyard. The front lawn had several classical sculptures arranged around a fountain garden. The grounds appeared neglected, as if no one had been there in quite a while.

Michael and Nasrin entered the home and made their way towards the back. They found a large seaside terrace with an empty swimming pool, and a dock with a boathouse. Inside the enclosure was a formidable looking speedboat.

Stansfield looked out over the Caspian Sea and thought of Adel Zia. He wondered about his friend's security, and whether he was engaged in the resistance fight for which he had been planning so long. Zia had offered this home in a noble attempt to get Michael and Nasrin out of Iran safely, so they could raise their children in freedom. Michael quietly prayed for Adel Zia, and for his survival in the developing Iranian democratic struggle.

The young couple returned to the villa for rest. They would plan their escape later, after a few hours of sleep. Michael was certain the Caspian Sea would quickly fill up with refugees, trying to escape Iran after the Allied land invasion. He would plan their escape to coincide with the refugee exodus.

At 5:30 AM on May 14, the Allies entered Iran from Azerbaijan (US First Infantry Division), Iraq (US Third and

Fourth Infantry Divisions, British First Armored and Second Infantry Divisions), Balochistan (US Fourth Marine Division), and Afghanistan (US First Armored Division).

At 7 AM, the US Second Marine Division assaulted northwestern Persian Gulf beaches, just north and south of Bushehr - Iran's chief seaport. Simultaneously, elements of the US Sixth Marine Division landed on beaches near Bandar Lengeh, and five miles west of Jask in southeastern Iran (western and eastern approaches to the Strait of Hormuz).

At 10 AM, the US 82nd and 101st Airborne Divisions parachuted into Dasht-E-Kavir - the "Great Salt Desert" - 200 miles southeast of Tehran. They were joined there by the US First Armored Division, which had crossed from Afghanistan five hours before.

A total of 240,000 first wave Allied assault troops were engaged in heavy combat throughout Iran. The United States had complete control of the skies and absolute domination of the seas.

Nevertheless, Michael and Nasrin's escape odyssey would be extremely perilous. Potential calamity could come from other refugees trying to commandeer their boat, or fire from Iranian gunship patrols along the Caspian coastline. Air attacks from both Iranian and Allied fighters were also major dangers. Yet freedom was calling, and there was no time to waste.

CHAPTER 22

Charybdis

A ship-devouring monster in classical Greek mythology, identified with a whirlpool off the north coast of Sicily.

The Odyssey-Homer (8th century BC)

PENTAGON INTELLIGENCE Bulletin No. 1741, May 14, 0837 Hours Washington Time, 1707 Hours Tehran Time, *Operation Climb Mount Olympus..... Code Bucephalus* in progress, Allied land invasion of Iran meeting intense resistance on the ground..... Air cover of F-18, F-22, and F-35 fighters over invasion routes little opposed..... US First Infantry Division crossed border from Azerbaijan into northwestern provinces of Iran near Caspian coast, racing to Rasht - northwest of Tehran..... From US bases in northeastern Iraq - east of Sulaymaniyeh and Kirkuk - US Third Armored and Fourth Infantry Divisions speed towards Kermanshah, Hamedan, Arak, and Qom, on way to Tehran..... From bases near Iranian border - southeast of Baghdad - US Third Infantry Division attacking Khorramabad, with plans to march towards Isfahan, Natanz, and Kashan..... CIA-supported Kurdish rebels disrupting communications and Iranian troop transports behind front lines in northwest provinces..... From Basra in southeastern Iraq, British First Armored and Second Infantry Divisions passed into oil-rich Iranian province of Khuzestan, rolling south towards seaport and nuclear reactor in Bushehr; SAS-led ethnic Arab rebels bombing munition depots and Iranian military bases behind enemy lines..... From Camp Patriot/Kuwaiti Naval Station, US Second Marine Division transported to landing beaches on Kharg Island and Bushehr; heavy fighting around offshore oil terminals and Iranian naval base..... From Bahrain, 10,000 Marines/Sixth Marine Division landed at Bandar Lengeh on Iranian mainland, west of Strait of Hormuz; another 8000 Marines/Sixth Marine Division from Oman assaulted beaches west of Jask, near eastern approaches to Strait of Hormuz..... US Fourth Marine Division race from Pakistani Balochistan towards Chabahar, east of Jask on Iranian coastline; plan to meet up with 6th Marines at Jask and move onto Bandar Abbas on Strait of Hormuz..... From bases west of Herat, Afghanistan, US First Armored Division crossed into plains of eastern Iran and Great Salt Desert of Dasht-E-Kavir, rendezvousing with 82nd and 101st Airborne Divisions..... Heavy losses, men and material, on both sides, in all areas of operations..... STOP.....

By mid afternoon on May 14, the Persian world was embroiled in a hell of a mess. Frenetic activity dominated the landscape from all sides. There were 240,000 Allied assault troops heavily engaged with Iranian forces throughout Iran. The 700,000 Iranian regulars, 400,000 Basij paramilitary militia, and 250,000 Iranian Revolutionary Guards were a formidable fighting force. The well trained and armed Guard Corps were particularly fierce warriors. Armed to the teeth with Russian and Chinese weaponry, they were fanatically loyal to the theocratic regime. Two full divisions of IRGC, "the Lovers of Martyrdom Garrison", were suicidal bombers used against advancing Allied armored columns.

In the northern Persian Gulf, the *George Washington* Carrier Strike Group defended the Marine landings on Kharg Island and Bushehr. The *George HW Bush* Carrier Strike Group in the southern Persian Gulf, and the *Harry S*

Truman Carrier Strike Group in the Gulf of Oman, covered the Marine landings at Bandar Lengeh and Jask, as well as the assault on Chabahar.

Additionally, the *Truman* was blockading the Chinese fleet at Gwadar, Pakistan, and assisting the US operations in Balochistan against the Pakistani army and 5000 Chinese troops flown down from Xinjiang. The US commando raids on the Karakoram Highway had prevented the PLA from moving several divisions south into Balochistan. This had freed up the US Fourth Marine Division to deploy into southeastern Iran in support of the Sixth Marine Division.

On the first day and night of combat operations in the Persian Gulf, sea mines in the Strait of Hormuz had claimed two US destroyers and the lives of 160 Americans. No oil tankers had been sunk.

By the third day, minesweepers had cleared the ship traffic lanes through the strait. Iranian and Chinese Houdang fast attack boats with C802 anti-ship missiles had damaged a guided missile cruiser and sunk a minesweeper in the southern Gulf, with over 200 more U.S. Navy sailors killed.

On May 15, the *George Washington* was hit by a Chinese-made DF-21 ballistic anti-ship missile from a mobile launcher several hundred miles away in south-central Iran. Nearly 300 sailors and officers were lost, but the surviving crew saved the ship and continued flight operations.

SCUD C and D missiles from mobile launchers and underground silos hit several friendly targets in Iraq, Azerbaijan, Kuwait, Saudi Arabia, and Oman, including Allied military bases and Gulf oil facilities.

Shahab-3 medium-range ballistic missiles, fired from underground silos in Iran, hit targets in Baku Azerbaijan, Baghdad, Kuwait City, Riyadh, Bahrain, and Muscat Oman. Four Shahab-3 missiles landed in Tel Aviv. There were several thousand civilians and Allied military personnel killed in the rocket attacks.

In the northern Gulf, a Kilo class Russian-made diesel electric submarine torpedoed and sunk a British destroyer with the loss of 160 fighting men.

By May 19, Iranian losses in the Persian Gulf included 10 frigates, 5 submarines, and over 80 fast boats. More than 2000 Iranian Navy personnel had been killed.

After the first five days of combat on land, more than 900 Allied troopers had lost their lives. Many of them died in fighting outside of Rasht in the north, and Khorramabad, Khuzestan province, Bushehr, and Bandar Abbas in the south.

At least 30,000 Iranian soldiers had been killed, mostly by air assaults on large massed troop concentrations. Hundreds of Iranian KIA came in suicide attacks against American tanks and armored personnel carriers.

The Allies had lost 68 tanks and combat vehicles. Over 500 Iranian hard tracks had been destroyed, most of them in an apocalyptic tank battle against the US First Armored Division in the Great Salt Desert on May 15.

Both sides had fought valiantly, but the Allies were well positioned after the first five days of *Code Bucephalus*.....

On the morning of May 14 in the eastern Mediterranean - after a night of aerial bombardments of military targets in Syria and Lebanon by the air forces of the United Kingdom, France, Turkey, and Israel - *Code Coeur de Lion* was activated. The operation - named after Richard the Lionheart ~ King of England from 1189 to 1199, Duke of Normandy, Duke of Aquitaine, great military leader, and the central Christian commander of the Third Crusade against the Saracens and their famous warrior king, Saladin - was an Allied marine and paratrooper invasion of the northern and central Levant region to rid it of Persian influence.

Highly accurate naval bombardments - after air to ground attacks by British F-35 Lightnings from the HMS Queen Elizabeth ~ a 66,000 ton super-carrier, and French Rafales from the nuclear powered Charles de Gaulle - destroyed most of the enemy defenses along the southern Syrian and Lebanese coasts.

Syrian MiG-23s, 25s, and 29s engaged in dogfights with the F-35s, Rafales, and Israeli F-15s and F-16s. Before the amphibious landings, more than two dozen MiGs splashed into the Mediterranean Sea. The Allies lost only one French Rafale.

An SA 18 SAM missile, shoulder-fired by Hezbollah ground troops south of Beirut, downed an Israeli F-16 over a densely populated area of the city.

Katyusha-122 rockets from coastal defenses in Tripoli sunk a French landing craft filled with troops. Two C802 anti-ship missiles struck a British guided missile destroyer, sinking her in less than ten minutes with few survivors.

At 6:50 AM, 3000 British Royal Marines from "3" Commando Brigade and over 5000 French troops from the First Mechanized Brigade began landing on beaches south of Beirut.

At Tripoli, 9000 combined troops of the French Army Special Forces Brigade and the French Second Armored Brigade met stiff resistance from over 5000 Iranian Revolutionary Guard Quds Force commandos.

The French Third Mechanized Brigade landed at Tartus, Syria, and quickly pushed back a defending Syrian Special Forces Regiment off the beaches.

As Hezbollah, Islamic Jihad, and IRGC-Quds forces fired Katyusha rockets into northern Israeli towns, Fajir-5 missiles began striking in Haifa further south; and several Zelzal-1 missiles landed in heavily populated areas of Tel Aviv.

Led by Merkava MK4 tanks, over 57,000 IDF Northern Corps troops quickly struck into Syrian territory from the Golan Heights. Their objective, Damascus, was only 40 miles away. Fifty thousand additional IDF forces crossed into Lebanon, and sped towards Tyre and Sidon.

The Allied plan in Lebanon was to trap the defending force of 56,000 Hezbollah, Islamic Jihad, Syrian, and Iranian Revolutionary Guard troops in a pincer between advancing IDF forces from the south and east, and the combined British and French Expeditionary Force from the north.

The heaviest and most dramatic fighting occurred in the Lebanese Bekaa Valley around the town of Baalbek, and in Adra, Syria - a mountainside town 15 miles northeast of Damascus. The Syrians had fortified SCUD missile bases at these locations with in-ground silos. Only 30 miles separated the bases. The SCUD C and D missiles were targeted toward Haifa and Tel Aviv in Israel.

At 4 AM, almost 3 hours before the Allied beach landings, Israeli Air Force C-17s dropped over 1300 35th Brigade paratroopers from a low altitude of 400 feet into the valley southwest of Adra. Armored personnel carriers (APCs), and Stryker and Namer infantry fighting vehicles, were also delivered by parachute.

Nine Sikorsky CH 53 heavy helicopters transported an additional 450 paratroopers to more mountainous terrain northeast of Adra. Twenty Apache attack helicopters provided air protection for the Sikorskys, firing their full complement of Hydra 70 and Hellfire air to ground rockets at fortified bunkers scattered along the hillsides. Two battalions of Syrian Special Forces defended the SCUD base. Within two hours, every silo and their contents had been destroyed.

At the same time, 30 miles to the northwest, across the Anti-Lebanon Mountains and into the northern Bekaa Valley, an assault on the ancient Roman sacred fortress town of Baalbek began. East of the Litani River (River of Lions), the classic Roman ruins of the Temples of Jupiter, Venus, and Bacchus sat at over 3800 feet elevation, facing the Bekaa Valley to the south. A World Heritage Site, Baalbek - known in ancient times as Heliopolis or City of the Sun, contained the largest and best preserved Roman ruins outside of Western Europe.

Descending into this "City of the Sun", next to the River of Lions, were dozens of military transport aircraft flying from the island of Cyprus. A vertical envelopment by 4700 French paratroopers from the 11th Brigade and 3000 French Army Chasseurs Alpins (Alpine Hunters) dropped from the sky at low altitude. Their dark gray parachutes were invisible against the cloudy night sky. French and British light tanks and APCs were dropped as well. French Rafales from the Charles de Gaulle and British Lynx Wildcat attack helicopters from the HMS Ocean assault ship provided air cover over the Bekaa Valley.

Five British Chinook transport helicopters ferried 240 members of the British Special Boat Service (SBS) from the HMS Ocean and onto the Roman ruins of Baalbek. They were met by 230 commandos of Shayetet 13 (S13) - the elite marine raider unit of the Israeli Navy.

The S13 Raiders were led by their famous commander, Ariel Peled, a 52-year-old veteran and the most decorated fighter in the history of the IDF. Two years before, he had refused the position of Commander-in-Chief of the Israeli Navy to remain in his combat role with S13. His men loved him and would have followed him anywhere on his command. On this day, they found themselves in combat with two Syrian Special Forces Regiments on the Roman ruins of Baalbek.

Lower in the valley, one mechanized division and two armored brigades of the Syrian Army defended the Bekaa Plain. They were joined by over 1000 Hezbollah fighters under the direction of Iranian Revolutionary Guard commanders. Over 200 tanks, including fifty-two T72s, were under Syrian command.

Shortly after 4 AM, a vicious battle began at Baalbek which continued until noon. Armed with US-made "Javelin" self guided antitank missiles, the Allied troops destroyed every Syrian tank in the northern Bekaa Valley. Higher above, among the ruins of the Roman temples, the British and S13 commandos engaged a fierce and determined enemy. The defending forces of the SCUD base literally fought to the last man.

As the S13 Raiders entered the encampment in an assault on the final two silos, Ariel Peled was shot in the head by a sniper and killed instantly. His body was carried to the base of the six remaining Corinthian columns at the Temple of Jupiter and wrapped in an Israeli battle flag. The bodies of his boys also killed were delicately placed around him. The 65 foot tall columns of the 'King of the Gods', built in the first century A.D. by Caesar Augustus - the first emperor of the Roman Empire, helped shadow the dead from the early afternoon sun. Just as Peled would have wished, his body was the last to be evacuated from the field of battle while his men sang "Shir Ha Shalom".

By 3 PM in the Bekaa Valley, over 8000 enemy troops had been killed, 12,000 had been captured as prisoners of war. The French had lost 920 killed in action. Forty members of the British SBS had been killed. Thirty-nine S13 commandos had lost their lives, including their beloved commander Ariel Peled - "The Lion of Baalbek".

The battles of Baalbek and Adra had eliminated the fixed SCUD threat on Israel's cities. Most of the mobile SCUD launchers had been destroyed by Allied air forces by the end of the first day of combat.

In the northern Syrian front, the VI and VII Corps of the Turkish Second Army advanced on Latakia, Aleppo, Idlib, and Homs. The fighting in the north had been less intense than the south.

By May 20, the bulk of the organized Syrian Army had been destroyed in the field by the Allies. However, thousands of Syrian irregulars, Hezbollah, and IRGC fighters remained in the southern front, engaged in brutal guerrilla warfare.

Late in the evening of May 20, I sat in my office at the Pentagon reviewing all the incoming intelligence with Lieutenant Commander Stevens. It had been a long and sad day for me. Earlier, I was informed that my good friend, Ariel Peled, had been killed in the raid on Baalbek.

"I must call Ariel's wife, Nava, in Jerusalem," I said quietly, before lighting a cigarette and stepping away from my desk.

I walked slowly towards the wall with several photographs of acquaintances from my career in the Navy. I focused on a black-and-white picture taken by Olivia in 2003, of Ariel and I saluting the *Tomb of the Unknown Soldier* at Arlington National Cemetery.

"How well did you know Commander Peled, Admiral?" asked Stevens, still seated at the desk behind me.

"Very well..... He was like a younger brother, Louis."

"I see, Sir," said the young officer, with his voice fading at the end.

I felt another tightness in my chest. It quickly spread down my left arm, tingling my hand. I opened and closed it several times, and the discomfort ebbed away. Louis noted my action.

"How do you do it, Sir?"

"Do what, Louis?" I said, still staring at the photograph.

"All the things you do, Admiral, for your country under the circumstances."

"What circumstances?"

"Your health, Sir....."

I turned and looked at him..... I could see the regret in his eyes for having asked such a personal question. He was actually afraid of my response.

I smiled at Louis and did not say a word. I returned my eye to the photograph and allowed my mind to bleed into it. I thought back to the first time Ariel and I met.

We were both young men from similar backgrounds. Although from different religions and cultures, we saw things more similarly than you would have expected.

In October of 1990, shortly after the Iraqi invasion of Kuwait, I was asked to go to Jerusalem to meet with Major General Uri Harkabi - head of Aman - the Israeli Military Intelligence Directorate. We were to discuss Iraq's mobile SCUD missile launchers, and the possibility they would be used against Israel with chemical and biological weapons. US naval aviators would target these launchers early in the Desert Storm campaign, beginning on January 17, 1991. The United States wanted assurance from Israel that they would not retaliate militarily if attacked with SCUDs. We felt an Israeli response would hurt the Arab Coalition we had worked so hard to develop.

Ariel Peled was an intelligent and confident assistant to General Harkabi. He was assigned responsibility for my well-being in Jerusalem. We spent much time together, discussing world geopolitics and life in the Middle East.

While younger than I, he had an old soul and much in common with me. We became instant friends, later visiting each other with our wives on multiple occasions over the years. Olivia was very fond of him. She considered him a consummate gentleman.....

"Can I get anything for you, Sir?" asked Louis anxiously.

"No, son..... It passed..... I'm fine....."

I took a long drag from my cigarette, tempting death to come for me again. He didn't return. I had scared off the 'Grim Reaper' yet one more time.....

"Louis, have you put my request in to Admiral Turner at the Office of Chief of Naval Operations (CNO)?"

"Yes Sir, I have.

"I don't think he'll be happy with your request to be transferred to Guam and participate in the battle for Taiwan, Admiral."

"I don't know why..... Vice Chief of Naval Intelligence, Admiral Culligan, is qualified to maintain the pace here at the Pentagon. Besides, I would be plugged in while on the fleet flagship. I could respond to any emergency just as easily as if still here in Washington. I'm in my sixties, for God's sake. How could I be that indispensable, Louis?" I asked angrily.

I took another deep drag on my cigarette and continued to stare at Olivia's black-and-white photograph.

"How about my sons, Louis?" I asked in a low voice.

"I spoke with Mark's doctor at Bethesda earlier today. He's improving from the urosepsis he developed two nights ago. Mark should leave the intensive care unit in the next 3 to 4 days, if there are no more setbacks.

"Julius and the *USS Oregon* were detoured, and are now off the coast of northern Vietnam. They're involved in a convoy action to support the Vietnamese offensive into southern China. Several attack subs have been grouped in a Tomahawk land attack missile (TLAM) assault on Chinese positions north of the Vietnamese border. After this mission, he's been ordered back to Subic Bay for resupplying before deployment to the Taiwan Strait.

"There's no word on Michael. We know he's still in Iran. His whereabouts are unknown, Admiral."

"Unknown..... I don't like that word," I whispered......

"Unknown?" I quietly asked myself, as I faded again into the photograph before me.....

On the last day of my trip to Jerusalem in 1990, Ariel Peled drove me to the airport early in the morning.

"Tell me about your family, Ariel."

"I married the love of my life and have two young daughters," he said proudly. "Nava, my wife, and I have decided to raise our family here in Jerusalem."

"How did you decide on a career in the military?" I asked.

"When I was a small child, my father was killed in the Six-Day War in 1967. He was a tank commander in the Golan Heights offensive.

"My brother Benjamin, a naval commando, was killed in southern Lebanon in 1982, while on a mission to destroy a Hezbollah communications center.

"I was the only man left in my family. I felt a duty to do my part in defending Israel.

"How about you, Captain Stansfield? Why did you become a career naval officer?"

"My father's father was a lieutenant in the 42nd Infantry RAINBOW Division under the command of Brigadier General Douglas MacArthur in France during World War I. He was killed in action when my father was a young boy. His body was never recovered.

"I remember as a child, my father would take my brother and I to Washington to see the *Tomb of the Unknown Soldier* at Arlington. My father truly believed my grandfather was buried there. I still make that pilgrimage very often to pray for both of them, and all the other boys killed in our wars of the past.

"My father was a military surgeon in World War II. He served two years in the Italian campaign. He died young, a short time after my brother Bobby died of rheumatic heart disease. I too was the only man left in my family.....

"I was taught by my father to respect the military life. After his death, I decided to follow that course," I explained.

"You know, Captain Stansfield, Israel doesn't have a Tomb for the Unknown Soldier.....

"In Israel, the living citizens are the unknown warriors. They do their part every day to make Israel a safer and better place to live. They pay taxes, educate their children, and support the Israeli Defense Force.

"There are too many unknown Jews buried throughout Central and Eastern Europe from the Holocaust. We do not want our soldiers to be unknown like those buried in Europe in unmarked graves. Every IDF soldier killed in action is repatriated back home, even if only small sacred pieces are left. Each warrior receives a hero's burial, and a name is always placed on the tombstone. The only unknowns in Israel are the collective citizenry."

At the time, I thought of how different this behavior seemed when compared to the individualism in the image-conscious societies of America and Western Europe. In the Western democracies, the citizenry rarely wanted to be unknown.

Olivia frequently reminded me of this story. She also believed that the unknown socially responsible citizens formed the backbone of democracy. The fabric of our society was woven and maintained by them. They were few in numbers but strong in spirit.

Through the years, the Peled and Stansfield families grew closer. We supported each other in times of crisis.

I would greatly miss my dear friend, Ariel......

I slowly returned to the present from my past.... I stepped back away from the photograph a few paces and took the last puff from my cigarette.

The concept of the 'Unknown' was uncomfortable for me. It had been this way since I was a child. I had never outgrown the discomfort of the thought.

"Unknown?" I repeated to Louis.

"Yes Sir. We don't know where Michael is. His status is unknown..... I'm sorry, Admiral....."

I lit another cigarette and looked over at my young aide.

"I'm going to tell you a story, Louis..... I haven't meditated on it for many years; but my concerns for the whereabouts of my son, and Olivia's photograph of Ariel, have reminded me of an event many years ago.

"In the summer after my brother's death, my father and I took a sailing trip into Lake Superior. I was eleven years old, and had been deeply hurt by Bobby's passing. We spoke much about him, while hooking north along Michigan's Upper Peninsula into the recesses of Wisconsin's northern coast. Although my father knew the region, I had never travelled this deep into Lake Superior.

"We experienced turbulent weather as we neared the Apostle Islands National Lakeshore. Large waves produced giant plumes of white spray and loud blasting sounds as they crashed into the caves along the high and majestic red sandstone cliffs. There was cold rain and dark clouds, and lightning streaked the sky. My father and I managed the wind well, but I was scared to death.....

"As night settled, so did the weather. The lake became calm. We had dinner under the stars and spoke more of Bobby.

"My father asked me to express the thoughts that hurt me most about not having my brother with me. I did, and he listened to all of it carefully. I finally said the 'Unknown' was most painful. The thought of not knowing where Bobby's spirit existed, and of not trusting that his soul was peaceful in a 'heaven', made me unhappy and unsure of his restful sleep.

"Under the bright star of Sirius, my father assured me that Bobby was in a peaceful heaven, that he was in no pain, and that he continued to love us as we loved him. Father urged me to not fear the 'Unknown'.

"The next morning, we awoke to a beautiful day. The sky was a light pastel blue, and the lake was sapphire. A dark emerald green forest rose up above the red cliffs.

"We took our boat close along the shore. Sunlight beamed into the caves, turning the water inside of them into an aquamarine. The red sandstone walls glistened into ruby.

"We explored on our boat for more than an hour, before coming upon the most magnificent cave opening of all. The rays of the sun seemed to shine more deeply into this one, creating a running river of turquoise. I shouted 'Love' into the cave, and it echoed loudly back to me.

"Father pointed at the current of blue water running into the opening. He said the cave must have a nearby exit returning to the lake. He suggested I go for a swim and find out. He reminded me not to fear the unknown.

"I was a strong swimmer, but would it be enough in a current of cold lake water inside a potentially endless cave?

"My father was urging me to swim into an unfamiliar setting, with only my survival instincts to protect me. He showed faith that I'd be safe. I trusted him.

"I pulled off my shirt and dove head-first into the cold Lake Superior. I swam slowly into the cave, allowing the mild current to take me further in. The red walls rose high above me. The beautiful turquoise darkened into navy and indigo, and finally, into midnight blue. The sun's rays ebbed away. It became dark, but not black.

"I twisted and turned through the maze until seeing bright light again. The dark water turned jewel. I felt the warmth of the sun on my skin. The cave opened out close to where I'd started. My father stood on the edge of our boat and waved me in.

"I had conquered the 'Unknown' for the first time in my life. I had trusted my father to guide me. He had known all along the secret of the cave. It was familiar to him. He had been here before."

I thought of Olivia. Even in her last breaths, she had understood the significance of the moment when I promised to safeguard the journeys of our sons. Olivia had a way of knowing such things. Her sensitivities were sharp and intuitive to the end.....

"So as you see, Louis, I may not know Michael's present status; but I have faith in his abilities to survive. I have taught him well to be fearless, and to trust his instincts in action. He will perform his duties and live....."

I closed my eye and dreamed of my girl. Olivia was my right and left hands. She was my heart. She was my soul. Olivia was my everything, and I was struggling without her.

I thought of all those I had lost in my life. Like a candlelight's flame slowly starved of oxygen, I had been diminished by each and every loss. The absence of Olivia had finally blown my candle out.

Olivia's spirit was still entwined with mine. But I could not see her, touch her, kiss her. I could not fall into her dark eyes. I could not hold her hand, or whisper in her ear and make her smile. I could not feel her heart beat against mine.

There was too much longing. The physical machinery of my being had lost its fire. The only heat remaining in me, I was rapidly using to save my country, my Navy, and my sons.

I gently said to Louis, "Drive me to Bethesda to visit Mark."

At this moment, the fear of losing my sons was too painful to bear.

CHAPTER 23

The Father, The Sons and The Holy Spirit

A true man of honor is humbled himself when he cannot help humbling others.

***Robert E Lee* (1807 to 1870)**

NOT ONE WORD WAS SPOKEN in the car ride to Bethesda. I entered the hospital surgical intensive care unit in the wee hours of the morning. It was filled with a dissonant cacophony of monitor alarm bells. Here, nurses and doctors attended to the needs of America's wounded warriors around the clock. The mangled bodies of brave Marines and sailors filled the unit, and demanded of the medical staff just as heroic attitudes. Ventilators, cardiac assist devices, dialysis machines, and intravascular catheters of all types kept the patients alive in their struggles to overcome their injuries. Every day, soldiers would succumb to their grievous wounds, regardless of their excellent medical care. The head wounds, the chest and abdominal trauma, and the catastrophic orthopedic injuries were often too great for their young bodies to overcome.

I had always feared the loss of a child, perhaps more than most fathers. Olivia and I had deep scars of torn families, broken down by unkind fate. We loved our children and never hid the fact from them. They were a reflection of what we had found in each other. We always hoped for their success and spiritual prosperity, and wished for them to have a full life.

I had seen the effects of losing a child on my parents. In a way, they both lost a desire to live after losing Bobby. They died from sadness, and I was left alone in the world. The tender emotions involved at a young age had become seared in my inner self. Hidden from view most of the time, but always there if one scratched deep enough.

I slowly made my way to bed number 17, where my youngest son was recovering from a Pseudomonas bacterial infection. It had disseminated throughout his body from his atonic urinary bladder, edging him close to death. In the past days, Mark had approached his end many times. But each time, his spirit to live had driven death away.

Mark lay asleep. He had a central intravenous line in his neck which provided needed antibiotics and alimentation, a Foley catheter collected his urine, and a large colostomy bag received his feces. Blood transfused through another intravenous line in his left subclavian vein. His paralyzed legs were covered with a warm sheet. Mark's face was pale, and his closed eyes appeared sunken into their orbits. I pulled a chair up close to him and held his swollen left hand in my palms.

A tall physician in his long white coat approached me. He seemed young like Mark. His face was also pale and drawn, and his eyes reflected the struggles and demons around him. Yet, he walked with confidence and valor. He impressed me as a strong warrior in the fight for life.....

"Hello, Admiral. I'm Dr. Stanley Thompson, the ICU medical director. I'm very proud to meet you, Sir."

"Likewise, young man," I said, rising from my chair and shaking his hand.

Dr. Thompson nodded his head and looked over at Mark. I could see him quickly reviewing in his mind all the numbers from moniters, pinging and panging around my son. He seemed to be satisfied with what he saw. The doctor again cocked his head slightly and smiled. It was reassuring to me.

"Although he appears to you to be gravely ill, your son is actually doing well. He overcame a critical septic episode without any major complication. His heart and lungs are working efficiently, and his remaining kidney has not suffered any setbacks. We've succeeded in avoiding hemodialysis. Neurologically, he is alert when awake and able to move his toes in both feet. We expect him to continue the present stable course and transfer out of intensive care in the next 3 to 4 days. Hopefully, he'll begin a rehab program in two weeks and walk in the near future. We'll continue to do the best we can here for him."

"Thank you very much, Doctor. My family and I are appreciative of the efforts given to Mark to keep him alive and in the fight. He's a tough boy, and with the efforts given here he should be alright, we hope. I will continue to pray for him. And I will also pray for you and your dedicated staff, Dr. Thompson."

"You can count on us, Sir, to keep fighting as hard as he is. It's an honor to help all of these brave soldiers."

The doctor shook my hand again and walked away. Mid-stride, Thompson stopped and commented, "Sir, there's something I want to give you. Mark asked me to hold this for his father in safekeeping until he would have a chance to explain. I know he brought this back from Pakistan, and it seems to have a great deal of meaning for him. It was emotionally difficult for him to release the item after his arrival from Germany. He said it had belonged to a very brave man who saved his life. He wanted you to keep it, in the event of his passing..... Mark will survive this, Admiral, I promise..... I'm sure he'll want the item back when he feels better."

Thompson returned a few moments later with a dark plastic bag. He led me to the nurse's station, a few feet away, and opened the bag over a white table. The doctor pulled out a colorful woolen cap, adorned with bright bands of red, green, yellow, and blue. The white of the cap was visibly soiled and bloodstained. The earth of the Hunza Valley was mixed with the blood of heroes. I could smell the purity of both.

I stared down at it. I passed my fingers into it. I closed my right eye, trying to sense what my son had lived. The blood-matted areas had hardened. They felt rough against my skin. I could feel the struggle in them.

In my mind, I saw the smoke and fire, and the red tracers flying in all directions. I heard the explosions and the rattle of machine guns. The cries of men in battle echoed inside of me. My heart became heavy.

The doctor looked at my face for reaction. He could not see the tears behind my black eye patch. We both understood the power of the piece.....

"Knowing of your son's infinite bravery, I'm sure this hat has quite a story to tell, Admiral."

Dr. Thompson saluted me and left me alone.

I carefully placed the cap back into the bag and returned with it to my son's bedside. I sat back down and waited for Mark to awaken.

Shortly before 6 AM, he opened his eyes to find me in vigil. He smiled and squeezed my hand.

Mark's gentle smile had been inherited from his mother. They both had smiles that could brighten a room with its sunshine and invite a crowd. It was a soft and attractive smile, making one feel 'easy' inside. You could only smile back.

I recalled how Olivia's smile had fascinated me at first sight. Its power made me fall in love with her before even being introduced. My son had this gift as well.

I stood over Mark and kissed his left cheek. I told him how much I loved him. Mark's eyes closed as a tear ran down the right side of his face to his chin.

"I'm fighting as hard as I can, Father."

"I know you are, Son. You're a fighter like your mother."

"It didn't turn out so well for her, Dad."

"I understand, Mark, but she was fighting a battle she could not win. You will win this battle, just like at Shishkat Bridge. You'll come through this in short time," I said encouragingly.

"I lost several men at Shishkat Bridge, Father. I couldn't save another man at the landing zone. Too many died. They were all heroes. I can't get their sacrifices out of my mind."

"Did this cap belong to one of them?" I asked, holding the pakol in front of Mark.

"It belonged to Marcus Callanan, our local guide. The bravest man I ever met. He saved my life, after I thought I had saved his. It's strange how life works, Dad.

"I found him wounded and unable to walk, and threw him over my shoulder. We raced back towards the landing zone. As I got closer to the helicopters, I sensed we were home free.

"I passed Marcus off to my lieutenant and provided aggressive cover-fire. I killed many enemy on that field, Father.....

"While withdrawing towards the helicopters again, I felt a sudden heat in my back. I lost all my breath and fell to the ground near Marcus and Lieutenant Thomas. I couldn't move.

"Men in the helicopters returned for us, but Marcus refused to go. He took my gun and told them to take me away. He looked me in the eyes and commanded me to take his sons back home to the United States, to grow up as free Americans. He stayed behind alone, taking on the entire Chinese Army.

"I was carried to the helicopter and watched the Chinese converge on him like a pack of hungry wolves. My last memory is seeing Marcus bayoneted on the ground, bleeding from multiple wounds. I observed this with his two sons, Martin and Gilbert, before passing out.

"Marcus Callanan saved all our lives by firing at the enemy as our helicopters escaped. I'll never forget his extraordinary selflessness."

I listened to Mark's humble description and admired how I could have such a noble son. He could not perceive how his own actions had changed history. He was oblivious to his own selfless courage and sacrifice. It didn't surprise me. Mark had been this way all his life.....

"They approved you for a Congressional Medal of Honor for your actions at Shishkat Bridge and the landing zone," I said slowly. "Your mission, Mark, helped save thousands of American lives. Several divisions of Chinese mechanized infantry were planning to go down that highway into southern Pakistan. They would have bottled up the Marines in Balochistan and prevented their invasion of southeastern Iran. The entire operation into Iran would have been altered negatively. The tide of war was tilted in our favor from the start. The United States is very proud of you, Son."

My son looked at me with his big blue-green eyes. They seemed to sink deeper into their orbits as we spoke. The struggles for life had taken their toll. His eyelids were edematous and dark-rimmed. They were not the same eyes of before. They were physically hollowed out by war.

But my perceptions of his spiritual depth, and the innocent and glorious sincerity of his eyes, made me weep silently. My son's soul was profound and strong. Mark had lived many lives in the Hunza Valley. Each and every one of them - every notable high and sorrowful low, each gain and loss, every sunrise and sunset, each flower and stream, every orchard and green field - all were imprinted in his stare. I could see into him with my only eye and feel his spirit. It was robust, just as I had hoped. His fire was still burning..... I now knew my son would survive. I felt it inside of me.....

"Father, please keep the cap for me. Find out about Marcus Callanan's sons. Make sure they are being taken care of. When I am healthy enough to leave the hospital, I want to personally return Marcus' pakol to Martin and Gilbert."

Mark closed his eyes and quickly fell asleep. I stayed at his bedside.

I pulled a piece of paper from the inner breast pocket of my Navy dress blue jacket. It was a poem, scribbled by Olivia a few days before her death. She had written the verses in front of me in less than a minute. She thought the poem reflected the love and honor of her family, and the virtues of her beloved adopted country.

I whispered the words into my son's ear:

Do not cry for me,
I will not fade, I will not die.

Like the words of the Prophet,
I am immortal.

Like scientific discovery,
I am illuminating.

Like the mighty old oak,
I am enduring.

Like the energy of the Universe,
I am eternal.

Like the march of Time,
I am irrepressible.

Like passion,
I am invigorating.

Like true love,
I am everlasting.

I am in everything that stands for justice
and the natural rights of free men everywhere.

I am American Amaranth.

I believed these words exemplified my sons. I frequently read them to myself and always carried the poem in my left breast pocket close to my heart. It reminded me of all the goodness Olivia had given our family. Of all the love she had left us with. There were many cherished memories in her words. I could sense her presence in them. They humbled and strengthened me for the great struggle to come.....

I kissed Mark's forehead, took a deep breath, and quietly exited this pantheon of heroes.....

CHAPTER 24

The Law of Technological Selection

In the struggle for survival, the fittest win out at the expense of their rivals because they succeed in adapting themselves best to their environment.

Charles Darwin (1809 to 1882)

FOR MANY YEARS, America and her NATO allies had planned for an inevitable war with Iran, North Korea, and the People's Republic of China. The sinking of the Aegis destroyer, the *Patrick Henry*, in the eastern Mediterranean Sea in the early morning of May 12, followed by the loss of US attack submarine, the *Spokane*, in the Indian Ocean a few hours later, made war a fait accompli.

Only minutes after the confirmation of the sinking of the *USS Spokane*, the President of the United States ordered the US Strategic Command and Missile Defense Agency to attack and eliminate enemy orbiting satellites, both military and commercial. US Ohio class ballistic missile submarines in the Mediterranean, Gulf of Oman, Indian Ocean, and western Pacific launched kinetic energy interceptors (KEI). Ground-based silos in Alaska, California, Wyoming, Montana, North Dakota, Hawaii, Poland, the Czech Republic, and Israel launched their ballistic missiles. Within a few hours, most enemy satellites had been destroyed. The only significant eyes and ears remaining in space belonged to the United States and its closest allies.

China, North Korea, and Iran had quickly countered with ballistic missile launches against American interests in the western Pacific and the Middle East. Targets included Israel, Saudi Arabia, Iraq, Afghanistan, the

Philippines, Guam, Okinawa, South Korea, and the Japanese main islands.

Without complete and proper GPS guidance, many of these enemy missiles went off course and fell harmlessly into empty ocean or uninhabited land. Aegis ballistic missile defense systems on naval ships, and land-based platforms of Patriot Advanced Capability (PAC-3) and Arrow-3 missiles, destroyed almost all of the more accurate enemy launches. Boeing YAL-1 airborne laser systems on modified military Boeing 747s in-flight were successful in destroying enemy ballistic missiles in the boost phase shortly after launch, when they were within 400 miles of the launch site.

The enemy would continue to launch satellites over the proceeding weeks, and the United States would continue to destroy most of them. On rare occasion, an enemy ballistic missile would land on populated areas and cause very significant loss of life. Even more rarely, an Allied orbiting satellite would be destroyed by an enemy missile. In fact, in the first month of the war, America had launched more satellites than it had had destroyed. The US developed a reserve surplus of orbiting military satellites.

The United States Strategic Command also implemented a lightning war cyberspace offensive which severely disrupted the command-and-control communication systems of their enemies. Top-secret mechanisms - unknown to the intelligence services in China, North Korea, and Iran - had essentially blinded their war making capabilities. Suddenly, there was a 100 year differential in the offensive and defensive technologies of the opposing sides in this war. Like Darwin's Law of

Natural Selection, the struggle for life was being won by the fittest, technologically.

Upon implementation of *Operation Climb Mount Olympus, Code Samurai* was activated and the assault on the North Korean terror regime began. American F-22 and F-35 stealth fighters based out of South Korean airfields attacked key nuclear and military targets throughout the northern peninsula. Stealth jets from the Iwami US Air Force Base in Masuda, Japan, on southwestern Honshu Island, followed these with further strategic attacks. Ten B-2 bombers out of Anderson Air Force Base in Guam and another five from the Misawa Air Base in Japan blasted the North Korean nuclear facilities with deep penetrating munitions, specially designed to cave in the structures and decrease radiation fallout around the facilities. These attacks were followed by B-52 raids on a variety of military targets, including mass concentrations of enemy ground troops. F-16 and F-35 fighters flew thousands of ground attack sorties against artillery emplacements within range of Seoul. Precision guided bombs silenced many of the well sheltered gun batteries which were raining down fire on the South Korean capital. Of the estimated 15,000 North Korean batteries, over 10,000 were destroyed in the first 48 hours.

Concomitant with the initial US air raids, Allied artillery pounded the North Korean Forces over the demilitarized zone (DMZ).

Within two hours, the South Korean First Army moved across the DMZ along the eastern coastal region, supported by the US 10th Mountain Division and the Japanese Fourth Infantry Division. Along the western DMZ, the South Korean Third Army poured over into

North Korean territory. They were supported by the United States Second Infantry Division, five regiments of Indonesian Special Forces, the Australian First Division, and the Japanese Seventh Armored Division. The South Korean Second Army and the Japanese Sixth Infantry Division remained around Seoul as a rearguard. The capital's civilian population was evacuated to the south.

US Task Force 91 - led by the *USS Gerald R Ford* Strike Group out of Yokosuka, Japan, and Task Force 92 - out of Sasebo, Japan, led by the *USS John F. Kennedy,* rendezvoused in the Sea of Japan on May 14. The combined fleet of 114 Allied ships delivered the US Fifth Marine Division and the US 29th Infantry Division on the beaches of Wonsan, North Korea, approximately 100 miles east of Pyongyang. Carrier-based F-18 and F-35 fighters provided a protective air umbrella for the advancing troops all the way to the North Korean capital.

The battle strategy of the advancing Allied armies was to bottle up and isolate pockets of North Korean and PLA troops, and destroy them with air attacks.

By May 16, US fighters controlled the skies over North Korea. The North Korean MiG25s and MiG29s, as well as Chinese SU-33s, J-15s, and J-20 fighters, were destroyed in the hundreds in the first four days of battle.

By the end of the first month of war, the Allies had suffered 32,000 casualties with 8000 killed in action. Of the 1.2 million North Korean and 340,000 PLA troops, over 400,000 casualties had been sustained with over 160,000 killed in combat.

The North Korean Navy had been eliminated. Chinese attack submarines continued to harass Allied naval ships, sinking fourteen of them, including a US cruiser.

Early in the landing operations off of Wonsan, concentrated air attacks by Chinese SU-33s had damaged two US destroyers and an Australian frigate.

However, the 700,000 Allied troops on the Korean Peninsula gained the early advantage in the war, and by June 8, they were 30 miles outside of Pyongyang. The air and sea were controlled by the United States.

Because of setbacks in the South China Sea and Korea, the Chinese delayed their planned invasion of Taiwan. US satellite images showed 200,000 PLA troops and hundreds of landing ships along the Fujian coastline of southeastern China opposite Taiwan, 100 miles to the east. America had not yet bombed the Chinese mainland in this region, hoping China would cancel their Taiwan plan and negotiate a settled peace.

Nevertheless, as the siege of Pyongyang began by mid-June, the PLA decided to proceed with their invasion of Taiwan - using most of their remaining naval and air assets. They believed an attack on Taiwan would relieve the pressure on Pyongyang, allowing for counter-attack out of the capital.

Taiwan was defended by 210,000 Republic of China (ROC) Army troops, trained in counter attacking amphibious assaults and urban warfare. Twelve of their forty brigades were armored with over 200 M1 Abrams tanks, and over 300 French Leclerc and Israeli Merkava heavy tanks. They had several hundred Blackhawk, Super Cobra, and Apache Longbow helicopters. Their infantry troopers were armed with Stinger ground to air and Javelin anti-tank missiles.

Earlier in the year, as part of *Code Nimitz* - the US defense of Taiwan, 30,000 US Marines from the First and

Third Marine Divisions had been transported by air from bases in Okinawa and Subic Bay to heavily fortified camps along the western coastline of Taiwan.

The Ching Chuan Kang and Hsinchu Airbases on Taiwan had a complement of over 190 F-16 fighters. The United States had deployed over 60 more F-16 and F-18s, as well as three B-1 bomber missile trucks, for air battle over the Taiwan Strait. The Kadena Airbase in Okinawa, 400 miles away, had fourteen F-35 and eight F-22 fighters assigned to the Taiwan Theater of Operations.

The island of Taiwan was ringed by many Patriot PAC-3 missile batteries to defend against Chinese ballistic and cruise missile attacks. The Taiwanese Navy had 16 diesel electric submarines patrolling the Taiwan Strait.

Most importantly, the United States ordered Task Force 93 to sail from Apra Harbor at Naval Base Guam to waters east of Taiwan, and cut off the exit routes north and south out of the Taiwan Strait. They were to isolate the Chinese invasion fleet in the channel and destroy it with naval air power.

Three carrier strike groups, the *USS Ronald Reagan*, the *Abraham Lincoln,* and the *John C Stennis* would depart Apra Harbor on June 13 with a complement of twenty-four destroyers, seven cruisers, eight LA class and four Virginia class submarines. In addition, eight more US attack submarines had been ordered into the Taiwan Theater of Operations to patrol the approaches to the strait from the north and south. Two Ohio class submarines, with an additional 320 Tomahawk missiles, would target military sites on the mainland of China and enemy ships sailing towards Taiwan.

Task Force 93 also included three old giant battleships, each completely reformatted into an agile and armored missile platform. The *Iowa*, *Wisconsin*, and *New Jersey* would provide over 1000 missiles with offensive and defensive capabilities.

My son - Captain Julius Stansfield - and his *USS Oregon* would sail from Subic Bay to help close the southern route out of the Taiwan Strait.

The *USS Ocala* command ship would serve as the control, communications, and intelligence center of Task Force 93. It would also support the commander and staff of the US Seventh Fleet. I had requested a transfer to the *Ocala* on May 19.

On June 6, I arrived for my early morning appointment with Admiral James Turner, Chief of Naval Operations. Turner had also graduated at the top of his Annapolis class, six years after me. Although friendly, our relationship had been strained on several occasions in the past.

Turner had disagreed with my designs for the raid on the Iranian missile base on Paraguana Peninsula in Venezuela three years ago. My plan was accepted, and it proved instrumental in winning the war for Colombia. It pushed the Iranians out of Venezuela and the Amazon Basin. Mark had been awarded a Navy Cross for his actions in the Marine raid on Paraguana.

Most recently, Turner had implied Navy Intel negligence in not keeping the *USS Spokane* away from the Chinese convoy in the Indian Ocean. He indirectly blamed me for the submarine's sinking and the start of the war. For months, and with great success, I had kept our subs in aggressive posture against Chinese ship convoys of contraband materials in open waters. I had not started the war with China; she had brought war to us.....There was certainly friction between Turner and I.

The admiral's assistant allowed me into the office, where I waited for Turner to arrive. I stood at attention as he entered the room 15 minutes late.....

"Good morning, Julian.....

"Go ahead and sit down.

"Get comfortable.....

"I'm sorry for my tardiness. I was at the White House, briefing the president on our plans for Taiwan.

"Have you heard the news from Russia and the Ukraine?"

"What news?" I asked.

"In the last two hours, seven high ranking Russian government officials have been assassinated in Moscow and Kiev.

"All hell has broken loose. It looks like the start of a coup," said Turner excitedly.

"It's not surprising," I said. "Our diplomatic negotiations on the Ukrainian situation over the past few years may have helped us get the Russians out of Syria and Iran, but the settlement also freed the Russians to clamp down on the Ukrainian freedom movement. Now, we have angry Russian nationalists who think their government was played in the Middle East, and pissed off Ukrainian freedom fighters who feel betrayed by the United States. Today's assassinations may have been conducted by either Russian Nazis or Ukrainian patriots. Either way, I believe both groups will want retribution against the United States. Particularly, the growing nationalist movement in Russia will be a major concern for all of us in the near future. The Ukraine is a powder keg ready to ignite. The whole goddam region could explode into a war."

"We can't handle a war in eastern Europe right now!" blurted Turner. "Let's hope our covert operatives in the region tame the situation. We must keep the Russian Neo-Nazis out of power."

"I have over a hundred agents working the area," I said. "And Joe Mitrano has another hundred. We'll suppress the nationalists for a while, but it won't be easy. They've reached a critical mass in the past months..... I foresee them taking control of Russia and eastern Europe before the end of the year..... That may be our next war....."

"There's nothing easy any more, Julian."

"I know....."

"Enough talk of the uncertain future of Europe," said Turner. "We have a hot war to fight right now. Our enemies are attempting to wrestle away from us the two most critical regions in the world. The oil and gas of the Persian Gulf and South China Sea are at stake, as are the trade routes in the eastern Mediterranean, Indian Ocean, and the Pacific. Control of the twenty-first century hangs in the balance.....

"In my discussions at the White House, the president showed extreme concern about Taiwan. He's worried our fleet will get too close to the Chinese mainland, inviting an assault by land-based anti-ship ballistic missiles. A rain of fire could exact a heavy toll on our navy. He's also afraid that our subsequent retaliation would cause massive Chinese civilian deaths and an escalation of the war to another level.

"What do you think, Julian, about the president's preoccupation?"

"Well, Admiral," I began to respond, before being interrupted.

"Hey!

"Hold off a moment!

"No formalities, Julian!" Turner barked back demandingly. "We're speaking as friends today."

"Alright, Jim.....

"Let me be blunt.....

"The president must remind himself to not be so apprehensive. War is ugly any way you cut it. If the US Navy takes action, it will be appropriate action in every case. If we are attacked, we will strike back with all our ferocity and determination. The enemy will pay a high price for interfering in our business.

"We're not going to allow a communist invasion of a friendly island nation ever again. Several decades ago, we permitted the Russians to plant nuclear missiles in Cuba. Sure, we 'settled' our way out, believing the missiles were retracted. But were they really?

"For more than forty years, there were Russian troops in Cuba, and nuclear Russian submarines coming in and out of the island. Each of those subs had numerous nukes aimed at our cities, just a few hundred miles away. In the event of battle, our counter-time against those nukes would have been reduced. We were sitting ducks.

"The Cuban communist center of operations subverted our interests throughout all of Latin America for more than fifty years. Our troubles in Mexico, Nicaragua, El Salvador, Panama, Colombia, Venezuela, Bolivia, Ecuador, and Chile would have perhaps been prevented, if only America had reacted in Cuba appropriately.

"Sure we 'solved' the 'Cuban Missile Crisis' in 1962, but only after screwing up big-time and allowing it to develop in the first place. It's incredible to me that America invited an enemy devoted to our destruction onto an island nation within swimming distance of our shores. What was our government thinking?

"So you bet your ass, Jim, I'm not allowing these PLA communist bastards to take Taiwan. It would set a precedent in Asia and the Pacific, costing many more American lives for a century. It would be the first in a long line of dominoes, all the way to Australia in the south and Japan in the north.

"My navy is not giving up any free islands to the Communists, no matter how far from America that island may be. If they hit us hard at Taiwan, we will obliterate them. It's up to them to deal with the consequences.

"Assure the president our strategy is strong, Jim..... Ask him to review his history, and unless he's prepared to abandon the Pacific to the Chinese for the remainder of the century, our only choice is to defend the invasion of Taiwan with all our might. We must be willing to escalate the war if need be, hoping all the while that the PLA sees action as futile."

"That's quite a mouthful to tell the president, Julian," laughed Turner. "But I agree with you. If we give an inch, they'll take a foot. Taiwan will be defended.....

"Now tell me how you see it played out....."

"I believe the Chinese will throw everything they have at our fleet in this upcoming battle," I said. "They feel the need to take Taiwan after their losses in the South China Sea and Korea. They must rush the pace before Pyongyang falls. Winning Taiwan would improve their negotiations later on at a peace conference. Maybe even allow for a re-establishment of a Communist Northern Zone in Korea.

"They will hit us with every plane and missile they have left. Certainly, without proper satellite control, their targeting is going to be poor. Nevertheless, the Chinese will score some hits, and we may need to surgically strike those missile platforms to the best of our ability. There may be some Chinese civilian deaths, as there have been on our side in South Korea, Japan, Guam, and the Philippines. It's an unfortunate fact of war.

"They may even threaten our civilian populations on the west coast of the United States. Two Chinese submarines have already been sunk off the coast of California in the past ten days. They may increase their operations in our coastal waters. We will have to defend against that. Without appropriate GPS guidance, targeting of US population centers is out of the question. Most missiles launched will not be properly directed.

"They will not use nuclear capabilities against our military or cities. The lack of satellite guidance and the certainty of our lethal retaliation are major deterrents.

"In the end, we will prevent a successful invasion of Taiwan. If given no other choice, we will bomb sites on the Chinese mainland.

"When this conflict is over, the United States must have a free democratic Korean Peninsula and an independent Taiwan. Japan must feel secure with the American defense alliance. And the South China Sea and its energy reserves must be under international law. That is the only conclusion that would favor the free world," I opined.

"What are your thoughts on the Chinese using electromagnetic pulse (EMP) radiation weapons?" asked Admiral Turner.

"The PLA still has some functioning orbital satellites over the Taiwan Theater. They're launching more every day. The US Strategic Command has destroyed many of these new launches; yet, the U.S. Navy can expect the Chinese to have some degree of targeting capability for this upcoming battle.

"They may try to detonate a low-yield nuclear device, 20 miles above the ocean east of Taiwan. The PLA would hope to knock out all US Naval electrical devices in the near vicinity for a radius of 280 miles. Our strategic military systems are hardened against EMP effects. We also have the ability to quickly replace and reinforce our computers, sensors, and communication equipment in huge numbers. Besides, it is impossible to target only your enemy's assets with a high altitude EMP detonation. The Chinese would most likely affect their own assets more than the hardened assets of the U.S. Navy, and they don't have the capacity to replace their critical equipment.

"If the Chinese were to detonate a high-yield EMP nuclear weapon, higher over the Pacific at 250 miles above the earth, only a few critical Low Earth Orbit (LEO) satellites would be affected in the short term. However, LEO satellites are not constructed to withstand high levels of radiation. Over months, surviving satellites would accumulate damage and malfunction. Luckily, America has substitute redundant technologies that allow us to retain most of our operational effectiveness. Higher orbital satellites, and high-altitude unmanned aerial vehicles in the combat theater, would assist the U.S. Navy in maintaining communications and tracking capabilities. Our precision strike potential would remain intact.

"In regards to the Chinese using a high-altitude EMP nuclear device in missile launch form over the United States mainland, I don't believe this would be a rational possibility. An ICBM detonation 250 miles over the American Midwest would lead to a 40% loss of electrical infrastructure throughout the continental United States. Our communications, food production, transportation, and general commerce would be thrown into chaos. Social anarchy would ensue. Possibly, millions of Americans would die. The US would immediately strike back at the enemy's homeland with full nuclear potential. China's annihilation would be the end result. I don't believe the enemy is suicidal.

"I specifically analyzed the Taiwan EMP scenario for the Navy in 2008. I reported my findings to a closed Congressional hearing in 2009. We have fully prepared for this contingency. If it occurs, it should not hamper our operations in and around Taiwan," I concluded.

"I again agree with you wholeheartedly, Julian," responded Admiral Turner.....

The Chief of Naval Operations swivelled on his chair and opened a file folder. He only looked at it for a few seconds, before closing it.

"Now, I believe you are here to speak to me about your transfer request to the *Ocala*," stared Turner.

"Why do you want a ship at this stage of your career, Julian? You're up in the years, sick and blind, and you want a combat transfer? Why?

"Your career is one of the most accomplished in the history of US Naval Intelligence. Your genius is mostly responsible for the advancement of our missile technology. Your work on Chinese operations has allowed us to take control of the present conflict. The U.S. Navy is what it is today mainly because of your research and insight over the past decades. There will be statues of you at Annapolis, I assure you.

"So, why a combat transfer at this stage of the game?"

I thought back to my conversation with Raul Sierra by the old freedom fighter's orchid house on Key Biscayne, so long ago in 1976. I remembered how Raul had simply needed to be close to his son in harm's way.

"Jim, it is not easy on the mind to know your son is in danger far away from you..... It's even worse when you ordered him to that danger..... You want him to stand strong and fight, but you don't want him to die..... The emotions are difficult to reconcile.....

"If one is still able-bodied, your only wish is to closely assist him in his struggles..... You also want to stand strong and fight. Particularly so, when your son's struggles are your struggles also.....

"It is almost impossible to sit back and direct the show from a distance, remaining composed as you move his stick on a map, pushing him further and further into the danger..... There is more fear from far away.

"If bombs are falling on him, then you wish them to fall on you also. There is comfort in shared physical danger. It is the closely shared proximity to death that alleviates the tension.....

"Perhaps, you say to yourself, they will take you instead of him..... The mind is an amazing mystery, and the emotions of a father are even more mysterious.....

"This is how I feel, not only in reference to my sons, but also with regards to all the young sailors and airmen about to go into harm's way..... They are all my children, and I wish to be with them.....

"Let me say this in the simplest terms possible. I am widowed and live alone. I miss my wife more than I can express..... My brain is getting old; my best thinking is behind me..... I've spent my life strengthening my country's position in this world. I believe I have done my duty.....

"I have three sons fighting for America..... One of them, my youngest, is in a hospital bed at Bethesda also fighting for his life..... Another is in a submarine, fighting the PLA in the South China Sea..... The third was dropped into Iran prior to the invasion and is unaccounted for. His status is 'Unknown'.....

"I need to finish my career the way I always envisioned it, fighting for the ideals that I have lived by..... If young warriors can risk themselves in this conflict - men and women with their whole lives still to live, with hopes and dreams, with small dependent children of their own to raise and teach, with young love still in their hearts - why not this old man?

"The United States Navy can and will live on without me....."

Admiral Turner sat back in his chair and smiled at me. He jutted his chin forward, pointing at a large painting on his wall. The oil-on-canvas depicted the mighty USS Missouri, firing her massive and powerful 16-inch guns at the Japanese in the Battle of Okinawa.

"Taiwan will be bloodier than Okinawa, Julian....."

"Much bloodier than Okinawa, Jim, and all the other battles ever fought....."

"I've thought about this transfer request for the past two weeks. I deliberately left it on my desk unanswered. I know your personal situation. I know the sacrifices you and your family have made for our country. For God's sake, your youngest son has won a Navy Cross and a Congressional Medal of Honor, and is now paralyzed at Bethesda.

"America respects you, Julian, and I do too..... I have approved your immediate transfer to the *Ocala*. You are in command of all intelligence for the Battle of Taiwan.....

"The fates of all the Navy men and women in Task Force 93 are in your hands. They can be in no better hands, I think.

"Godspeed to you and your sons. I salute you with admiration, for your ideals and your unbreakable will to defend them. But most of all, I honor you for what you signify to the United States of America.....Undying loyalty.....

"God bless you, Julian....."

In the afternoon, I met my daughter, Rebecca, for lunch at *El Castillo*, a Cuban American restaurant in Georgetown. Olivia and I had dined here many times with our family over the years. We were friends with the owner, Mario Posada, a Cuban immigrant.

I made my way to the back of the restaurant, to the usual private table, and found Rebby (for rebel) waiting. My Rebby was a 30-year-old world-renowned classical concert pianist. Her Chopin and Rachmaninoff piano concertos sold out in all the music capitals of the world.

She had just arrived in Washington from two weeks of concerts in Paris.

Rebecca had studied music at Juilliard, and her great talent and confidence had propelled her to the top of the profession. She was tall and elegant like Olivia. Her facial beauty, often compared by people to Ava Gardner, more closely resembled her mother. Although single, she was usually accompanied by handsome, educated, and rich gentlemen. Because of her stubborn determination and passion as a child, I had nicknamed her "Rebby" for the southern Confederate rebel general - Stonewall Jackson.

"Hi, Daddy!

"What took you so long, *Padre mio*?" asked Rebecca, as I sat across from her at the table.

"There is a war going on, Rebby. My schedule is not easy to time," I smiled.

"I ordered you a Daiquiri, Daddy. Just like you like it."

"Thank you, Rebby."

"I saw Mark this morning at the hospital," she said warmly. "He's looking well. They're moving him to a regular room this afternoon."

"This was his third stay in the ICU in the last three weeks; I hope this time he can recover more fully and begin his rehab," I stated.

Mario Posada brought my Daiquiri personally and greeted me with his usual, "Good afternoon, *Capitan*."

"Hello, Mario. It's good to see you again. I haven't been by in several months," I said.

"I know, *Capitan*..... We've missed you," said Mario nostalgically. "Will you be having the *Paella* like old times, *Capitan*?"

"Yes..... Bring us both the *Paella*, Mario. That would be wonderful."

I gazed at Rebecca, admiring her way. She was a happy, lively girl, and I enjoyed her company. She often made me forget my troubles.

"You know, Rebby, the *Paella* here is the best I have ever had, other than your great-grandfather Raul's on Key Biscayne in the 1970s. Your mother always loved it."

"Why has Mario always called you *Capitan*, Daddy?"

"Your mother and I first came to this restaurant in 1983, before you were born, to celebrate my promotion to captain. Mario took good care of us, and the name, '*Capitan*', stuck."

Rebecca was strikingly beautiful like her mother. She also had inherited the 'Olivia' smile. A big smile and a wink of her dark eyes could conquer anyone in an instant, including her father. Rebby had an ebullient personality that could set fire to a man. She would use it with great expertise to get her way all the time. I had fallen victim to her charms often, as I had with her mother. I stared at her face while we sat in the restaurant talking, and thought of all the joy she had brought me in my life. She was a gifted girl in all respects. And I loved her.

"I'll be leaving Washington late tonight, and I won't return for a while," I commented.

"When the Director of Naval Intelligence leaves Washington during wartime, I can presume you're not going on vacation, Daddy?"

"No, Rebby..... I'm not going on vacation.....

"Please keep in touch with Mark as much as possible. Don't mention anything about my leaving. I'll telephone him in a few days.

"Go by and visit his wife and children. Be as helpful as you can. They're going through a rough time," I said.

"I promise, Daddy.....

"How are Julius and Michael doing?" she asked.

"Oh, they're both well and safe; they have asked me about you often," I deflected, hiding their true dangerous situations.

"When this war is over, we'll all get together again and share some love time, Rebby," I vowed.

Mario brought the seafood and yellow rice *"Paella"* to the table, and Rebecca and I enjoyed our meal together. We spoke warmly of family and 'old times'. We talked of Rebecca's music and the power of love in sound. It was a gift she had since childhood, to bring joy with music, to alert the senses with her piano. Her interpretations of great classics were considered better than those of the master composers themselves. Beethoven, Bach, and Chopin, Schubert, Liszt, and Mozart could all sleep in peace, listening to Rebecca's beautiful performances of their music. It was her offering of peace to the world.

While Rebby spoke passionately of her music, I listened contently to her voice and smiled. Her mother had loved her playing as much as I. Olivia would lay with me in bed for hours and listen to Rebecca's recordings. We'd marvel at the depth of sounds and her expressive tonalities. With all of Rebby's travelling, we didn't see her much. We had missed her together, Olivia and I. Today, I was enjoying Rebecca. But at the same time, I was missing Olivia.

Our family had eaten *Paella* at Mario Posada's restaurant many times over the past several decades, usually all together. The absence of so many on this afternoon was clearly felt by Rebecca and I.

After lunch, Rebby drove me home. As I rested on the living room couch, she went to the piano. She turned her body towards me as she sat, tossed her beautiful jet-black hair, and winked at me with her right eye.

"I'm going to play for you what you've always loved so much, Daddy. Don't forget me."

I watched Rebecca transform into the great artist. She allowed her heart to control the keys. Rebby dominated the piano like she dominated me..... How could I ever forget her?

She leaned into the piano and made magic with Rachmaninoff's "Piano Concerto Number Two, Second Movement".

Rebecca cast her spell. Her mystical charms were released to me in her beautiful sounds. Her sacred heart floated into me.

I closed my eyes and thought of my sons, Julius and Michael. I could see them in my mind's eye. I remembered back to their early birthday parties as children, Christmas mornings, school graduations, and old times spent together with Olivia.

Rebecca was gifting this vision to me. Such was the power of her music. She could make me remember and feel even more strongly.

The emotions also brought tension. I had never sensed fear like this in my life. Not knowing my sons' conditions, and fully appreciating the dangers they faced, I hoped for their safety and well-being in our titanic struggle..... I had promised this to Olivia.....

CHAPTER 25

The Ocean Deep

Most Holy Spirit! Who didst brood
Upon the chaos dark and rude,
And bid its angry tumult cease,
And give, for wild confusion, peace;
Oh, hear us when we cry to thee,
For those in peril on the sea!
US Navy Hymn

***William Whiting* (1825 to 1878)**

I SAT ON A US Navy transport plane flying at 35,000 feet above the western Pacific Ocean. For hours, I had been reading a book of Navy hymns given to me long ago in childhood by my father. The book's aged yellow pages had many earmarked for Father's favorite passages. He had particularly liked William Whiting's 1860 poem, "Eternal Father, Strong to Save", used by the British Royal Navy and later adopted in 1879 as a hymn at Annapolis. At the academy, it would conclude each Sunday's Divine Services..... Through my window, I looked down at the Pacific below and thought about all the American sailors lost in battles through the years into the ocean deep. My mind drifted more to those lost in the past month of conflict, and to the many more who would perish in the near future. In deep contemplation, and with an injured heart, I remembered the last words my mother spoke to me before she passed from this world ~ "Peace on Earth".....

I pondered all the decisions made in *Global Directive 93*. For years, I had led the secret military commission charged with securing the future global order in the twenty-first century. In our organized collaboration with the White House, State Department, CIA, and Wall Street, we had hoped for an organized and unified world – an Earth with justice, religious and cultural freedoms, and economic prosperity for all. The *Directive* was to establish a *Pax Americana*, safeguarded by US diplomatic, military, and economic power. The institutions of *Lady Liberty* would be shared with the world, hopefully preventing future global wars, mutually-assured nuclear destruction, and the end of life on earth..... We all hoped for 'Peace on Earth' to be eternal.

The seven military commanders and I on the commission had been hand-picked by the Office of the President of the United States. Our terms of service were open-ended, with durations decided by another secret select committee, but I had served and led since inception. I had known every military member personally through the years. All of them had been fiercely loyal to the Constitution of the United States, never wavering from their devotion to America, and never siding with the 'Left' or 'Right' in the developing schism in our country. I had always held faith in each and every member's allegiance to America.

Since the beginning of the *Directive*, and not unexpectedly, we had faced resistance from radical Islamism, Chinese Communist State Capitalism, a Germanic European Union, and resurgent Russian Nationalism. However, the course of affairs had been more complicated, turbulent, and aggressive than even I had anticipated. It had not been an easy road to global freedom.

With the economic debacle of 2008, world social chaos ensued. Revolution and civil war spread to every corner of the earth. Enemies outside our country, and those within, increased their drives to weaken and damage America. Our American political process and loyal allegiance to institutions began to unravel. Dishonor and distrust spread across our nation. Destabilization even spread to the US military.

The great upheaval - a continuously degrading continuum from the fall of the USSR, through the radical Islamic terror of 9/11 and beyond, world economic depression, Chinese expansionism, and the destabilization of the European Union and Russia – culminated in world war.

Tremendous pressures were placed on the American military machine. The members of the *Global Directive 93 Pentagon Commission* were not spared from the anxiety and insecurity. I began to sense more division and disagreement among my peers. Perhaps, Sam Powell and Joe Mitrano had alerted me to be more aware of dissension.

I thought of all this as I flew over the Pacific Ocean, preparing to lead my beloved Navy into the most horrific sea battle in world history..... With the weight of the world on my chest, I fell asleep and passed into an unsettling dream.....

I walked down the long narrow hall, like I had countless times before, and entered the Global Directive 93 conference room at the Pentagon. It was a familiar room, where my colleagues and I had decided the fate of the world on many occasions.

The cold and silence of the space was startling. The room was infused with a somber darkness I had never sensed before. Each of the seven members of the commission sat around the table with their heads bowed. Like testy and fiery stallions in winter, their hot breaths were visible to my eye. I could feel their aggressive power misdirected towards me. There was hatred and rebellion in the air.

I stood at the head of the table and shouted, 'For Lady Liberty, there is no dissolution! There is no decay or death! We must persevere, or all is lost! There is no disunion in the United States of America! If we do not live, the world does not live!'

I called each of my colleagues out by name. One by one, they directed their dragon's fire at me, each of them faceless.....

It was still early morning when the plane crossed the northeastern coast of Luzon Island in the Philippines. I had asked to go to Subic Bay for a few hours to see my son, Julius. The *Oregon* had arrived at the US naval station two nights before for a rearmament of torpedoes and missiles in preparation of the Taiwan campaign. I hoped to spend time with Julius before flying on to Guam.

We passed in a southwesterly direction across central Luzon, toward the island's South China Sea coastline. I looked down on Mount Pinatubo, site of a massive volcanic eruption in June 1991 that had hastened the closure of US Naval Station Subic Bay the following year.

When relations with China worsened a few years ago, the United States negotiated with the Philippine government to re-open the naval base. Over the past two years, Subic Bay had strengthened into America's third-largest base in the Pacific - after Pearl Harbor and Guam. It was the American Navy's center of operations against the PLA in the South China Sea.

Originally won from the Spanish after the Spanish-American War in 1898, and briefly lost to the Japanese in 1942, Subic Bay had later served America well during its 20th-century conflict with Communist North Vietnam. I had spent time there during my submarine deployment to the Pacific in the late 1970s. I had not returned since.

The C-17 descended over the Zambales Mountains, separating Luzon's central plain from the South China Sea. I could see the Bataan Peninsula and Corregidor Island far to the south, site of Douglas MacArthur's fighting strategic retreat from advancing Japanese forces in early 1942; and later, the infamous Bataan Death March of American and Filipino prisoners of war back into the interior of Luzon. As now with China, Japan had also claimed the energy riches of the South China Sea and had invaded the Philippine Islands to protect its southeastern Asian flank.

Flying low over the Zambales Mountain range towards Subic Bay, the rolling carpet of verdant hills reminded me of one of the last times our family had been together. The lush tropical green vegetation, meandering rivers, and magnificent waterfalls brought back the memories of our family trip to a free Cuba, two years past.

The Amazon War had ended in the defeat of Venezuela, and the fall of its Iranian and Chinese supported socialist government. Democratic reforms in Venezuela led to a discontinuation of free oil shipments to Cuba and a rapid disintegration of Cuba's aging communist elitist regime.

The transitional government in Cuba decided to honor Olivia's grandfather, Raul, and father, Jorge, for their sacrifices to resurrect a free democracy in their native land. Hacienda Sierra near Trinidad, Cuba - birthplace of Raul, Jorge, and Olivia - would be consecrated as a National Historic Site. The green promontory of the Morro Castle overlooking Havana Harbor and the Caribbean

Sea, where Olivia's father and many thousands of freedom fighters had been executed, would be ceremoniously declared sacred hallowed ground by the Archbishop of Havana.

Only months before falling ill, Olivia and our family travelled to the old Spanish colonial town of Trinidad in south-central Cuba for five days of public ceremonies. The US Government flew us from Homestead Air Force Base to Cienfuegos Airport and provided protective escort throughout the trip.

Travelling by car from Cienfuegos to Trinidad, fifty miles away, we toured the region and the Hacienda Sierra – built in the late 1700s within the beautiful Escambray Mountains. Founded in 1514 by the Spanish Conquistador, Diego Velazquez, Trinidad and its adjoining Valle de los Ingenios had seen the origins of the Cuban sugar cane industry.

We visited the Iglesia Parroquial de la Santisima Trinidad where Olivia had been baptized. We also took the old steam railroad through the sugar cane fields to Manaca.

Birthplace of Raul, Jorge, and Olivia - Hacienda Sierra had belonged to eight generations of the family before Fidel Castro's revolution.

We went to Caburni Falls, where the Caburni River cascades from a 200 foot rock wall into a series of freshwater ponds. We swam where Olivia's father had taught her to swim as a young child.

Our family travelled by train north to Varadero and Raul Sierra's beach home. The coral limestone house facing white sands and blue-green waters, where Raul gathered with family for special occasions and frequently entertained Ernest Hemingway, had been stolen by Fidel Castro. The regime used it for lodging foreign communist dignitaries.

Finally, we visited Havana and the Morro Castle. Our family watched Olivia place a wreath of red amaranth flowers at the base of a giant iron cross, marking the spot where Jorge Sierra had fallen and his legend had risen. At the end of the formal ceremony, the Archbishop of Havana sanctified the site with approval from the Pope.

On our last morning in Cuba, we watched the sun rise over the Caribbean Sea from the castle promontory, just as Olivia's father had done seconds before leaving this earth so many years before. An old iron bell was struck six times heavily and forty-two times lightly by Olivia, tolling the exact hour – 6:42 AM - of her father's last breaths on his sacred soil.

For Olivia, the whole experience had been emotionally draining - but necessary. She had lived to see her homeland free. I suffered and rejoiced with her.

Our children also had a chance to appreciate their mother's deep faith in the United States of America. The truest meanings of freedom had become clear to them during this pilgrimage to their mother's birth country.

All these memories came to me while my transport plane descended over the Zambales Mountains.....

The C-17 flew past the mouth of Subic Bay and circled south back towards the Cubi Point Airfield. I looked down through my window and could see a destroyer squadron returning to base after ocean convoy patrols in the South China Sea. I could also see five F-18 Super Hornets flying over the mountains north of the entrance to Subic Bay, part of an air shield always over the naval base.

I landed at Cubi Point shortly after 9:30 AM. As I exited the plane, I saw my son waiting for me in a Navy Humvee. We greeted each other with a warm embrace and drove to the Officers Club for breakfast.

"It's good to see you, Father," smiled Julius behind the steering wheel.

"But why the hell did they send you here to Subic?

"I was surprised when Vice Admiral Johnson told me you'd be arriving this morning.....

"There must be something big brewing for you to have come so far into a war zone," stated the inquisitive Julius.

"You think I'm too old to fight?" I laughed.

"No, Father. I didn't say that..... I just thought it was unusual that the Navy sends their senior people into a hot missile area."

"Julius, the entire world is a hot missile area..... I could have my ass shot off while having lunch at the Pentagon. I could just as likely get assassinated in a Georgetown restaurant.....There are no safe zones in this war."

"I guess you're right," he said.

"Of course I'm right! I'm your Dad, Director of Naval Intelligence!" I laughed out loud.

"When did the *Oregon* come into Subic Bay?" I asked, trying to tame my son's interest in my visit.

"Come on, Dad! You just said you're Director of Intel! Am I to believe you don't know the *Oregon's* position at any given time?" smiled Julius.

I didn't answer.....

"We came in two days ago, Father, after two months in the South China Sea. I've been on four combat patrols in the past month. There's been a lot of destruction.....

It's shocking to see how much disruption an American attack submarine can inflict in a few short minutes. You have to be crazy to go up against us.....

"We've had our losses too, Dad. We've lost a lot of good men in the past month."

"I know, Julius..... We've had our losses," I quietly acknowledged.....

We arrived at the Officers Club and sat at a table by the window overlooking the naval station. A tall flagpole outside flew a large American flag. A strong wind whipped it violently, almost separating the Stars from the Stripes.

"How long are you going to be here, Dad?"

My eye fixated through the window at a missile cruiser sailing out of the bay towards the South China Sea. Her 400 officers and enlisted sailors were dressed in white. All stood at attention on the battle deck while saluting the base's flag.

Will this ship survive the coming onslaught? I asked myself in my mind. How many of these brave Americans will return to their families? How many can I save? I silently murmured to myself.

"What did you say, Father? I saw your lips move, but I didn't hear what you said."

My mind had wandered again..... I retrained it on my son, the object of my visit.

"I'm here only for three hours, Julius."

"What can you get done in three hours?" he asked.

"Well, I can eat a good breakfast and enjoy your company," I said, before ordering sunny side eggs, Canadian bacon, and two pancakes.....

"I've come here only to see you, Julius....."

"You've come all the way from Washington to see me for three hours, Dad?

"What gives?"

"Order your breakfast, Son," I requested, again trying to tame my son's developing curiosity.

After eating, we drove to Lookout Point - an elevated rocky outcropping at the southern end of the bay as it met the South China Sea. At 900 feet above sea level, it gave a great panoramic view of the area. One could see forever across the blue-green waters and lush mountain tropical vegetation.

The horizon we saw with our eyes was crystal clear, unlike the one I sensed in my mind. Here on the side of a mountain, Julius and I sat together and talked about family and my son's hopes for the future. A future I understood to be insecure and in doubt, no matter how hard I hoped for the better.

"I heard Mark's condition is improving, Father."

"Yes, I think he's going to be all right," I said into the wind. "The doctors believe he may walk again after a few months of rehabilitation. I sure pray he will."

"I was told Mark was approved for the Medal of Honor.....

"He was always a hero," smiled Julius.

"Well, he was forced to stand tall and meet up to his older brothers," I reminded.

"How about Michael; what information do you have on him?"

"None," I responded. "He was dropped into Iran months before the invasion. He was operating out of Tehran and basically disappeared after the bombs started dropping. He's very smart and has been trained to survive in all sorts of adverse conditions. The CIA hopes he'll either get to American lines or escape north into Central Asia. Those are my hopes too," I added.

The wind blew strongly on our rock as a new squadron of F-18s took off from Cubi Point Airfield to the east. The jets quickly rocketed over our heads, drowning out our voices and ringing our ears. They sped out over the South China Sea in search of the enemy.

"Father, you didn't really come down to Subic Bay only to spend a few hours with me," doubted Julius. "What else is going on?"

I looked into my son's eyes. A father often does in these moments..... In life, there are moments where the great magnitude of the event stops time. The intervals can not be measured by a watch. They have no real beginning and no real end. They are both fleeting and everlasting. They stay with you for both only an instant and an eternity.... Stirring and dramatic as they may be, these touchstones of our lives are never tangible. You can not capture them with any of the senses; you devour them only with your heart. At the end, we measure the quality of our lives by these moments.....

Julius' eyes told me everything. They reflected his soul. I saw no fear in them. They were prepared. He understood what was happening..... In them also, I could see his concerns for me - not for himself..... I had devoured all this with my heart.....

I gently nodded at him and said, "Tonight, you'll be ordered to leave port before sunrise and sail the *Oregon* toward the Taiwan Strait. I'm flying to Guam and taking control on the *USS Ocala*, the command ship of Task Force 93 with three carrier strike groups.

"Task Force 93 will meet up with elements of Task Force 94 out of Subic Bay, east of Taiwan on the evening of June 15. The PLA marines will attempt to invade Taiwan with all the remaining naval power they have left at their disposal. We're going to stop them, Julius.

"The *Oregon* is part of the attack submarine wolfpack assigned to blockade the southern route out of the Taiwan Strait. Another wolfpack will cover the northern approaches. No Chinese ships will be allowed to leave the strait. We're going to bottle them in and destroy them from the air.

"They will come after you with aggressive anti-submarine tactics..... Take my advice..... If the *Oregon*'s location is discovered, silently drop to the bottom and wait it out. Don't try to evade in the open. Find a thermocline. Let them pass you by, then come after them. Play it smart.....

"This battle will last several days. It will probably involve more munitions than any naval battle in history. That means more pounds of explosives than the Battles of Leyte Gulf and Okinawa. There will be much destruction on both sides and many lives lost. Victory always has its price..... These are the costs of freedom.....

"Stay sharp and live by your intuitions. Don't try to be a hero. Use your stealth intelligently. Be silent and quick. Hit them with all you can and don't expose yourself to retaliatory fire. They can't hit what they can't see.

"Remember all the things I've taught you through the years..... Survive this and you're going home to your family....."

My face expressed and conveyed multiple emotions to Julius. Aggression, hope, fear, love, and despair were all registered easily by my son. I could see it in his eyes. I had expressed myself open-heartedly. I had made the reason for my visit plainly clear. I wanted and needed my son to survive and come home. I did not want him to die in the abyss.

I embraced Julius and brought him close to my chest. I then softly cupped my right hand over his heart and felt his heartbeats on my fingertips. I had given him life with Olivia, and now I was sending him off into the Acheron. A true underworld river of pain was awaiting him, and he was going there on my orders..... I did not want to withdraw my hand, but I did.

I smiled and said, "All right. Take me back to the airfield, Captain, and let's get to work."

We now understood each other completely.

Julius and I did not speak while we drove down to Cubi Point. On the tarmac, I embraced him again.

"I love you, Son."

"I'll see you soon, Father, back home in the States."

As I boarded the C-17, Julius saluted me. He had fully appreciated the reason for my visit - a father's love for a brave son in harm's way.

CHAPTER 26

The Rising

Man is free at the moment he wishes to be.

***Voltaire* (1694 to 1778)**

MICHAEL AND NASRIN rested inside the Caspian seaside villa safe house. They planned to escape later that evening under cover of darkness. The trip by speed boat northwest to Azerbaijan could reach either Astara or Lenkeren in three or four hours, if unimpeded by Iranian gunships or attacks from the air.

In the late afternoon, Stansfield was awakened by the sound of automatic weapons and loud explosions. He grabbed his binoculars from his backpack and ran up the stairs to the small third-floor attic. The room had windows facing north to the sea and south to the center of Chalus.

To the southeast, he saw a column of Safir-74 tanks (Iranian T-54 upgrades) and tracked Boragh armored personnel carriers entering the Chalus township. The heavy armor was followed by walking Iranian infantry. Civilian refugees, who had swarmed the streets of Chalus in their escape from fighting to the south and west, were being shot down by their own soldiers.

To the north, Stansfield saw Iranian gunboats firing on refugees trying to escape Iran by sea. Along the coastline, east and west, many boats were sinking. Survivors, including women and small children, drowned in the choppy waters.

The Iranian military was systematically murdering their own people, disallowing them to escape the chaos.

Every person, every woman and child, was expected to stay and fight the American invaders.

Nasrin joined Michael in the attic and sobbed as she viewed the horrific spectacle. She slammed her fist against the wall.

"What madness!

"They are animals!

"How can they shoot down innocent women and children?

"These poor people, Michael, are defenseless!

"How can this massacre be permitted?" she cried.

"I've seen this many times, Nasrin, in many countries!

"All it takes is one bad judgement by a junior officer under pressure. Perhaps his troops came under fire from partisans in the melee. Confusion takes over and rational thought disappears. One soldier shoots, and then another, soon a frenzy evolves into a slaughter. The officers lost control of their troops."

"That's bullshit!" screamed Nasrin. "These bastards are enjoying it. It's an intentional extermination of people who disagree with their government. Muslim Nazis killing innocents who wish only freedom. It's a travesty of humankind!"

At that moment, three American F-16s flew over Chalus and fired rockets at the armored columns. Explosions shook the villa. A-10 Warthogs jetted over the coast, dropping bombs on several Iranian gunboats. Surface to air missiles streaked the sky.

A Warthog was hit and crashed in a ball of fire into the sea. Three gunboats exploded and sank rapidly. Iranian underground resistance fighters opened up on the Iranian military from buildings near the town center.

An A-10 passed low over the villa, almost scraping its belly on the roof. Its power of flight trembled the floor and shattered two windows. The American bomber shot a rocket at a gunboat close to the shore behind the safe house. The projectile flew off course and landed in the villa's boathouse, detonating violently in a fiery display. All hell had broken loose.

Michael covered Nasrin with his body.

"Don't move!" he shouted, as pieces of burning boat and house rained down on the villa's roof and sculpture garden. Black smoke entered the hall outside the attic from a broken window downstairs.

"Let's get down to the ground floor behind the concrete stairwell for protection!" he yelled. "Crawl on the floor all the way down!"

Nasrin shaked uncontrollably as she tucked herself under the protected nook. Michael embraced her tightly, bringing her face against his chest.

"Don't panic, Baby," he whispered in her ear.

"This is all going to be resolved.... You must stay within your wits, Nasrin. Our survival depends on our abilities to reason. You can't lose control of your mind.

"We must accept what's happening for now. You and I alone can't change it. War is this way. It's an ugly process.

"We're marooned for a while..... We may need to fight to get out of here..... It won't be easy..... I need you clear in the head. A jumbled mind won't cut it."

Stansfield stared out the back windows. The Caspian was dotted with the burning hulks of civilian and military sea craft as far as he could see. Thousands of dead and dying crippled bodies floated on the water, speckling the blue and white with crispy black. The vestiges of the boathouse burned, sending fiery wooden embers in arcs of red light onto the terrace. The speedboat had vanished.

Michael's escape plan had vanished as well. They were now trapped inside the safe house.

Gunfire and explosions continued for several hours into the night. The young lovers held each other behind the stairwell and pondered their options.....

In the early morning, Stansfield removed Nasrin's leg wound dressings. He visually inspected the hole with the aid of a flashlight. He smelled the wound. With a gauze, Michael expressed a small amount of serosanguineous fluid from the torn flesh. It wasn't purulent. After confirming it was healing well without infection, he applied more antibiotic and clean dressings.

Michael returned to the attic with his binoculars. He carefully surveyed the situation.

Looking south towards Chalus, Michael saw young men being lined up against a wall. In groups of ten, they were shot by firing squads. Resistance fighters were being executed in front of their own people. The bodies were thrown into trucks and transported for burial in mass graves east of the town.

Iranian Army regulars took up positions throughout Chalus, fanning out through all the major streets.

Sections of the small city remained unsecured. Resistance fighters had taken positions on rooftop terraces and in upper floor apartments. The stage was being set for a major battle inside the city center. The freedom fighters were not giving up. A civil war was evolving inside of Iran. Brother versus brother and sister against sister would become the routine.

Stansfield focused his eye-pieces on the executions. An Iranian Revolutionary Guard Corp officer methodically fired his pistol into the heads of dying partisans in front of the firing line. The bodies were dragged away, and new unfortunates were pushed with their backs against the white cement wall.

Michael scanned the white concrete. Hundreds of bullet holes pockmarked the crimson-splashed wall. Fresh red blood dripped down onto the green grass at its base. The Iranian regulars' boots sloshed in the bloody pools as they dragged their victims' bodies to the waiting cadaver trucks.

The American CIA agent had seen uncontrolled sectarian killing in the Middle East. He had experienced it from all warring sides. Murder was not the dominion of only those groups which America deemed enemies. Michael lived it first-hand from America's "allies" in the civil wars of North Africa and the Levant. Genocide was rampant in Libya, Egypt, Lebanon, and Syria.

On one of his first missions, Stansfield infiltrated into Aleppo, Syria, with a CIA team of five other Americans. The city of over two million people was engulfed in brutal house-to-house fighting. Syrian Army forces were attacking from all directions. Confusion on the battlefield was stifling the Syrian Rebel Army. Stansfield's orders were to provide intelligence and special tactics to the rebels. The Iranian Revolutionary Guards were providing similar help to the Syrian regime troops.

During a particularly rough day of battle in and around an old apartment complex, many warriors had died on both sides. Civilians had also suffered. By late afternoon, the Syrian regulars had been defeated. Over 350 bodies littered the grounds of the six-story building.

The rebels had captured 46 enemy troops, including 6 Iranian officers. Michael Stansfield asked to interrogate the Iranians. A command post was established on the first floor of the apartment complex. Stansfield finished his intelligence gathering by the early morning of the next day.

While drinking a cup of cold coffee, he heard commotion outside. He sprinted out and found the rebels passing a rope between the second floors of two adjacent buildings. Several other rebels beat the Iranians with their rifle butts. Civilians had gathered around to yell at the Revolutionary Guard officers.

"Death to the infidels!" they screamed. "Let the dogs eat them!" others shouted.

Stansfield attempted to control the mania, but his Syrian liaison instructed him to withdraw. The Americans were forced to stand back and watch the legal process take form. In all war, but especially in civil war, civilization disappears and humanity is forgotten.....

Meat hooks were thrown over the second-story ropes. The physically bruised and scared Iranians were stripped from the waist up and shot in both shoulders. Ropes were tied around their feet, and they were hoisted upside down from them. Blood from their shoulder wounds dripped to the ground, attracting the starving neighborhood dogs. The skinny canines barked in a frenzy.

A decree of violence and criminal abuse perpetrated on the innocent people of Syria was read aloud by a rebel officer, sentencing each crying Iranian to death.

Another rebel, with a long sharp butcher knife, stepped out in front of the screaming crowd. The people chanted as the rebel lifted the large blade into the air. The wild civilians became louder. The rebel walked to the Iranians in orderly sequence, striking each one near the umbilicus and ripping downward. Their eviscerated entrails fell to the ground, feeding the hungry dogs. The larger alpha canines pulled the intestines in different directions. The smaller dogs followed their leads. The rebels cheered, and the people cheered. Stansfield and his men cringed.

Michael had learned that in Muslim sectarian war, there were no prisoners. Torture and murder were commonplace. Mercy was rare. Civil war was always ugly. But in the Middle East, it was hellish. It was often impossible to differentiate the "good" guys from the "bad".

Stansfield peered through his binoculars at the scene in Chalus. Iran had now become hell's playground. There would be no mercy here either. Thousands would die on both sides in this war.

In many ways, the American felt deep empathy for the victims of both sides. In recent history, there had been much confusion in Iran, as in the rest of the Middle East. There was little political organization throughout the region. The pathetic victims of eternal sectarian wars were wasted without ever reaching logical, peaceful, long-term solutions to the religious and tribal discords. These were the lands of perpetual disagreements, and the young people kept paying the ultimate price for the irresponsibilities of their 'leaders'.

Michael hoped Adel Zia's 'boys' would win the day with grace. That they would implement justice and lasting freedoms for their people. He prayed for the profound greatness of the Iranians to be realized, and for their integration into the world community of nations.

He knew the potential of the Iranian youth. The woman he loved, Nasrin, was the shining example of Persian beauty, brilliant intelligence and creativity, and humane kindness. These were the values that the Iranian nation could easily propagate across the planet.

As in many wars of world history, Western and Eastern, Christian and Muslim, the young warriors often fought without even understanding the reasons why. Religious zealotry dominated actions. Most were boys, really wishing simply to be home with their parents. Good or bad, these young boys were still soft between the ears. They couldn't reason the whys and hows of world geopolitics. And they certainly couldn't reason their own deaths. Without understanding the full significance of their own sacrifices, these boys were charting the course of 'freedom' in their lands. That was the methodology of how freedom was usually won – through blood and sacrifice – even if 'unknowingly'.

Yet, freedom would last only if the causes and reasons for it were well understood. Michael hoped Adel's fighters would recognize these basic truths. Only 'thinking minds' could secure true liberty long into the future.

Indeed, even with noble and wise warriors, freedom can remain elusive - never to be captured by the worthy. Humble chivalry, intelligent planning, brave war-fighting, and even supplication to the 'Almighty' may not guarantee success in the achievement of eternal freedom.

In sharp emotional perspective, Michael thought back on his trip to Cuba a few years before. His grandfather had died in another civil war, half-way around the world. The patriot had known fully well what he had died for – beginning to end. There was no misunderstanding in his mind. He fought and died for freedom in his native land. He struggled to replace a communist dictatorship which had hijacked his way of life. He sacrificed so his wife and daughter could live free in the land of their birth. There was never any confusion in Jorge Sierra's head. But he didn't succeed in acquiring that most evasive of all of man's natural rights – living and dying 'free'.

Michael was by his mother's side when she laid amaranth flowers at the site of his grandfather's execution. He felt her pain when she cried silently in front of the giant iron cross atop the Morro Castle. Olivia appreciated how difficult true freedom was to acquire and maintain. She impressed these realities on her husband and children. Freedom could only be bought and preserved with blood and sacrifice – 'knowingly', and even then, there were no guarantees.....

Stansfield checked his pistols and loaded extra magazine clips into his pockets. They would remain in the villa for now and wait for an opportunity to escape. He believed it would only be days before American troops arrived at Chalus. To protect Nasrin, he would fight only if their safe house was breached. There was enough food and water to last several weeks, and the only sensible plan was to hunker down and avoid discovery by the enemy.

The weeks passed. US fighter-bombers flew over Chalus and attacked the Iranian positions several times a day. Resistance fighters kept constant pressure on the Iranian regulars throughout the city.

In early June, Stansfield observed two brigades of Iranian Revolutionary Guards enter Chalus from the west. He knew they were in retreat from advancing American forces, approaching central northern Iran from the northwest. Freedom was close.

The next night, as Michael and Nasrin slept beneath the dark stairwell, they were awakened by noise. The front door of the villa opened, and the sounds of footsteps echoed through the house. Stansfield raised his pistols in both hands and waited for a clear shot. In a flash, he recognized Adel Zia's voice and lowered his guns.

"Adel!

"It's Majid.... Don't shoot!" yelled Stansfield.

The two men met and embraced.

"I thought you would be in the USA by now, Majid," said Adel Zia as he hugged Nasrin.

"We lost our escape boat to a misdirected American rocket," explained Stansfield. "We have been hiding here for more than three weeks."

"You were wise not to leave, Majid. The battles around Chalus have been hard. Many Americans have died west of here. There is no escape by land. It is best to stay and fight in Chalus with me."

"What brought you here, Adel?"

"My underground commanders need me to organize the resistance and prepare Chalus for the Americans. Your brothers are close, Majid.

"Chalus and the northern passes to Tehran are heavily defended by the Revolutionary Guards.

"I am here to command the attacks on the Guards while the Americans make their final push into Tehran," stated Zia.

"They have killed many of your fighters in Chalus," said Stansfield. "Execution squads murdered hundreds of them. I saw it with my own eyes."

"Majid, in Tehran, they have executed many thousands of citizens. But in street fighting, we have killed many of them also. The resistance will not surrender to these beasts. We want freedom more than life. There are many like us, who will fight the regime until their last breath."

"So we shall battle together, Adel. Chalus will stand as a symbol of freedom for the Iranian people for all times."

"From your mouth to God's ears, Majid," smiled Zia.

Michael understood his situation clearly. His children with Nasrin, one day, would be half Iranian, just as he was half Cuban. Future Stansfield blood would be partly Persian blood, and it needed to be free. Chalus would help decide that freedom.

"Where are the Americans, Adel?"

"The US First Infantry captured Rasht, 150 miles west of here, and will begin a new offensive towards Chalus this morning.

"American forces are fighting for Arak and Qom to the southwest of Tehran, and the British have taken control of Khuzestan province further south.

"US Marines control the Persian Gulf coastal plains after days of deadly battle. They are moving north to Yasuj and Shiraz in the west, and Kerman in the east.

"Heavy combat in the Great Salt Desert claimed many American lives; but the US 82nd and 101st Airborne Divisions, spearheaded by the First Armored Division, are only 65 miles southeast of Tehran.

"The Revolutionary Guards fought bravely in the desert with heavy armor. Great tank battles led to the loss of thousands on both sides. There were hundreds of suicide attacks against American tanks.

"US Marines also suffered large losses around Bushehr and Jask, before defeating several divisions of Iranian Army Special Forces and Revolutionary Guard Armor. They say the Iranian 55th Paratroop Division at Bushehr, and the 12th IRGC Infantry Division at Jask, fought to the last man. There were no prisoners," responded Zia with glee.

"How is Pedro Salazar?" asked Stansfield.

Zia looked down and shook his head.

"Shortly after the first bombs fell on Tehran, Pedro was taken from the Spanish Embassy by Iranian Intelligence and executed on the street while embassy officials watched. I was told he bravely looked his killers in the eye as they shot him down like a dog."

"Do you know if he talked before his execution?" asked Stansfield.

"Pedro was a brave supporter of Iranian freedom, Majid. He died with his tongue silent," sighed Adel......

Accompanied by four freedom fighters, Adel Zia led Stansfield to a small bedroom near the back of the house. The Persian patriot moved the bed to one side and pulled open a trap door from the floor. They stepped down into a basement filled with arms, munitions, water, food, and medical supplies. Russian Kalashnikov and Chinese QB2-95 assault rifles, Russian handheld RPG-32 grenade launchers, pistols, and hand grenades were concentrated in the center of the room.

"We have been preparing a long time for this day, Majid!" declared Adel Zia, holding a rocket launcher.

"You and I will destroy many tanks with these RPGs," smiled the Iranian.

"By the time your comrades reach Chalus, Majid, it will already be free....."

For a month, organized bands of resistance fighters fought Iranian regulars and Revolutionary Guards around Chalus. Enemy positions were overrun, and many tanks and armored personnel carriers were destroyed. The town was turned to rubble, shrouded by the stench of death.

Adel Zia and Stansfield commanded a formidable force of freedom soldiers of all ages. Boys as young as sixteen, and men as old as fifty-five, fought in the surrounding countryside with great valor. Supplied with more weapons by the Americans, brave volunteers from all over Iran reinforced the resistance brigades. By early July, more than 15,000 patriots were fighting under Stansfield. Chalus had become legendary.

Nasrin turned the villa into a medical aid station. Many wives, sisters, and daughters helped care for the wounded and dying. Three doctors performed rudimentary surgery to save lives. All their efforts were made more difficult by constant mortar attacks and the occasional artillery barrage.

Communicating with American forces by satellite radio, Stansfield helped US bombers target Iranian positions in front of the advancing US First Infantry Division. Battle intensified as the Americans reached the outskirts of Chalus.

By July 4, elements of the Iranian 23rd Special Forces Division had driven the freedom fighters back towards the villa. They were cornered within the walls of the compound.....

In the late morning, during a short interlude in the fighting, Michael found Nasrin on the terrace washing her blood stained hands in the Caspian Sea.

"The enemy will push for the villa this afternoon," he said. "Unless the Americans break through, we'll likely be taken down. I don't have enough men to hold the compound."

Nasrin embraced her love firmly as he kissed her.

"Take this," he said, passing her the small box with the poison pills.

"You mustn't be taken prisoner, Nasrin.

"If we are overrun, and I am killed, and all the other resistance fighters are dead, bite down on two of the pills in the box. Within seconds, you will pass from this world and join me in the next."

She quietly nodded in agreement.

"Without you, the earth is silent and dark," she said. "Like a flower without rain or sun, I would wither away."

"I will wait for you on the other side," whispered Michael.....

With the roof of the house gone, and the walls blasted by shells, Nasrin and her team of valiant helpers moved the casualties into the basement. Surgeons tried to perform little miracles by candlelight.

"We're running out of ether, Doctor," said Nasrin, while dripping the last drops of the volatile liquid anesthetic onto a porous cloth over the patient's face.

"We have a box of chloroform upstairs!" shouted the surgeon. "Someone go get it!"

Michael Stansfield held a flashlight over the exsanguinating young boy's belly. The doctor searched frantically to find the bleeding vessel without success. Large puddles of blood formed under the make-shift surgical table.

"I don't see it, but it's likely to be the inferior vena cava. I can't fix such a critical vessel," whispered the surgeon in English to Stansfield.

An Iranian 155mm howitzer landed a high-explosive projectile near the corner of the basement, causing dust and debris to envelop the operating area. The surgeon vigorously washed out the belly with water.

The seventeen year-old fighter had fallen outside the perimeter wall, shot by a Guard sniper. Stansfield had carried the boy into the basement only minutes earlier.

"He's not breathing!" screamed Nasrin.

The surgeon stopped his work..... "Get to the next one, Nasrin!" he yelled.....

Enemy mortars rained into the sculpture garden, and many more rebel fighters died. Machine guns positioned on the unprotected second floor of the villa rattled at the approaching Iranian forces. Several dozen men of the resistance grouped behind the security wall, firing their rifles and grenade launchers.

The ruins of the eastern wing of the villa became engulfed in flames, obscuring the battlefield with black smoke. The situation had turned against the freedom-fighters.

Adel Zia and Stansfield fought side by side near the front perimeter wall. United in arms, they defended the entrance gates.

The American fired his assault rifle between two large iron railings. He targeted a small squad of Iranian troops inside the building across the street. Return heavy machine gun fire blasted the concrete wall next to him. A flying piece of sharp concrete embedded in his left lateral thigh, causing significant bleeding.

"Keep your head down!" hollered Stansfield at Zia. "Shoot at the second floor!"

"I'm moving to the other side of the driveway, Majid! I'll have a better angle of fire!" shouted Zia.

The Persian patriot sprinted to the far side of the drive with his RPG. He crouched beside a statue of Zeus and shot his weapon at the open window across the way. Thunder and fire consumed the enemy in an instant.

"To hell with you all, you vipers!" yelled Zia, while preparing another rocket. "To hell where you all belong!"

The second rocket levelled the top of the building, killing any survivors from the first blast. Yet, Iranian troops streamed closer to the villa from down the street.

A mechanized brigade of the US First Infantry Division approached the rebel compound from the west along the coastal road. American tank fire suppressed and slowed down the Iranian attack on the resistance.

An Iranian Boragh APC exploded into a thousand pieces, barraging sharp metal into the infantry soldiers down the block. A truck full of Iranian troopers was hit by another shell and disintegrated beyond recognition. Dismembered body parts scattered down into the compound. A chunk of torso landed at Stansfield's feet, inducing him to check his own body for injury. Chaos had descended upon the patriot stronghold.

"Direct your fire on the machine gun down the road!" Stansfield yelled at his men in Farsi. "Don't let their fighters get past that point! Hold them for an hour, and Chalus is ours!"

A light Iranian tank came rolling down the road. It sped toward the entrance gates of the villa.

"I'll stop them!" shouted Zia, prepping his rocket launcher. The projectile ricocheted off the front of the tank without exploding.

With wide eyes, Zia screamed at Stansfield, "To the house, Majid! To the house!"

The tank tore through the front gates before they could run, firing on the freedom fighters with its 12.7 mm mounted heavy machine gun. More than a dozen men were mowed down.

Stansfield pushed Zia to the ground.

"Stay down in the dirt, Adel! Don't move!" yelled the American.

Trailing blood, Michael sprinted behind the tank. He knifed a Guardsman in the neck and shot two more with his pistol. He pulled himself onto the tank turret and dropped a grenade through an open hatch. A mighty explosion stopped the killing machine in its tracks. In control of the mounted machine gun, Stansfield opened fire on the advancing Iranian troops. Scores of enemy were peppered with bullets.

A-10 Warthogs strafed the Iranians with cannon and rocket fire from above. A missile hit Stansfield's position, hurtling him several feet away. American troops flowed into the street in front of the villa and overran the remaining Iranian forces.

Regaining consciousness, a disoriented Michael lay on the ground unable to move or hear. The blast had blown his eardrums. Cold and weak, he looked down at his right leg and saw a large wound bleeding profusely. White bone was exposed. An open artery shot his blood from his body like a fountain. The grass next to him was soaked in a pool of crimson. Michael probed with his finger for the bleeder, but couldn't find it. He was bleeding to death.

With long columns of US infantry marching into Chalus, Nasrin ran from the villa to Michael's side in the sculpture garden. He waited for her where he had fallen, lying by a sculpture of Nike - the ancient Greek 'Winged Goddess of Victory'. Stained by battle, the base of the white marble was red with Michael's blood.

Adel Zia applied pressure on two large wounds in his friend's thigh and leg. Nasrin caressed Michael's face while US medics attempted to stabilize him.

"Stay with me, Michael!" pleaded Nasrin as she kissed his lips.

"Don't leave me!

"Don't die, Michael!" demanded Nasrin.

Stansfield's Iranian comrades crowded around him and prayed. Adel Zia yelled at the heavens for his friend to live.

Nasrin weeped. She softly spoke into his ears, but he could not hear her words. She kissed his face over and over again, but his eyes did not open.

Nasrin looked up to the skies and screamed, "Please, God! Save one of your angels! Please give him back to me!"

She tenderly passed her hand through Michael's blood matted hair, and told him how much she loved and needed him. She commanded him to live.....

Michael motioned with his glassy eyes for Nasrin to come closer..... The Persian princess brought her sweet face next to his, and the American 'David' whispered, "I came to this country in duty to mine..... Now, I'm in love with you, and we've defended Iran for your people..... Our children will be the better for it..... FREEDOM."

CHAPTER 27

The Homeland

I am not an Athenian or a Greek, I am a citizen of the world.

***Socrates* (469 BC to 399 BC)**

THE CHINESE CRUISE MISSILES came from the southwest at nearly the speed of sound. In the darkness of early morning, they passed - one by one – overhead at low altitudes, alarming the fishermen off the southern coast of California. The buzz and boom of the rocket engines over the Pacific Ocean, flying only 15 feet above the sea line, startled the sleepy men on their boats. They watched in horror as explosions rocked Camp Pendleton near San Diego. The lights of fires spreading on the US Marine base lit up the black sky in a red glow. The American homeland was burning.....

With many of the American sportsmen still holding fishing rods, hooks in water, they heard and felt detonations underneath them nearby. Their small boats bobbed in the suddenly turbulent seas. A PLA attack sub received a terminating blow from a silent American aerial torpedo. A gush of foamy white water formed on the surface of the dark Pacific, marking the spot of death for many Chinese sailors. A US Navy P-8 Poseidon submarine chaser jet flew low over the station and confirmed her kill.....

Yes, without a doubt, war had come to America in a big way, thought Lieutenant Commander Louis Stevens in Guam, as he reviewed the initial bulletin on the Chinese assault. In addition to the carnage at Marine Corps Base Camp Pendleton, numerous US naval installations and ships in San Diego were burning out of control. Several hundred sailors and Marines were already dead, and perhaps many civilians. Even worse, more bad news was incoming.

While flying to Guam from the Philippines, my transport plane was ordered to remain radio-silent. It was not an unusual command under the circumstances of war, but the true reasons were not communicated to me. At the time, I was unaware of the Chinese strikes on San Diego.

I read saved reports from the FBI on general homeland security, a CIA review on anti-terror direct actions in Latin America, and a US Navy assessment of enemy actions in American coastal waters since the start of war. Information from "The Task Force For Prevention Of Mass Casualty Terror Events On The Homeland" was thorough and complete, as were the papers on US Special Activities in Central and South America. While I read, my own thoughts edited the reports.

Since the "Terror Attacks of 9/11", the United States mainland had been kept free of mass casualty events. The single gunman terror shootings at Fort Hood, Texas, in November 2009 had claimed the lives of thirteen US soldiers. The dramatic "Boston Marathon Bombing" in April 2013 killed three people and severely injured more than two hundred and fifty. After Boston, more than four dozen attack plots had been foiled by US security services before their final development.

Stakes were raised last Thanksgiving night when seven heavily armed terrorists attacked the White House perimeter in Washington. Using automatic weapons and suicide explosive vests, the Iranian-trained Shia zealots killed ten US security personnel on White House grounds.

In the past six months, attacks on soft targets in the United States included hotels, public transportation, and entertainment venues. They had led to the deaths of over 150 civilians. The FBI traced most of the attacks to Iran-supported groups such as Hezbollah, Islamic Jihad, and Hamas. More than 800 terror cells in the United States were tracked by the FBI. Most of their recruits had entered the US through its southern border with Mexico.

In 2002, Iran began courting leftist socialist governments in Central and South America. By 2007, the Iranian Revolutionary Guards were infiltrating terrorists into Venezuela and dispersing them throughout the region. Cuba and Nicaragua assisted the anti-American actions.

Terror lines of communication developed from Venezuela into Brazil and Bolivia, as well as into Costa Rica, Nicaragua, and most importantly, Mexico. Drug smuggling tunnels across the southern US border were used by terrorists to enter the United States and disperse to their assigned sleeper cells.

Iranian intelligence services were involved in the uranium mining operations in the Amazonian region of Venezuela and in Potosi, Bolivia, providing for most of the uranium needs of Iran's nuclear programs. Although ideologically different, the radical theocracy of Iran and the Marxist socialism of Venezuela, Bolivia, Ecuador, Nicaragua, and Cuba shared a deep rooted enmity toward the United States.

America had aided Colombia in its long war with the Venezuelan-supported FARC movement (Revolutionary Armed Forces of Colombia). Because of Venezuela's ties with Iran, and its involvement in establishing terror networks and uranium provisions, America developed military bases in Colombia in 2010.

The Tolemaida and Palanquero Airbases near Bogotá were updated for US Air Force specifications and heavily fortified. A US naval presence was established in Cartagena on the Caribbean Sea and Malaga on the Pacific coast. Several thousand American troops were stationed at these bases in Colombia in preparation for war with Venezuela.

US Southern Command in Miami, Florida, directed the US Fourth Fleet to develop naval bases in Belize, Honduras, and Panama. Naval airbases were established on the islands of Aruba and Curacao, as well as Punta Cora in southern Panama.

Iran soon began building a missile base on Paraguana Peninsula in Venezuela. The United States ordered unmanned surveillance vehicle drone overflights to follow the progression of construction.

CIA political teams were infiltrated into Cuba, Nicaragua, Ecuador, Bolivia, and Venezuela. A slow development of opposition groups was initiated to purposely lead these countries to civil war. Freedom seeking rebels were armed and prepared for combat with the Marxist regimes in power.

After the completion of the Iranian missile base on Paraguana, clandestine Iranian freighters delivered medium and long-range ballistic missiles to the port of Amuay. The dangerous rockets were transported fifteen miles north along a coastal road to the fortified underground silos on the northwestern side of the peninsula. The area was guarded by over 2000 Iranian Revolutionary Guard commandos and a regiment of Venezuelan Army regulars. Heavy artillery gun emplacements, anti-ship missile batteries, and surface-to-air missile units along the coast protected the area against attacks from the sea and air.

Inevitably, and as programmed by the US, the Amazon War between Colombia and Venezuela began. A US Special Forces Marine Raider paratroop unit from Camp Pendleton, California, waited on airbases on the islands of Aruba and Curacao - only a few miles northeast of Paraguana. A US Amphibious Task Force led by the assault ship, *USS America*, sailed from the naval base at Guantanamo, Cuba, into position off the northwest coast of Paraguana.

Minutes after 1 AM, on a late winter Caribbean evening more than two years ago, six F-35 Lightnings off the *USS America* began bombing missile batteries and fortified gun emplacements on Paraguana. Colombian Mirage-5 jets from Cartagena attacked the port of Amuay, south of the Iranian missile base.

US F-16s and Colombian Mirages from the Palanquero Airbase near Bogotá bombed FARC and Venezuelan Army bases along the border, and Iranian terror bases deep in the Venezuelan Amazonian jungle.

An hour later, ten Viper attack helicopters off the *America* swept low over the coastal defenses of the Iranian missile base on Paraguana, rocketing military barracks and beach machine gun emplacements.

At 4 AM, eight hundred US Marine paratroopers were dropped near the causeway on the southeastern end of the peninsula to block enemy troop reinforcements from the Venezuelan mainland. Another 500 paratroopers descended from low flying C-17s into an area four miles east of the Iranian missile base.

At 5:20 AM, over 2500 US Marines from the First Expeditionary Brigade arrived on the northwest coast of Paraguana by landing crafts, amphibious assault vehicles, Super Stallion helicopters, and MV-22 Osprey tilt rotors.

Lieutenant Mark Stansfield's company of paratroop raiders were the first Americans to encounter the Iranian Revolutionary Guard commandos along the southern perimeter of the base. After crossing a minefield and breaching an electrified barbed wire fence, they met heavy resistance from dug-in machine-gun positions inside the camp. Using bayonet charges and hand-to-hand fighting within foxholes, reminiscent of World War II Marine tactics, Stansfield's unit overpowered and collapsed the southern defenses.

US Marines soon broke the perimeter defenses in the east and northwest sectors of the base. It became a bloodbath for the Iranian defenders.

Further south, the Americans cut off the causeway to the mainland and advanced towards the port of Amuay, twenty miles to the west.

M1 Abrams tanks, delivered from the *USS America,* drove 15 miles south from the landing beaches toward Amuay's port oil terminal facilities.

By late morning, Paraguana Peninsula was under American control. The US Marines had suffered over 400 casualties and 62 men killed in action. The Iranians had lost over 1900 killed. Of 3000 Venezuelan Army regular troops, over 500 had been killed or wounded early in the fight. The remainder surrendered quickly in the Amuay assault.

The Iranian missile silos were found to be nearly operational with long-range ballistic missiles easily capable of reaching the United States mainland. In addition, port facility warehouses at Amuay contained chemical and biological weapons of mass destruction.

Further south, CIA-led Colombian special forces crossed into Amazonian Venezuelan jungles, attacking FARC and IRGC camps. The uranium mines were overrun within a week.

Before dawn on the first day of the Amazon War, over 38,000 US paratroopers from the 82nd and 101st Airborne Divisions dropped into the Orinoco River Basin in the Venezuelan provinces of Guarico and Anzoategui - approximately 100 miles south of Caracas. Quickly securing the Orinoco Oil Belt, possibly the world's largest proven oil reserves with over one trillion barrels of heavy crude, tank supported columns of US paratroopers assaulted the capital.

Within three weeks of the US invasion, the Marxist government of Venezuela fell. All of the FARC and Iranian terror camps were destroyed. The uranium mines were under US control, and all of Venezuela's oil facilities were protected and safeguarded from enemy attack.

On cue, rebel uprisings against Marxist regimes in Central and South America formed with US assistance. A war between Nicaragua and US-supported Honduras quickly led to the fall of the leftist government in Managua. The rule of gangsters in Bolivia and Ecuador fell in ashes. After two months without oil subsidies from Venezuela, and the complete collapse of its economy, the decrepit dictatorship in Cuba was removed by a CIA backed rebellion.

Cuban freedom fighters took control of Havana and invited the U.S. Army to help them stabilize their country.

Three US infantry divisions entered Cuba at ports in Havana, Cienfuegos, and Santiago. A new Cuban Constitution took shape with the aid of the US State Department. Democratic elections were scheduled for the end of the year.

On the first day of summer that year, the Mexican federal government - assisted by the CIA and U.S. Army Special Forces - eliminated the last vestiges of the Iranian terror networks in Mexico. Drug and terrorist smuggling tunnels across the border with the United States were destroyed. Over 15,000 additional Homeland Security agents were assigned to patrol the Mexican border with Texas, New Mexico, Arizona, and California.

July 4 was celebrated in the United States as a day for independence across the entire Western Hemisphere. For the first time in nearly 60 years, Latin America was free from Marxist and foreign enemy influence. Democratic elections were held across the region, and most countries asked for US assistance in developing their constitutions and justice systems. A new "Rule of Law" became the people's choice. Freedom reigned. Raul and Jorge Sierra's dream had finally been realized. Neither was alive to enjoy the final fruit of their labors.

Perhaps the most dangerous region in the Western Hemisphere that summer was the United States of America. Still mired in political disunity and a deep economic slump, America had over 5000 sleeper terrorists within its borders. They were living, working, and planning their next move in support of the Iranian terror regime.

Twenty months later, in early March of this year, terror networks again began to infiltrate teams of Iranians into the United States. They carried disassembled parts of many nuclear devices. The separate pieces were taken to regional safe houses and specially trained engineers, who would organize the bomb parts into fully functional nuclear weapons of mass destruction. On orders from Tehran, sleeper terrorists would then deposit these bombs at selected sites across the United States. They would wait on stand-by, to be detonated if an American attack on Iran became imminent.

US intelligence services began tracking many of these infiltrators since discovering their presence in April. Nuclear engineers of Muslim background with recent suspicious activities were detained by Homeland Security across the United States. Safe houses in West Palm Beach, Philadelphia, New York, Richmond, Denver, and Los Angeles were discovered and terminated. By late May, the FBI was confident that all nuclear cells had been shut down.

Since the beginning of war with Iran, North Korea, and China on May 12, the *Nimitz* Carrier Strike Group had protected the waters around Hawaii. The *Eisenhower* Strike Group patrolled the Pacific Ocean off the western United States.

In addition, "Ghost" stealth ships (GSS) - radar evading 150 foot long fast boats which could cruise for long periods of time at 70 mph, and carry MK 48 AdCap torpedoes and cruise missiles - patrolled the littoral waters around the United States. They roamed from Panama to Alaska on the West Coast, and covered the Caribbean Sea island chains, the Gulf of Mexico, and the Atlantic US seaboard to Greenland.

In the first three weeks of the war, two Chinese submarines had been tracked and sunk by US destroyer convoys off California. Ghost ships sank several false-flag clandestine freighters in Pacific coastal waters, Gulf of Mexico, and the American Atlantic nearshore.

On June 3, a type 095 Chinese nuclear attack submarine in the Gulf of Mexico evaded US convoys and attacked the Louisiana Offshore Oil Port (LOOP) - a deepwater oil terminal off the coast of Louisiana which handled 13% of the nation's foreign oil imports (1.2 million barrels a day). The terminal disappeared into the Gulf of Mexico.

The same submarine, on June 4, attacked the US Strategic Petroleum Reserves in Freeport, Texas, with supersonic high explosive land attack cruise missiles using prerecorded contour maps of the terrain (TERCOM). Several missiles, not needing GPS guidance, heavily damaged the facilities in Freeport which contained over 250 million barrels of oil - 33% of the nation's reserves.

US GSS-13 finally tracked and sank the attack sub on June 5. That same day, another Chinese submarine attacked port facilities in the Panama Canal Zone before being sunk by a convoy of "Ghost" ships.

This was the condition of the American homeland, critical but stable, as my plane landed at Andersen Air Force Base Guam in the late afternoon on June 8. Lieutenant Commander Louis Stevens waited for me on the tarmac.

"How was your reunion with Julius, Admiral?" asked Stevens.

"Very fine," I answered.

"I saw what I needed to see. He was prepared. I saw the invincibility in his eyes.

"Yes..... I saw what I needed to see..... It was comforting.....

"You young people amaze me, Louis. It's good to have youth. The word, 'fear', is not in your lexicon.

"As you age, you tend to recognize fear more frequently. The risks of things become more apparent to you. You worry more and sleep less.

"It's unfortunate, really. The youth have much more to worry about, I think. Old men like me have already lived their lives. It's the energy of the young people that the world depends on. You all are not dispensable like I am. You are the essential ones, not I.

"What would the world be like without the energy of youth and young love?

"I don't know, but I certainly wouldn't want to live in it. No..... I wouldn't want to see that....."

We drove southwest towards Apra Harbor and the Naval Base Operations Center. We passed an old World War II airbase which had sent thousands of B-29 sorties against the Japanese home islands in 1945. I looked out the window at World War II battlefields which had claimed thousands of American and Japanese lives in the Second Battle of Guam in the summer of 1944.

After driving past the security checkpoints at the entrance to Naval Base Guam, Louis calmly interrupted my daze.

"Admiral, Chinese submarines have attacked our bases in San Diego and Pearl Harbor. It happened just an hour ago. There's been an almost complete radio silence on the news. We don't want the PLA to hear any casualty reports.

"The US Marine base at Okinawa is under attack as we speak. I don't have any significant reports from

Okinawa, but the word from the other bases is ugly, Admiral."

Lieutenant Commander Stevens was always subtle when he would break bad news to me. He would be slow and deliberate in his presentations to hopefully mitigate the stress on my heart. I didn't much like it, but I understood his concerns about my health. I had adapted to this form of news delivery.

"Tell me the details which have been confirmed, Louis."

"Type 095s with reduced acoustical signatures, in small packs, attacked with CJ-10K cruise missiles using TERCOM. The attack in San Diego came at 2 AM local time, and two direct hits on the Marine barracks at Camp Pendleton have caused heavy loss of life. The men were asleep in their bunks, Admiral. They estimate more than 300 deaths and over 400 injured.

"Three ships in San Diego were badly damaged. So far, we have confirmed 248 dead and over 500 injured on the naval base.

"A destroyer and minesweeper were hit in the West Loch at Pearl Harbor and quickly sank. Casualties are still undetermined. There are many dead bodies floating on the water, and there are reports of men trapped in the submerged hulls. Search and rescue dive teams are looking for survivors. But we don't know if we'll have enough time to save any of them, Admiral.

"It appears the Okinawa base has sustained only minor damage and fewer than 30 casualties. But the attack is still ongoing and reports are incomplete.

"Admiral Turner instituted *Code Bravo* and ordered retaliatory strikes on the Chinese mainland. US submarines are getting into position to launch Tomahawks at Chinese oil facilities and naval targets in Dalian and Qingdao in the northeast, naval bases at Zoushan and Fujian along the east coast, and military targets at Yulin and Sanya on Hainan Island in the south.

"Orders were also given to destroy the naval bases at Gwadar Pakistan, Sittwe Myanmar, and Sri Lanka. Turner wants all their ships-in-port sunk without mercy.

"We're entering a new, more dangerous phase of the war, Admiral."

While we walked to the Operations Center, discussing the rapidly changing conditions of conflict, air raid sirens began to blare. The camp loudspeakers repeatedly shouted, "This is not a drill! Get to bunkers immediately!"

Guam was under a ballistic missile attack. Within seconds, the underground bunkers had filled with Navy personnel.

Patriot PAC-2 and PAC-3 missile batteries on land, and Aegis systems on ships, fired interceptor missiles into the sky. We heard explosions outside the bunkers.

Louis and I sat in the signals room, listening to all the activity reports coming from ships in the harbor and missile batteries on land. The many chattering voices painted a grim picture of the realities outside the bunker.

I sensed Louis' concerns for our situation. He was worried, and his face depicted doubts of America's future. It was understandable.

At that precise moment in time, we were seriously on the defensive. Our major bases had been attacked. America had sustained heavy loss of life. There was a bad storm outside, and there wasn't much he or I could do about it.

I was old enough to understand these emotions in a young man. I had been young once. Although it seemed so long in the past that I could hardly remember it.

These concerns for my country at that instance of time had not crept into me. I had faith in the resilience of the 'American Spirit'. "American Amaranth" was a hard thing to break. And I held much truth in that reality.

I looked over at Louis and held out my right hand. He shook it and immediately captured my intentions. He smiled and I smiled.

"I'm beginning to think that military intelligence is much like meteorology, Louis. No matter how many satellites and high tech devices you have, the element of the unknown is constantly staring you in the face. Surprise seems to be always around the corner. Planning can only take you so far, then fate intervenes.

"Before losing Olivia, we'd spend parts of every summer at our home in South Florida. We lived through many hurricanes. Weather reports were usually accurate, but never perfect. On rare occasions, the data provided to us on the island was completely wrong. There was always a sense of the ominous with an impending storm.

"Olivia and I would sit on the beach and stare at the gathering clouds. Over time, they would blot out the sun. The blue would turn to a dark gray. One could feel the barometric pressure drop.

"Often, we'd marvel at water spouts as they formed offshore. Their spinning water fountains showed you the power of nature in revolution. You saw fish rising from the sea inside the churning winds and waters.

"The wind picked up slowly at first, then rapidly to a strong gust. A howling tempest developed seemingly over minutes. It became difficult to walk in the sand.

"The ocean swelled, almost as if God was pouring more water into it. White foam capped the black sea. The waves crashed at the shore, slowly rising on the beach. When the water touched our toes, Olivia would look at me and nod. It was time to go.

"Leaving the beach, we'd walk past Raul Sierra's orchid house. Years before, Olivia's grandfather had enclosed the flower farm in an extremely weather resistant glass. He protected his orchids more than his own life. Raul would say to me often that his orchids symbolized the freedom of his family to him.

"Olivia would close the door to the orchid house and smile at me. We both knew no matter how bad the storm would be, the orchid house would be standing intact when we returned to our home.

"Regardless of the dire weather reports or eventual actual storm, we knew in our hearts that Raul's 'Freedom House' would stand. No hurricane ever destroyed the Sierra orchids. The flowers lived through them all.

"The way Olivia and I saw it, either the meteorological intelligence always overestimated the strength of the storms, or more likely, Raul's orchids were damn well protected. We always chose to believe the latter.

"No matter the storm, Louis, it's impossible to bring down freedom. If you protect it, it will stand.

"Our job is to defend freedom, like Raul Sierra defended his flowers. We must always have the confidence of victory in our minds.

"Regardless of how bleak the intelligence reports may be, they don't begin to tell the whole story. The 'Free Man' defends his turf to the end, and he is rarely unsuccessful.

"The size of a nation's heart can not be measured in an intelligence report. No satellite in the sky can pick up those data points. These are the intangibles which decide the fates of nations."

Fifteen minutes later, an "all's clear" siren sounded. Lieutenant Commander Stevens and I came out from underground to a panorama of fire and smoke. Several buildings at the base were ablaze. A frigate and destroyer were sinking in the outer harbor. Fire and rescue teams converged at all the casualty sites.

I looked at Stevens and said, "Yes, Louis..... I think we have entered a new phase in this war..... It may be a more difficult and dangerous phase for America. But rest assured, the 'Freedom House' will stand."

CHAPTER 28

Into The Abyss

Hell is empty and all the devils are here.
***William Shakespeare* (1564 to 1616)**

AFTER THE CHINESE MISSILE ATTACKS on American naval bases in San Diego, Pearl Harbor, Okinawa, and Guam, US submarines retaliated with Tomahawk cruise missile barrages along the Chinese coastline. In addition, Chinese naval bases at Gwadar Pakistan, Sittwe Burma, and Hambantota Sri Lanka were flattened from the sea and air. US attacks over the next several days destroyed China's "String of Pearls" naval base network in the Indian Ocean and South China Sea. America also increased the intensity of her attacks on Chinese oil convoys from Africa and Brazil along this route, essentially depriving China of more than 90% of her energy needs. American B2 and B-52 bombers out of bases in Japan and Guam bombed Chinese port facilities along the Fujian coast opposite Taiwan, day and night. The large PLA naval bases at Zoushan and Ningbo, 300 miles up the coast, were heavily damaged as well. Taiwanese F-16s and US F-22 and F-35 fighters out of Okinawa flew continuous sorties over the eastern Chinese coastline, attacking all targets of opportunity. Chinese MiG29s, SU-27s, and J-20 fighters regularly confronted the Americans over the East China Sea, leading to dogfights visible from coastline beaches on the Chinese mainland.

Chinese ballistic missile attacks directed at US air and naval bases on Japanese home islands, Okinawa,

Guam, and Taiwan intensified. Most of the missiles were intercepted by Patriot batteries or fell harmlessly into the ocean without proper GPS guidance.

Chinese JH-7A bombers, escorted usually by Sukhoi and J-20 fighters, made regular bombing runs over Taiwan. They hit airfields, ports, oil facilities, and military bases. The loss of personnel and equipment mounted on both sides.

Chinese PLAN attack submarines wreaked havoc on Allied shipping around Taiwan. American subs dealt heavy blows to enemy shipping along the Fujian coast. Sixteen Swedish-made Taiwanese Navy diesel electric submarines ran quietly through the Taiwan Strait, attacking Chinese military convoys. Ship losses for both sides increased through early June.

On June 11, Chinese cruise missiles fired at the city of Los Angeles by a PLAN submarine off the California coast were intercepted by Patriots and destroyed. Four "Ghost" stealth ships converged on the sub and sank her with MK 48 torpedoes, a hundred miles west of Catalina Island.

On the other side of the world on June 12, armored and mechanized elements of the Indian Army crossed into eastern Pakistan's Indus River plains and sped towards Lahore. Indian troops also invaded Pakistan's northern highlands, breaking out within six hours and advancing towards Islamabad. US Special Forces had secured Pakistan's nuclear arsenal a short time prior to the Indian invasion. American planes out of air bases in Afghanistan and western India ruled the skies over Pakistan, destroying large Pakistani troop formations before they could get to the invasion fronts. Killing zones along highways led to an estimated 300,000 Pakistani Army casualties in the first 48 hours of the invasion.

Over 800,000 Indian troops crossed the borders into Nepal, Bangladesh, and Burma, engaging Chinese forces in those countries. The United States aided India by providing satellite intelligence and additional fighter support for the Indian Air Force. Heavy fighting broke out along the Himalayan border with China in the Indian province of Arunachal Pradesh, the site of the Sino-Indian War of 1962.

Resource, economic, and demographic competition had forced India to pragmatically decide to join the Allies against China in a clash for supremacy in Asia. Fighting the Indians along her vulnerable western flank and the Vietnamese in the southern provinces would draw over 3 million Chinese troops away from fighting the Americans in the South China Sea, Taiwan, and Korea. Mainland China was now completely encircled by enemies, and her energy supplies had been choked off by the United States Navy.

On the morning of June 12, the *Carl Vinson* Carrier Strike Group - supported by F-16s and F-35s out of Woody Island - attacked the Chinese naval base at Sanya on Hainan Island. This operation would tie up what remained of the Chinese Southern Fleet and prevent their support of the East Fleet in the upcoming battle for Taiwan. US Task Force 93's left flank was now protected. On the same morning, Vietnamese forces broke out towards Nanning, the capital of the southern Chinese province of Guangxi. Chinese forces were in retreat along all fronts.

Also on June 12, the German First Armored and 13th Mechanized Infantry Divisions, along with seven

Canadian infantry regiments, crossed into Iran from Afghanistan and sped towards Tehran through the "Great Salt Desert". On their way, they passed the burnt out hulks of Iranian tanks destroyed in the Battle of Dasht-e-Kavir. These 60,000 additional Allied troops would support the Americans in their assault on Tehran.

In my stateroom on the *USS Ocala*, late in the evening of June 12, I reviewed the American casualty reports for the first month of combat in this terrible war. Over 15,000 Americans had lost their lives around the globe, fighting for their country.

I had earlier learned from Rebecca that Mark was progressing in his physical rehabilitation program at Bethesda. Julius and the *USS Oregon* were already in combat operations, south of the Taiwan Strait. I still had no word on Michael out of Iran.

The *Ocala* was quietly anchored in outer Apra Harbor, its bow facing northwest towards Taiwan. I walked out on the afterdeck facing the ship's stern and the Guam shoreline, a quarter-mile to the east. The night sky was dark with overcast rain clouds. A warm humid breeze from the south stretched the Stars & Stripes atop the ship's mast behind me. To the north, I could see the carriers along the pier still taking on supplies. To the south, battleships *Iowa, Wisconsin,* and *New Jersey* were finalizing their preparations for war.

I lit a cigarette and leaned on the deck's bulwark. Along the shoreline, several destroyed buildings were still smoking from the Chinese missile attack four days earlier. White smoke from the base rose up into the caliginous sky, slowly mixing with low-hanging black clouds.

The tops of the masts of the US destroyer and frigate sunk on June 8 were clearly visible, rising above the waterline in the harbor - five hundred feet south of the *Ocala*. Salvage crews worked through the night to recover what they could from the dead ships. The search and rescue teams had long given up on finding survivors in compartments of these ladies of war. The masts would remain as tombstones for the watery graves of over 300 American sailors who had served on their now sunken decks.

A misty rain began to gently fall. The clouds were finally letting out their tears. Wetness moistened the skin of my face.

The wind shifted and I could suddenly smell the tropical organic scent of Guam's rich soil. A soil made richer with the iron of our young warriors' blood.

The scene before my eye was tragic. The clouds and smoke, the darkness, the drizzle of rain, the aromas of the earth, the gravestones, all told the story of what had happened here. Many boys and girls had met a violent end. Some had died in an instant without pain or suffering. Others had gone slowly and desperately, bleeding out their last visions of life, or drowning into the sea. There was much about this that troubled me. I could not reason the loss of loved ones. And I had loved all these young Americans.

I quietly stood smoking my cigarette and paid my respects to the brave ones who had given everything for their country. I also gave my condolences to America for having lost her sons and daughters. We had all lost much in this place.....

"Good evening, Admiral," said Lieutenant Commander Stevens as he joined me on the afterdeck.

"Hello, Louis.....

"How are you feeling?"

"Scared, Sir," said Stevens truthfully.

"Scared of not performing my job to the best of my ability," confided the young lieutenant commander.

"Shit, Louis! We're all afraid of that," I stated, looking over at him with my one eye.

"I want you to close your eyes for a moment, Louis," I said.

"Feel the warm breeze and cool rain on your face. Smell the earth. Listen to the sounds of Americans at work, preparing their ships for the fight. Listen to the snap of our flag in the wind behind us. It is the call of our Stars and Stripes to war. The senses of feel and olfaction, the power of audition, all present to your mind's eye a picture of a natural state of confidence.

"Now open your eyes, Louis. Take a moment to absorb what you see.

"Look at the tombs in the waters around you. Observe the white smoke and dark clouds above you. The foreboding picture that you see is fear-provoking, Louis. It is threatening and evil.

"War is this way, Louis. Moments can be felt very differently at the same time. The good and the evil mix in a strange inexplicable way. For this reason, minds are torn by war. The contradictions poison the souls of warriors.

"Always stay within your wits, Louis. You are a great young man. Let your conscience rest. I am certain that I will continue to see only the best of you...."

I took a long drag on my cigarette and slowly exhaled the smoke into the wind. I wiped away the rain from my right eye. I could sense the bucking up of my lieutenant commander.

I pointed with my right index finger at the Guam coastline and swept it from left to right.

"Along that shore, three miles north and two miles south of this harbor, over 2000 US Marines lost their lives fighting to recapture this island for us in 1944. The Japanese lost 19,000 men. We wouldn't be here tonight if not for the sacrifices of those Marines.

"We'll all do our jobs to the best of our ability, Louis. Americans always have and always will. It's in our genetic code. It's the only way we know how to do things."

I paused and took another deep pull from my cigarette. The thought of the consequences of war to people's lives had always made me feel ill.

As I had aged, I realized further that love was the only essence of life which really mattered. War and killing had no place in the ether of existence.

Human toils in war were often wasted efforts, recycled over and over again in history. Winners and losers switched places with each other along the road. Human military history was full of recycled parts. Everyone had passed time at the top and at the bottom. The leading actors changed occasionally. But the continuum never allowed any one power to stay at the top.

What was the reason for all this?

With the sick weapons of modern war, the future of man was either of extinction or common bond. We would eventually all die in war together, or all live in peace. Our minds had to evolve to this reality. There was not much choice. We could either decide to return to Earth's primitive origins and start over from scratch with clubs and rocks, or unite in peace and allow the human mind to explore its potential greatness for a brighter future.

At times, I felt like a policeman trying to do his job in a rough neighborhood. My function was to keep the order for society. My credo was to uphold the concept of orderly and free government for the people. The rights of man had to be protected. Warring gangs had to be either pacified or put down. Their anarchy could not be allowed to spread throughout the community of nations.

America and I had a difficult job, coaxing the world into a brighter future. A future of peaceful prosperity for all under one banner, flowing with freedom and 'rule of law'.

Universal law that would allow free and fair expression. Where our minds could be used only to benefit societies, not to destroy them. Where freedom to worship in any religion was accepted, without allowing any particular faith-based doctrinal thinking to stifle the young people we depended on to advance humanity. Earth had to become 'one' world in every sense of the word.

To accomplish our duties, America recruited her youth – our best and brightest. Those forces opposing us, the enemies of human freedoms and creativity, did the same. Wars were fought by the young.

Losing young boys and girls, friend or foe, from any nation, in any conflict - past, present, or future – made me sick to my stomach. They were the true treasures of our societies. They were the glory of our respective nations.

How could mankind continue to throw our glory away? Why couldn't we 'fix' our problems with the power of the word rather than resort to the more malignant force of the sword? I wondered these things.....

In my old age, my psyche had become one of healing, not killing. Like a physician or surgeon enveloped in the struggle to save the sick, I was determined to do good in this world. I wanted to participate in a 'great change' that would move the people of our planet to a better consciousness. I saw my country's mantle of freedoms as the best medicine for the ills of the world. I didn't like the use of military force, but it was my scalpel.....

"It seems we can't stay out of war, Louis," I said in a low voice, before taking another long drag from my cigarette.

"In three days, the most destructive battle in naval history will take place in the Taiwan Strait. Over 200,000 Chinese troops will try to land from hundreds of landing ships onto an island defended by over 250,000 well-trained and armed defenders. Battle fleets on both sides, composed of aircraft carriers, battleships, cruisers, destroyers, and submarines will put more destructive metal into the air than any other time in history.

"Our fleet - consisting of only 60 ships – has more firepower than the US fleets at Normandy, Leyte Gulf, and Okinawa combined. Our three carriers, and airbases on Okinawa and Taiwan, will put up over 600 planes into the battle - all more technologically advanced and destructive than our competitors. Thousands of anti-ship and anti-aircraft missiles will be fired by both sides, and thousands more will defend against them.

"Because of China's lack of suitable satellites, their planes will have to get closer to our ships before they fire their rockets. I am certain the Chinese will attempt to knock out our electronics with an EMP weapon. Even with redundant systems and replaced equipment, our planes may also need to get closer to their targets before they fire their missiles. Aerial dogfights will likely be within visual range of the pilots involved. From the ships below, we will watch the most catastrophic air combat in the history of man.

"This battle will resemble more those fought against the Japanese in World War II than any other naval battle since. There will be great losses on both sides. It will be Armageddon. Many good men will find their final resting place in the watery abyss around Taiwan.

"Even if the Chinese can land troops on the western shores of Taiwan, they will be overwhelmed by the multiple layers of killing zones in place on the beaches. The weaponry and fortifications assembled on land are unassailable. I can't conceive that Taiwan will be overrun.

"When you analyze all the specifics for this battle, it can only be considered a suicide mission for the Chinese. There is no point in their attempt.

"The Ocala will be an important target for their planes. If they can eliminate our intelligence relays, fleet decision-making may be slowed down enough for them to hurt us. You can expect a lot of fireworks around us, Louis. Keep your head down," I urged.

I threw my cigarette butt into the Pacific. I continued to stare into its blackness. The sea, I thought, was ominous enough. To battle on it was pure fear. Warfare on water was a creation of man's lunacy. It was furious and unforgiving. Defeat on water was very final. It was difficult to regroup from the bottom of the sea. Only the fish could lick your wounds.

"I'm old, Louis," I murmured....

"The *Ocala* is the first ship I have commanded in battle. Several decades of Naval Intelligence, Chinese studies, and missile research have come to this - my final exam. This is my life's work."

As dawn broke on June 13, Task Force 93 left Apra Harbor for Taiwan. The *Ocala*, along with the carriers *Ronald Reagan, Abraham Lincoln,* and *John C Stennis,* were escorted by the missile battleships *Iowa*, *Wisconsin*, and *New Jersey*, seven cruisers, 25 destroyers, and 12 attack submarines. Eight more US attack submarines waited near Taiwan to join the task force, including the *USS Oregon*. Two additional Ohio class Tomahawk platform submarines with a total of 320 cruise missiles waited east of Taiwan in the Philippine Sea. The most firepower ever assembled in a US battle fleet sailed into the western Pacific Ocean to meet an enemy determined to save face and finally win back the island of Taiwan.

In the late morning of June 13, Captain Julius Stansfield stood in the command-and-control room of the *Oregon,* watching a video display of two Chinese carrier battle groups heading south down the Taiwan Strait towards his position twenty-five miles away. The *Huo Li* and the *Tai* were new 60,000 ton aircraft carriers, carrying a combined 130 Sukhoi-33 and J-15 multi-role fighters. Their escort of 29 destroyers and frigates were actively engaged in defending the fleet from attacking Republic of China F-16s and US F-18s out of Taiwan.

Stansfield could clearly see two of the guided missile frigates go up in flames as they were hit with multiple Harpoons and Tomahawk anti-ship missiles. Chinese destroyers fired torpedoes at nearby Taiwanese submarines. The Chinese carriers collected their jets returning from bombing runs over Taiwan.

Stansfield figured the carriers were heading towards the South China Sea to battle with the Carl Vinson Strike Group, which was presently attacking Hainan Island. The captain ordered his pack of four attack subs to sail south and stay 25 miles ahead of the Chinese battle groups.

At ten minutes before 4 PM in the afternoon - 35 miles southwest of the Pescadores Islands, as the Taiwan Strait opens into the South China Sea - Captain Stansfield turned his submarines toward the lead destroyer squadron of the PLAN task force. His subs fired a combined twelve MK 48 AdCap torpedoes at the first three destroyers.

While the torpedoes neared their targets eleven miles away, the American submarines fired several Harpoons at the carriers.

In coordinated fashion, land-based batteries on Taiwan fired supersonic Tomahawks; and US F18s, north of the Chinese fleet, released more Harpoons.

Minutes later, the ocean surrounding the *Oregon* shook violently. Multiple US torpedoes and missiles had hit their targets.

As Chinese anti-submarine helicopters detected sonar identifications on the US wolfpack, Stansfield dove the *Oregon* to 600 feet and hid in a thermocline. He waited to escape.

Several Chinese YU-7 anti-sub torpedoes were fired by frigates, while Stansfield piloted the *Oregon* out of the area under cover of the ocean's natural thermal layers. Quick thinking and the undersea cloak of stealth had helped save his ship and men.

A YU-7 severely disabled a sister US submarine, causing it to surface. It was immediately attacked and sunk by destroyers. There were no survivors.

Now miles away, Captain Stansfield looked at the *Oregon*'s photonic mast video display of the carnage he had left behind. Both Chinese carriers were dead in the water, ablaze from bow to stern, and listing 45° into the South China Sea. Several destroyer and frigate escort ships had also been hit, and were rapidly in different stages of sinking.

A US wolfpack of four attack submarines, combined with land and air based anti-ship missiles, had decimated two Chinese carrier battle groups in the southern Taiwan Strait. An American sub had been lost, along with 18 Taiwanese and US jet-fighters. The Battle of Taiwan had begun in America's favor.

Shortly after 11 PM on June 14, China unleashed the largest ballistic missile attack in history. Hundreds of DF-15 and DF-21 missiles carrying high explosive conventional warheads landed on Taiwan, Okinawa, Luzon, and Guam.

Over 1100 Chinese planes flew bombing sorties over military and civilian targets on Okinawa and Taiwan. JF-17, J-15, SU-30, and SU-33 fighters fired subsonic C802 and hypersonic (Mach 2) C803 anti-ship missiles with 400 pound warheads at any remaining Allied shipping in the Taiwan Strait and its approaches. The small Taiwanese Navy was annihilated.

At midnight on June 15, the lead elements of the Chinese invasion fleet left their ports along the Fujian coast and headed towards the northwestern beaches of Taiwan. By 3 AM - several hundred fighting ships of all categories, carrying an initial landing force of over 120,000 Chinese troops, had crossed a point of no return.

At precisely that moment, American forces unleashed a hell of their own. Hundreds of Tomahawk anti-ship cruise missiles were fired by Ohio class submarines in the Philippine Sea and land based batteries on Taiwan. Over 300 land-based F-16, F-18, F-22, and F-35 fighters attacked the Chinese fleet with Harpoon and highly accurate Joint Strike Missiles. Aerial dogfights between hundreds of aviators within visual range of each other could be seen in the night sky. The combat stage above was brightly lit by the raging ship fires below.

Far to the east, I had just finished writing a letter to my children. It read as follows.....

Julius, Michael, Mark, and Rebecca:

If you have received this letter, it is because I cannot be present to convey my love to all of you in person.

You have all been the greatest gift of my life. Your mother and I always worshipped each of you as a true reflection of our love.

I cannot express in words what your mother meant to me in my life. She was truly the spirit of my existence.

As a young boy, I lost my older brother to disease. Shortly after, I lost my father to a broken heart. My mother faltered under depression until cancer claimed her. I was left alone.

I graduated from Annapolis and made the United States Navy my family.

My life changed forever when I met your mother in 1975. Her beauty, inside and out, was breathtaking. Her character was as flawless as the most flawless diamond.

Her smile could literally stop your heart. Her love made you wish for immortality so that you could enjoy it for an eternity.

All of you were a product of this love, and the memories you gave us both were cherished.

Julius was a most noble boy. Your legendary high school baseball prowess led you to be chosen in Major League Baseball's Amateur Draft upon graduation. The Pittsburgh Baseball Club offered you a large sum of money to be their future shortstop. Instead, you chose to attend Annapolis and make the U.S. Navy your career. Stunned by your choice, Baseball could only celebrate you, as I did. Your noble calling now has you leading a ship of American warriors in the present struggle. I've loved you with all my heart.

Michael was a most determined boy. You always strove to be the best at everything. You needed to be the best student, the best athlete, the best son. As you grew older, you also needed to be the best lover of women. Your smile not only conquered the girls, but also your mother and I. I have loved you with all my heart.

Mark was a most courageous boy. You always stood up for what you believed in and fought for it, if need be. I worried that if war came, you would not return to me. Your courage, I thought, would cause you to take risks beyond the call of duty. Now your courage has been honored with a Congressional Medal of Honor. I have loved you with all my heart.

Rebecca was a most passionate girl. Your love of everything beautiful led you to a career in music. You often express emotions with your piano, which I cannot even attempt to communicate in simple words. The magnificence of your power allows others to see the beauty in their lives. Your gift is precious, and you are precious – to me. I have loved you with all my heart.

You're all accomplished adults now. You have your lives to live. I've lived out my health and don't have your mother at my side. I have finally returned back to where it all began, on a U.S. Navy fighting ship. I cannot ask for anything more.

Remember always the costs of freedom. Your mother taught me these costs long ago. Always believe in America. It is truly the best nation the world has given. Let Lady Liberty live on for the betterment of mankind, standing tall and free for all to see. And with every effort in our minds, bodies, and souls, let us strive boldly to preserve her original beauty.

With My Love Everlasting, With My Spirit Undaunted, And With My Dreams Fulfilled.....
Your Father

I slipped the letter into a waterproof plastic envelope and placed it in my right pants pocket. My 'day of reckoning' had arrived. I would lead a gallant collection of naval warriors in a desperate struggle for justice and freedom. The future course of our world would be predicated by the result. A conclusive American victory could perhaps pacify humankind for a time. Many successive generations of children, of friend and foe alike, would benefit from 'Peace on Earth'. I could only hope with my life. But before the peace, there would be war. We were prepared for the challenge.....

Upon entering the ship's bridge, I gave a copy of my hand-written thoughts to Louis Stevens. I looked into his eyes and I saw no fear. There was a great calm in him which I found in myself. I smiled at him and shook his hand.....

I stood among my officers and saw the same serenity in all their faces. They understood what they were confronting, but they were all at peace with it. It would be victory with honor, or – death. I took the time to shake all their hands and show my deep respect for their bravery.....

I then turned to face Lieutenant Commander Louis Stevens and ordered him to sound "General Quarters". In seconds, horns blared and speakers shouted, "All sailors, man your battle stations....."

Two hundred and twenty miles east of Taiwan, the US carriers turned into the wind and catapulted their planes towards the battle. AWACS radar planes from Luzon and Taiwan flew over the naval battle group, seeing everything within 200 miles of the fleet.

Shortly before 4 AM, the Chinese mainland launched a low yield nuclear electromagnetic pulse weapon which detonated 120,000 feet above Task Force 93 in the Philippine Sea. The explosion led to little damage aboard the hardened ships below. Some communication relay systems were slowed on the *Ocala* until equipment was replaced.

In retaliation, Ohio class submarines off the Chinese mainland fired two high-yield electromagnetic pulse weapons over eastern China. The missiles blacked out all civilian electrical circuits and much of the PLA military communication infrastructure. Chinese invasion fleet ships and planes were now fighting mostly blind. Attacking planes would need to visualize their targets and fire their weapons at close range. Fireworks would be seen up close and personal.

As Chinese landing ships neared the Taiwanese coast, over 200 X-47B unmanned combat aerial vehicles approached the invasion beaches from their bases in Okinawa. Flying in low at 480 mph through a thick wall of anti-aircraft fire, each of the surviving X-47s dropped their 4500 pounds of guided bombs on the Chinese troop carriers.

F-18 and F-35 fighters from the American carriers arrived shortly after, and shot Harpoons and Joint Strike Missiles at the invading force. American AIM-9 Sidewinder and Chinese PL-10 air to air missiles filled the sky, while American and Chinese aviators dueled over the invasion beaches at close range. F-22s from Okinawa joined the fray as planes on both sides were hit and fell into the ocean below.

Hundreds of Chinese fighter jets approached Task Force 93 after overflying Taiwan. Because of the poor quality of their surviving orbiting satellites, and the use of US EMP weapons over the mainland, the Chinese planes were ordered to approach their targets at close range. F-18 fighters, flying protective cover over the US task force, quickly engaged the Chinese. Heavy metal filled the air space as the orange sun began to rise over the western Pacific.

Close-in weapons on American ships - such as the US Phalanx defensive systems, shooting 3000 depleted uranium rounds per minute; and the Rolling Action Missile (RAM) defense systems, using infrared homing surface-to-air missiles - fired at dozens of Chinese hypersonic C803 and SS-N-22 Sunburn anti-ship projectiles, approaching the US carriers at Mach 2 speed.

Three Sunburns, using violent end maneuvers to elude American Aegis radar defenses, slammed into the *John C Stennis*. The direct hits ignited aviation fuel depots and ammunition magazines. A giant ball of fire and smoke rose 1500 feet into the morning sky. Men were torn apart and thrown overboard by the blast as hundreds of sailors were instantly incinerated. While fire teams worked to save the American carrier, a nearby cruiser and destroyer were hit by multiple missiles. They both sank within minutes of each other. Hundreds of US sailors struggled in the rough seas after losing their ships.

"There's a large flotilla of Chinese jet-fighters approaching us from the south, Sir!" shouted Stevens. "They seem to be honing in on us!"

"Bring all our fire on them!" I shouted from the front of the bridge. "Is the F-18 umbrella available to us?"

"No, Sir," answered Stevens. "They're over the carriers, engaged with a large enemy force."

I walked outside, and looked to the south and west with my binoculars. I could see six J-15s approaching us at super-Mach speed. A lone American Super-Hornet was beginning to engage.

"Fire every missile we've got at them!" I ordered. "All defensive close-in weapons fire at will!"

The first two J-15s were shot out of the sky by the *Ocala*'s rockets. The next two were shot up by the lone F-18 close enough to engage. The fifth veered off at the last second after failing his missile fire. However, the sixth J-15 came home to us.

With Lieutenant Commander Stevens and I standing outside on the bridge of the *Ocala*, the remaining J-15 attacked on our port side and fired a C803 from eight miles out. The ship's defenses could not deter the anti-ship missile traveling at 1100 mph. At twenty feet above the waterline, it tore into the middle of the *Ocala*, setting off a huge explosion and destroying much of the bridge.

Fires spread through the ship quickly. The engine room was destroyed by a secondary explosion. The ship rocked on the water and heaved as the blast tore a large hole on the starboard side. The *Ocala* began to list. Another explosion tore a five-inch gun turret off our bow and into the sea.

Stevens found me unconscious, pinned under a collapsed structural iron beam. With the assistance of two sailors, he removed the heavy pillar of metal and freed me.

"Can you hear me, Sir?" Stevens shouted over me.

"Yes I can, Louis," I said in a broken voice, while regaining my bearings.

"How's the ship? Is she going to live, Louis?"

"No, Sir! I think we're going to lose her quick!"

"Have we lost many men, Lieutenant Commander?"

"Yes, Sir..... Many men," Louis answered sadly.

"We need to save as many as we can, Louis...."

"Yes, Sir. Let me start with you, Admiral!"

"But I can't move my leg," I said.

"Save all the others, Louis..... Let me be..... I've had my day in the sun..... Help them!" I shouted.

"Admiral, I'm not going anywhere without you, Sir..... Let me help you off this ship..... The leg looks pretty bad, Sir. You can't walk on that leg. I see the bone and there's a lot of bleeding," said Stevens, before removing his belt and tightening it around my right thigh as a tourniquet.

"Let me get you up and out of here, Sir. There's not much time, Admiral! The ship's going to go down soon!" Stevens warned.

The lieutenant commander lifted me up from the floor, and carried me on his back aft towards the stern which was free of fire. While we retreated, a large explosion amidships instantly killed the fire teams working near the bridge.

Stevens ran with me as far as he could. He set me down and looked into my eye. "Do you want us to abandon ship, Sir?"

I could hear further explosions as he stared into me. The cries of the injured and dying were all around us.

"Yes, Lieutenant Commander..... Abandon the *Ocala*!"

The 630 foot long command ship listed heavily to its starboard side. Lifeboats were dropped into the ocean, and sailors jumped overboard to escape the raging fires.

While Stevens continued to help the injured, I was carried onto a lifeboat by my crew. Being lowered into the water, I caught a glimpse of a plane in my peripheral vision.

An SU-33 approached the starboard side of the sinking *Ocala* at a high rate of speed. It came close and fired bursts of 30 mm cannon into the defenseless sailors on deck. Lieutenant Commander Stevens and three dozen other men were obliterated before the Chinese jet passed over the *Ocala*. The blood of my men and my good friend, Louis, splattered me in the face.

Moments later, I sat on a lifeboat with twelve other men and watched the Ocala - a quarter mile away - sink beneath the waves at 6:50 AM.

Looking further north, I could also see the 102,200 ton *John C Stennis* sinking into the Pacific Ocean. Lifeboats and sailors filled the sea. Oil burned on the ocean surface as warriors swam toward floating debris.

Halfway around the world at Carnegie Hall in New York City, Rebecca Stansfield and her escort of the night had just settled into their seats. Mozart's "Requiem Mass in D Minor" began to play. Her phone vibrated, alerting her to a Washington emergency newsflash text message:

> ***"The Battle of Taiwan has begun. American air, land, and sea forces are actively engaged in a struggle to defend Taiwan against Chinese invasion forces. More news will be forthcoming as they develop."***

Rebecca closed her eyes tightly after reading the flash and instantly knew where her father was. She held the phone to her heart and wept silently. Mozart's music played on.....

American aviators finished off the few Chinese fighters which remained after two hours of combat in the Philippine Sea. The blue sky was pockmarked by the smoke rings of aerial explosions.

Silence temporarily crept over the western Pacific. Destroyers began to pick up survivors of the four US ships sunk in the battle.

By 6:30 AM, Chinese invasion troops were landing on the beaches along the 20 mile length of northwest

Taiwanese coastline in the townships of Bali, Linkou, Lujhu, Dayuan, and Guanyin. American M777 howitzers pounded the first wave of 40,000 Chinese marines with air burst anti-personnel shells. US Marines and Taiwanese regulars, in fortified positions 800 to 1200 feet inland from the beaches, used M252 A1 mortars and XM806 .50 caliber machine guns to decimate the Chinese as they emptied from their landing crafts.

While continuous US air assaults culled the second phase of the Chinese invasion, the battleships *Iowa*, *Wisconsin*, and *New Jersey* fired over 600 Tomahawk anti-ship missiles into the Taiwan Strait in the largest show of naval bombardment with cruise missiles in history. Dozens of PLA surface vessels sat ablaze, as US submarines swept north and south through the devastation and applied torpedo "coups de grace" with MK 48s.

The sea was blanketed with dead and struggling Chinese sailors. Many of the transports carrying the 80,000 Chinese troops in the second phase of the landings went to the bottom with their human cargoes. The reinforcements for the Chinese marines already battling on the Taiwanese beaches would never come.

From my lifeboat, I watched a second wave of Chinese jets approach Task Force 93 in the western Philippine Sea. Surface-to-air missile batteries on Taiwan, an unsinkable carrier, had heavily damaged the flight of over 300 Chinese warplanes. US surface vessels fired hundreds of Sea Sparrows into the sky before dogfights developed between the American F-18s and F-35s, and the PLA Sukhois, J-15s, and J-20s.

Although US Aegis ships defended themselves well against dozens of anti-ship missiles, a few hit their marks.

Another American cruiser and two more destroyers received crippling blows. The cruiser sank within 25 minutes, only two miles away from my lifeboat.

Planes from both sides fell into the Philippine Sea as the sky above filled with smoke and fire balls. Sailors still in the water worried that falling metal debris would rain down on them.

A J-15 flew over my station at low altitude with an F-18 on her tail. The Super Hornet fired a rocket at the Chinese jet and destroyed it. As the American plane veered off to the side to gain height, another PLA jet-fighter purposely crashed into it. The mighty explosion over my head deafened me for an hour. I watched in horror this modern naval warfare killing spectacle.

Meanwhile on the beaches, the heaviest fighting became concentrated in Dayuan Township - two miles west of the Taoyuan International Airport. Four brigades of Chinese marines assaulted a heavily fortified area defended by over 15,000 US Marines. Using Javelin missiles against amphibious PLA armored personnel carriers and light tanks, the Americans prevented the overtaking of the airport. Heavy hand-to-hand fighting continued through the night and into the following morning. By daybreak, over 14,000 Chinese marines lay dead just west of the airport. The Americans had lost over 2500 killed in action in Dayuan Township alone.

Over 70,000 Chinese troops had managed to reach the Taiwanese beaches in the initial assaults. An estimated 40,000 troops had been lost in transport sinkings during the first phase of the invasion. Of those landing on Taiwan, nearly 37,000 had been killed by the end of the second day of battle.

The second phase of the landings was annihilated in the Taiwan Strait. Of 80,000 Chinese troops on transports in the second phase, more than half were lost into the strait due to ship sinkings by Tomahawks, jet fighter attacks, and torpedoes. The rest safely returned to ports along the Fujian coast.

By June 18, the Battle of Taiwan had been decided. The physically blood-stained Taiwanese coastline was silent. The surrounding sky and seas were calm. American and Taiwanese military morgue details picked bodies off the beaches, and started the long accounting process so characteristic after major battles with such loss of life.

In the end, more than 100,000 Chinese marines lost their lives. Nearly three hundred PLA ships sank with the loss of 50,000 sailors. Over five hundred PLA planes were destroyed. Most of their aviators were dead.

The defending Taiwanese Army suffered over 28,000 killed. Their small navy composed of frigates, corvettes, fast boats, and diesel-electric submarines essentially evaporated in the first day of battle. Their air force was decimated.

America had 4800 Marines killed in action. The aircraft carrier, *John C Stennis*, two cruisers, three destroyers, and three submarines were lost, along with over 2800 of their fighting men and women. Seventy-two US planes were destroyed with the loss of 64 aviators. We paid for victory with the heavy treasure of our youth. Many would not dance or sing again..... Or love again..... Or live again.....

My warriors and I, the survivors of the *Ocala*, waited in the Philippine Sea until the morning of June 17 to be retrieved. Severely sunburned and dehydrated, I had lost much blood. I had an open fracture of my right leg.

I was urgently transferred to the *Ronald Reagan* for medical care. Two days later, they transported me in a C-2 Greyhound to the US Naval Hospital in Okinawa for further surgical care of my broken tibia. Still, my odyssey in the Battle of Taiwan was not finished.

CHAPTER 29

American Amaranth

Our dead are never dead to us, until we have forgotten them.

George Elliott (1819 to 1880)

Dear Mr. and Mrs. James Stevens:

I hope you will forgive me for the delay in writing this letter, sending my deepest sympathies for the loss of your great beloved son, Lieutenant Commander Louis Stevens. For you see, I have been unconscious for most of the past two weeks, struggling with infectious complications of an open compound fracture of my right leg. Only a condition as grave and incapacitating as osteomyelitis could have kept me from expressing my sincerest condolences to you any earlier.

I had the great honor of working with Louis for the past three years. He exemplified all that is good in America. He was noble, conscientious, intelligent, and dedicated to the preservation of our great country. He possessed what my late dear wife termed - "American Amaranth" - a hard to describe quality found in the American spirit which is responsible for the making, preservation, and advancement of our unique republic. Our close working relationship allowed me to understand these qualities more completely in the person of your son. He was truly a magnificent young American.

On the first day of battle for the defense of Taiwan, our ship, the USS Ocala, was attacked by Chinese Air Force jet planes. A missile destroyed the ship's bridge where both Louis and I were stationed. After regaining consciousness, Louis searched for me. He personally saved my life, extricating my injured body from under a fallen iron beam. Using his uniform belt, he applied a pressure tourniquet to my leg to inhibit excessive arterial bleeding from an open wound. He carried me to a safe location on the ship and continued to save as many injured sailors' lives as he could. Several of his comrades and I witnessed his heroism under fire. We are living testaments to his courage and selfless devotion to duty.

Only moments after I had ordered the failing ship abandoned, a Chinese plane flew low over our position and delivered cannon fire at our men at close range. Louis was sadly a casualty of this attack.

For his bravery and actions in the Battle of Taiwan, I have personally recommended that Louis receive a Navy Cross, posthumously. I know this cannot be any consolation for your bereavement, but do so to further express our nation's gratitude, and to honor eternally his "American Amaranth". I will cherish his memory for as long as I live.

My Deepest Regrets and Sympathies
Admiral Julian Stansfield
Commanding Officer, USS Ocala
US Naval Hospital, Okinawa

I DRIFTED IN THE western Philippine Sea and watched the Battle of Taiwan unfold with an open fracture of my right leg. By the time of my rescue two days later, the leg wound had become infected. I spent two more days on the carrier, *Ronald Reagan*, being treated with intravenous fluids and antibiotics. My wound was surgically cleansed as best as possible. As sepsis developed, I was emergently transported to the naval hospital in Okinawa for more intensive care. Losing consciousness shortly after arriving in Okinawa, two surgeries and targeted antibiotic therapy had finally stabilized the situation. I came out of my coma in the evening of July 3. The first thing I requested from my nurse on the morning of July 4 was pen and paper to write a letter to the parents of my aide and friend, Louis Stevens. While I recovered over the next several days, my sleep was often interrupted by nightmares of the attack on the *Ocala* and the loss of the lieutenant commander.

In the early evening of July 12, I received the most joyous phone call of my life. Michael called me from a US military hospital in Baku, Azerbaijan, to inform that he was alive and well. He had sustained wounds in Iran which required surgery, but now were healing without complications. He expected to be home by late July.

Although fighting continued in Iran, a cease-fire between the armed forces of the People's Republic of

China and the United States went into effect at midnight, July 19. On July 24, the *USS Oregon* was inactivated; and Julius made plans to fly from Subic Bay to Okinawa. He wanted to see me.

My nurse helped me dress into a formal white uniform.

"Don't remove your oxygen, Admiral," she ordered, watching me strip off my mask. "The doctor wants you to keep it on downstairs."

"The doctor is a captain, and I'm an admiral," I reminded the nurse with a grin. "And this hospital is still on US Navy territory. I will not wait for my son, looking like a sick old man misplaced in a military uniform. Even if I turn blue, I'm not going to the reception area downstairs on oxygen and in a wheelchair."

After making my comments, I took the words back in my mind..... I beat them down with a stick..... How could I have said such a thing?.... My son Mark was in a wheelchair.....

Julius arrived in the late morning of July 26. He found me standing with crutches near the entrance of the hospital, framed between a giant bronze eagle and an American flag. I was short of breath but tried not to show it.

"Hello, Father!" said Julius as he embraced me.

"You truly are an old warrior," he whispered.

"Too old," I whispered back.

"I heard about Louis Stevens," he said, looking into my eye..... "I'm deeply sorry, Dad....."

I stared back at Julius in the face and silently thanked the Almighty for sparing his life. He was in one piece, and I was grateful. Many young men just like him had not been so fortunate.

"I'm happy to see you healthy, Son.....

"I've been told of your exploits in the Taiwan Strait. We're all very proud of you. Your crew is very proud of you. You did your duty and got them all home to their families. That is quite an accomplishment in this war."

"We had close calls, Dad..... We had many frightening moments..... But through it all, I remembered your words. They helped me survive more than once."

"That was my intention, Julius..... That was my hope."

"When you're down there in that blackness, Father, the world collapses on you. You're unsure if you'll ever see the brightness of a day again. There's a lot of doubt that goes through your head. But your words helped me..... Thank you."

I understood the blackness of doubt. It had come upon me many times in my life. It was not your friend. In peace, it created melancholy. In war, it could make you flinch at the wrong time and cost the lives of your men. It could cost one's own life. It needed to be beaten down by careful mind control and strategic clarity, both virtues in short supply when in combat deep in the sea. I had tried to help Julius with this. I was content that I had been successful.....

"I finally heard from your brother, Michael. He had a rough time in Iran but is well now in Azerbaijan. He was wounded while fighting with the rebel army in Chalus, north of Tehran, and required surgery at a US hospital in Baku. He's on his feet and sounded full of energy on the phone. He'll be home by the end of the month.

"Mark is walking short distances with assistance. Although the road to recovery will be long and arduous, he'll be discharged from hospital care by early August.

We're all hoping for the best. He, Sarah, and the boys need our prayers.

"I'm grateful all of you have made it through this war as I had hoped. My mind is at peace."

I had finally caught a respite from the tempest. Perhaps, the world could stay at peace for a while, and my sons and I could stay at peace. At the very least, I had an interval of relief from my worries and time to see my family again. I was greatly looking forward to it.

We sat at the cafe and ordered coffee. Julius and I were happy for the opportunity.

"You were two-for-two with two home runs," I said to him.

"What do you mean, Father?" asked Julius with a curious grin.

"The two times in your life that I gave you advice, you listened. Both times, you hit it out of the park," I beamed.

"You never needed much advice, Julius..... You always seemed to know what to do in any situation. I simply sat back and enjoyed watching you run through life..... But on two occasions, I couldn't help myself.....

"You listened to me at Subic Bay, a few weeks ago. I advised you to use your stealth in the Taiwan Strait. I told you to seek the thermoclines. I urged you to keep your head down and come out fighting when the time was right. You were aggressive when you needed to be, and passive when you were required to be. Those are the signs of a great leader, Julius. You saved your men and yourself. You performed your duties with distinction for your country in wartime. I am very proud of your abilities to control your mind and emotions, Julius...."

"Thank you, Father. Your advice was well taken.....

"I realized your concerns for me. I appreciated your visit very much.

"Under the sea, your words kept coming back to me. They were helpful.

"It's not easy to maintain mind control in a submarine under attack. You do your utmost to present a calm exterior to your men. You refrain from emotion as you proceed with your duties. But inside, your heart races and your stomach tightens into a knot. You become nauseated, Dad. You understand the consequences of being hit by the enemy. There is no way out. One touch by the enemy, and that's the end of you. There are no lifeboats from the bottom of the sea."

"I know, Julius....

"Long ago, when I was a submariner, I'd sense the fear every time my ship submerged. I never experienced being attacked underwater, but I was often suffocated by the anxiety of the possibility. Mind control became a mastered exercise. I have great respect for combat under the sea. As far as I'm concerned, the submarine service is one of courage beyond the call of duty. It's for special people, Julius. People like you."

We sat silently awhile. We drank our coffee and collected our thoughts.

"What was your second instance of advice, Father?" asked Julius curiously.

"It was years ago, at the Virginia State High School Baseball Championship Game," I responded.

"What was the name of that pitcher you faced? The big guy with the fastball and tight curve? The one everybody was afraid of?"

"Stobbs, Dad..... His name was S t o b b s," Julius repeated slowly with a big grin.

"He was a mean SOB. He was known for hitting batters he didn't like. He had a fastball that could twirl your cap, and a curve that would drop your pants!" laughed Julius.

"I remember your advice, Dad.

"Stobbs was known for sneaking his curve when he had left-handed batters with two strikes. He used his fastball to get you there. The fastball was his money pitch, though. It's what got him to the Major Leagues and eight All-Star games," Julius said nostalgically.

"So what did I tell you? Do you remember?" I asked.

"The morning of the game, you said I was the best hitting shortstop in America. That if Stobbs got me with two strikes, he would never throw me a curve. That he would throw his best fastball to strike me out in the biggest game of our lives. That he would go with his money pitch against the biggest money ball-player in the country," said Julius, still grinning.

"What did you tell me, Julius?" I asked, relishing in the moment.

"I disagreed with you. I told you that all the scouting reports on Stobbs said the same thing. Against left-handed power hitters with two strikes, he threw his curveball," answered Julius.

"What happened?" I asked, already reliving the glory in my mind.

"I came to bat in the bottom of the eighth inning with my team down a run, a man on first, and two outs. I took Stobbs to a full count. I called a time-out to compose myself and tighten my batting gloves. I stood there for a few seconds as I wiped sweat off my brow. I looked over at you and Mom, sitting above the third-base dugout. I remembered your advice to look for the fastball. I forgot the scouting reports, telling me to expect the curve. I got back into the batter's box and loaded up for the fastball. Thousands of fans in the stands screamed, waiting for the pitch.

"I can still see the pitch in slow-motion. Stobbs' long arms going into their wind-up. His left leg kicking high into the sky. His eyes from beneath his cap glaring at me, and challenging me to swing. The dirt of the mound shooting up from the ground as his left foot came crashing down on it. The white ball appearing like a small dot, coming low at me, and rising towards the plate. My tight, compact, level swing meeting the ball over the inside of the plate with a loud crack of the bat. The ball shooting out of the park on a line over the right field wall. The seven thousand fans shouting as I circled the bases with a glint in my eye. As I neared second base, I looked out at the American flag behind center field, waving briskly in the wind. The flashes of cameras all around me. The baseball scouts along the first and third base lines, clapping their approval of me. I see it all in slow-motion, Dad.

"I remember coming back to the dugout, surrounded by my team-mates, and looking up at you. You smiled and pounded your heart with your fist, before shouting, 'Remember the moment.'

"Thank you, Father, for the advice, and for the memories," said Julius warmly.

We ordered another coffee. We continued to talk of life. We had a strong need to be together.

Next to us, at another table, were the parents of a young boy who had died in the hospital earlier that day. The boy, severely burned in the Battle of Taiwan, had been transported with me from the *Reagan*. I had closely followed his condition since coming out of my coma. He had gone through weeks of intensive care and multiple skin graft surgeries. Infection had taken hold several days prior, and he had not responded to any antibiotics. Sepsis evaporated all hopes of recovery. The boy had been released from ICU to a regular room, allowing his parents to remain with him all the time until the end. The mother wept as the father held her in his arms..... I walked over to them.....

"I'm deeply sorry for your loss, Mr. and Mrs. Blenheim. My name is Julian Stansfield. I was an officer on a ship in the Battle of Taiwan. Young William fought very bravely to keep his ship afloat. He and his men succeeded. Their destroyer survived the battle, and many sailors were saved. He is a hero. Our country loves him for his service and bravery. I hope you can find some solace in this knowledge, some comfort in the sorrow. I will pray for him," I said gently, before slowly returning to our table.

"Did you know the boy, Father?" asked Julius as I sat down.

"I know all of America's boys, Julius. And I know of all their courage. That boy, William, died doing his duty to the best of his ability. He gave his all when it was required. He paid the costs of freedom. Like all the other brave souls, William was a patriot. I needed to express that to his parents. They needed to know how much America loved their son."

Julius quietly stared at his father. He thought of how his father had lived his entire life. The admiral had a profound respect for sacrifice. The 'high road' for him was the only road. There were no detours. Impediments to sincerity and 'truth' did not exist for him. The noble measure of a man was the only measure that counted. Chivalry in action was paramount.

"What are your thoughts, Dad, on the conclusion of the war?" asked Julius.

"It seems like the Chinese miscalculated," I said. "The peace negotiations beginning in Singapore on August 1 will not be kind to them.

"They lost control of the South China Sea. All their bases on the Paracel and Spratly Islands have been destroyed, and the energy reserves will be evenly distributed between China and the other claimant countries of Vietnam, Singapore, Indonesia, Malaysia, Brunei, Taiwan, and the Philippines.

"Their ally North Korea was utterly defeated, and the peninsula will be reunified under a single democratic government. All the Korean people will prosper as a result.

"Taiwan was successfully defended and will remain free. Perhaps true freedom will now spread to the mainland.

"They lost Tibet and their influence in Pakistan, Nepal, Bangladesh, Burma, and Sri Lanka. Their military bases in these countries have been eliminated.

"We should now assist China with the modification of her crumbling political system. We must help them avoid civil chaos.

"It was a short bloody war as they had predicted, but they lost. Now they understand the power of the United States of America," I stated, before sipping my hot coffee.

Although fighting continued in Iran and Pakistan, their political and military infrastructures had crumbled; and their regular armies had been devastated in less than two months of combat. Their nuclear programs were dead. The people of Iran had rebelled against their government, and were now working with the Allied nations to establish a free and democratic system.

The terror regimes in Syria and Lebanon had also fallen, and democratic interim governments were being organized. New Muslim nations in northern Pakistan, Balochistan, Kurdistan, and Khuzestan were being planned and developed. The map of the Middle East was changing to better accommodate ancient tribal cultural regions. The mistakes of the Versailles Treaty of 1919 were being corrected.

A global democratic process kindled throughout Latin America, Africa, the Middle East, and Asia. Freedom had taken hold, and it was spreading quickly. Many years after the 9/11 terror attacks in the United States, the world was finally changing for the better. The global economic collapse had receded from the plural consciousness, and hope for a more peaceful planet became the people's most pervasive thought.

While Julius and I spoke, it became clearly evident to him that I was pale and markedly short of breath. I would pause between sentences to regain strength. Fatigue made it difficult to express my words. I didn't have any energy left to hide the true state of my health.

I noticed my son's concern. It was written on his face.

"Julius, don't worry about me..... I've lived a good life. I've had more than I ever expected..... I am satisfied.....

"One is born with a limited number of heartbeats. It seems I've reached my limit. My heart is beginning to fail me. All my life, it's beaten strongly. I can't complain or ask for more.

"The doctors are shocked I had the stamina to withstand what I did this past month. I think I willed myself to survive. I had much to do. Much to protect and save. Desire can take you almost anywhere, I suppose.

"My heart muscle is flabby and mostly dead. It's not functioning efficiently. My vital organs aren't receiving enough oxygen. The vision in my only eye is worsening, and my kidneys are failing. The specialists believe my battle wounds caused severe muscle cellular breakdown, contributing to the poor function of my kidneys.

"Something has changed..... I feel it..... An extreme weariness has grown over me.....

"The cardiologist says medications can improve my heart function temporarily, but soon I'll need a heart transplant. Imagine, they want to give me the heart of a young man. How unacceptable that sounds to me. I've taken enough hearts of young men.

"I told them that I was not interested in a new heart. Besides, I gave my heart away to your mother many years ago. It's no longer mine to give away again."

I smiled serenely and asked Julius to help me return to my hospital room. We walked slowly back together, talking about friends lost, love, and hopes for the future. Julius realized my end was near, and that I had willingly accepted it.....

As my son walked away from me down the hall, I shouted his name. He turned and looked back at me.

"Julius, there's something I want to return to you!"

I reached into my pocket and pulled out a baseball. I tossed a perfect strike to him. He caught it with one hand.

"You still have the touch, Son!

"I had it shipped over from Washington. I always slept with it next to me. It brings me a bit of happiness.

"That's your home run ball from the state championship game. Your coach gave it to me after the big game and advised that I hold it for Cooperstown, one day. I guess it'll never get there. But it has great value for me, as it should for you.

"It has a good dent on the side of it. You did hit that ball damn hard, I recall. Keep it for your kids and tell them the story of you and your 'old man'. It's a good story.

"I love you, Julius."

I saluted my son and went into my hospital room.

Julius stayed standing in the hall for a while. He felt the dent on the side of the baseball. He turned the ball in his hand and saw the inscription on it, "Remember the Moment".

He stared at his father's hospital room door, smiled, and cocked his head. A father's love could never be forgotten.....

On August 2, Julius and I flew from Okinawa to Pearl Harbor. The next day, we left for Washington. I was going home for the last time.

On the long trip, I fell asleep and dreamed.

I was a young man, running on an early morning in Annapolis. My friend Joe Mitrano was with me, as he was every dawn before reveille. We sprinted, side by side.

It was cool and foggy on our jog, and I sensed summer was ending. Though the scent of flowers was still in the air, the smell of the ocean nearby had weakened.

Joe slowed down and faded away behind me. He waved me on. I kept going, following a path I'd run a thousand times.

Out of the white fog, my father joined me for a while. We talked as we ran, of our old home and Mother. He thanked me for being such a good son. He seemed strong and happy, as I had always remembered him. He expressed his love for me and disappeared from my eyes. I kept running.

I was greeted by my brother, Bobby. He ran right next to me. He had grown into a man, bigger and stronger than I. I had always wished for that. He thanked me for loving him so deeply, and for being the finest brother a boy could hope for. He bid me luck in the great life he saw for me. Bobby was joyous for my future. He also disappeared from my eyes. I kept running.

The bugles sounded loudly, calling me back. I had done my duty, and it was time to return home. I couldn't be late for the rest of my life.

The sun broke the horizon. It's golden half ball of fire warmed my skin and my heart. The fog melted away, as did much of the pain. I would triumph and achieve a special happiness, reserved only for a lucky few. A wealth of love was coming my way. I was to be anointed with a sacred gift of immeasurable glory, where all hopes and dreams came true.

I sprinted faster to my promise. All would ease when I would arrive. There was no sickness or heartache where I was going, no shortness of breath or fatigue. All eyes could see in this golden land. I would have my love with me for all of time. There would be no more longing or desperate loneliness. No more war, only peace. I hoped to arrive soon, before the turning of the leaves.....

I awoke as we descended into Washington. I looked out my window into the dark night. Black-out conditions were still in effect over the city. It was like staring into an unfamiliar cave at dusk; its inner workings were black and mysterious, unwilling to divulge direction or course, stony-walled but fragile. It was not unlike my future, and perhaps even reflective of my past.

I had lived an interesting life. My work had taken me to the four corners of the earth. Behind a black screen, I had fought for my country on water and on land. I had risked my life for freedom in the highest mountain ranges, and the hottest tropical jungles and deserts in the world. I had battled on the seven seas. I had seen all types of enemies, of every race, religious creed, and political ideology. I had vanquished all of them for America.

But the central core and vital essence of my life had not been my work. My past, and that was all I thought of now, had been filled by Olivia. She had been my life, my inspiration, and my reason for all.

I thought of Helmut Pfaeffle and our long talks years ago in China. His life had also revolved around a woman, even decades after her passing from the earth. I had come to understand Helmut's undying love for Camilla much better over the past two years. The timeline of life was a zig-zag, and it did need the soothing beauty of Mahler's music and the passion of the red rose.

My view down the unpredictable timeline into the future had ended. I was no longer interested in looking forward. I had stopped my trek down the path, turned, and stared into the past. It was the past that I held closely against my breast. It was calling me home with every heartbeat.....

Julius and I were thrilled to find the entire Stansfield family waiting at Andrews Air Force Base.

Less than three months after the start of global war, we had a homecoming. All those dear to me were alive and together..... Except Olivia..... She was not there, and I felt her absence.

Mark and his wife and children, Julius' wife and children, Rebecca and Michael, all waited on the tarmac while Julius helped me from the plane. Standing next to Michael was the beautiful Nasrin. Walking slowly with crutches, I stepped up to them. I tightly embraced my children one by one, leaving Michael for the end.

As Michael approached me on his crutches, I could not restrain my emotions. I kissed him on the forehead and silently wept on his shoulder.

"I am so relieved to see you alive," I said. "I had feared the worst. Not knowing where you were, or if you were needing help, was very difficult. I'm happy to see you home, Son."

Michael could see the devotion in my face. I could sense that he could in his expression. The love was deeply mutual.

"Dad, let me introduce you to my wife, Nasrin. We were married in Baku."

I kissed Nasrin's left cheek and congratulated them both for finding love in such terrible times. Nasrin's exotic beauty reminded me of Olivia when we first met so long ago. She was striking at first sight. I could perceive her aura. She possessed rare qualities. She was familiar to me.....

"Father, I'll get you a wheelchair," said Julius, seeing me exhausted and weak.

"I'll reluctantly accept it," I laughed without much choice.

"I'd be honored to assist you, Admiral," said Nasrin.

"Please call me Julian," I urged. "The honor would be mine. It's not often that an old man is graced by such beautiful presence."

Nasrin and I became quick friends as people often do when they deeply love the same person. Julius pushed Mark's wheelchair next to mine.

Michael asked, "Were you afraid, Father?"

I gazed across at him and answered, "Afraid of not fighting, Son..... Not unlike you....."

Michael smiled.

We had dinner at "El Castillo". Mario Posada personally waited on our table like old times, enjoying our presence together as he had done many years earlier.

The Stansfield family was physically banged up, but not defeated. I looked around the table and saw joy on everyone's face. Their spirits were strong and hopeful. This brought great peace to me.

I continued my conversation with Nasrin, learning more about her interesting life and her desires for a large family in the future. There was no talk about the war.

"Michael has told me much about you, Admiral. In Iran, he spoke about you and his mother often."

"Please, Nasrin..... Don't call me, Admiral..... I'm Julian from now on..... 'Admiral' sounds too authoritative and impersonal. I'm neither both."

"I prefer, Julian, also," she laughed.....

"I understand you have a science background," said Nasrin.

"My father was a physician, and my mother a nurse. There was a lot of medical talk at home as I grew up. At Annapolis, I concentrated on chemistry and physics. Later at Navy Intelligence, I worked with rocketry. So, yes..... You could say I have a science background. I wish it would have been of the more constructive kind, rather than the destructive. It's always better to create than to annihilate."

Nasrin nodded her head and smiled at me. We continued to talk of family and the good things of life.

As the evening ended, I said to Michael, "I'm happy you found such a wonderful woman. Fate is an amazing thing. Love is a gift that seems to drop from heaven when you least expect it. If one is lucky enough to find love, protect and nurture it for all your life. Once lost, young love rarely returns."

"I know, Father," he said with sparkle in his eyes.

I kissed my sons goodbye. I tightly embraced each and every one of them. My boys were special; each was kind and courageous, and a great source of love and pride. I hoped to see them again on my long journey. I had faith their souls were entwined with mine, never to leave the fortress of my heart. I could not help but believe in the mighty justice of eternity.

Rebecca drove me home. I felt an overwhelming physical and emotional fatigue. Like a runner finishing a marathon, I was weary and consumed. I was in need of repair. But I did not wish this.....

A part of me wanted to see my family evolve. My predominant remainder desired something else. I needed Olivia. In this life, on this earth, I could not have her.

My life was complete. I did the best I could. I gave all my energies to live a 'good' life. I was content in knowing my boys returned from war alive. My promise to Olivia had been kept.

In the car ride home, Rebecca's perfume reminded me of the same scent on Olivia when we first met. One doesn't always associate these things with love, but scent is part of the chemistry required. All sensory stimuli related to the initial moment become permanently fixed in your mind. The visual, aural, olfactory, tactile, and gustatory perceptions create a wonderland of the mind. All the senses keep coming back to you in cascades of emotion. For me, it was both beautiful and devastating.

Rebecca inherited a great joy of living from her mother. Like Olivia, she had distinctive personal qualities that set her apart from everyone else. These two women in my life also shared a unique perfume. The scent in the air brought me back to a familiar place. It was a perfect place, where time stayed still. Where youth reigned and never was lost. Where love controlled everything.....

On a December evening in South Florida many years ago, Olivia's beauty captured me in a supernatural way. Her dark eyes swept me into her soul. Her smile locked into my heart and never let go. Her perfume's fragrance remained on my shirt collar till the next day, and into my next life. Always after, the elegant scent caused me to envision Olivia's smile. It was a heavenly potion made specially for her, and for me. Forever more, this scent of anticipation was irresistible..... Now, however, it was just one more reminder of loss.....

"Father, I have never found love like you and Mother.....

"What does it feel like?

"And how do you find it?" asked Rebecca as she drove home.

"Those are difficult questions to answer, Rebby.

"Let me see if I can explain myself.

"The Universe was formed nearly 14 billion years ago. From an unknown original 'Singularity', an infinite expanse was formed. Hundreds of billions of galaxies were created, each with hundreds of billions of stars.

"Our solar system was formed almost five billion years ago. Millions of asteroids and comets have crashed into our planet over the eons. The 'stuff of life' was slowly created. Single-celled organisms evolved into multi-cellular forms. Large life came to the oceans then onto land. Human beings evolved over the past several million years from more primitive creatures.

"Throughout all this time - the billions of years of biochemical creativity - the seeds of human existence were sown. The organic chemistry required for the workings of the human brain developed over these billions of years. All the neurotransmitters involved in the human mind to produce emotion, and both good and evil, are evolved from molecules present on the earth at its origins. Love, Rebecca, is chemistry.....

"But at the beginning and at the end, we have mostly questions. Ultimately, we neither know where it all came from, nor where it all will go.

"Love, like the rest of the 'Big Picture', is a complex unknown. You can't search for it, Rebby. You don't find love. It finds you."

I smiled gently at my daughter and held her hand the rest of the way home. She was a talented girl with great emotions. Love would one day find her.....

Arriving at our house in Georgetown had seemed peculiar to me since Olivia's death. I felt out of place and alone without her. The weight of the loneliness, and my promise kept, now seemed to take all the life out of me. It was like my world had suddenly ended.

I struggled up the steps with my crutches. Rebecca assisted me from the street to the first floor landing. While fighting my way up, I felt a sudden pressure pain in the middle of my chest. It was not dissimilar from other anginal episodes I had suffered in the past several years, and kept a secret from my doctors and family.

I entered the empty home and sat at the living room couch. I was out of breath.....

"Rebby, please pour me a cognac. It will help me sleep a little deeper tonight."

Rebecca placed the soothing spirit on the table in front of me. She sat down and held my hand.

"Several weeks ago, Father, I attended a Mozart Requiem Mass concert at Carnegie Hall in New York. Shortly after the start of the program, I received a text message announcing hostilities in the Battle of Taiwan. Shocked, I began to cry. I suddenly realized you were there. I can't explain my emotions on a mere presumption, but they were real; and I was afraid to lose you, Daddy."

I gently caressed my daughter's face and kissed her forehead. I eased her mind, like she eased my soul with her music.

I said to her, "Play Debussy's 'Clair de Lune'..... Play it slowly, as your mother liked."

"Why did Mother love this song so much?" asked Rebecca as she sat at the piano.

"Your mother always said it reminded her of our early-morning sailings together on Biscayne Bay when we were young. We would go out before dawn and capture that special time when both the moon and rising sun are in the sky together. She found that very special....."

Rebecca created magic. I closed my eyes and thought back to an earlier time. Her music made me feel more easily and strongly.

"Clair de Lune" always seemed to take me where I wished to still be..... I felt the cool South Florida air in December. I smelled the sweet scent of pink jasmine. The roar of the Atlantic surf was in the background. The terrace was crowded with beautiful people. I walked through them with my champagne, feeling young and strong. I stood by the pool and listened to the music. From across the way, my life changed..... I caught only her profile at first. She was tall and elegant. Her skin was white and her hair black. She was graceful in all her movements. Her arms and hands were feminine. Her nose was regal. Then, she turned and gazed at me..... Her eyes were dark and deep. Her face was gentle but sensuous. Her lips were the most beautiful I had ever seen. And then she smiled..... What she did with a smile was unlike anything I had ever known. I could read her soul through it. I could see the love in her. She was desirable to me in an extreme way. Her smile had mystical power. She was stunning. My heart stopped.....

As Rebecca touched the last notes, I felt a strong pain like no other. I dropped my glass of cognac and faded away from this world. Rebecca ran to my side and pleaded for me to wake up. But I could not resist the calling..... It was time.....

We were in a dream. Our sailboat cut across the bay. There was no sound or color. Everything was in black and white. There was an overwhelming sensation of tranquility and serenity. The full moon was still clearly visible in the sky, while the sun rose above the horizon. The warm ocean wind softly touched our young faces. Olivia leaned over to me and whispered in my ear, 'You kept your promise as I knew you would. It's the end of one day and the beginning of another.' She held my hand tightly, and I sensed she would never leave me again. Through the sea spray, and the reflected light of the sun and the moon, the name on the sailboat's starboard bow was exposed for all the world to see..... American Amaranth.....

Acknowledgements

I would like to convey my deepest appreciation to my father and brother for all the years of interesting conversation on history and geopolitics, and the mutual sharing of books which were essential in forming and trying to foretell future history. I would like to thank my parents and grandparents, and the rest of the Cuban Exile community, for sharing an oral and photographic narrative of the true meanings of losing one's homeland. I would like to thank the United States of America for accepting me as a young child, and allowing me to become a citizen of the greatest country on Earth. I give further gratitude to America for providing my wife and I the opportunity to live in a safe and secure home, where we raised our children with the freedom to express their opinions and pursue happiness without oppression. It should never be taken for granted. Specifically, I would like to thank my children for giving me the highest purpose of my life.

Most importantly, I am eternally appreciative of my wife for her support in the long and winding road of my first vocation - to become the most proficient physician I could be, and practice the art of medicine as I had always envisioned it. Additionally, her love throughout my new venture of writing this book of speculative historical fiction was my fuel to express my thoughts in words as best I could. Her insights and perspectives throughout the creation were critical in its development.

I give thanks every day that we crossed paths so many years ago; she is truly the most beautiful person I have ever known.

Selected Sources

When writing a work of historical fiction, the reader must be familiarized with the historical background involved. When that "historical fiction" is set in the future, where the history has not yet been made, the reader must be convinced by the writer of its possible occurrence. This is often a difficult task and requires intellectual projection. *American Amaranth* is set in the near future, but the reader is transported back in time throughout the book to Ancient Greece and Persia, Rome, and Imperial China. The reader also gets personal glimpses into America's conflicts in the twentieth century, particularly World Wars One and Two, Vietnam, and the Cold War against Communism in Europe and Latin America. With an understanding of the past, and knowledge of the present, the reader is also transported into the future and the possibility of a limited conventional world war. Being a lover of history helped me tap into the hundreds of books I had previously read on the subject of war, past and present. Being a clinical physician has taught me to understand human nature. This experience, and an understanding of the world conditions at the present time, leads me to believe that forward projected "historical fiction" may become fact.

Military, historical, and geographical reference sources for *American Amaranth* included military defense equipment reviews in Jane's Defense: Air and Space, Land, and Sea; Wikipedia; Encyclopedia

Britannica; and literally thousands of internet information sites, including international newspapers, cultural sites, and even extremist opinionated blog sites.

Excellent concise sources of information on the internet included the CIA World Factbook, GlobalSecurity.org, and Dr. George Friedman's Stratfor.com.

Being a surgeon myself, I found particularly enlightening Dr. George W. Tipton's account of a combat surgeon's experiences at Anzio during World War Two in the Bulletin of the American College of Surgeons, "Surgery Under Stress: World War II, Anzio Beachhead".

Other selected sources included:

On China

- Sun Tzu's "The Art of War"
- The Cambridge History of China
- "A History of Chinese Civilization" by Jacques Gernet
- "Ancient Chinese Warfare" by Ralph Sawyer
- "Modern Chinese Warfare" by Bruce Elleman
- "The Rise and Fall of the Great Powers" by Paul Kennedy
- "On China" by Henry Kissinger

On Iran

- "Forgotten Empire: The World of Ancient Persia" by Curtis and Tallis
- The Cambridge History of Iran
- "A History of Modern Iran" by Ervand Abrahamian

On Ancient Greece and Mythology

- "Persian Fire" by Tom Holland
- "The Greco Persian Wars" by Peter Green
- "The History of the Peloponnesian War" by Thucydides
- "The Peloponnesian War" by Donald Kagan
- "Ancient Greece: A Political, Social and Cultural History" by Sarah Pomeroy
- "The Campaigns of Alexander" by Arrian
- "Alexander the Great" by Alan Fildes
- "The Complete World of Greek Mythology" by Richard Buxton
- "The Greek Myths: Complete Edition" by Robert Graves

On the United States

- "US Navy: A Complete History" by M. Hill Goodspeed
- "Marines: An Illustrated History" by Chester Hearn
- "The Battle of Anzio" by T.R. Fehrenbach

Made in the USA
Lexington, KY
04 October 2016